INDIAN SUMMER

C. James Brown

ISBN: 978-1-7337498-1-7

cjamesbrown.com

for
Madlyn

1

I like to make decisions and move forward. No hemming and hawing, and no second guesses. This means I run into trouble every so often, but I tried slow and deliberate, and I made just as many mistakes while wasting a hell of a lot of time. Now I make the call and act.

So, I haven't spent a single minute of the six months since Joanna Hill walked into my office thinking about what I'd do differently. When a woman like Joanna asks a man for help, he has no choice in the matter.

She crossed her legs, and my eyes traveled from the tip of her red heel up past the curve of her ankle to a shiny nylon clad calf. She caught me looking and didn't mind. She had something to sell. I had money to burn. "What can I do for you, Miss?"

"Joanna Hill," she said uncrossing her legs and shifting in the second-hand leather club chair I recently purchased to class up the joint.

I extend my hand across the desk, "Earl Town." She leaned in, gave it a shake, then sunk back into the soft, worn cushion.

"I think my boss is in trouble. He's missing." That seemed simple enough, why the sales pitch?

I leaned back and pressed my fingertips together to show I was listening. Sounds stupid I know, but people react to these nonverbal cues, and it moves things along. I arched my eyebrows, and she continued.

"I work for Wayne Trust on Federal Street. My boss is James Mac-Arthur. I think something bad may have happened to him."

She turned and looked at the pictures on the rusty file cabinet to my right.

"Is that Clint Eastwood?"

"Yes, it is."

"How do you know him?"

"It's a long story. We go back a-ways." Back to me watching his movies on tv. A friend sent the photo as a joke. The guy Clint had his arm around was my doppelganger.

"But, you're not that old."

"I'm old enough to have worn a few hats. How'd you hear about my services?"

"I see the sign in your window all the time. I live on Columbus."

I worked out of my apartment in South Boston. The only advertising I'd ever done was placing a small sign in my window, but with all the foot traffic in the neighborhood, it drew a fair amount of walk-in business. It read Gumshoe for Hire. I didn't care to work for anyone who didn't know what a gumshoe was.

"Please, tell me why you think your boss, James, is in trouble."

"Mac, everyone calls him Mac, was supposed to be in New York last Monday to give a speech that morning. He didn't show up to the event, and no one's seen him since."

"That was seven days ago. Surely, you've contacted the police."

She brushed her hair aside. She had thick, shoulder-length, auburn waves of it, which set off her emerald eyes. She was young, mid-thirties, and pale, and made even paler by the application of candy apple lipstick. She was all business. Black jacket and skirt over a white silk blouse, upon which lay an oversized stone necklace. Amethyst, perhaps? I don't know. I find geology boring. A rock is a rock unless it's used as a weapon, in which case it's a more useful rock. Miss Hill was in fine shape in face and figure. She knew how to use both to her benefit.

"No, no one believes he's in any danger. Except for me."

"Why not, Miss Hill?"

"He sent his boss and me an email last Sunday that said he was taking a break and not to worry. That's all, no other details."

"Really?" I said.

She took out her cell phone, fiddled with it, then reached across the desk. I took it and read the message. That's all it said. The sender had an email that ended in @waynetrust.com and the time stamp was 6:03 pm.

"This is not like him. Something's wrong, I'm certain of it." She lifted her purse from the floor and removed a pack of L&M's and a lighter. "I see your ashtray there, okay if I smoke?"

"Go ahead." I reached back and switched on the small air purifier I kept on a cabinet under the window behind me, which was also cracked open a couple of inches. I don't smoke myself, but I don't care if others do. I like that it puts people at ease. That's why I keep the ashtray on my desk. I don't like breathing smoke, and I certainly don't like kissing a smoker, though I make exceptions for women like Joanna Hill. But what really pisses me off is how society treats smokers like serial killers. Therefore, I say smoke them if you got them. I consider this a public service.

She took a long pull, held it for a while, and let out a dense plume. I also loved watching women smoke. I guess I've seen too many old detective movies.

"I'm sorry," she said. "I'm not really a smoker, but when I'm stressed out." She shrugged and looked around some more.

"So, the email was a week ago, any word from him since?"

"No," she said defiantly, as though I doubted her.

"Have you spoken to his family, or gone to the police?"

"He doesn't have a family. Well, he has two ex-wives, no kids though. Both exes say they haven't spoken to him. I've asked them to call me when they hear from him, and neither has."

I started on my next question, but she cut me off and added. "He pays substantial alimony to one and keeps the other, who's remarried, in comfort. At least, that what he's always complaining about. So, they have a vested interest in his safety, and would call me if they heard something."

"And the police?"

"They told me there's no evidence of a crime, and there's the email."

"So, they aren't looking into this at all?"

"No." she sighed.

"So, what is it you would like me to do?" Other than avoiding eyeballing your calves some more. I noticed she wasn't wearing a wedding ring.

She looked at me as a mother to her confused child. "Well, find him of course. Isn't that what you do?"

"Yes, finding people is part of the job of a licensed detective, which I am, but I'm not convinced he needs finding. Maybe the approach the cops are taking is correct, and he'll turn up soon."

"No! Something is wrong here. Mac doesn't just disappear. He's a top executive with a billion-dollar trust company. This is not normal behavior."

"Okay." I held out my hands in surrender. "I hear you. You mentioned his boss at, what's the name of the company?"

"Wayne Trust."

"What does his boss at Wayne Trust say?"

She looked relieved. Like maybe this caveman is finally getting it.

"That's another odd thing. Mac's boss is Whitman Endicott. He's the other person who received the email. Mr. Endicott is concerned, but not enough." She stubbed her cigarette out, then leaned back into the brown leather.

"He told me Mac was probably worn out from a deal they've been working on, is just blowing off some steam, and will be back soon enough. He said he has people looking into it."

"What kind of a deal?"

"I'm not supposed to talk about it. It's a merger, possibly with a foreign bank, but insider trading rules mean everything that can be kept secret, must be, even from co-workers."

"So, is anyone concerned about James?" I caught myself and added, "Other than you?"

"Mac," she said correcting me. "Everyone calls him that."

I shrugged.

"Not really, no. But, no one else knows him as well as I do." I raised my eyebrows, and she shot me down.

"We're not sleeping together. That's all you men think about." Well, she didn't say that last part, but I could tell she was thinking it.

"I've worked for Mac for fourteen years. He wouldn't just run off and leave things like this. He takes pride in his work." She reached over the desk and touched my arm. "Something is wrong."

"My fee is $1,000 a day with a three-day minimum payable up front. If there are expenses, I'll bill you for those later. If less than three-days are needed, I'll reimburse you for the difference. If it takes more than three days, we can discuss an extension. Are these terms agreeable?"

She smiled for the first time, and it was a beauty. "Yes."

She took out her checkbook and pen. It wasn't even 9 am, and I had a case and an alluring new client. Not a bad start to the week.

2

I t was a warm late-September morning. One of those Indian summer days when the temperature spiked into the 80s, and you tried to stay outside all day because you knew in three months-time you'd be yearning for heat and light like that again. It was summer's last hurrah, and it was glorious.

The leaves had started to turn in Andover, which is about 25 miles north of Southie. I was on my way to meet Maria Moore, formerly Maria MacArthur, as in Mac's first-wife. Joanna called her and set it up, but not until after we'd argued about it.

"What's the point? He was last seen in Greenwich, why not start there?" she asked.

"The point is, I'm the detective, you're the client. You pay me to find your boss; then you let me do my job." As I said this, I got up, removed my holster and Glock G20 from its cabinet, and put it on followed by my sports coat. I did this rather obviously to illustrate that this was serious business and it seemed to work. She made the call right there in my office.

Her point was, however, valid. But, before I went too far, I wanted to talk face to face with someone else about this 'supposed' disappearance. I needed to make sure that Joanna wasn't some nut wasting my time, even though she was paying me well for it. You'd be surprised at the people that come into my office with a story to tell. Usually, the crazy ones leave when I mention my fee, but not always. I'd learned after a flight to Miami once, that it paid to probe things close to home first to make sure there really is a case to be investigated.

I'd been to Andover before and knew it was a ritzy town. Hell, all the best people, including former Presidents went to Andover, before going onto their Ivy league school of choice. But the street I'd just turned onto was beyond what I had imagined. The houses all had to be at least 10,000 square feet. They had rich, perfectly manicured lawns, lush flower beds, and flawlessly aligned cobblestone walkways. The street had a granite curb, which tells you all you need to know about Regency Ridge. Few residential streets in New England have curbs, and those that do, usually come with sky-high prices and outrageous property taxes. Just thinking about the monthly nut on a place like this made my heart race.

Maria Moore's home was a big brick box, a colonial style palace set about a hundred feet back from the road. It had a three-story center section flanked by two-story wings. There were six copper-topped dormers across the center and two chimneys in each wing. A walkway in red brick led me to a set of wide stone steps topped by an intricately carved oak door. I was about to depress the doorbell when I heard a voice behind me and turned to see a grubby young man in shorts and flip-flops. He was in his mid-teens and wore a necklace with a shark tooth on it.

"You need something?" he asked, with a look that said get off my porch. Yeah is your mommy home?

"I have a meeting with Mrs. Moore."

"You the detective?" He looked me over as though he was sniffing something that had been in the vegetable drawer too long.

"Mmm hmm." Now, he looked at my car and then me, and then back to my car. I was in a navy and plaid sports coat, dress pants, and loafers. What can I say? I like to look good, but I drive a beat to hell 2002 Chevy Caprice with 173,000 miles on it. It's a damn reliable car, it's paid for, and most importantly, it's inconspicuous. Business was good, but I still had to take the occasional insurance fraud or cheating spouse job, which required surveillance in something people aren't likely to notice. As my father used to say, the bills don't pay themselves.

The car didn't fit the man, or the clothes didn't fit the car, but I liked it that way. People are too obvious. Contradiction makes life interesting.

Plus, it was an ex-cop car, which meant the suspension, transmission, and engine was beyond what you get in a regular Caprice. It was a smooth ride, had a lot of power, and I didn't need to worry about dents and scratches, it was loaded with them. Not caring if you have a fender bender gives a man a clear advantage over other drivers. Especially in Boston.

"So, Mrs. Moore?" I said it real slow, enunciating each word. Was he stoned?

"She's out back. It's easier to go around." He pointed to a walkway that ran to the front edge of the east wing and turned the corner. I nodded and he began jogging across the lawn towards the mailbox.

I took the walkway to the corner and turned to find a fence taller than me. It was made of horizontal cedar planks and was much too modern for this house. I stepped through a gate and found myself in a gorgeous Japanese garden. I knew it was Japanese because it had those finely manicured little trees and a lot of boulders and gravel, and it was calm and peaceful. It even had a statue of Buddha in a little nook on my right. They can have the house; I'd live in the garden. I followed a path that weaved in and out of tree clusters and past a koi pond with one of those bamboo water fountains that slowly fills up with water then tips over with a loud knock every so often. At its end, I found a set of stone steps that led to a gap in a tall hedge. I stepped through the gap and entered a sunny backyard.

Two women, one of which I hoped was Maria Moore, sat in the shade of an umbrella by a round metal table on the edge of a rect-angular swimming pool. It was long and narrow and looked as though a giant had taken one end of a regular sized pool in each hand and stretched it out like taffy. I approached the women and decided to lead with a joke.

"Who took the other half of your pool?" I smiled and held out my hands to put them at ease.

"It's a lap pool," said the one on the right, who clearly hadn't gotten the joke.

"I'm ..."

She cut me off. "Chief Earl Town. Please sit." Clearly, this lady was Maria. Mrs. Moore was younger than I had anticipated. Joanna said Mac was 56, but his first ex couldn't have been more than 45. She had a thin face with a sharp jawline and tanned skin, which I could see a lot of. She was wearing a one-piece swimsuit with some sort of wrap around her waist. My eye wandered to the deep shiny crevice between her breasts.

"Thanks," I smiled. "Please call me Earl. I gave up the chief business a long time ago." She pointed to a wrought iron chair, and I sat.

"Why'd you give it up?" asked the one on the left.

Now Maria cut her off too, "Madison," she said sharply. "Please go and check on that damn gardener. Make sure he isn't making a mess of my calla lilies again."

Madison, who looked no more than 20, didn't appreciate being told what to do. She stomped off towards a large greenhouse just steps from the back of the west wing. She filled out her blue bikini, and I had to avert my gaze. What is it with this day?

"Stepkids," she muttered as she watched Madison go. "You look hot," she said, turning to me. "Please, take off your jacket." I did, and she did a doubletake at the sight of the Glock, but she didn't comment on it.

"You need some water?"

"That's okay Mrs. Moore. I'm fine. Thank you."

She waved me off, picked up her phone, and said something about aqua.

"So, it's Earl these days?" She wasn't really asking. "I like Chief better. Chief Town has a nice ring to it."

"Are you from Princetown?" I had been the chief of police in a small New Hampshire border town for a decade, but I'd retired five years ago.

"No, but I remember your case. I was a reporter with Channel 9 when I met Mac." Channel 9 was the ABC affiliate out of Manchester NH. The case she referenced was largely the cause of my retirement. Princetown was about 30 miles south of Manchester just north of the New Hampshire/Massachusetts border.

"Now, I remember you—you're Maria Montez!" I said surprised at the recollection. I remembered her for one reason, and that was how she great looked back in the day. I assumed when I no longer saw her on tv, that she had gone onto a bigger market and fatter paycheck. But I guess marrying a guy like James MacArthur must pay well.

"As you said, that was a long time ago." She returned the smile that had unknowingly come over my face as I thought about a young Maria Montez. She was still a looker.

"So," she said. "What is old Mac up to now?" She moved a copy of the Wall Street Journal from the table to an empty chair just as a middle age Hispanic woman appeared and placed a tray down between us. On it was a pitcher of ice water in which floated strawberry slices.

Maria said, "Thank you, Camila." Camila bowed slightly and left us. I turned to watch her and noticed the house looked even more significant from the back. It reminded me of the Breakers in Newport without the beachfront.

I turned to face her. "You've spoken with Miss Hill, no?"

"Of course, Chief." There was that smile again. I felt a bead of sweat forming on my brow. She went on. "I know he's supposedly missing, but the question is why? And, with Mac, there could be many reasons."

"That's why I'm here Mrs. Moore. The other question is where? Maybe you can help me with that as well."

"Please, call me Maria."

"Well Maria, I'd like to hear about all of those reasons, so I can determine which one is the correct one and find him."

She filled two water glasses and placed one in front of me, then leaned back into the sun and affixed a pair of cat-eye sunglasses to the bridge of her nose. Sweat glistened at the base of her throat and collected in a shiny pool on her chest.

"Well it's everything, isn't it?" She made a dramatic sweep of her left hand. "It's women; it's business, it could be a bet he made with his idiot friends at the club. And, of course, when Mac is involved in something, it's usually about money." She turned and watched the kid I'd seen out front, who was now banging a tennis ball off a wall beside a court that lay on an elevated piece of land about 30 yards beyond the pool.

She said. "Joanna may be blowing this out of proportion. As a rule, Mac's girls are flighty. Excluding myself, of course."

"Do you think she's one of Mac's girls?"

"She may not be now, but if she's Mac's type, and he'd never hire someone who wasn't, you can bet he's bedded her at some point. Mac always gets what he wants. And he always wants women like ..." She looked down at her moist cleavage, and my eyes happily followed. Then she brought them up, and I met her stare. She asked, "What does she look like?"

"You've never met Joanna?" I was shocked, given how long she'd worked for Mac.

"No, not in person. Mac likes to keep his girls away from one another. It keeps him out of embarrassing situations. That's another reason I figure he slept with her. If he hadn't, he would've introduced us at some point."

She looks like you, but younger, and with red hair, I thought, but it's honey that attracts the fly, so I played nice. "Let's just say, not everyone has a face for television."

She responded with a brilliant smile; it was the one I first saw on tv twenty years ago. "I don't believe you."

I changed the subject. "Your ex-husband, what exactly does he do?"

"Do?" A knowing grin extended out from the center of her mouth and she averted her gaze as if recalling a specific event. "Mac makes deals. Big deals." That was it? Maybe I needed to try this another way.

"I don't know anything about the trust business, but this is some place," I added looking around.

"Oh, you mean, how did Mac pay for all of this? That's your question. You know, as a former reporter, I'm used to bluntness. You can be direct with me, Chief."

"Okay."

"Do you know how Mac got to be second in command at Wayne Trust?"

I shook my head.

"He sold his father's company to Wayne Trust in 2001 for one hundred and fifty million dollars." She paused and smiled at the thought of all that green stuff. "Some people like to say it was his daddy's company, but it was Mac who built it into what it was, all through a series of acquisitions in the nineties. Mac has a knack for making money. It just always finds its way to him."

"That's a nice knack to have."

"Mmmm." She moved back into the shade of the umbrella and peered at me over her cat-eye glasses. "This house was a present to me. A wedding gift really, as it was part of the negotiation of our prenuptial agreement. In the event of divorce, he retained the family fortune, while I got the house, enough money to manage it, and a little extra for the finer things in life. Mac's taken good care of me." She leaned in to pour herself some water, and I could smell her shampoo. It was clean and sweet, and it rolled around in my nostrils.

"Please understand. I am concerned about him. I just doubt that he's in trouble, at least not anything he and his lawyers can't handle. I'd say odds are good that he'll be back soon. This has happened before you know."

"It has? Please tell me about that."

"Mac is a complicated guy. He grew up rich, went to the best schools, and never had to want for much of anything. It sounds great right? Except, it all comes with enormous expectations. He expects to excel in business, and he always has. But, the kind of pressure he's under causes him to let off a little steam from time from to time." She picked up a spray bottle and spritzed her arms and chest. It was difficult keeping my eyes trained on her face, and I sensed she was enjoying my discomfort.

"After he sold Wayne Trust the first-time, he went to Acapulco on a ten-day fishing trip and stayed for three months. I'm not even sure he was in Mexico the whole time. He certainly wasn't fishing all that time, not for marlin anyway. Senoritas perhaps."

"So where do you think he is now?"

She laughed. "I have no idea. If I were you, I'd check with his friends at the club." Suddenly, she sat up and shouted. "Camila, come here!"

I spun around and saw Camila jogging across the yard. She had the look of a dog approaching an owner holding a rolled-up newspaper.

"Yes, Ma'am?"

Maria smiled, but it wasn't sweet. It was acid. "What have I told you about checking the glassware? Look at this?" She pointed to one of the empty glasses on the tray. I couldn't see anything wrong with it.

"I'm sorry, Ma'am, I'll get another right away," Camila said head bowed.

"I don't want another one," said Maria through gritted teeth. "Just take this away please."

Camila took the dirty glass and moved quickly back towards the house. Maria turned to face me.

I nudged her back onto the subject at hand. "You were saying something about his friends at the club. Is that the Andover Country Club?"

She laughed an insulting sort of laugh. "Andover, God no! He golfs at Brookline."

I should've known. I hear the caviar is fresher at Brookline.

"No, I meant Indian Head in Greenwich. It's a yacht club. Mac keeps his boat there. This time of year, he spends his off days sailing the Long Island Sound, evenings in the club, and nights on his boat, which he parks there. It's quite a setup. During the week he stays at his apartments in New York and Boston."

"So, you think he may be staying at the yacht club?"

"No, apparently not or you wouldn't be here." She looked at me like I had two heads. "His closest friends, I guess I'd call them friends, fraternity brothers might be apt. They're Indian Head members too, and they spend a lot of time there during the season."

"The season?"

"Sailing season."

"Anything else you can tell me? You mentioned women."

"Mac likes to surround himself with beautiful, usually young, women. He promised me he was done with it when we married, but the prenup was a bit of a giveaway, now wasn't it? His second wife, Beth, got the same treatment, but the poor girl, she believed him. It came as a shock to her."

She saw the curious look on my face and explained. "Look, I don't know who he sees these days, but he's prone to sweeping women off their feet with a trip to someplace exotic. You'd be surprised how well this works with young girls."

No, I wouldn't actually.

"What I'm trying to say is, his friends at the club probably know where he is." She held her phone in front of her and asked someone named Anne to print out contact information for Gibby French, and Nate Sterling.

She looked up at me and said, "You can go back around through the garden, Anne will meet you out front." I thanked her and took in the view one last time, and I don't mean of the pool, then made my exit.

3

I checked messages while making my way back to Boston and found one from Joanna. I called her office line.

"Miss Hill, it's Earl Town. Did things not go well with Endicott?" Whitman Endicott, as Joanna had informed me this morning, was the CEO of Wayne Trust, and Mac's boss. I wanted to talk to him.

"He had to go to our New York headquarters, and will be there for the rest of the week."

"Okay, so I'll meet him there."

"I don't think a meeting is possible right now."

"Well how about a phone call? It's important that I speak with him."

There was a lengthy pause, so I asked if she was still there.

"He's not amenable to speaking with you at this time. There's a lot on his plate with the thing I mentioned this morning. By the way, please don't mention that to anyone."

I was sure the deal, whatever it was, was important, but how about a missing executive?

"I know you wrote the check for my services this morning, but is anyone reimbursing you?" I thought I might've insulted her, so I added, "I ask because you mentioned the sensitivity at Wayne Trust about this. If Wayne Trust is reimbursing you, then I would think Endicott could give me a couple of minutes on the phone."

"No, as I said earlier. The company is not involved in this. They are looking for Mac in their own way."

"What does that mean?"

"I've been assured that the company has someone investigating it, but they also don't want to do anything that will draw attention to his absence, so it's all very hush-hush."

"Okay, I'm going to Greenwich, and then to Manhattan. One way or another I'll track down Endicott."

She started to cut me off. I said over her. "I'll keep you abreast of developments" and hung up.

If I moved fast, I could make it to James MacArthur's yacht club tonight. I called my sister Emily's kid Ed, a thirty-year-old basement dwelling momma's boy with little reportable income, but who is fast on his feet and obsessive about doing good work, though he does as little of it as possible. His laziness worked to my benefit. If I needed something done, he was usually available to do it, and he was smart enough not to turn away easy money. He was also a smart-ass.

"Hello."

"Ed."

Long pause. "What do you need Earl?"

"Why can't I just be calling to see how you and your mom are doing? We are family you know."

Another lengthy pause followed by a sniff of the nose. The little bastard was waiting me out.

"I'd like you to do some research for me this afternoon. Scrape the Internet for information on a few people."

"You really should learn to use Google, it'd save you some money."

"I'm driving to Connecticut, or I'd give it a try."

"Okay, it's $200 an hour. I have a busy afternoon planned. You're inconveniencing me."

"Really? What is it you're planning to do, Ed?"

"Fine, $150," he snipped.

"I'll give you a buck a minute, no more no less. Get it done and don't drag it out. That's it, pal. I can do this myself when I get to Greenwich."

"Okay *pal*," he replied. I gave him a quick rundown of the case and a few names to research.

"It's almost one now, I'll call you at three," I shouted over the noise of a semi truck I was passing.

"Make it 3:30. I gotta eat!"

I left Boston heading west on the Mass. Pike. It wasn't long before I felt my stomach growl and recalled that I'd only eaten a couple of hard-boiled eggs that morning. I had about five-hundred feet between me and an exit to the Westborough service plaza, so I checked behind me, saw it was clear, and, at 75 miles an hour, veered across two lanes onto the off-ramp. As I was approaching the parking lot, I heard tires squealing and noticed, in my rearview, a silver sedan cutting off an SUV and taking the ramp as I had.

I pulled into a space along the east side of the main building and watched a late model BMW slide into a spot six over to my right and two rows behind me. I was in its line of sight. The silver four-door looked expensive. I stayed in my car watching for several minutes while pretending to use my phone. No one got out of the BMW.

I walked inside and bought a sandwich and an energy drink. I'm a coffee guy, but a bus full of college students from New Jersey had just pulled in, and every damn one of them was in line at Dunkins. I got my food and took a window seat in a large atrium. There were no good views of the parking lot from inside, and I didn't want to go back out and make it obvious I was onto them. I waved an elderly janitor over to my table. He looked like he needed a break.

I said, "Hi, I would like to pay you $20 for a simple, perfectly legal task that will take you no more than five minutes."

He moved slow, so it wasn't until almost ten minutes later that I called my dear friend Ron Hines. Ron must have seen my number on the caller ID.

"Chief, how's it going?"

"Hiney, it's good, but you're the chief now."

"You're still chief to me."

"Thanks, Hiney."

He'd been my deputy in Princetown until things took a turn for the worse and he was forced out, but that's a story for another time. Now he was the chief of police in a quaint, affluent town on Cape Cod.

"Earl," he said, getting serious. "I'd like to catch up, but I'm on the scene right now. Got a rollover to deal with."

"No problem, Hiney. Could you do me a favor and look up a plate for me? When you have a chance."

"Of course. What are you onto?"

"I'm not sure yet. It's a new case. I'm headed to Greenwich of all places, and I think I may have a tail."

"Greenwich? That's some serious fish out of water shit. You ever been to Greenwich?"

"Hell, no. I'm not sure they'll even let me in. I may have to buy a new suit and get a haircut along the way."

I read Ron the plate number of the Beamer from the photo that the janitor had snapped a few minutes before, and he promised to call back when he had something.

I finished my five-dollar footlong and walked to the west side of the building where there was a convenience store. From here I could see the ramp that led back to the pike. I thought that if the guy in the Beamer had any brains at all, he'd leave some space and wait a minute before following me back onto the highway, and I saw what I needed to lose him.

I nonchalantly made my way across the pavement to the Caprice. The BMW was still in the same spot, and I couldn't see through the windshield thanks to the sun's glare. The element of surprise would be my friend in this exercise, so I got in, started the engine, immediately put it in gear and tore out of my spot.

There was a line of semi trucks parked along the edge of the lot just before the onramp, and I had spotted an opening between the last two. I swung the Caprice into the gap, put it in reverse and backed up until I was within an inch of the semi behind me. Unless the BMW's driver was looking to his left at the precise moment he passed by, he'd never see me. I put it in park and waited. About 60 seconds later my tail raced onto I-90. If he noticed me, he sure didn't show it. I counted to thirty and moved out behind him.

I kept a reasonable distance between us. At first, he was doing 80, but after about a mile of searching for me, he put the pedal down, as he tried to find my car in the traffic ahead. The Beamer was flying now. It broke 90, then 100, and I let the string run out a bit. It must have reached about 120 before the driver let up. The Mass State Police barracks was only a couple of miles ahead, and the silver sedan slowed to a more reasonable speed as we passed it.

I slid in behind a Subaru 4x4 with a co-exist bumper sticker and used it as a buffer for a while. However, I would soon need to decide between exiting the pike for I-84, which was my preferred route or keep up the tail. I was wishing Hiney would call back, so I'd have some information on who the Beamer belonged to.

We were about 5 miles from I-84 when the BMW moved sharply into the right lane and then onto an exit ramp. I got in behind a black SUV and followed. I stopped at a traffic light just four cars back, but the SUV kept me concealed. The Beamer went through the light and then hung a quick left into a McDonald's. There was a gas station across the street, so I pulled in and parked behind a set of fuel pumps well back from the roadway. I needed to fill up anyway. I got out, slid my card into the pump and peered through a zoom lens attached to a Nikon D850 that I keep behind the passenger's seat.

The driver's side window was half-down, and two people were having a discussion in the Beamer's front seats. The driver was a determined-looking young woman, in a white blouse and dark gray jacket. She had an oval face, dark complexion, thick full lips, and black shoulder-length hair. Her companion's face was difficult to see, but he appeared to be a middle-aged white guy. He had on a blue oxford shirt and dark jacket, but no tie. They were arguing.

It went on for a minute, and then she put her phone to her ear and gave him the Heisman. He got out and walked into the restaurant, and I got a couple of clear snapshots of him. His was an imposing figure. Plus, he had a bulge under his jacket.

I finished filling up and prepared to move out quickly, all while keeping one eye on the action across the street. The driver stared straight ahead, tapping her fingers on the steering wheel.

Just then, a young mother swung her SUV into the station and decided she wanted to use my lane. She hit her horn, and I ducked behind the pump. I didn't dare stand up, so I yelled to her from a crouch, "It won't start, waiting for triple A!" Her face told me just how much she cared about my problems, but she left me alone only to then drive to the other side of the pump and block my view across the street.

I peeked around the minivan, caught the pain-in-my-ass staring at me and gave her a big sarcastic smile. The Beamer was approaching the parking lot exit. I thought for a moment that they had spotted me and were coming across the street, but they hung a right out of McDonald's and turned onto the Pike heading east for Boston. I decided to follow. It was only 2 o'clock, Greenwich could wait. I jumped into the Caprice and moved out in pursuit.

When I caught up to it, the BMW was in the left lane and moving at about 80 miles per hour. I sat back and kept tail. After about 10 minutes, my phone rang. It was Ron Hines.

"Hiney!"

"Chief!"

"Whaddaya got?"

"It's a 2015 BMW 3 series, registered to a Boston-based company called Wayne Trust."

"You don't say."

"What are you involved in Chief?"

"Missing persons, but it may be something bigger. The people in the Beamer are armed. Sound like private security to you?"

"Jeez, I don't know. It's possible I guess a big financial company must have serious security, but why are they following you?"

"I'll let you know when I find out."

"You do that. And, be careful."

We disconnected. I squeezed my smartphone which activates the voice-controlled assistant. "Hey Google, please look up Wayne Trust Company in Boston, Massachusetts."

The artificial female voice I'd chosen came back within seconds, "Wayne Trust Company in Boston Mass. Here you go."

An address and phone number appeared on my screen: 150 Federal Street, right in the heart of the financial district. I wrestled with the decision to keep following them, likely all the way to 150 Federal, or turn around and go to Greenwich. I decided to take the next exit and reverse course.

I called Joanna on her office line. She picked up on the second ring.

"It's Earl Town. Why is Wayne Trust security tailing me?"

"Oh."

Was her surprise about the fact that there was a tail, or that I had spotted it?

"Let me call you right back from a more private place."

My phone buzzed a minute later, and Joanna's voice came through my speakers.

"Why do you think someone from Wayne Trust is following you?"

"Two people, a middle-aged man, and a younger woman tailed me, presumably from my place in Boston, down the Mass Pike until I caught on and lost them. They appear to be heading back to Boston. The car, a silver BMW 3 Series, is registered to Wayne Trust. What's going on?"

"I don't know anything about this. Do you think I was followed to your office this morning?"

"Possibly," I replied. "Look, you need to level with me. Is Wayne Trust looking for Mac, or hiding Mac?"

"I don't know why they'd hide him. His absence is not a good thing. Not right now."

"Why did you hire me?"

It took her a couple of seconds to respond. "I told you, I'm concerned about him. It isn't like him to just disappear." She raised her voice, "I don't know why more people aren't as concerned as I am!"

"I'm sorry," I said. "I'm concerned too. Questions like these are just part of the process. Who else at Wayne Trust is looking for him?"

"I don't know. As I told you, they don't include me in those discussions."

"Alright, I gotta go. It'll be okay, I'll find him."

"Thank you."

My phone rang a while later, as I was approaching Bridgeport. It was 3:29, and I was supposed to call Eddie in a minute, but he beat me to the punch.

"Edward, my favorite nephew."

"Earl," he said with disdain. That was his whole reply. No favorite uncle comment in return. He was waiting for me to ask him for the information I paid him to gather. The money wasn't enough. He needed me to ask for it. So, I did.

"Okay, what did you find?"

"I sent you a package of documents. About thirty of them. Mostly about Wayne Trust and the firm that's supposed to be buying it, but I also found a lot of background on MacArthur, Endicott, Sterling, and French. Oh, and Maria Moore too, and I even dug up a couple of things on Elizabeth MacArthur. She's really something."

"What's so great about Elizabeth?" This was Mac's second ex-wife. She kept his name after the divorce.

"She's the same age as me. Mac married her when he was 47, and she was 23, and had just graduated from UCLA, where she was on a volleyball scholarship." He said this last part as though she had gone into space or won a Super Bowl. He added, "There are videos of her playing on YouTube. She's lit."

"Lit?"

"Yeah, you know fresh, hot. She's a prize dude. Are you going to interview her? Need some help?"

"Keep it in your pants Ed, or I'll tell your mother." Despite living in my sister's basement, the kid actually had a decent rap with the ladies and usually had a girlfriend. He had a ton of self-confidence. Not from earning it of course, but because my sister gave him far too much praise and far too few kicks in the ass. He was a good kid though. I'd seen a lot of messed up kids in my cop days. I saw quite a few who got on hooked on hard drugs and never reached thirty. There are worse things than youthful arrogance.

"Alright, enough about your fantasy girl, I'm not gonna have time to read what you sent for a while. Give me the bullets. Start with James MacArthur."

"Okay, here we go. Number one, James MacArthur is rich AF."

"Please, save the slang for the next time you hang with your crew," I said.

"It means as fuck. He's rich as fuck. This guy sold a business he inherited to Wayne Trust for $150 million."

"I know that."

"Okay, but you didn't let me finish. The deal he struck paid him in Wayne Trust stock too. He owns stock options that convert to about a fourth of a percentage point of Wayne Trust common stock upon the sale of the firm to another entity. Only the CEO, who's also on your list, one Whitman Endicott, has more Wayne Trust stock."

"So, they both own a little stock, what's the point?"

"The impending deal is rumored to be a merger with a Swiss Bank."

I heard him flipping through papers. "Shit, I can't find the name of it – it's an acronym, and it's in what I sent you. Rumor on the street is, this bank is looking to buy Wayne Trust for $14 billion!"

"Holy shit. What do those percentages work out to?"

"Almost $100 million for Endicott and about $60 million for MacArthur."

I let out a long whistle.

"Tell me again Earl, what exactly are you investigating?"

"The disappearance of Mac, aka James MacArthur. Everybody calls him Mac."

"That's what I thought you said, but why on earth would he disappear, when he's about to make another $60 million?"

"I don't know." I considered the question. "Maybe someone wanted him to disappear."

"Surely, not Endicott with $100 million on the line. He can't be happy that a senior executive is missing when a deal like this is in the works, can he?" See, he's a smart kid.

"Okay, good stuff so far, what else you got?"

"So, one is, he's rich, two is, the deal will make him richer, and three is, he's the only one in his family getting rich. For now, anyway. His ex-wives aren't likely to see any of the new windfall."

"Oh, Miss Montez didn't mention this, tell me more."

"Miss Montez? You mean Maria Moore?"

"Yeah, that's right." I had a vision of young Maria anchoring the weekend desk on channel 9 on my mind. I added, "You wanna see lit, look up some old video of Maria Montez on the channel 9 news."

"I will," he replied a little too enthusiastically. "Well, the first ex-wife is well-taken care of and has no ownership stake in anything. The second ex-wife is in the same boat, but she's not happy about it. She filed suit against Mac in New York last year. That's where she lives in a $3 million co-op paid for by James, I mean Mac, but she wanted a bigger piece of the pie, including some of his Wayne Trust stock, and challenged the prenup on the grounds that his behavior during the marriage negated it."

"What kind of behavior?"

"That's not too clear, but the allusion is the usual stuff, you know, adultery. Though there's one article I found that said the agreement was designed to cover precisely that kind of behavior and her lawyer is trying to set a precedent that will seriously alter divorce law in New York."

"Where's the suit at now?"

"It got thrown out last month. Mac has better lawyers. Elizabeth threw a lot of shade at him in the tabloids. I sent you a couple of enlightening pieces from the New York Post. One is about a cocaine-fueled, late-night swim meet between Mac and a model in a Central Park fountain. What a life. She hasn't refiled the suit though so he may have fought her off for good."

"Hmmm, okay, so he's rich and getting richer, has lots of women in his past, including at least one angry ex-wife. What else you got?"

"Number four!" He said it as though he were introducing an athlete to a roaring stadium crowd. He enjoyed this work, but he wouldn't admit it and give me any leverage.

"Gibson French and Nathaniel Sterling are rich too."

"No kidding Ed, they all hang out at an exclusive yacht club in Greenwich."

"You interrupted me again. Wait until I finish." I tightened my grip on the wheel and bit my tongue.

"MacArthur and French have known one another since they were schoolboys. They went to Milton Academy together, and then both went onto Dartmouth. They've also been members of Indian Head for decades. I found an extract of a story about them winning a sailboat race in their teens, and the fathers of both James and Gibson are listed as former commodores of Indian Head."

"What does a commodore do?"

"You see Caddyshack?"

"About a dozen times, but I'm surprised you have. It's from before your time."

"Yeah well, new movies suck if you're not into guys in tights. I think it's like Judge Smails. The Commodore is the top dog, sort of runs the place. But, here's one more thing for you."

"Uh huh." I was trying to get around a slow driver in the left lane, what is it with these people, and was distracted.

"Nathaniel Sterling is the current Commodore." There was silence as I finally got around the idiot blocking about 15 other drivers and me from getting where we need to go, and he asked. "What do these guys have to do with this anyway?"

"Hopefully, they can tell me where he is. If I can get in to see them."

He said, "I sent an article about some problems at the club that should help you help with that."

"Excellent, thank you. Anything else?"

"Yup. Gibson French is a partner in a big-time New York law firm founded shortly after World War II by his grandfather. The firm is Holman, French, and Clark, and among the firm's prestigious clients are both Wayne Trust and the Indian Head Yacht Club."

"That's good to know. Anything else?"

I was trying to process everything and wanted to get off the call and think things through, but Eddie said: "Well, you asked me to tell you what Mac actually does. Here's a quick summary. Mac runs the retirement division for Wayne Trust. It's a big business. Annual revenues are about twenty percent of the total company take. His unit includes a bunch of business lines, the biggest of which is administering hundreds of billions in retirement plans for corporations and managing about a half trillion in mutual funds and other investments."

All this in two hours, the kid is actually worth $100 an hour, but no matter what I give him, he always asks for more.

"Four class action lawsuits were filed against the company since the start of last year. All four are targeting Mac's division."

"This is common for a big company, no?" I asked.

"Not in this case. These aren't like slip and fall at the office suits. They allege that Wayne Trust violated its duty as a fiduciary on four retirement plans with billions of dollars and tens of thousands of investors."

"What are they accused of doing exactly?"

"Well, the state of Tennessee ..."

"The state itself?"

"Yeah, their retirement plan for state employees. They allege Wayne Trust recommended its own mutual funds for 401(k) plans, when better and less expensive options were available, thereby earning millions more in fees for itself at the expense of company employees."

"Wow. That sounds serious."

"The articles I sent you show some of Wayne's competitors being hit with similar suits. You gotta think Mac might be under a lot of pressure with this stuff going on."

"This is good work, Ed."

He said, "I know. Well, that's everything, gotta go," and ended the call just like that. That's my nephew. Lazy, yet efficient. Why spend more time working than you absolutely have to?

I called him back. "Edward, you hung up too soon, how you would like to make another fifty?"

"You want me to look into French's law firm. I could tell when you paused."

"No, it's not that. I'm going send you photos of two people who I believe work for Wayne Trust, possibly in security, but maybe in management. Work your magic and see if you can find out who they are."

"Okay, I'll do my best."
"I ask for nothing more, Ed."

4

I checked into an Extended Stay, just outside of Greenwich, to keep the cost down for my client. I unpacked my overnight bag, cleaned myself up a bit, then went into town. There was no checkpoint at the Greenwich border to keep out the riff-raff, so I drove into the belly of the beast. Someday they'll wall this place off and only let in the help.

It felt a little conspicuous driving an old cop car through the land of excess, but no one seemed to notice me. They were too busy shopping at Hermes, Chanel, and a bunch of other stores that wanted nothing to do with Earl Town. I cruised the main drag in what they call "Old Greenwich" and marveled at the cheese, juice, and crepe shops. Where I'm from, they don't have shops like these. Hell, where I'm from crepes are called pancakes.

I found a coffee shop with free wi-fi and parked at a meter that had the nerve to charge me a buck for fifteen minutes. Inside, I ordered a double espresso and took up residence at a table in the corner. There I reviewed what Eddie had emailed me. Of particular interest was a story on some recent strife at Indian Head:

Employee Strike Threatens Indian Head Regatta
Chip Van Holden, Greenwich Standard, August 25, 2015.

Strong headwinds are threatening the sailors at Indian Head Yacht Club this weekend. Indian Head's nearly 100 employees are threatening to walk off the job if working conditions aren't improved, they say. This means the club's annual fall series regatta and Commodore's Cup races may have to be put on hold or altogether canceled. This is not the first time Indian Head faced a grave challenge. The adjoining tennis club burned to the ground in 1972, but the current rebellion may be even tougher to extinguish.

"This has been a long time coming," said Javier Pena, who works in the bar, and is an unofficial leader of the group. "We are fed up with being mistreated. We are human beings, and we have families to feed," said Mr. Pena at a Wednesday afternoon protest just outside the club gates. "They pay us slave wages, take away our benefits and lay off many hardworking people in the winter. We don't mind picking up after these people and their children, but they need to treat us with dignity and respect."

The group is asking for a living wage, overtime pay, guarantees that more employees will be kept on year-round, and to be treated with respect. Indian Head's vice commodore Nathaniel Sterling told the Greenwich Standard that club members were "saddened to learn about unrest among the staff, who are considered family to each and everyone who enjoys the history and beauty of Indian Head." He added that "club members have the utmost respect for the employees and plan to discuss, and address, these issues right away."

Another member told the Standard that several events have pushed the employees to take action. Among them is a recent incident in which a member of the wait staff was apparently thrown into Long Island Sound when a mistake was made in a drink order. The employee, a recent arrival from Guatemala, does not swim and nearly drowned before being pulled from the water by a group of participants in the teen races being held that day. There was another incident in July in which an Indian Head employee was reportedly injured, but town officials, citing privacy laws, would not disclose any details. According to an anonymous source familiar with the situation, the group who allegedly tossed the worker into the water includes several officers of the club. "Looks like rough seas ahead for the IHYC," that source said.

I nursed my coffee and scanned more documents, but I only had time to skim most of them. A more thorough review would have to wait until I got back to my hotel.

Homes in the center of Greenwich are stately, and probably sell for millions, but as I got closer to Indian Head, property values soared into the stratosphere. The houses I passed now were set well back from the street, but still easy to see because they were enormous. Some looked more like hotels or colleges than homes. Andover was beautiful, but this really was a touch of Newport during the gilded age. These were the homes, perhaps just summer cottages as with Newport, of today's robber barons. The men and women of Wall St., Madison Ave., and American media. People whose primary responsibility was to keep the stock price high and the public in the dark. People who professed to care genuinely about those less fortunate, while using their wealth and influence to keep those same people at a distance, except for the ones they paid to clean up after them and raise their children. I try to keep an open mind and not prejudge, but my blue-collar childhood left me with a big chip on my shoulder, and at that moment I felt envy-fueled anger at the conspicuous wealth around me.

The street came to a dead end, at which point I found a sign and gatehouse for Indian Head Yacht Club, established 1883. I set my old cop badge on the dashboard where it would be seen and made my approach. The guard was quick to step out and stand in front of the gate. Did the Caprice look that bad? I leaned out of my window. "Hey, let me through. We've just received a call about another assault on one of your employees. This is urgent."

"What?" The guard, who was probably barely in his twenties, was slow on the uptake.

"Look, I don't have time to explain, but apparently a couple of your members grabbed one of the female staff, stripped her naked, and forced her to be a human sushi platter for a private event on the patio. What is it with you fucking guys and the help? Now, let me in."

"I can't." He was in a panic and looking around for someone to help him, but there was no savior in sight. "Hold on a moment," he said and headed back to the gatehouse. He makes a call, and the jig is up, I thought. But, instead of going to the phone, he unhooked a clipboard from the wall, looked it over, then returned.

"Can I see some I.D. please," he held out his hand.

I handed him my driver's license and left the badge on the dash. "I'm not gonna be on there, I told you I got a call."

He looked it over for no more than a couple of seconds, then leaned into my window.

"Okay, you're all set, Mr. Town. You can pull up. Visitor parking is on the left. The main entrance is straight ahead from there. Have a good evening. I hope everything is okay."

"What, I'm on the list?" I threw it in park, climbed out and grabbed the clipboard out of his hand. There I was, five down from the top of the page.

Who told them I was coming? I could've asked Joanna to set up a meeting with Sterling, but I wanted to have a look around first and perhaps catch him off guard. They were a step ahead of me, multiple steps. Hell, they started to tail me only hours after I met Joanna.

I drove in, head spinning, and parked not far from the water's edge, but my view of it was obscured by row after row of sailboats. The big ones were on trailers, while the small ones were stacked five-high in steel racks. As I approached the farmer's porch that wrapped around the clubhouse, I looked out at a sea dotted with dozens more sailboats, including a couple that must be worth millions.

When I reached the steps, a timid looking man in deck shoes, tan pants, and a blue windbreaker over a pink polo shirt approached me with his right hand out. He was average height, middle age, thin, and balding on top with a hair island in the front. On his windbreaker was the Indian Head Yacht Club crest.

"Mr. Town. I'm Larry Ferncroft, Indian Head's rear commodore. Commodore Sterling is running late and asked me to escort you into the bar until he's free."

"Why that's nice of you, Larry," I shook his hand, and wondered just what a rear commodore does. "Say, how did Mr. Sterling know I was coming this evening?"

He ignored my question and motioned me to follow him inside. We entered through a set of doors into the lobby. Indian Head looked nothing like any clubs I'd been in before. It was cavernous, plush, and imposing. It was the kind of place where a group of teenagers goes to party and have sex and ends up being killed off one by one.

Directly in front of us was a dark wooden staircase, and to the right of that was a trophy case that would surely be the envy of any high school principal or university dean. It was filled with trophies, plates and assorted vessels made of sterling silver and fine crystal, and there were photographs of championship-winning crews sprinkled alongside the hardware. There was a separate case with a set of huge Tiffany & Co. sterling silver serving trays with the names of races and racing crews etched into them. There were oversized urns made of fine metals and intricately cut crystal vases. All of it sparkled under the glow of small spotlights. It was the history of the club illustrated through its victories.

I was staring dumbfounded at all the shiny objects when Larry suggested we move into the bar. But then my eyes focused on the restaurant next to it, which was filled with the sound of voices and laughter. Their source was a collection of well-dressed couples and families inside dining on white tablecloths. Every male in the restaurant wore a tie, even the boys, while the wait staff had on white jackets.

The back of the room opened onto a patio, and beyond that was the Long Island Sound. Life looked incredibly good here. I hesitated and took it all in before following the rear commodore into the lounge.

We entered a cozy pub with the requisite sailing theme. There were photos of boats, models of boats, paintings of boats, blueprints of boat designs, and parts of boats attached to the walls. And flags, lots of small flags of varied colors hanging from the top of the paneling. There were chalkboards with race results and daily club activities. This was summer camp for the rich and fortunate, and I found myself hating on Larry and everyone in this place. I understand that these could be some of the nicest people in the world. Who am I to judge? But dammit I did, and when Larry smiled and asked if I wanted a mojito, because Rooster, apparently that was the bartender's nickname, made a mean mojito, I briefly considered pulling my gun and shooting him.

The dress code was weekend at the Kennedy compound. Surprisingly, I fit in pretty well here with my standard blazer, oxford shirt, slacks, and loafers. There were lots of white slacks and shorts, polo shirts, and those French shirts with white and blue horizontal stripes. Oh, and salmon, the rich love to wear salmon. Everyone had an even tan and perfect teeth. Even the kid's clothes were clean, pressed and color coordinated.

We took seats at a four top along the interior wall under a couple dozen plaques listing the names of the winners of past races and regattas. I made a mental note to look up 'regatta' later. Larry stared at me with a dopey smile, and I couldn't decide if he was nervous or just stupid. He was still going on about the mojitos.

"Ah, no thanks. A glass of water will be fine for me, it's a work night." I said with a wink. I was trying to catch what Larry was saying while also eavesdropping on the conversations around me in the hopes that someone might say the name Mac.

"Is Mr. Sterling meeting us here?" Larry looked relieved that I'd asked, as he seemed to be struggling to come up with something to say.

"No, I believe you are to meet in the Commodore's office. He's unfortunately in another meeting at the moment, but he should be done soon. Are you sure you wouldn't like something to drink?"

I watched a waitress pass by with a tray of cocktails for a group of middle-aged women yucking it up around a fire pit on the patio. This was the life, and I wanted a taste too.

"What the hell, Larry. I'll have one after all."

"Splendid!" he called out. "Rooster, dos mojito por favor!"

"Si!" replied the Rooster.

In the moment, I regretted being so weak, but looking back I don't regret it. After Rooster, a diminutive Hispanic man in a white jacket, delivered the drinks, Larry suggested we move out onto the patio, and there have been several times in the months since, when I've caught myself thinking about the taste of that mojito and the view of the sun setting on the Long Island sound on that warm September evening. Then I recall the events that followed and my mood sours.

"Maybe I can help you. I hear you're looking for Mac?"

News travels at warp speed around here. "Seen him around?" I replied.

"Not since the races last Saturday. I had to be in New York that night, so I left while he was still on the water and haven't seen him since."

"Well, how is it that you may be able to help me?"

"I could introduce you to some of his other friends at the club."

"Can you tell me where Mac is? That would solve my problem."

"No, I'm sorry I don't know him that well." Larry leaned in close, and whispered, "But rumor has it he took off to the Caribbean with a European model. He has a reputation, you know."

"So, I've heard. Is Mr. Endicott here tonight?"

"Whit? I haven't seen him, but he might be out there on the Lush Life." He pointed to a massive yacht anchored in the Sound about a football field away. "If so, he'll probably come over later, after dinner hours. The patio scene gets pretty rowdy here, even on a Monday night." He grinned.

"Are you married?" he asked, with a look at my ring hand, which was free of jewelry.

"No, not for a while now."

"Well, we have many single female members. I'll bet you'd enjoy the patio later this evening."

"Which of these boats belongs to Mac?"

"The Hylas 70, there." He pointed to an enormous sailboat anchored not far from Endicott's craft.

"Jesus, that's a big one too." This thing was twice the length of the house I grew up in. "What does something like that go for?"

"Go for?" He had a pained look on this face like a bad smell had wafted in off the water. I had committed a faux pas. Like I cared. "Well, the Hylas is actually inexpensive compared to similar boats of its size, and it depends on the options and age. That one's new, Mac launched it in the spring, and he's not one to skimp on the features, so

I expect it's worth a couple million."

I whistled.

"How about Mr. French? Where's his?"

He pointed another large yacht, though smaller than those of End-icott and MacArthur. This one was moored to a dock.

"Nice," I said. "He around tonight?"

Larry surveyed the room. "Gibby? Nope, I don't see him. After Labor Day, he seldom comes during the week. He's what we call a summer sailor. I sail until Halloween weather permitting." As he said this, a slender mid-thirtyish brunette woman with big brown eyes, requisite white pants, white and blue striped top, and deep tan came up behind Larry and placed her hands over his eyes, one of which featured a huge diamond and a wedding band.

"Guess who?"

"Ah, not my wife," he said. "She'd never press her chest against me the way you are." Nice one, Larry.

She came around to face him, and they hugged. Then she turned and looked at me expectantly.

Larry did the honors. "Tinsley Saunders, this is Earl Town. Earl, Tinsley Saunders, a long-standing member of Indian Head."

"Hi there," she said, looking me over. "Are you a newbie?" She knew I wasn't.

"I'm the new tennis pro," I said feigning a forehand.

"Really? Well, I don't need any lessons, but maybe we can play a set sometime." She smiled two thousand watts, and I saw fire burning in her eyes.

"Okay, but I should warn you, I've got a killer overhead smash."

She giggled while I feigned clobbering a tennis ball, but then Larry's damn phone buzzed against the table and the moment was over. He answered, and an angry male voice could clearly be heard coming from the speaker. Larry said, "Okay, yes, very good. I'll bring him right up." He disconnected and turned to me. "Ah, Mr. Town, the Commodore is ready for you."

I looked at Tinsley. "What a shame. Perhaps, I'll see you on the court."

"I'd like that," she winked at me, and I felt a jump in my step that I hadn't felt in months.

Larry encouraged me to take my drink as we departed, but this was a business meeting, it was time to focus. We made our way back into the lobby and then up the staircase, and I thought about teen slasher movies again. Just what awaited me on the top floor?

5

I found Commodore Nathaniel Sterling waiting for me outside his third-floor office. He wore a navy sports coat with gold buttons and the club's crest, over a white polo shirt and perfectly-creased pants. All of this was mounted on a pair of impeccable boat shoes, and plaid socks. The socks screamed party animal, and I wanted to ask him where he got them but bit my tongue.

I had imagined him older. He had neatly trimmed blonde locks parted on the left. This made him look more surfer than sailor. He was nearly as tall as me, which pissed me off as I'm 6'3, and used to looking down on my prey. I amped up the pressure in my handshake out of a need to impress on him my dominance as an alpha male, and he gave me a knowing smile that said, 'I know what you're doing, and you don't scare me.'

Without breaking our stare, Sterling thanked Larry and turned his back to him. It took the poor guy a couple of seconds before he got the message and headed back downstairs.

The office had the obligatory dark wood molding and featured a small collection of model sailboats under glass. His desk and two brown leather club chairs sat in the middle of a space that was about twice as long as it was wide. Behind the desk, was a set of French doors through which soaring masts were visible.

He announced, "It's a gorgeous evening. Let's talk on the balcony and enjoy the sunset." Despite the Ken doll looks, he was an elegant sort.

He walked over to one of the more opulent bar cabinets I'd ever seen. It was veneered in an exquisitely polished burled wood and accentuated with an intricate serpentine design across the front. The veneers likely took hundreds of hours of hand craftsmanship to create. My ex-wife was a furniture restorer and dealer, and I was sure she would've appraised this piece for at least thirty-grand.

He scooped ice into a crystal rocks glass. "It's been a long day, and I'm going to have a taste of the Dalmore. Would you like one?"

Everyone wants to get me off my game, I thought. But it wasn't every day I got offered finely aged scotch. "That'd be great, thanks."

"French chinoiserie, 1930's," I said, referencing the bar. He tilted his head confused for a second, before smiling. "That's very good. Mr. Town. You catch a lot of furniture thieves?" He opened the doors to the balcony and extended his arm, at the end of which he held my scotch.

"I've asked my assistant to hold my calls. Let's go outside."

I didn't move. "Your assistant is still working?" It was nearly 7:00 p.m.

"Yes, the place requires long hours during the season. Soon it'll quiet down though." He puffed his chest like he was on stage and added, "The days, they do grow short."

"How did you know I was coming here this evening?"

He took his eyes off the setting sun and looked over at me with a cocky smirk. "We're concerned about Mac too, Mr. Town. He has a lot of friends here at the club, including me." He stepped out onto the spacious wooden perch, and I followed. On the deck sat a small teak table and set of Adirondack chairs, and a small gas fire pit, with an already flickering flame. He had everything he needed for a romantic evening, but the right partner. He wasn't my type.

He stretched out in the chair nearest the fire and directed me to one opposite it.

"You didn't answer my question, Mr. Sterling. I was hired this morning, and haven't had time to speak with many people, yet you were aware that I would be coming by the club tonight. Are you having me followed?" I said this with a smile.

"I reached out to Joanna Hill this afternoon. I wanted to know if she'd heard anything from Mac. She mentioned hiring you, and that you planned to speak with Mac's ex-wife Maria. So, I assumed she would send you here and had you put on the list. Next time though, you really should just give the guard your name. It took some effort to convince him that a female staffer hadn't been assaulted tonight." He wasn't smiling now. So much for my impending membership.

He sipped his scotch and gazed out at the water through a clear glass railing. Waves were breaking against the club's docks and a cluster of boulders that protected the shoreline, creating a steady hum. The whitecaps caught and reflected the sun's dying rays. Snippets of conversation and laughter drifted up from the patio below. It was the perfect fall evening on Long Island Sound.

"Did you speak with Maria Moore?" I asked.

"No, I haven't spoken with Maria in a long time. I have no reason to."

He was nothing if not a cool customer. He was in no hurry to get to the point, and the balcony offered an excellent vantage point for him to point out the various areas within the club grounds, which were more extensive than I'd thought. There was an Olympic size swimming pool, with high dive platforms, and about a dozen tennis courts. Beyond a boathouse, I could see a series of fire pits burning along the beach. I knew that the club was on Indian Head Point but now realized that the club was Indian Head Point. They owned the whole damn thing. The real estate alone must be worth tens of millions.

I went back to the mission. "When did you last see or hear from Mac?"

"The Saturday before last. He was here at the club racing that afternoon, and, as I recall, he spent that evening in the restaurant and the bar. He was in good spirits."

"Did he leave alone?" He eyed me for a second and averted his gaze back to the setting sun. I noticed that many of the boats had solar lights that had kicked on as the darkness grew. The water was illuminating like a starry sky.

"I'm not at liberty to say, Mr. Town. Privacy is essential to the Indian Head experience. What goes on at Indian Head, stays at Indian Head." He smiled at his little joke and swirled his scotch.

"Was he perhaps with a woman who is technically *with* someone else?" I asked, sensing he was hiding an indiscretion.

"He was with several people that night. Then I believe he took a small craft out to his yacht."

"The Hylas 70?" I asked while pointing at the boat Larry had shown me.

"Yes, that's the one," he reluctantly admitted. "You're familiar with boats such as these, detective?"

"No, not at all," I replied.

"Oh, well the Rebecca is a real beauty. Mac is very proud of her."

"Rebecca, is that her name?"

"Yes."

"Is that his mother's name? It's not one of the ex-wives, and he doesn't have a daughter."

"I'm not sure, he was elusive about the name."

"But, you're a good friend of his?"

"Yes, I joined the club twenty years ago, and Mac has been a member since childhood. We spent many days sailing together."

"But you don't know if he named the boat after his mother?"

"His mother wasn't named Rebecca," he relented. "Isn't this beside the point Mr. Town?"

I pressed on. "Where do you think Mac is?"

He stared out at the last remnants of the sun's fire. "He's probably with a girl or two. Maybe in Rome? He likes Rome. Or maybe Bellagio? He loves Como too. He isn't on his boat, I can tell you that. And, as I said, he hasn't been to the club."

"How do you know he isn't on that boat right there?" I pointed to the Rebecca.

"The security of our members and their property is paramount to us Mr. Town. Our staff investigated Mac's craft when his whereabouts became a concern. We've since made sure it's locked up tight."

"So, someone has visited the boat? Made sure everything is kosher?"

"Yes, several times."

Most of the boats moored in front of Indian Head were tied to a set of long docks that stretched out into the Sound. Each had extensions to the right and left with additional moorings. But, the largest yachts, including the Rebecca, were anchored in deeper water a good distance from the docks. "How does someone go back and forth to a boat like the Rebecca?"

"We have smaller craft they take back and forth."

"Did Whitman Endicott ask you to investigate the Rebecca?"

He turned and gave me his best *fuck you* smile. "I'm not going to discuss the conversations of the club's members with you, Mr. Town."

"I'd like to find Mac and put my client's mind at ease."

He shook his head, dismissively. "Let's get to the real point, detective. If it's money you're after, the privacy of our members is important enough that I will be more than happy to pay you to go away. Is that what you really want, a check?"

I reacted with anger, which doesn't usually go well. "Listen. I made a commitment to my client. I'd like your help, but I sure as hell don't want your money."

He smiled, pleased with himself for setting me off.

"Is he with Rebecca?"

Sterling pulled up his left shirt sleeve, revealing a sparkling gold wristwatch, which he eyed. "I have other matters to attend to this evening and must take my leave, Mr. Town. I'll call you when I hear from Mac, which will likely be any day now."

He stood up and motioned for me to depart via the French doors, as he said, "Mac is a popular man, with friends all over the world. He could be with any number of them."

"That boat there with all the lights on." I pointed to Endicott's beastly craft. "Is Whitman Endicott on it?"

"No," he lied. "That belongs to another member."

"Is Gibson French here this evening? I'd like to speak with him as well."

"I haven't seen him at the club tonight, but I'll give him your information if I do."

"Which one is his boat?"

He smiled at me, said nothing, and led me through the office to the top of the staircase, where I gave him hard eyes. "You're not being straight with me."

He shook his head and gave me another dismissive smile. "I've been very generous with my time Mr. Town. Good night."

"Did Mac leave alone that last night or not?"

He brushed past me and started down the stairs, speaking over his shoulder as we went. "Yes, he left by himself. That's all I'm going to say about the business of our members, Mr. Town."

We reached ground level, and Sterling walked me to the door. I said, "I'd be a lot more concerned if my friend disappeared."

"You're not like us, Mr. Town. If your mate had the kind of resources at your disposal that Mac does ..." As he said this, he opened his hands and looked around the lobby, then he looked down his nose at me. "You'd know that he'd just dropped out for a little breather and will drop back in whenever he's ready. This kind of behavior sometimes upsets people, but they forgive us, as long as we keep picking up the check."

As he walked me out to the front porch, he brought the B.S. to a crescendo.

"Mr. Town, Indian Head is a historic and exclusive club. Our members demand a high level of privacy. I will help you any way I can. But please, you must be discreet. There are many powerful people here who will react very badly if they believe someone is rummaging through their trash, so to speak."

"Mac is the trash?"

"You know that's not what I meant, Mr. Town."

"Are you threatening me?" I had to ask.

"No, of course not." He was all smiles again. "I just don't want to see either one of us having to deal with headaches we don't need."

"Headaches. Okay. I have a migraine, and the only fix is a tour of Mac's boat. Take me out there and let me have a look around."

This caught him off guard, and he stepped back almost bumping into a woman who was exiting the club with her teenage kids.

He held up his hands and said, "No, Mr. Town. This is what I mean about invading the privacy of our members."

"Have you yourself been on the boat since he disappeared?"

He shook his head.

"Why don't we go out and take another look now? We could swing by Endicott's boat too. I think I saw a light on."

"I've really got to go. It's been a pleasure. Roger will see to it that you get out of here safely." He looked over my shoulder, then spun around and headed for the staircase.

I turned and found the kid from the gatehouse waiting for me.

"I got it, Roger," I said, as I brushed past him.

On my way into Indian Head, I had driven by a place called the Ridgeway Shore Club. It was a large white shingled building constructed above a private members-only beach. It was only about a half mile from the yacht club. I drove the short distance to it, pulled into the parking lot and maneuvered the Caprice under a gargantuan maple tree at the far end, where it was dark. Then I hopped out and got down to business.

6

The Caprice was built for performance and was inconspicuous, but there was another benefit to driving it. The huge trunk offered storage space for a wide range of useful items, and I kept it well stocked and organized. I had yet to use some of its content, hello Pocket Fisherman, but others, like the rations, solar battery chargers, and high-powered binoculars had come in handy, mostly during stakeouts. Tonight, I had an opportunity to use some very special gear.

About a year prior, I had a case that called for me to surveil a cheating husband on his boat in Chatham. Since then, I had stored a small inflatable raft underneath the main trunk compartment in that space around the rim of the spare tire. A pair of oars were strapped to the inside of the trunk lid, along with a small boat motor with plastic propeller and 48-inch shaft. It ran on a couple of 100-watt lithium batteries and wasn't fast, but in tonight's mild surf, it would glide the small raft to where I needed to go. The oars were a back-up.

I removed my jacket and shoes and stepped into a dark jumpsuit. This offered excellent concealment in the dim moonlight. It also had numerous pockets, including several that were waterproof. Into these, I stashed my phone, a flashlight, my gun, a knife, and several zip ties. It pays to be prepared for anything. I put on a pair of black running shoes and slid the raft into a large pocket, then used a couple of bungee-chords to strap the small motor to my back. I grabbed the oars and headed for a small patch of trees to the right of the Ridgeway Shore Club, beyond which I could see the Sound. Once at the water's edge, I quickly inflated the raft via a CO_2 cartridge and slipped into the water.

While on Sterling's balcony, I had counted the boats moored in the Sound in front of Indian Head and had come up with about 60. A couple dozen of these were big enough to be anchored away from the docks in large clusters. All of these boats had cabins, and thus the potential for passengers who might not appreciate me sneaking around in the dark. Mac's boat was in the rear corner of the cluster furthest from the Shore Club and thus would be among the more difficult to reach without alerting anyone.

Rather than row straight out to Mac's boat, I plotted a more circuitous route to avoid detection, and it took about 20 minutes to reach the front edge of the group of boats in which Mac's craft, the Rebecca, was moored. The electric motor was crucial as the nearly silent engine made moving through tight passages less nerve-racking.

There was only a sliver of the moon out that night, but the sky was clear, and the stars were out in force. They sparkled above me and were reflected on the surface of the waves over which I stealthily guided the raft, staying in the shadows as best I could. Then I spotted trouble up ahead. I was approaching a huge catamaran when the sound of laughter alerted me that a couple was seated on the boat's deck. I killed the motor and drifted over into a gap between two huge single-hull sailboats and considered whether to wait or go back around and approach from the other direction. This would take considerable time, and I risked running the motor's battery down to nil, which would leave me having to row back to shore.

Fragments of their conversation were picked up by the ocean breeze, carried from wave tip to wave tip, and dropped into my ears, and I realized they were young. The male was awkward, but undaunted, in his pursuit of the girl, and it wasn't long before I heard the unmistakable sounds of lovemaking. I took advantage of their distracted state and made my move. Keeping my head low, I passed within about fifteen feet of their copulation. It sounded like Romeo was more than making up for his awkward come on. After a few more minutes of gliding over the water's surface, I had reached the Rebecca. I tied my raft to the stern of the long, sleek craft and climbed aboard.

Coming here without permission was a risk I had to take. I needed to see if Mac was onboard or had been recently. I stayed low and surveyed my surroundings. I listened for voices and watched for movement and anything that seemed out of place. All was quiet on the Rebecca.

I crawled up to an elevated area below the main mast, laid on my belly, and took out my high-powered field glasses. This vantage point gave me a terrific view of Indian Head's patio as well as into the pub and restaurant through several sets of open French doors. An hour until closing time and the place was still crowded. I caught sight of the Commodore on the patio. He was seated around a fire pit with two men and two women, one of whom was my new friend Tinsley Saunders. Though sitting together, the men and women were having separate conversations. The women laughed at times while the men wore serious expressions. Twice I saw them look towards the Rebecca.

The man sitting closest to Sterling looked an awful lot like the photos of Gibson French that Eddie found online. There was a sprig of mint in his glass, he was drinking a mojito.

I stashed the binocs, and stepped down into a rectangular seating area, at one end of which was the padlocked entrance to the cabin. I fished a packet from inside my jumpsuit and using its contents, made quick work of the lock. I'd inherited the set of picks from a man named Calvin whom I'd busted a decade ago for a string of break-ins. He was a hell of a picker, and fortunately not one to hold a grudge. Not when I made him an offer he couldn't refuse for the set and a few lessons shortly after becoming a P.I. As an ex-cop, I knew what I was doing was wrong, but like it or not, some cases can't be solved if one stays within the constraints of the legal system. When someone is missing, and potentially in danger, it's not hard to justify a B&E. I wasn't going to steal anything, just looking for clues.

I opened the hatch and peered in, wondering as I did, if boats as sophisticated as the Rebecca came with alarm systems, and wishing I'd asked Eddie to look into it. It was too late now.

I took six steps down into a dining area. A table and banquette were on my left, and a built-in workspace with requisite communication equipment was on my right. Straight ahead was a door, while behind me was a small galley kitchen, at the end of which was another door. The woodwork, which was everywhere, was a rich, well-polished maple that reflected the low light emitted by my pen-sized flashlight.

I began my search with a detailed look around the main room, which was immaculate. No papers were lying about or dinnerware in the sink. The trash cans, often a good source of information, were empty. It looked like a cleaning crew had been through, and I wondered if the club hired a cleaning service for their members' boats and when they last serviced this one.

I walked over and opened the door that was under the steps I'd taken to get down into the cabin. Behind it was a small bedroom. The bed was just big enough to fit two people if they knew each other very well. It was set on a platform and underneath this were a couple of small doors that concealed a set of drawers filled with men's clothing. There was more storage built into the walls above the bed and along the sides of it, but I found nothing out of the ordinary in any of it, except perhaps a couple of adult toys that I was careful not to touch. I noticed that the bed was freshly made, and I didn't come across any dirty laundry.

After about ten minutes, I began to grow concerned about my inability to see or hear if anyone was approaching. This wasn't like a house, where there are multiple exits. There was only one way out of the cabin. As I made my way back towards the compartment at the opposite end, I decided to go back up top and take in the scene.

I heard voices as I hit the top step and ducked back down into the stairwell. Were they on the deck? I listened intently for a bit, then slowly made my way back up and discovered the source. The young lovers had just passed by on a small craft and were a good distance away now. I crept back to the elevated platform by the main mast and scanned the periphery. All was clear, though the group I'd seen earlier was no longer seated around the firepit. I went back down into the cabin and across to the other door.

Behind it was another bedroom, with a similar layout, only this one had an even larger cabinet bed. Inside, I found plastic storage bins containing a couple pair of boots, rain slickers, flares, some maps, and pieces of equipment I took to be spare parts, but no clues.

I noticed a set of picture frames above the bed and trained my light on them. From left to right, Mac had assembled the important women in his life. There was a black and white photo of a distinguished woman with 60s clothes and bouffant hair, must be Mac's mother. Next to Momma MacArthur was a picture of Mac and Maria Moore on a tropical vacation about 15 years ago. Maria was in a tiny white bikini and holding a coconut with a straw sticking out of it. The early sanguine days of a failed marriage. Next to this was a shot of Mac and wife number two, Elizabeth. She was young, tan and a couple of inches taller than Mac. He looked like a proud father dropping his daughter off at college, but they were holding hands, and she was eyeing him in such a way that it was clear the relationship was carnal. There were no other frames. Where's Rebecca?

I had seen everything and found nothing suspicious, except that is for the cleanliness of the cabin. It was too sterile, as though it had been scrubbed, and that left me feeling unsettled. I backed out and closed the door.

I ran my light around the main cabin for a second time, and when I scanned the galley, it caught an odd reflection from the base of the banquette in the corner. Something shiny protruded from behind the cushions. Hidden behind it, I found a pair of stainless-steel racks like the ones used in an oven. I turned and shined my light on the high-end stove, but it was a compact model and too small for these racks. However, they looked to be just about right for the ship's sub-zero refrigerator. They don't cut corners on these million-dollar boats, I thought, as I tugged on the stainless-steel door handle.

The first thing that hit me was the smell, and I spun around immediately and vomited into the sink opposite the fridge. When I recovered enough to turn back around, I saw, in the eerie glow of the refrigerator light, the late James MacArthur. He had been rolled in plastic and folded into the small space, hands on knees, knees against chest and chin. His bowels and bladder and God only knows what else had released and pooled in a plastic bin in which the body was seated.

I pulled out a handkerchief and held it tight over my nose and mouth. Mac was in profile, so my view was of his left-side. It was difficult to see through the material wrapped around him, but it looked to me like he had a sizable wound on the back of his head. His eyes were closed, and he appeared peaceful. The air in the fridge was cold but not cold enough to stave off decomposition, and I thought for a moment that it would've been better if Mac had splurged on a large freezer as well.

I snapped a couple of photos on my phone, then closed the door. I needed time to consider my next move. Things had suddenly become complicated. Just then I felt the boat dip a little, as though someone had come aboard. I killed my pen light and froze.

I waited in the pitch dark, with the smell of decaying flesh and vomit thick in the air and I wondered if the odor was strong enough to reach the nostrils of someone deck side and alert them that the refrigerator had been breached.

Nothing moved for a good two minutes, and I was about to chalk it up to nerves and make my way to the stairs when I heard the unmistakable sound of footsteps approaching the cabin entrance. I patted my pockets to make sure nothing would jingle, then started to creep over to the space behind the stairs so I would be in position to sneak past the intruder and out of the cabin after they descended. Or, at least surprise them if it became necessary to stand my ground.

But as my gloved hands groped in the darkness for the railing, there was a sudden flash of light, and I knew I'd made a mistake. I spun sharply to my left and felt a taser dart slice through the air just past my neck. I'd avoided fifty thousand volts, but now I was facing away from my attacker, and the shooter closed the gap between us in a split second. Before I could avoid a second attack, something heavy struck the back of my head, and I fell forward, my mind spiraling down into a cold, dark abyss.

7

It was night, and I was in my bed upstairs at the old cottage on Lake Winnipesaukee. The voices of my parents and siblings wafted up through the ancient pine floorboards. My family was playing penny-ante poker by the big stone fireplace. Tomorrow we would fish and swim in the warm, dark water.

Then the voices grew louder, and I sat up. My ears caught hold of a creak in the well-worn stairs, and my mind raced. Footsteps accelerated down the hall. Someone or something knocked, then pounded on the door. A woman's voice, her words muffled, I strained to make sense of it. Her voice rose, and the words became clear. "He's dead."

The door swung inward, and a bright searing light ripped me from the sheets and engulfed me. It dragged me back into consciousness.

I was lying face down on the floor of my raft, my cheek adhered to the rubber by dried spit, throat and lips desiccated.

I blinked and was slammed by a searing pain across my brow. I tried to force my eyes open. They resisted. A high-pitched squeal filled my right ear, a wavering hum consumed my left. I felt another wave of pain, this time from the back of my skull. I stayed still while the ache swept from the deep recesses of my brain to my eyes, and back again. I heard a woman say, "Okay, so he's not dead, but he doesn't look too good."

Something tugged at my feet, and a man said, "Buddy, are you okay." Then I heard him say, "He's bloody, call 9 1 1."

I gingerly rubbed and opened my eyes. Amber leaves and sunlight reflected off the surface of the water. I tried to focus on the waves, but little fireworks started going off. I squeezed them shut as I tried to recall how I'd come to be here.

My mind rolled back to yesterday morning and waking up in my apartment in Southie, but I struggled to recall what happened after that.

I opened my lids again and rolled onto my back. I lifted my head, rested it on the side of the raft and felt a shockwave of intense pain ripple from the top of my head to the small of my back. It was so strong it made my teeth ache, and I called out in pain.

I sat up and wrapped my arms around the side of the small craft and squeezed until the pain relented. I heard the man's voice again. "Don't move, son. You got a head injury. My wife is getting help."

Memories came rushing back. I recalled meeting Joanna Hill and driving south on I-95. I remembered entering a Japanese garden through a tall fence with horizontal planks and meeting the anchor-woman. I released my right hand from its grip on the raft and gingerly touched the back of my head and felt a mat of dried blood.

Slowly, I slid my body backward until my legs were hanging over the side. I touched solid ground and lifted myself onto a patch of grass along the shore. I stayed there, on all fours, trying to find the strength to stand. The man was next to me now, insisting I stop moving. He had stale breath, and I gagged as he helped me sit on the embankment.

"Where am I?"

Then his wife was by his side, and they started arguing. Neither had brought their phone. He told her if I died it was on her for forgetting it, and she told him he was off his rocker.

The man looked to be in his 70s, had sparse white hair, loose and spotted skin, and wore a blue tracksuit. The woman was about the same age and wore a similar outfit with a matching visor that read 'The Good Life.' She had a mouthful of gum and said around chews, "He's hurt. Look at the blood on his head."

The man turned to her and said, exasperated: "I know he's hurt, Bernice. That is precisely why I asked you to call 911."

I tried to get up but fell back to my knees after the first step. I rested my head on the ground in front of me and summoned the courage to stand again. I finally managed to pull myself up onto my feet and immediately felt a wave of nausea roll over me. I took a couple of steps, dropped to my knees again and deposited the contents of my stomach onto the grass.

The man said, "Buddy, you got a concussion. You wait right here, and I'll go and get some help." He gently placed a hand on my shoulder, and added: "Okay?"

I nodded and felt nauseous again.

He stood up to go, and Bernice said: "He needs to go to a hospital."

"Jesus, will you please turn up your hearing aid Bernie!"

I announced, though I'm not sure they understood me, as I was slurring: "I'm okay, thank you. I just need a minute." I stood and held up my hand. They stopped bickering and stared at me.

"Where is Indian Head?" I asked.

"Indian Head?" The man said it as though he'd never heard of it. "Why it's about a mile up that way." He pointed in the direction I was facing. Now he looked at the woman. "How many times have I told you that place is trouble, and now look what we have here."

"You weren't telling me anything I didn't know."

"I'm okay. Thank you for your help," I said. "I'm going to get my car and come right back for the raft. Don't worry about me or this stuff. I'll take care of it." I started walking towards the street.

Bernice said, "Alan, stop him; he needs help."

"What the hell do you expect me to do?" he replied. I didn't look back.

The walk to the Caprice felt as though it would never end. I had been washed ashore in an affluent neighborhood not far from Indian Head Point. The previous night's events came flooding back as I stumbled along the roadside. I recalled my conversation with Sterling, taking the raft into the Sound, exploring the Rebecca, finding Mac, and being struck on the head.

The more I recalled, the less I wanted to have to answer questions from the cops about any of it. So, I compartmentalized the pain and bouts of blurry vision and drove back to the hotel post-haste. That is, after I stopped, deflated the raft, and quickly threw it and the motor back into my trunk. I also stopped to puke several more times on the way.

The hotel was sanctuary. I barged into my room, turned up the air conditioner and lay face down on the bed for a long while. I wanted so badly to sleep, but the throbbing in my head wouldn't let me, and I knew it was the wrong thing to do if I had a concussion. Eventually, I pulled myself up and stumbled into the bathroom. I dug through my overnight bag for pain reliever and was in such a rush to open them that I flung half the bottle onto the floor when the cap finally released. I stared into the mirror and saw a sorry mess reflected back at me. I needed to see what was up with the back of my head and would use my phone to take a snap of it. Unfortunately, my phone was nowhere to be found.

After patting myself down and going through my pockets several times, I scanned every surface in the room. Then I got on hands and knees and checked the floor, including under the bed. Nothing.

It must be in the car, I thought. I stepped into my shoes, grabbed my keys, clutched the doorknob to the outside world and braced myself for the light of day. I turned the knob and squinted outside, waiting for my eyes to adjust, before finally making my way to the Caprice. I looked everywhere, but no phone. I got out and opened the trunk. I pulled out my jumpsuit and the raft and examined them, but no luck.

I went back inside, sat on the bed and called my cell number from the hotel phone. It rang, and I put the receiver down. I opened the door to the parking lot and listened intently for my ringtone. I recalled taking the snaps of Mac's body in the fridge and just knew that the phone hadn't gone missing. It had been taken from me. My evidence was gone.

I decided to call my voicemail. Maybe someone found my phone and called me to tell me he had it. Maybe Alan and Bernice did. I found a message waiting for me. It was left at 7:33 that morning. A bright female voice said, "Mr. Town. This is Elizabeth MacArthur. I understand you're looking for my husband. I think I can help you. Please call me as soon as possible." She left a number with a Manhattan area code.

I needed water and caffeine and lots of it, but I needed to clean up first, so I made my way to the bathroom and started the shower. My head throbbed, and I felt nauseous, but I climbed in and let the water run on my chest and then on my head and face. I carefully probed the back of my skull, where I found a lump the size of a golf ball and a cut about two inches in length running southeast to northeast through the center of it.

The water helped the clouds part. More of my meeting with Joanna came back to me, then I flashed on Maria Moore again. First, I recalled talking to her poolside, then I remembered the picture of her in a bikini on Mac's boat. I let the hot water run on the back of my head for a while to clean the wound, then got out, toweled off and dressed slowly. The pain had dulled, but not enough, so I popped two more pills. I couldn't bear the thought of trying to shave, given how unsteady my hands were, so I left the stubble.

I needed a new phone, stat. I fished my tablet out of the overnight bag in the closet, got online, and located a nearby dealer. Then, since I had no mobile with GPS app, I wrote down directions for the first time in years. I would first go back to where I washed ashore and look for my phone. If I didn't find it there, I'd go buy a new one. I grabbed my keys and wallet and opened the door.

I found myself staring straight into the face of the large man from the BMW. Before I could move, he reached in with a big hairy mitt, took me by the throat and slammed me into a dresser. I started to reach for my Glock, but the girl had moved swiftly in behind him, and she took hold of my right wrist and twisted my arm up behind my back until I thought for sure it would break. She grabbed my other wrist and cuffed the two of them together with tremendous efficiency. While she did this, the tall man reached into my holster and removed my weapon. He then tossed me into a worn lounge chair in the corner, and the two of them loomed over me.

I should've been nervous, but my training, and experience as a cop, had taught me to remain calm in these situations. I assumed they were my attackers from the prior evening and deduced that if they had wanted to kill me, they would've done so already. Therefore, they needed me alive. I decided to go on offense and didn't wait for them to start the conversation.

"You jerkoffs must be tired after lugging my ass off the yacht last night. I'm surprised you didn't sleep in."

The man, who was standing over me like Ali to Liston, looked at the woman and shook his head. "What did I tell you about small-town cops and private eyes?" She was parked at the foot of the bed taking the room in. She shrugged, unimpressed.

"What about small-town cops? You're such a tough guy. You and your girlfriend knock me out when I'm not looking and then jump me when I open my door. Give me a chance next time. I'll teach you some things I learned as a small-town cop."

He smirked at me, and I tried to stand up so I could look him in the eye, but he quickly shoved me back down. He pushed so hard that the chair slid back until it met the wall. My head hit the chairback, and I winced in pain.

"Take these fucking handcuffs off me, this is kidnapping," I said through gritted teeth as my skull began to ache again.

He looked at me with pity. If they hadn't taken my Glock, I would've shot him in the face and kneecapped his partner. I wanted a fight, and they weren't going to allow me to partake. Now he spoke again.

"You are a dumb ass redneck small-town Cow Hampshire shithead." He turned and looked incredulously at his partner, then turned back to me. "You have stumbled into something much bigger than you can imagine." I held his stare and did my best not to show the confusion I was feeling.

He leaned in closer, but not close enough for me to kick him, which was my only move given my hands were shackled behind me.

"You're so stupid that you think we kicked your ass last night. What else do think you know, former Chief Town? Please enlighten us." He said chief, as though it was a joke I'd once held that title. While he smirked at me, she showed no emotion. She was an uninterested observer hanging out on the periphery taking in the room and its contents.

His calling me chief meant they had done their homework. I wished I'd had the chance to circle back to Ed. I wondered if he emailed me something I could use now. "You're just pissed that I lost your tail yesterday. You two couldn't even follow a simple redneck."

Neither one betrayed any annoyance at that, so I turned it up. "You know, I followed you and watched while you stopped at McDonald's and then got back on the Pike."

Surprise, then anger, rolled through the man's eyes like a small tremor, but he snuffed it out fast. So, I went further. "I could've followed you two all the way back to Wayne Trust and surprised you." He turned sharply and glared at her, laying all the blame for the loss of their anonymity on her. She frowned back, not accepting it. She might be young, but she wasn't about to take any bullshit.

I had broken their facade, but I'd also said too much. If killing me was an option for them, then announcing that I knew this much about them, significantly increased the odds. I needed to learn to shut up when I was ahead.

He moved closer and stood over me grinding his teeth.

"Want to know who beat your ass up last night, smart guy? Well, we could've told you who took you out, if it wasn't for your little stunt on the Pike."

"You seem to know all about me, who the hell are you, and what do you want?" I looked from him to her hoping to see some empathy from the kinder, gentler sex, but she gave me ice. "Why did Joanna Hill hire you?"

"That's privileged information. I am a licensed private investigator."

"You have no privilege here pal."

"Wait a minute," I said. "How do you know I got my ass kicked last night if you didn't do it?"

The woman finally perked up. She poked her partner in the arm and whispered something to him. The man took a couple steps back, and they conversed in hushed voices.

Both reached into their jackets as they turned to face me. They were going to shoot me. Fortunately, each removed a leather I.D. case. My uninvited guests were special agents Ronald Sullivan and Amalia Garcia of the FBI.

"Thanks," I said. "Now, I think you'd better uncuff me, or you're gonna have a hell of a lawsuit on your hands."

Sullivan looked at Garcia as if to say go ahead, and she did the honors. I stayed in the chair rubbing my wrists and waited for them to answer my question. "I want my gun back," I said staring up at Sullivan.

Sullivan addressed me. "You'll get it back, later. To answer your question, we found your car at the Shore Club last night and kept an eye on it. We saw you return there this morning and followed you here. You look like you got a real ass-kicking. Probably well-deserved too. Look, we don't like idiot detectives messing up our work and wanted to get your attention. You're off this case."

"The fuck I am," I said, then recoiled as Sullivan looked like he was going to backhand me.

Sullivan started back in. "So, we played nice and told you who we are. Now it's your turn. What are you doing for Joanna Hill, and where were you last night?"

I live by a code, which is to always put my client's interests first and to maintain their privacy at all costs. That is, provided they were being straight with me, which I believed Joanna was. These were Federal agents, who, for reasons I did not yet know, were interested in the case I was working on. I needed to understand what Sullivan meant when he said I was involved in something much bigger than I could handle. Therefore, I believed it was in my client's best interest that I shared certain information with these people, as long as they shared back. At least that's what I told myself on that morning. And, if I had trouble sleeping that night because of what I'd done, I could've blamed the head injury, but I didn't need to, I slept just fine.

"Okay," I said. "I tell you something, you tell me something."

Sullivan chuckled. "Let's start with you telling us something, and we'll see if we want to play the game or just arrest you for interfering in our investigation." He leaned in and slowly enunciated: "Miss Joanna Hill." Her name was left suspended in mid-air, as though if I didn't say something soon, it would crash to the ground and shatter, and my opportunity to get out of this situation would be gone forever.

"She wants me to find her boss. She's concerned about him."

"And, her boss is?"

I reared back in the chair and threw my hands up, "James MacArthur of Wayne Trust Company. Surely, you guys have figured this out?"

"Yeah, we know Sherlock," he leered at Garcia, but she ignored him and kept her gaze on me. He went on, "But we wanted to hear you say it."

"Now, it's my turn. Why were you following me yesterday?"

Sullivan leaned against the dresser and looked at Garcia. His expression was 'do you believe this guy?' Instead of empathizing with him, Garcia took the lead.

She said, "Mr. Town, we're gonna need a little more from you, and then if we decide to share any information, it will be because we think it's in our best interest. We have reason to believe you committed a crime at the Indian Head Yacht Club last night and we will ruin your week if you keep dragging this out."

I rolled my eyes like a six-year-old and waited for the next question.

"What did Maria Moore tell you?" Garcia surprised me with that one.

"How do you know about her? Were you tailing me then too?"

Sullivan sighed. "Answers, that's all we want from you."

"She didn't say much of relevance. She thinks he's banging a piece of arm candy on a beach somewhere. Apparently, he's done this drop out of sight routine before."

"Then why did you drive all the way to Greenwich?"

"Come on, give me something," I pleaded. "If you're not going to buy me dinner before screwing me, at least buy me a drink. Why were you tailing me in a car registered to Wayne Trust?"

Garcia turned and looked at Sullivan for approval, and he nodded. She said, "We are looking into some potential issues inside of Wayne Trust," then she clammed up and stared at me.

"That's it! No way, that's not cutting it," I said. "You guys can do better than this. Come on, why were you tailing me in a Wayne Trust car? You look like Feds, you act like Feds, hell, you even smell like Feds, but I can't fully believe you're Feds, at least not honest ones, if you can't tell me what the hell you were doing in the Beamer."

Sullivan cleared his throat. "Our original mission yesterday would've been compromised by the obvious nature of our automobile, which as you might expect is a standard issue unmarked sedan."

"So, you boosted one from the firm you're surveilling?"

Sullivan shrugged, while Garcia smiled. It was a nice smile.

"Wow, you Feds don't mess around," I said.

"We didn't steal anything," a frustrated Sullivan exclaimed. "A contact within Wayne Trust supplied the company car to aid our investigation."

"They gave you a BMW, so you could tail me?"

"Look, this is that last thing I will say on this subject," Sullivan said all serious. "We did not plan to tail you, that was a change in plans."

"You were tailing Joanna? Why would you need a BMW for that?"

"That was not in our plans either," said Garcia.

"Where did you think she was going instead of seeing me? To see Mac?"

Blank stares, no comment, I'd hit the limit.

"Is there something I should know about her? Is she working with you?" More blank stares.

"Okay then, what are you driving now?" I asked, still not entirely sure they were on the level.

"Look for yourself," he said motioning to the window.

I got up out of the chair and moved past them. I peered out through the window and saw a late model black Caprice parked two spaces from my car.

"Yup, that's a Fedmobile," I said. "Look, I'll tell you about last night, but first I need a cup of coffee to clear my mind, and you need to get someone out to MacArthur's yacht because unless the blow to my head produced some very realistic dreams, I found James MacArthur stuffed into a refrigerator last night. Hell, I took a few snaps of it."

Garcia was the first to ask. "Where are the snaps?"

"On my phone, and I'll be damned if I know where that is. I think whoever hit me over the head took it."

They shared a look to see if the other believed me. Garcia went out to the parking lot for a few minutes, which I took to mean she was calling someone to investigate. When she came back, the two of them made me walk through the whole night, in excruciating detail, which they recorded. I left out the part where I picked the lock on the cabin of the Rebecca. At one point, I nearly asked for a lawyer, which, take it from an ex-cop, would've been the smart thing to do, but my lawyer was five hours away and costly, and I needed to make some money on this one and get back to solving it. The events of yesterday meant the trail was hot.

Even without calling in legal representation, it took well over an hour to complete my statement.

With Mac gone, this was now a murder investigation. As the fog that had permeated my mind dissipated, I wondered if this would also mean I was off the case. After all, I had found Mac, so technically I fulfilled the mission I'd been hired for.

However, I also wanted to find the perp who killed him and cold-cocked me. When Joanna heard about Mac, would she cut me off, or would she keep me on to find his killer and my attacker?

As it turned out, my new friends were determined to make the decision for her.

When I finished by telling them about waking up on the shore with

Alan and Bernice, Sullivan leaned back, arms folded and announced, "Okay Town, now that we have your statement, this is where your road ends. Go home to Boston and forget about this. We don't need you screwing up our investigation."

"What do you mean? You don't own me, Sullivan, I'm off the case when my client says so, not you."

"No! You get in our way again, and I'll have your license," he spit back at me.

Garcia's phone buzzed, and she left the room while Sullivan and I went back and forth. She cut us off when she returned and asked Sullivan to step outside, and they left me alone for several minutes. Sullivan's face was crimson when they reentered, and I knew something was very wrong.

"You lying piece of shit," he growled while standing over me.

"What?"

"The yacht is clean!" He shook his head, loathing the sight of me. "Stand up, you're under arrest for providing false information to a federal agent."

"Are you kidding me? He's not in the fridge?" I shouted. "You guys checked the Rebecca, right? There's a lot of boats moored there, are you sure they got the right one?"

He motioned for me to stand with his middle and index fingers. I did as he asked but kept on talking. "They must have moved the body. Surely, your people could smell the rot. The stink was unbelievable. I left my dinner in the sink."

"Turn around," Sullivan said, cuffs in hand.

"You're going to bust me for this. Why would I make it up, when it was so easily checked? How stupid would I have to be? I'm not crazy!"

Then something amazing happened. Garcia put her hand on Sullivan's arm and whispered in his ear. He continued to stare at me while she talked. On his face sat a mask of disgust. Finally, he gave me a hard stare and said through gritted teeth, "My partner believes booking you is a waste of time, and you're lucky I'm in agreement. We've got other things to do. But listen to me carefully, Town. You are off this case. Go back to Boston. If I catch you sniffing around here again, I will kick your ass and take you to jail, in that order."

Then as fast as they had entered the room, they left. I was dumbfounded but overjoyed to be free. I was going to leave Greenwich alright, but I wasn't going home.

8

I went out to the parking lot and removed the raft, motor, and oars from the trunk of the Caprice along with my fingerprint kit and carried all of it back to my room in two trips. I dusted the whole lot of it and found no prints other than my own. My head throbbed, but the nausea was gone, and the interrogation had given me some energy. I had to admit that I kind of enjoyed watching Sullivan and Garcia work, even though it was on me. I missed police work, especially working with a partner. They were a good team.

It was nearly 12:30 and checkout was at noon. I threw my belongings together and handed in my key. Then I drove back to where I'd met the delightful Alan and Bernice that morning and scanned the area for my phone. I found nothing and became convinced my attacker had taken it.

I made my way to a strip mall, dropped $400 I didn't have on a new phone and set it up while scoffing down a Monte Cristo and a quart of coffee at an old-fashioned diner on the edge of town. Once it was set-up, the phone alerted me to a new voicemail that had come in while I was in transit. It was Joanna, checking in. I needed to talk to her, but I called Ed first. He picked up on the fourth ring.

"What's up?"

"Is there a way to access photos on my old phone?"

"Your *old* phone?"

"The one I had yesterday. I'm talking to you on a new one."

"You lost your phone?"

"More like my phone lost me, Ed."

Ed asked me some more questions, and I told him my password so he could check the "cloud," whatever that is. After a few minutes, he told me nothing had been uploaded in weeks, and thus, unless I found the actual phone, I was out of luck. As we spoke, something else crossed my mind.

"Ed, how is the security on your computer?"

"Security? You mean against hacks?"

"Yes, is it well protected should someone try to access it from the outside?"

I heard him fumble for something, probably a snack. "Uh, yeah. You know me, I use a solid VPN, and I go through a strict firewall." I had no idea what he meant, but it sounded good. "Why do you ask?"

"Somebody may have taken my phone because I had evidence on it. This means they may have also read your emails, and, I don't know," I paused trying to avoid arousing his concern. "They may try to hack into you or something. It's just a feeling I have."

"Yeah, but they can't access your emails, because your phone is password protected, right?"

"Uh, I may have turned that off at some point."

He sighed. "You're an ex-cop, what it is you don't understand about the need for security, Earl?"

"Sorry, typing a damn password became inconvenient."

"Said the thousand-year-old man. What kind of people are we talking about?"

"The worst kind Ed, rich people. Hey, what'd you come up with on the duo in those photos?"

"Ah, that would be zero. If they work for Wayne Trust, the company sure doesn't want anyone to know about it. I managed to work my way into the H.R. system. It was surprisingly easy for a company of that size. They should hire me as a security consultant. I would fix that shit right up."

"I'm sure you would, Ed."

"Anyway, I didn't see anyone matching the woman's description."

Did I mention that Ed was an experienced hacker? Actually, he's part of a hacker network of sorts. As I said, Ed's smart, just too smart for his own good. He went on. "There are a few middle-aged men that didn't have photos in their files, who could be a match for the guy, but they're not in security, so I doubt it's any of them."

"That's okay. I didn't need you on this one after all. Their names are Ronald Sullivan and Amalia Garcia. They're special agents with the Federal Bureau of Investigation."

"The FBI! How do you know this, Earl?"

"I had breakfast with them this morning,"

"Really?" He exhaled into the phone. "Breakfast with the FBI? Nope, not buying it."

"I need you to find anything you can on these guys. They say they're working on something big at Wayne Trust. That someone on the inside loaned them the company car. I need to know who that was and what they're working on. First off, I'd like to know what division of the FBI they work in. That should be easy for someone of your talents, and that information might give us an idea of what they're investigating."

"Okay, I'll see what I can do."

"I need it today."

"Okay, okay."

"See if you can get me a copy of Whitman Endicott's calendar too. I'd like to see the last few months and the next couple."

"I got other things to do, you know. This is gonna cost you more," he said.

"Fine $60 an hour," I countered.

"$100."

"Nope, I need to make a little money too here, Ed. You know my rate."

"Okay, but you're lucky. Who else do you know who can get into the company network? If my mother didn't love her little brother so much, I'd charge you for the information, not my time, and that would cost you a grand."

"I know. I appreciate it, kid." Sometimes you gotta be humble.

"Hey, wait, when are you gonna pay me? I could use the cash." So, could I, I thought as I crossed from Connecticut into Westchester County, New York, and a collection of some of the wealthiest towns in America.

I wrapped it up by promising to transfer the cash to him that evening via something he called Venmo and hung up. Then I fumbled around with the radio dial until I found a decent jazz station playing Cubano-Be, Cubano-Bop from Bird and Diz at Carnegie Hall.

It was another beautiful fall day. I admired the turning leaves until I hit the outskirts of Manhattan and the trees gave way to urban sprawl and graffiti. I used my new phone to record my thoughts as I drove and outlined what I knew and the big questions I needed answers for. Then I called Joanna.

She called me back a few minutes later from a more private location.

"Other than me, have you contacted anyone from outside the company about Mac?"

"No, I told you I wasn't supposed to even hire you."

"Do you know any reason why the FBI might be interested in Wayne Trust?"

There was a lengthy pause. "Why are you asking me?"

"The man and woman who tailed me in the Wayne Trust car yesterday also paid me a visit this morning. They're FBI. When I asked why they were following me in a vehicle registered to Wayne Trust, their inference was they're working with someone on the inside. They wouldn't tell me who, or if Mac had anything to do with it."

"Joanna, are you there?"

"Yes, uh, sorry. This is quite a shock. I was told there was nothing to worry about, but obviously, management is concerned too, assuming they brought them into this. This must be what Whit meant about having people looking into it."

"I'm not sure they're only looking into Mac's disappearance. I think they may already have been inside Wayne Trust when he disappeared."

She gasped. "You're kidding."

"No, I'm not. Can you think of anything else they might be investigating?"

"No," she said without hesitation. Then she recanted. "Well, it might have something to do with the merger, I guess. I mean that's what everyone is focused on right now."

"Who do you think they're working with?"

"Well, nothing like that would happen without the CEO being aware."

"Is Endicott still in New York?"

"Yes, he's supposed to be there all week." Then she asked, "Are you okay? I didn't expect this would involve the FBI."

"Yeah, I'm okay," I sputtered while reaching back and dabbing at the egg on my head. I examined my finger-tips for blood, they were clean.

"You sound a little worse for wear today? Did you stay at the club after you spoke to Nathaniel?"

"No," I said, dismay in my voice. "The commodore practically walked me to my car. I don't think he sees me as club material."

"Ah," she paused. "These people live in rarefied air, Earl. They don't much like outsiders, especially when they have the nerve to ask questions. Be careful." I could've used the warning 24 hours ago, I thought. Back then I would've proffered a smart-ass comeback. Now I knew there was real danger afoot.

"I'll be fine, thank you though. Hey, what do you know about Rebecca?"

"Rebecca?"

"Yeah, Mac named his new yacht after her. Who is she?"

"I'm not sure. I learned long ago to keep things with Mac strictly professional. I don't know a Rebecca."

I considered telling her about my trip to out the Rebecca, discovering Mac and all the rest of it, but the apparent lack of a body and hard shot to the head left me with questions. How would I explain it all? She may not believe me, and frankly, I wouldn't believe me. I decided to wait until I had things sorted out. She'd paid me for three days. I'd work through tomorrow and then tell her everything I'd found on Thursday morning. Until then, I'd keep asking questions. Next up was Beth MacArthur, and then Whitman Endicott, whether he wanted to talk to me or not.

9

Beth MacArthur agreed to meet me at a Starbucks in Tribeca at 6 pm. I arrived in Manhattan via the Brooklyn Bridge an hour earlier and checked into a hotel I'd found in the East Village for only $280 a night, which is cheap for NYC. It was a drab place not far from the East River. I parked three blocks away for the bargain rate of $45 a day. Even though I was trying to keep costs down by staying in a fleabag downtown hotel, I still pictured myself breaking the news about Mac to Joanna, then handing her an itemized invoice for my expenses, and I felt scummy. The young woman behind the counter smiled at me and told me to enjoy my stay as she directed me to a tiny stall that looked more like a coffin than an elevator.

After checking for bedbugs, I unpacked the few things I brought and cleaned up a bit. My head was pounding again, so I swallowed a couple of aspirin. As I dressed, I wondered what Sullivan and Garcia were up to. Were they watching me? What about the people who attacked me, were they watching me? I went to the closet and grabbed my Glock. I removed the belt I'd been wearing and put on my knife belt, which boasts a buckle with a hidden six-inch blade. It also had a bottle opener, which is nice. When you're done killing for the day, and it's time to relax …

I wasn't far from the address Beth had given me, so I walked, arriving about ten minutes early. At 5:58, I saw Beth. She was in the middle of West Broadway, crossing the street in my direction. Eddie was right, she was tough to miss. She was tall, blonde, and stunning. Her hair blew about in the breeze catching the evening light, and her casual clothes were stylish and likely came with designer labels. She was young, but she walked with the confidence of someone who's experienced life. I stood and signaled her as she came through the door.

She came over and thanked me for meeting her. I thanked her for calling me, and she sat down and got right to the point. "Have you turned up anything on Mac?"

I shook my head. "I wish I could say that I have Miss MacArthur. In your message, you mentioned that you might be able to help me?"

She turned and scanned the room as though looking for spies. I had done the same thing myself upon arriving. "Is someone watching you?" I asked.

She seemed to be expecting the question, and she answered me with one of her own. "Have you had the pleasure of meeting Gibson French?"

"No, I had hoped to see him last night, but no luck. Do you know him well?"

She looked around some more and said, "I don't think this is a good place to have this talk. My friend has an apartment nearby, we can go there."

I leaned in close and looked her in the eye. "Do you recognize someone? Are we being watched?"

She slid a small piece of paper across the table. On it was an address and apartment number. "Fifteen minutes." She then got up and left.

I plugged the address into my phone, it was only five minutes away, so I stayed put for another ten, trying to wrap my head around what had just happened.

As I walked a couple of blocks to the new meeting place, I considered the possibility of ambush, and mentally prepared myself for an attack. Beth seemed genuine, but after last night and Joanna's warning, I was determined not to be taken by surprise.

The place was an old brick warehouse on Greenwich Street. The apartment number she'd given me was seven, which meant the top floor. I looked for a name as I rang the buzzer, but there wasn't one, just the number seven. The lock clicked, and I stepped into a modern lobby, with an excess of abstract art. I found an elevator straight ahead and stairs to my right. Thinking about an ambush, I took the elevator up to five and the stairs the rest of the way. She was waiting for me when I reached the top floor. She said nothing, but her look read confusion.

"Gotta stay fit in my business," I said. She didn't buy it.

She held the door open, and I stepped through cautiously but wasn't tasered or hit over the head.

I'd walked into a spacious room with sky-high ceilings and phenomenal views. The walls were red brick, except for the one with three arched floor-to-ceiling windows in which the Vitruvian Man could have stood without touching an edge. The floor was freshly stained but left rough, so it still contained hundreds of scuffs and scrapes from decades of human activity. I guessed this was kept for character and authenticity, and several other buzzwords that people in this neighborhood paid a premium for. A series of thick dark beams crossed the ceiling. The room was divided into kitchen, dining, and entertainment areas, the latter of which was denoted by thick shag rug. An array of modern art pieces had been purposefully scattered about.

"Your friend has a nice place."

"Thank you, I'll tell her you like it. You made quite an impression on her."

"Really? I know the owner?"

"Yes, Tinsley Saunders."

"Oh," I said, surprised. "She made an impression on me too," I added, perhaps a little too quickly. Tinsley was more clued into what was going on than I thought. Word gets around at Indian Head.

"I'll tell her you said so." She pointed to the dining area and asked if I wanted a glass of wine. She had begun to pour one for herself. I asked if coffee was an option. She pressed a couple of buttons on a built-in appliance next to the oven, and I heard beans grinding. "It's espresso, I hope that's okay."

"Very, please make it a double."

We sat kitty-corner at the end of a long marble table. From this vantage point, I could see both the Empire State and Chrysler buildings through the arched windows. Tinsley had serious money.

Beth sipped a cabernet, then spoke. "I know everyone thinks Mac will turn up soon, but this feels different to me."

"Do you still see him often? The divorce was a couple of years ago?"

"Yes, we've stayed close, despite the divorce, and other things."

"The lawsuit?"

"Yes, that."

"It sure sold some newspapers."

"Parasites." She looked up as though asking for divine intervention against the media bloodsuckers.

"You mentioned that you might be able to help me?"

"Yes, back to that. We had a meeting at my lawyer's office the week before last. He felt bad about the way things had gone. He was like that. His lawyers got the case thrown out, and he still wanted to make sure I was okay. He also didn't want me to refile, which I'm still considering. So, we spoke for a while about how he could make things right, and he was not himself."

"How so?"

"He kept giving in to me, which wasn't like him at all. Mac's a fighter. Personal conflict is fun for him, and he likes to battle. It was a bone of contention between us. He never gives in, even when he's clearly in the wrong."

She stopped and collected her thoughts. "So, something was wrong with him?" I prodded.

"Yeah, so much so that I went against my lawyer's advice and asked to speak with Mac alone."

"And?"

"At first, Mac denied anything was wrong, but when I pressed him, he finally admitted that things were strange at Wayne Trust. He wouldn't elaborate, but that's what he said - *things are strange*. When the meeting was over, Mac made another odd comment. He said he wasn't sure he could trust Gibson French anymore, and that I was focusing on the small fish. My inheritance was the big fish and that I should be more concerned about that."

"Why would he bring up your inheritance?"

"I don't know," she said.

"Did you ask him?"

"No, I thought he was being melodramatic. Then a couple of days later, he disappeared."

I considered this for a while. "So, you think he was trying to tell you something. Like, if something happens to me, look at French?"

"I don't know," she said. "I just know he wasn't himself. He wasn't as feisty. And, the comment about the inheritance, why would he say that? You have to admit that in hindsight, it sounds like he thought something might happen. This is why I've been feeling dread about his disappearance. The longer he's missing, the more convinced I am that something bad has happened."

"What about Whitman Endicott?" I asked. "Was Mac concerned about him?"

She thought about this for a bit, then said, "When it comes to Whit Endicott, Gibson is Mac's competition. The two of them compete for Endicott's attention."

"If you don't mind my asking, just, approximately, how much is the inheritance?"

"Depends on the stock price, somewhere around $30 million, last I checked."

"Is it Wayne Trust stock?"

"Yes. Mac told me his shares would be mine, but I don't need them. I still love Mac, just not as a husband."

"Have the authorities talked to you?"

"Yes, of course, I've told them everything I can."

"Have you spoken with the FBI?"

"The FBI?" She finished her glass of wine and got up to pour another. She was lean and athletic, but with curves. "No, are they looking into it?"

"I'm not sure. Do you think Gibson French has someone following you?"

She rested against a long marble countertop and swirled the ruby wine around her glass, "I haven't seen anyone watching me, but I've felt eyes on me several times. This morning I went for a run in the park, and at one point I just knew someone was watching me. I mean more than the usual guys." I smiled and nodded, acknowledging her beauty. "I stopped to tie my laces and tried to look around without making it too obvious, but I didn't catch sight of anyone. It gave me the chills though. I got the feeling again when I entered Starbucks. Things just don't feel right."

I nodded, thinking about what I'd found on Mac's boat.

"Did Whitman Endicott hire you?"

"No," I said, defensively. "Joanna Hill did. Do you know her?"

"Sure, she's known Mac longer than I have. I never trusted her."

"Really?"

She nodded, seeming bored, perhaps when one is married to a guy like Mac, not trusting other women becomes old hat.

"Why did you assume it was Endicott who brought me in?"

"He's the CEO. He's usually the one giving orders."

"Who's Rebecca?"

"Rebecca, I don't know. Why do you ask?"

"Mac named his latest yacht after her. She must be pretty special to him, but no one seems to know who she is. Did he have a close relative or friend named Rebecca?"

She considered this for a while and shook her head.

"How long have you known Tinsley?"

"You're really giving me the third-degree now." She smiled, and it was a doozy. She knew how to disarm with a look. She was well-practiced in it and could've won medals.

"Yeah, sorry, force of habit. But it's odd, my meeting her in Greenwich last night, and ending up in her apartment with you tonight."

"She's a good friend of Mac's and is concerned about him. She was excited to tell me that someone is looking for him."

"But surely, if you don't trust Joanna, then how do you?" I paused realizing that the question I was about to ask was impolite, but not knowing how to put my foot back in my mouth. Beth bailed me out.

"I never trusted Tinsley either, detective. But sometimes it's easier to go along with the program than risk being excommunicated."

"Does Tinsley have that power? To excommunicate you?"

Beth gave her answer some thought, then said, "Yes, I believe she does."

10

I left after nearly an hour, feeling that I'd gotten as much as I could from Beth MacArthur. The sun had nearly set, its last rays straining to stay above the Hudson as I walked along West Houston Street. I took out my phone to see if Eddie had sent me anything, and then used selfie mode to watch behind me for a tail. Within seconds, I noticed a male figure in dark glasses. He wore a baseball cap pulled down tight and was noticeably trying to look inconspicuous. I stepped into a small bodega and bought some mints. After I started walking again, there he was, still about ten paces behind me.

Up ahead, I spotted a group of young women, seven or eight of them. They were gabbing and laughing and moving like molasses. I wrapped the fingers of my right hand around my belt buckle and released the double-edged blade. I quickened my pace and slipped through the throng, then ducked into a deeply recessed doorway. The women slowly passed by, then him. I waited until I saw his back, then leaped out and wrapped my arm around his throat. I lifted him off his feet and pulled him back into the doorway, turning as we went and pressing him face-first against a wall. He struggled, so I squeezed tighter and growled, "I have a six-inch knife pressed against your right kidney. The last 24 hours have been very unpleasant for me, and I am itching to hurt someone. Who are you?"

He tried to speak, but I had my arm so tight around his neck that he couldn't form words. I loosened my grip, and he gasped for air. When he caught his breath, he said: "It's me! It's Larry Ferncroft!"

"Larry, what the fuck are you doing? I nearly sent you to the ICU."

I released his neck, and he tried to spin around, but I pushed him face first against the wall again. "Not so fast, pal," I said. "Hands up and out, spread the feet."

"What are you doing?" he cried out.

"Checking you for weapons, Larry. This is what happens when you stalk an ex-cop." I patted him down. He was clean. "Alright, tell me what you're doing here, Ferncroft."

He turned to face me. His lower lip quivered. "I came here to talk to you, no, to warn you." Great another warning. Yesterday, it was beautiful women, today it's warnings. I preferred yesterday.

"You could've just called me, Larry. I gave you my card. Besides, how did you know I was here?"

He leaned past me and poked his head out of the doorway, looking intently to his right and left. "Can we do this somewhere else?" It was Beth and the spy routine all over again.

"There's a bar over there." He pointed over my left shoulder, and I turned and took in the place.

It was a hole in the wall. The kind of place with a faux brick exterior and dirty windows. The torn green awning above the door read Whiskey Pub. It looked like a dump. "Let's go," I said pulling him by the shoulder.

We crossed the street and entered a narrow dimly lit dive. I felt at home, but Larry looked weirded out. It smelled of stale beer, and the floor was sticky. The bar and about a dozen stools, most filled with what looked like professional drinkers, were on the left, while a couple of beat up oak tables and mismatched chairs were on the right. I pushed Larry towards the rear table. "What'll you have," I asked him.

"A beer I guess," he said meekly.

Something told me this was a Pabst Blue Ribbon kind of place, so I pointed to the big neon PBR sign behind the bartender and held up two fingers.

The androgynous barkeep, who had a tattoo that began on the right side of his neck and ran all the way to his fingertips, said, "You just caught the tail end of happy hour, so this round's two for one." Things were looking up.

Besides the ball cap and glasses, which were now resting on the table, Larry wore a navy windbreaker with a Columbia logo, blue jeans, and sneakers. He avoided eye contact at first, looking down at the table instead. I handed him a PBR and sat down across from him.

"So, this is your spy uniform, Larry?"

"Sorry I didn't mean to spy."

"Do you realize the Indian Head crest is on your cap? Did you think I wouldn't see you?"

"No, I wasn't planning on spying. I saw you come out of Tinsley's and I just got the urge to see where you were going. I was going to stop you. It was a stupid thing to do. Look, the reason I came here is to warn you, for the Commodore." He stopped speaking and turned to see what had captured my attention.

A couple of young women had entered. One of them looked like a young professional just getting off work, while her friend looked like a ball of yarn wrestling with a pin cushion. Her black hair was streaked pink, blue, and green, and she had piercings in her nose, lips, and eyebrows. I had discovered the Millennial odd couple. As I observed them, a cheer went up for the Felix of the pair. Of the two, she was the regular. Go figure.

"Warn me about what, Ferncroft? Let's have it."

"Okay. Commodore Sterling asked me to tell you that Federal agents came by the club this morning asking questions about you."

The guys checking on the body. So, they were there. Unless Sullivan and Garcia paid a visit later. "Were you there at the time?"

"No."

"Did he tell you their names?"

"No." He leaned in. "But Caroline, my wife, she overheard Mrs. Albrecht talking about them, she and her husband Hirst are among our oldest members. She was with a group of ladies on the patio, and Caroline heard her say they were a couple of big boys; if that helps?" Surprisingly it did. It wasn't Sullivan and Garcia.

"What did they ask him?"

"I don't know."

"Cut the shit, Larry. What the fuck did they want?"

"I really don't know. Commodore Sterling doesn't tell me anything. Other than what to do." He looked down at the table again. "I should find a new club. I would've already if it weren't for my wife. Her great uncle was a founder."

"Where were you last Saturday night?"

He reared back so sharply that he struck the back of his head on a dartboard hanging on the grimy paneling. "Ow," he said rubbing it.

"You know the last time anyone saw Mac, was last Saturday night at the club. Sterling told me he was on the docks with a group of people that night. Were you there?"

He held up his hands palm out. "No man. Jeez. I was in New York that night. My father received an award for his work for the victims of the 9/11 cleanup. It was at the Yale Club. I spent the night there, then drove back Sunday afternoon."

"Okay. You said, 'a warning,' what exactly was his warning?"

"Just to be careful now that the Feds are involved. He's very concerned about the club's reputation."

"He made that clear last night," I said. "He cares more about Indian Head than the life of his dear friend James." If he disagreed with my assessment of Sterling's priorities, Larry didn't show it. "Why send you? He could've called me too."

"I work nearby on Chambers Street, and he thought it would be best if someone spoke with you directly. This is a topic that's best discussed in person."

"How did Sterling know I'd be here tonight?"

"Tinsley said so. Elizabeth told her she was meeting you. Tinsley told her she could use her place."

"Why meet at Tinsley's place?" I said this aloud, but I was really asking it of myself.

Larry had an answer. "Sterling thinks the Feds are watching Beth's place for Mac. He didn't want them to see you again and start asking more questions."

I processed this for a bit. The Feds were investigating Wayne Trust and looking for Mac? What are these guys involved in?

I said, "You didn't tell me Mac's boat was named the Rebecca. Who is she?"

"I don't know," he replied while picking at his beer label.

"Are there any members named Rebecca that might have caught Mac's fancy?"

"No, I don't think so. There was a Becky who worked in the kitchen, but she was not Mac's type. She was a senior citizen, and that was a long time ago."

I leaned in close to get his attention. "French and Endicott. Tell me everything you know about Gibson French and Whitman Endicott."

He filled me in while I sipped my beer, but I didn't get much of value at first. He said Endicott joined the club eight years ago and he and French were already very friendly, having known each other for years before. The three amigos, including Mac, were thick as thieves, with Endicott being the pack leader. Their position at the club was such that they had the run of the place. Sterling had become the pseudo fourth mate but was as much an employee as a friend to the other three.

What finally caught my ear was when Larry changed the subject to Monday night.

"I'm sorry if Rooster went a little overboard on the drink Monday," he said, making small talk now that he'd bored the anger out of me.

"What do you mean? That was a damn good mojito."

"It was?"

"Yeah, why?"

"I overheard him talking with another bartender yesterday, and he said something about taking special care of the cop, which I assume meant you, who was here the previous night. At least I think that's what he said, and my Spanish is pretty good, I learned to speak it fluently as a child."

"Yeah, what was your nanny's name?"

"Marisol."

"You were saying?" I nudged him.

"Well, I thought maybe he'd spiked your drink to mess with you. Sometimes Mac and the others will tip him to make the ladies drinks extra strong. It helps loosen them up."

I was never a good poker player, and my reaction was reflected on Larry's face, as he realized he said something significant. "What did I say?"

"I got jumped after leaving the club last night, Larry." I turned to show him my wound but didn't bother to mention where it happened. "You think special care could have had something to do with this?"

"No," he protested. "Jorge, that's his real name, wouldn't do that. He's a good man, a family man. He's been with the club for twenty years."

"Uh huh. Well, it looks like I have to go back to Greenwich." I had hoped to brace French and Endicott the following day, in their offices here in the city, but discussing this comment with its source took precedence.

"He won't be in Greenwich."

"Why not?"

"Endicott's annual charity ball is tomorrow, and Rooster is working the event, as are many club staff."

"Really? Where is this happening Larry?"

"Right here in Manhattan. Well, uptown, not down here. Endicott's brownstone is on the Upper East Side. It's quite the place."

"Is this tomorrow day or tomorrow night," I asked.

"Night, of course. Lots of Wall Street and Silicon Valley heavy hitters attend. The Wall St. guys wouldn't attend during the day, and it's for charity."

"Will French and Sterling be attending?"

"Oh yeah, they'll be there."

"Well, well," I said. "This is a gift horse."

"You can't just stroll in there, Earl. They hire a ton of security, plus some of the guests bring their own. We're talking government bigshots and corporate titans. Seriously important people." He leaned in and whispered. "Rumor has it, a former Senator and First Lady is attending."

I had no reply. I just looked at him, and he sat back in his seat, hands up. "No way Earl, I can't get you in. I don't have that kind of pull. I only get in because of my wife, Caroline. She's the connected one in my house. I can't help you."

"I don't need your help, Larry. I got my own connections."

11

"What do you mean, you can't get me on the list? Come on Ed, you told me you could hack anything."

"I can hack anything," he said, exasperated. "I'm in the Wayne Trust system, but the list for this event is not here. If I could find it, I could add you to it, but I can't find the damn thing."

"Okay," I said. "I've got a plan B. I was just hoping I wouldn't have to use it, but it is what is."

Eddie reminded me that he spent an hour trying to find the attendee list, and I owed him, and I told him to add it to my tab. Then I asked, "Hey, what did you come up with on my G-men?"

"I don't know if I can find my notes, a little cash in my pocket would help."

I responded in frustration, "I'll venom it to you after I hang up, Ed. Now, help me out here."

"It's Venmo," he shot back. Then he put the phone down, and I heard the sound of rustling papers, followed by a cat's loud meow, as Eddie apparently shooed it off his notes, before coming back on the line. "Ronald D. Sullivan, age 47. Hey, he's actually older than you, Earl."

"Your act needs work," I replied.

"Sullivan is based in the Boston field office. He's a senior special agent, whatever that means, while Amalia M. Garcia, age 34, is a special agent from the main New York office at 26 Federal Plaza. Looks like both are assigned to a special agent in charge – a.k.a. a SAC – also out of New York named Darnell Bowden." He giggled at Bowden's acronym.

"Here's where it gets interesting."

"Finally," I said.

"They work in the National Security Branch, which handles terrorism, foreign intelligence and espionage, and even WMDs. What is Wayne Trust involved in?"

"I don't know, but I have a feeling that's the key to unlocking the answers to my questions."

"That's all I found," he said. "There's nothing in the news about these guys regarding cases they've worked on, but the FBI doesn't tell the press about that stuff very often. I've got a friend. Well, he's more of an acquaintance, who's a lot more proficient on the dark web. He may be able to find out more if you need it."

"Thanks, I'll keep that in mind. One more thing, Ed."

"Yes, Earl."

"What'd you find on the three amigos?"

"If you're referring to meetings between Endicott, French, and Sterling."

I sang, "You know I am, Ed."

He groaned, "I found several meetings between Endicott, French and others that appear to involve this deal they're working on."

"Nothing with Sterling?"

"No, sorry," he actually sounded sincere.

"Alright, well it was worth a try."

"Ah but here's something you're gonna find *really* interesting."

"I'm all ears, my favorite nephew."

"Your only nephew. On Sunday, September 16th. The day before Mac failed to show for his speech." He paused, savoring it.

"Yes, and shortly after he was last seen. Go on." I was laying on my bed staring out of the window at a flock of pigeons perched on one of those old wooden rooftop water towers in lower Manhattan.

"Endicott and French met with a big group that Sunday afternoon, including the Suisse Bank that's trying to take them over. It's called JKB SA. Executives from the two sides and a bunch of investment bankers from Goldman Sachs, Morgan Stanley, and Nomura Securities, along with bigshots from French's law firm were present." He paused again.

"Okay, get to the pertinent part, Ed."

"The meeting started at 10 am and ran past midnight. At 4:00 and 4:10 pm, Endicott's assistant sent urgent messages to him, saying that Nathaniel Sterling desperately needed to speak with him and/or Gibson French."

I sat up so fast I nearly fell off the bed. "Whoa!"

"Yeah, whoa," he echoed. "Apparently Endicott spoke to the assistant, and probably Sterling by phone shortly after, because there's no digital record, such as an email or text, of them interacting."

"You can read their emails and texts?"

"If they're using Wayne Trust accounts, yes? If not, no."

"Okay," I said.

"At 4:33 p.m. Endicott sent an email to the assistant asking that a car be ready to pick up Mr. French ASAP."

"Does it say where the car was to take him?"

"No, but they emailed a receipt later that night at 9:30. No details on where he went, but the bill was over $400, so it must have been a long drive. It was car number four of The Big Apple Car Company based in Hoboken, New Jersey."

"Fantastic work, Ed. Thank you."

"I'm well aware of that, Earl, and you're welcome. Send my money!"

It was Wednesday morning. I felt great, aside from the constant ache coming from the back of my skull. I'd had an early night. After leaving Larry, I grabbed a quick dinner while sitting at a bar watching the Red Sox beat up on the Orioles, then went back to my hotel where I managed to get nearly eight hours of sleep. I had figured that with Endicott's shindig and all, it would be a long day and I'd need the rest, but now my evening plans were in doubt.

I opened my contacts and pulled up the number for Harriett Goldstein, a.k.a. Plan B. Harriett and my ex-wife, Roxanne, had been roommates at Bard College, and when Harriett's eighteen-year-old daughter Shoshanna went missing three years earlier, Roxanne talked Harriett into hiring me to find her. That was the first time a case had taken me to New York, and until two days ago, I thought it would be the last.

The police hadn't turned up anything in the weeks after Shoshanna went missing. Harriett had substantial means and had hired several private agencies to find her, but they'd burned up a lot of precious hours supposedly chasing down leads with nothing to show for it, but big invoices, of course.

The theory was that the girl had gotten pulled into a white slavery ring and was likely turning tricks somewhere around Manhattan, but prostitution is a billion dollar a year business in New York and New Jersey, and finding her in that cesspool was proving impossible.

I decided to take a different approach and left the haystacks, like scouting prostitution rings and drug dens to the police and big agencies. Instead, I applied my primary methods of finding a missing person – consumer credit and personal contacts. I called Carla Rincon, an old flame of mine in the consumer credit business and told her about Shoshanna, and she agreed to help me track her down. When that didn't work, because there hadn't been any recent activity on her credit or debit cards, I went to Harriett's apartment on the Upper West Side and went through her things in the hopes of identifying a few personal contacts that had been overlooked by the police.

I got my break when Inez, Harriett's housekeeper, complained about the mess I was making in Shoshanna's closet. She said offhandedly that the place looked like it did when Shoshanna was getting ready for a date, so I took the opportunity to ask a few questions about her dating habits. Inez was a real snoop and had been closely monitoring Shoshanna's social life. She told me a lot of things I didn't need to know, but also mentioned someone Shoshanna had met via a dating app in the weeks leading up to her disappearance. Thanks to Nephew Ed and his computer hackery, I quickly had a name, address, and several photos of the guy. He was a young smart-ass named Craig Mann, who I caught up with soon after in front of his apartment building.

Something was off about Craig. He was in his early twenties and living in a dump on the edge of Chinatown, but he wore a Patek Philippe watch worth at least fifteen grand and drove a new Audi. He had studs in his ears, a tattoo sleeve on his right arm, and an attitude derived from a life of indulgence where no one had ever put him in his place.

I asked him if he'd seen or spoken with Shoshanna, and he said, "No man, why would I want to spend time with that slag." When I said she'd been missing for over a month, he said, "Maybe she joined the circus, she was kind of a clown."

He couldn't have cared less about her, and I wanted to punch his teeth down his throat. I didn't necessarily think he was involved in her disappearance though. Guilty dudes usually deny knowing their victim, and he hadn't, but I decided to keep an eye on him for an hour or two anyway. Not because I was confident it would lead to Shoshanna, but because I wanted to catch the little shit doing something, anything, illegal, and fuck him over.

Within minutes he left his Chinatown craphole, and I followed. He was too stupid, or too cocky to look for a tail, and I soon watched him pick up a young-looking Asian girl in front of a knockoff designer handbag shop on Canal Street. It didn't look like a guy picking up a date, it was business, and the little prick drove his passenger up to a hotel in midtown. He double parked on one of the '40s between Seventh and Eighth Avenues and I did the same. After about a half-hour, she came out and hopped back in his car, and off they went to her next appointment at a nice place on Madison.

Less than an hour later we repeated the process and this time her assignation was at an apartment building on the Upper East Side. Again, he waited in the car, mostly staring down at his phone, while she went in and made the donuts. This time I found a lot a couple of blocks away and paid the forty bucks of extortion money to park the Caprice.

When the girl came out of the building, I took Craig by surprise, opening the drivers-side door as he counted the money. I put one hand on his left shoulder and grabbed a handful of his shirt with the other and tore him out of his seat, throwing him face down onto the sidewalk. As I pressed him into the filthy concrete, I turned to the girl and told her to relax. I figured I'd be in trouble if she turned on me and attacked or started screaming for help, but I didn't need to. She was too out of it to protest. She just sat in the passenger seat watching through the open door.

He, on the other hand, vigorously tried to protest, but stopped once I pressed his arm up behind his back until the pain told him it'd be best to shut up and stop squirming. I went through his pockets and found a knife and a bottle of pills that looked like some sort of tranquilizer. Being on a busy New York City street, I had to work fast, so I presented him with two options.

"Okay, you little scumbag. I've got you and your girl here on procuring and prostitution, but you and I know that ain't shit. What is shit, is pimping out underage girls, which from the looks of your friend is what you've been doing." I looked at her again. She was staring in silence, possibly not understanding what I was saying, possibly catatonic. She had hair that was long and straight, too much makeup, and a profoundly stoned look in her eyes. She wore a plaid mini-skirt and a pink jacket and looked like she should be planning a school dance, instead of turning tricks uptown.

Craig decided he had something to say. He started mouthing off, so I pressed on his arm again until he begged me to stop.

"I don't have time for any more of your bullshit, Craig. You speak again, I break your arm. Now, as I was saying, you're going to tell me where Shoshanna is, you pimp piece of shit, or I'll turn you in. If my hunch is right, your friend here is not seventeen." I leaned down, so my face was close to his, the left side of which was pressed against the sidewalk.

"Here's my impression of you, for the rest of your life: Hi, my name is Craig, I just moved into the neighborhood, and I'm required by law to inform you that I'm a registered sex offender."

Unfortunately, I had drawn the attention of a couple of thirtyish men that were hanging around in front of the next building. They were well-dressed and didn't look like a threat, but more of a pain in the ass if they called the cops. The taller of two wore a gray plaid sports coat and a pink button-down shirt. His shorter friend wore an expensive looking leather jacket. Plaid called out, "Hey, you okay over there?"

I decided to use this to my advantage, and said, "You know, I could use a hand. This guy here's been pimping out young girls, and I'm taking him in. If you wouldn't mind, come here, and tell me how old you think this girl is. I want a second opinion."

"What's your name?" I asked the girl. She stared straight ahead but mumbled something that sounded like Alyssa.

"Alyssa, how old are you?" I asked. No answer. "Where are you from?" Again, no answer.

Plaid and Leather arrived, and Craig tried to lift himself off the ground, but I pressed down harder. "Come on man, let me up," he cried out.

"Jesus," said Plaid. "She's really young." Then he asked her, "Do you need help?" She said nothing, and he turned and stared at Craig,

"You're a piece of shit," added Leather.

"Look at you, making friends," I said to Craig.

"You need a hand taking him in?" Plaid asked.

"No, thank you, guys, I'm good." I increased the pressure on Craig's arm, bent down, and made my pitch in a low whisper, "Here's the deal pimp. Your friend gets the rest of the day off. You and I go for a drive to wherever Shoshanna is, and maybe, if all goes well, you get to stay off the sex offender list."

Craig took the deal. We said goodbye to his new buddies, then got into his car with him behind the wheel and me riding shotgun. Alyssa climbed into the back seat and closed her eyes.

Craig very nicely informed me that, as a police officer I was not allowed to treat him this way, and that he would see to it that my career in law enforcement came to a quick end. I showed him my Glock and informed him that my career in law enforcement had already come to a quick end. Then I added that, as a private citizen, I was going to shoot him in the face if he tried anything stupid. He stopped talking and kept his eyes on the road.

He was heading for the East River. I asked him where we were going.

"You said to take you to Shoshanna, so I'm taking you to Shoshanna."

"I got that, idiot. Where is she?"

He looked at me and smirked. "In Queens, but if you think you can walk in and take her out of there like some movie hero, you're mistaken. The people she's with will waste you."

"You know whose problem that is, Craig?"

"Yeah, it's your problem."

"No, Craig, it's yours." I held up my phone. "I just sent a text message with your photo attached to a friend of mine in NYPD vice. If something happens to me, the cops are coming for you. You understand what I'm saying?" He threw his head back in frustration. "That's right, chump, you can either make sure I leave wherever it is we're going in one piece, and with Shoshanna, or you're fucked."

He slammed the steering wheel. "We can't just walk in there and take her. They'll kill both of us!"

"You know their operation, pimp. Surely there's a way to do this. Think about it."

"We gotta get her out of the house," he said after only a minute or so. "She's more of an in-call girl, but we gotta get her to come to us."

"Great, so how are you gonna make this happen?" We were now headed north on FDR Drive and would be crossing into Queens soon.

"You gotta call and request her. Not her specifically, but someone like her. She's the only one like her right now. Most of the girls are Asian. If you ask for a Jewish American Princess type and tell them you have money to spend for outcall, they will send her to you."

"Sounds reasonable," I said. "So, they'll call you to pick her up, and you can hand her over to me."

"No, they won't call me to drive her. I should've had her at the next appointment by now." He pointed over his shoulder to the cargo in back. She was sound asleep, head slumped, chin on chest. "They're gonna be looking for me. Someone from the Triad will drive her. You gotta keep me out of this. If they find out I helped you, I'm a dead man."

"My heart bleeds for you, Craig. After all, you're a real humanitarian." I pointed my thumb at Alyssa. "This had better be a nap and not an O.D."

"She's a junkie whore, man. She's asleep."

"She's a junkie because you feed her drugs, so she'll turn tricks all day," I replied. Then I lowered my voice, so she wouldn't hear what I was about to call her, and added, "She's a prostitute because you pimp her out. Don't you fucking dare suggest otherwise. Now, what's the number? I'll call them."

"Where are we gonna meet? We gotta get a hotel room and call from there. They need to call the hotel and get connected to your room via the front desk, or they'll know it's bullshit and they won't send her." What he said made sense. I made him give me $300, and he and I checked into a Days Inn not far from where Craig said she was being kept. The close proximity would make the deal even more appetizing for the pimp, as he wouldn't have to deal with Midtown traffic.

A woman with an eastern European accent answered when I called the service a short while later. So much for female empathy.

I told her I was looking for a good time. What is one supposed to say when ordering sex as though it was pizza? I said I needed a specific type of girl, and, because I was a prosperous business guy with lots of important meetings, I needed the girl delivered to my hotel room quickly and would pay extra to make all of this happen.

And what do you know? She said she had just that type of girl and could have her there in less than an hour. Forty-five minutes later, Shoshanna Goldstein knocked on my door and stepped into salvation.

Harriett leaned on some of her connections in New York City and got the authorities to break up the prostitution ring, but I followed it in the press, and few of the men behind the ring even received a slap on the wrist. There are far too many backroom deals and political alliances in a city like Manhattan for true justice to be done in cases such as these.

Harriett did manage to get help for Alyssa though and eventually she went home to her parents. Turns out, she was from New Jersey, and legal, though barely. She's now enrolled at CCNY. Craig was arrested the next day and did a measly eight months at Rikers. He's probably pimping again. I made a mental note to keep an eye out for him while in Manhattan. I'm sure he'd love to see me.

* * *

Harriett was born and raised in Bronxville, a wildly wealthy town in Westchester County, fifteen miles north of Manhattan. Her father made a great living producing television in the early days of the form. When the networks packed up the bulk of their original programming and moved to Los Angeles, Harriett's father stayed behind and parlayed his wealth with investments in commercial real estate. When he and Harriett's mother left this world in the 1990s, Harriett inherited a fat nest egg, and a lot of goodwill from the politicians her father had generously supported. Harriett continues to bankroll city politicians in their election campaigns to this day, so when Eddie couldn't get it done, Harriett was plan B.

Her phone rang three times before she picked up. We exchanged hellos, and she caught me up on Shoshanna's current situation, which was good considering what she'd endured, then I got down to business.

"Harriett, I'm calling because I'm hoping you can help me with a case I'm pursuing in the city."

"You know I saw Roxy a couple of weeks ago, she's worried about you. Says you're not returning her calls."

"Everything is fine, Harriett. I've been swamped."

"Yeah, well you should call her. She worries about you. You're still very important to her you know, even if she is straight out with her business now." And busy making time with a rich guy.

"I know Harriett. Look, I've got sort of a big ask, and if you can't help me, it's okay."

"Call her."

"Okay, I will call her, *soon*. Are you familiar with Whitman Endicott?"

"The financier?"

"That's the one."

"I've met him. He was a big Bloomberg donor, not so much with De Blasio."

"He's hosting a charity event at his Upper East Side home tonight. Lots of powerful people will be there."

"Okay."

"I'm working a case that involves some of his guests, and I'd really like to be there too. It's the break I need on this case."

"What kind of a case is it? That's a serious bunch."

"It's a disappearance," I hesitated before realizing that I needed her to want to help me and the details could be a motivator. "It started as a disappearance, but it's turned into a murder investigation. It hasn't hit the press yet, but will soon, so I need to act fast."

"A murder, involving that crowd? That's amazing!" I imagined her telling her yenta friends about it over tea at the St. Regis.

"Do you know anyone that can get me in? In return, I'll keep you abreast of the case." I knew that would clinch it.

She thought about it for a moment. "Yes! I know just who to call."

I went out to find some breakfast and enjoyed walking in the city. There's an energy that is unique to New York. This is especially true on weekdays when millions travel into the city to work. Even in Tribeca and Greenwich Village, which is between the office skyscrapers of Midtown and the Battery, the streets pulsate with human life. Boston also has tremendous energy, which is fueled by the tens of thousands of students who attend college there, but New York is a far more powerful force. Every kind of person – rich, poor, black, white, young, and old, is joined together on the sidewalks, in the stores and restaurants, and in the buildings that tower over the wide avenues and narrow side streets. It's an authentic melting pot, and a thing to behold and be thankful for.

I was leaning over a counter in a little diner in the West Village and eating my way through an omelet when Harriett called back, with a strange question.

"Are you familiar with Harriman's English breakfast sausage?"

I stared at my plate, then fought the urge to look over my shoulder. "Uh, yeah, I've seen their commercials."

"The matriarch and keeper of the family fortune, Eleanor Harriman, is willing to let you accompany her to The Fight for Life Ball tonight."

"The Fight for Life Ball?"

"Yes, that's what Mr. Endicott's annual gala is called. It's to raise funds for cancer research, more specifically, a rare type of lymphoma."

"How old is Eleanor?" I asked, picturing myself wheeling a decrepit old woman around all night.

"What kind of a question is that? You said you wanted in, I got you in."

"And I thank you very much for that Harriett. I really do, but I need to be able to move about. If she's in a wheelchair or something."

"She's in fine shape. It won't be a problem. You walk her in, have a cocktail, then hand her off to one of her many society friends and do your thing. When she wants to leave, you see her safely home. This is Eleanor's social circle, she won't need any nursing from you."

I breathed a sigh of relief and thanked her.

"Where are you staying?"

I asked why it mattered.

"You don't think you can waltz in there in a sports coat, do you? This is a black-tie affair, Earl. I'm sending a man named Phillipe over to take your measurements. He'll be there within the hour."

I hadn't even considered the dress code.

"You need to pick up Eleanor at eight on the dot. She won't put up with tardiness. Therefore, I will have a car service at your hotel at 7:15. Can you be dressed and in that car at 7:15?"

"Yeah, of course, but I'm not sure I can afford your guy Phillipe, maybe I can find a tux somewhere."

"A rental?" She got a real kick out of that and cut up laughing. "Have you met these people?"

"Of course," I said getting defensive. "I spent Monday night at Indian Head Yacht Club in Greenwich."

"Well then, you must know that if you walk into Whit Endicott's gala in a rented tuxedo, you will be mocked and shunned all evening. Now, don't worry about paying Phillipe, just be ready for him."

"I can't thank you enough for your help, Harriett."

"Cut it out, you don't need to thank me for anything. Just be good to Eleanor. Be a proper gentleman."

Phillipe came by as promised and was a real trip. He was a decade or more past middle-age with a small thin frame, nearly white hair, round tortoise-shell glasses and impeccably tailored navy pinstripe suit with pink bow tie and matching pocket square. He looked both ways before entering the room, then sniffed loudly as though something offended his olfactory senses. I felt a little like a baboon in a cage receiving a check-up from the zookeeper, but I refrained from cracking wise. Inside of two minutes he had run his tape up, down and all around. He was efficient in words and motion until he was leaving when he paused to ask me a question.

"Have you ever attended a function such as the one tonight?"

I laughed nervously, which caught me off guard. I'm not one to suffer nerves. "No, and I guess it's obvious isn't it?"

He stepped back and looked me over sympathetically. He stared up at me, placed an index finger under my chin and lifted it, then said, "Don't let them intimidate you. Keep your chin up and smile. You'll do fine."

"Thank you, Phillipe, I appreciate the advice," I said.

With that, he patted me on the shoulder and left.

❋ ❋ ❋

A short while later, I was back in the Caprice heading west through the Lincoln Tunnel on my way to visit the New Jersey-based Big Apple Car Company. After emerging from below the Hudson, I discovered that this stretch of Jersey isn't a dump anymore. Who knew? I guess gentrification had made its way across the Hudson.

BACC was a family business being run out of a two-story home a couple of miles inland from the river. The address took me to a large ranch-style house on a small plot of weedy, overgrown grass. There was a long driveway to the left of the house that stretched to a cinder-block garage in back. Access to the back yard was blocked by a tall chain-link fence with two beware-of-dog signs. Seeing no clear indication of a business office, I knocked on the front door.

A middle-aged woman with dark thinning hair and splotchy skin tugged it open and leaned her considerable girth against the frame. She gave me a good looking over with a pair of suspicious eyes.

I held out a business card. "Hi there, I'm hoping to speak with the dispatcher for BACC."

She plucked it from my hand, read it over carefully, then eyeballed me again. "Says you're from Boston? You a Red Sox fan."

"Guilty as charged ma'am." I gave her my best smile.

"Mmm hmm. I'm the dispatcher, what it is you need?"

"The Sunday before last, your number four car picked up a passenger at Wayne Trust on Third Ave. in Manhattan at roughly 4:30 p.m. I need to know where they took him."

"Why on earth would I tell you that, Mr. Red Sox?"

"It's related to a murder investigation ma'am."

"Is that so?"

"It is. The passenger may have had something to do with the crime."

"Then why are you here instead of the police?"

I considered my answer carefully, deciding which way to go.

"The police aren't good for much of anything but handing out tickets and harassing taxpayers ma'am."

"Ain't that the truth," she said with a grin. "Hold on." She closed the door, and I stood on the porch wondering where the dog was and if they even had one.

She opened the door a couple of minutes later and stood there with a yellow Post-it in her hand, but she didn't offer it to me. Instead, she said, "You know, we could use a little help paying a few tickets."

"Of course." I took out my wallet and removed a twenty-dollar bill. "Would this help?"

"Not so much. Our fines are big here in Yankee country." She smiled when she said Yankee country. The Sox and Yankees were battling it out for first place in the East Division with about a week to go and were expected to meet in the playoffs. I started to take out another twenty, and she prodded, "keep going."

So, I did, and she didn't let up until I had five of them in my hand. "Okay, that'll do." We traded cash for sticky note. "The Yankees are gonna kick your boys' butts," she said with a laugh and closed the door.

The note read G. French, 4:50 p.m., starting at Wayne Trust, 457 Third Ave, to Indian Head Yacht Club, Greenwich and then 8:55 p.m., start return trip, G. French to 457 Third Ave. from IHYC, Greenwich. It sure looked like I had uncovered a conspiracy to hide a body until a merger was completed.

I arrived back at my hotel at about 4:00 p.m., and there was a knock on the door not long after. I scrambled off the bed to answer it. In the hallway, stood a gaunt, feminine young man with long wavy hair, full lips, and prominent cheekbones. He said nothing, handed me a garment bag and a pair of sparkling patent leather shoes and turned to leave. I told him to wait and grabbed my wallet from which I extracted a ten. He looked at it as I held it out to him, shook his head, turned and left. I called after him. "Thank you, how do I return this?"

He called over his shoulder, "You don't. It's yours."

12

My phone buzzed at 7:05 p.m. "This is your driver, Vinnie. Just informing you that I'm in front of your hotel."

"Vinnie! Do you know how to tie a bowtie?"

"What? Uh, yeah I can do that." Vinnie had a thick accent, not so much Italian as it was Brooklyn, or Brooklyn Italian. An image of Travolta in his white suit boogied across my eyes.

He double parked and waited for me in the lobby, where I put him to work on the bowtie. It wasn't even a challenge for him.

As soon as we reached the sidewalk, I spotted our ride. The one with VNZ-CAH on the license plate. Vinnie held the door open for me, and I slid onto the soft black leather. He walked around back and climbed in behind the wheel.

"This is a nice ride, Vinnie."

"Thanks, Mr. Town." He held up his phone. "So, this text says I'm supposed to take you to 800 Park Avenue, to pick up a Mrs. Harriman. Sound good?"

"Perfect."

He pulled out, and I leaned back and considered what I was about to do. I'd never been afraid of much of anything. If I had, I wouldn't have gotten into a line of work that creates enemies of immoral people who don't value property rights and human life as much as I do. My experience at Indian Head in dealing with that little snot, Commodore Sterling, and the subsequent events of that night had made me angry, and anger can lead me to feel invincible. It's righteous anger that drives me at times like this, but now I had to wonder if I may have bitten off more than I could chew. Worrying about this was doing me no good. Doubt is death. I decided to check back in with my new friend.

"Vinnie, you have your own business, and you can tie a bowtie with the best of them. These things don't fit your youthful age and ah, accent. What's your story?"

He laughed. "I know, right. Brooklyn kid makes good." We were moving north on the Westside Highway. As he spoke, Vinnie's eyes bounced between watching me in the mirror and the road ahead.

"It's my dad's business. He's Anthony, so most of the cars are named after him, Anthony 1, Anthony 2, only it's spelled ANTNY on his plates, so people think he's into insects, you know *ant-New York*." He said "York" like it was the center of an egg.

"So, when I started working for him, he got a plate just for me. That's my pops."

"That explains the car, but not the bowtie," I said.

"Ballroom."

"Ballroom?" I asked.

"Yeah, ballroom dancing. I was a junior champion in the tri-state region when I was a kid. I love to dance, and I love being around girls who dance." There you go – Travolta.

"A smart man gets his priorities straight. You're a smart man Vinnie."

"Hey thanks, Mr. Town. Mind if I put on some music?"

"Not at all." He fiddled with his phone and Barry Gibb's legendary falsetto wafted into the ether. Perfect.

❊ ❊ ❊

Harriett had informed me that etiquette required I go up to Eleanor's sixth-floor apartment and collect her. To ask a woman of her station to come down unaccompanied was simply not done in polite society. As I made my move to exit the Town Car, Vinnie reached over the seat with a small bouquet of flowers. "Mrs. Goldstein asked me to give you these."

I must've looked surprised because he added, "You know, to give to Mrs. Harriman."

"Thanks," I said taking them and feeling a little like a kid going on his first date with his old man acting as chaperone. "What about condoms?" I asked.

He laughed hard and said, "That's a good one, Mr. Town."

Eleanor lived in a grand fifteen-story pre-war number with imposing stone facade and uniformed doorman. I had to show ID to get past lobby security. Eleanor's place took up all of the sixth floor, and when the doors opened, I found myself inside her apartment. I was in a small square room with inlaid tile floor and a round rosewood table. On the table was a red vase with a bouquet of white tulips. Ornate black-lacquer doors were to my right and my left, while the wall straight ahead was lined with fine pink silk adorned with cherry blossoms. Neither door had a number or otherwise stood out as the one I should enter. I decided to go right and just as I made my move, the door on the left opened, and I held up. A pretty young woman, probably college age stepped into the room and looked me up and down. She wore running shoes, black yoga pants and a neon green top under a white fur vest.

"You're not Leonard."

"No," I replied. "Leonard went that way." I pointed to the door on the right and smiled.

She rolled her eyes, stepped to the side and, with a bored wave, motioned me to enter.

She led me down a long glimmering hallway. The lighting was tucked behind thick crown molding and radiated down from a vaulted gold-leaf ceiling. On the right, we passed by a kitchen the size of a gymnasium. It had miles of white tile and a marble-topped island that seated eight.

The girl, who I'd been dutifully following, looked over her shoulder at me. "My name's Alex, what's yours?"

"Earl," I said glancing into a dining room with a parquet floor and French fireplace mantel.

We took the next left, and I found myself in a sitting room backed by floor to ceiling crimson curtains, in front of which sat a semi-circular white leather sofa. Eleanor Harrison was poised on one end.

I gave her my winningest smile and was about to speak when Alex cut me off.

"This one's different grandmother. You'd better be careful, he looks heterosexual."

The lady of the house glared at her for a split second, then caught herself and turned to smile at me. She looked to be in her sixties and was striking.

"Thank you, Alexandra." She gave her a look that said, 'Why haven't you left already?' and the kid winked at me as she strolled out.

"Great kid," I said.

Eleanor stood up. "Eleanor Harriman pleased to meet you, Mr. Town." She held out her hand on a flat plane, and I didn't know if I was supposed to kiss it or shake it. I went with a soft shake, and that seemed to satisfy her.

"Please call me Earl."

She looked me over, then smiled warmly, and it completely disarmed me. She looked as though she was thinking of a sweet child-hood memory. She had manners and charm that had been learned over decades of living amongst the rich and powerful. I felt sweat forming on my brow and told myself I was Cary Grant, and to act accordingly. She sat down again and pointed to a spot on the sofa a couple feet away. I did as I was told, but instead of sitting comfortably with my knees apart as per usual, I straightened up, crossed my right leg over my left knee, and turned my head to face her, just like Cary would've.

She wore a shining silver dress that fit snugly. Knee length, it was more high fashion cocktail wear than granny goes to tea. Her blonde shoulder-length hair and red lipstick looked good against the silver. She only had a couple of wrinkles around the eyes and looked more like a mom than a grandmother, and I realized that I'd seen women at Indian Head with a similar look. She'd bought a few more years of youth through surgery and fillers, and God knows what else. Her voice pulled me out of my thoughts.

"Are those for me?" She pointed to the flowers.

"Yes," I said. "Thank you, Eleanor, for allowing me to accompany you to this ..." She cut me off with a wave of her hand and sniffed loudly. A door opened on her left, and a servant entered. She walked across the room and took the flowers from me. "Pilar will put those in a nice vase." She looked at the girl and nodded, and she quickly left the room.

"Great," I muttered to myself, then, thinking of Cary, I uncorked an enthusiastic "Splendid!"

Pilar came right back with Eleanor's coat and handbag. I guessed I wasn't getting a tour of the place. She stood up, and I followed her lead. She paused and examined me as though she was looking over a child in his Sunday best.

She instructed, "Stand up straighter, and pull those shoulders back." I did as I was told, and I must have passed because she moved onto my next shortcoming.

"Pardon me for saying so, but Earl may be a bit too Kentucky for this crowd. What is your middle name?"

I almost said Cary, but I went with the truth instead. "Leland."

She rolled her eyes, groaned, and walked past me towards the hallway.

"I have a nickname," I proffered. She stopped, turned, and raised a single eyebrow. "Chief," I said.

"Mmm, Harriett mentioned you were a policeman."

"I was, once."

We moved from the gilded hallway to the elevator, which we rode in silence all the way down. I was trying to think of what Cary would say when she broke the ice.

"Just so you know, I'm not doing this as a favor to Harriett. I don't do favors."

I nodded but didn't ask. She was going to tell me anyway. She waited until Vinnie placed us safely into the back of the Town Car and began to drive.

"I know that you brought Shoshanna back. I've lost a child, Mr. Town, forever. I know what that's like and I'm not going to repeat it with a grandchild. You may have noticed, Alex doesn't take things very seriously. She is fearless because she's never been in danger. If anything ever happens to her, and God knows the way she carries on. Well, I'm going to call on you and you better damn well answer."

I gave up the Cary act and uncrossed my legs. I looked her in the eye. "If that happens, I'll do everything I can to help you."

"I'm counting on it," she replied, then looked away. We drove in silence for a bit before I spoke again.

"How far back do you and Harriett go?"

Vinnie was already turning onto Endicott's street. Eleanor only lived about ten blocks away.

"Do you mean, how did an Upper East Side Blueblood and an Upper West Side Jew become great friends?" That wasn't exactly what I meant, but I nodded.

"Politics makes strange bedfellows, Mr. Town. In fact, practically everyone you meet tonight is attending for a political reason. You'd be advised to keep that in mind. There are no innocent conversations. Every guest at an event of this kind has an agenda. I guess you do too, don't you?"

I nodded, and she went on. "Ultimately, it all comes down to money or status, but at least you're here for a noble cause. You are here for a noble cause, aren't you?" She took my measure with another hard stare. I nodded again.

"So, Eleanor," I said with a sly grin. "What's your angle?"

Vinnie had stopped the car and gotten out. Eleanor gazed up at Endicott's five-story stone mansion, as Vinnie opened her door, then looked over her shoulder at me. "Wouldn't you like to know?"

Getting into the affair took some doing. First, we waited while two couples ahead of us gave their names to security staff, then it was our turn. Security was tight and seemed to be designed to send a message to non-invitees that it would be a mistake to try and gain access. There was an NYPD squad car parked about 50 yards from the front door, and two pairs of cops were stationed in front of aluminum barricades on the sidewalk about a car-length from either side of the stone steps that led up to the second-floor entrance. A couple of paparazzi stood behind them. They didn't seem all that excited to see me.

At the base of the steps were two men in dark suits. The shorter one was older, maybe mid-forties, olive skinned and chubby, and about 5'7". He had a clipboard and was checking names. The second one held a wand in his right hand, which he was using to check guests for weapons. This would be a problem, as I was strapped. After what happened on Mac's boat, I wasn't taking any chances around these people.

Wand man was tall enough to have a couple of inches on me and was ripped and bald as a peeled Idaho Spud. He had a bulging jaw and neck muscles that suggested he took lifting weights a little too seriously. The crispness of his suit and stiff, perfect posture implied he'd done a stint in the service.

Our turn came, and my date took charge. "Eleanor Harriman and guest."

The short one looked over his list, then flipped a page, and said, "Yes, Mrs. Harriman. And your guest is?"

"My guest," she said.

"Could I have a name?" he pleaded. She wasn't in the mood to acquiesce.

"Earl Town," I interjected, not wanting to stand witness to a pointless pissing match. She gave me a look that suggested I'd let her down and turned to start up the stairs.

I tried to follow, but the tall one stepped in front of me.

Eleanor looked back and saw what was happening. Before I could engage with the wand waver, she'd grabbed his wrist and said loudly "Just what in the hell do you think you're doing?"

He smiled, a little too cocky and familiar. He lowered the wand to his side. "Just doing my job ma'am. It's my responsibility to ..."

Eleanor cut him off. "You will not search my guest. If you try again, you'll no longer have a job." His smile twisted into a look of disappointment and he stepped back, but as he did, he muttered something about Eleanor or me.

"What did you say?" I pressed him.

"Come on," said Eleanor, tugging on my wrist.

"What's your name?" I asked him. He grinned at me but extended no reply. It was what my mother used to call a shit-eating grin, and I wondered why he was so cocky.

Eleanor tugged a second time, and I let her lead me up the steps and into the viper's nest.

13

We stepped into a wide marble-lined hallway with soaring walls, a coffered ceiling, and elaborate plaster moldings. It was more cathedral vestibule than foyer. However, the art was anything but iconographic. To my left was a pink neon sign that said in cursive 'The heart has its reasons.' A few feet away was either a large-scale Jackson Pollack or something a six-year-old made while pitching a tantrum in the paint department.

We moved at a sluggish pace, as Eleanor waved and said hello to a number of guests. This included several older women who I was surprised could hold themselves up, given the amount of jewelry heaped upon their necks and wrists. Harry Winston must have been low on inventory that evening.

The entry hall led us into a colossal atrium. A marble staircase wound its way across the back of the room and stopped in its center. An immense crystal chandelier was suspended from the underside of the staircase. Under this sat a grand piano and an attractive female singer who'd had a few hits back in the eighties.

I said to Eleanor, "Is that?"

She interrupted. "What's her name. Yes, she's an old flame of Whit's, and damned annoying. Looks like he's relegated her to the entry hall this year, thank God."

I held onto Eleanor's arm and took the stairs slow at first. She seemed to appreciate my concern, but she was in good shape and by the time we reached the action on the second level, I needed her for support more than she needed me.

The second floor mostly consisted of a single large room that had likely been a grand ballroom a century ago. In the farthest corner from us was a jazz quartet. The bass player was laying down a serious groove while the piano man rhythmically plinked and plunked the high keys.

In the opposite corner was a sleek semi-circular bar made of stainless steel and leather. A set of red leather stools sat in front of it, and all were full. Two bartenders in white jackets were mixing drinks, one mixed for the crowd in front and the other for the wait staff that was walking throughout with silver trays held high. Neither of the two was the Rooster.

In the lengthy span between the bar and the jazz group were four sets of French doors topped with arched windows. All four were open, and beyond them lay a stone patio where many more guests were mingling in the warm September air.

A waiter came by with champagne. I was about to take a glass when Eleanor spoke up.

"What is this?"

"Bollinger, ma'am."

"I know it's Bollinger," she sighed. "Whit drinks Bolly like it's water. What year is it?" She looked at me, and added, "He only drinks vintage."

I pulled back my outstretched hand and put it in my pocket.

The waiter said, "I'm sorry, I misunderstood. It's 2008, a wonderful year."

"Ah, yes that'll do," she said. She nodded at me, and I took two.

In the middle of the room sat a long brown leather sofa set. Beside the end nearest us stood a tall sculpture comprised of repurposed scrap metal and other industrial materials. The assemblage appeared to be two figures in an embrace. One looked like late-in-life Walter Matthau and the other an angry Hervé Villechaize. Each also looked like it was melting in a searing sun. Later in the evening, I checked the plaque attached to its pedestal. The work was called 'The inevitable decline of western civilization under the forced capitulation of bourgeois social mores and twentieth-century gender roles,' and I thought to myself: 'Damn if this guy didn't just nail it.'

Eleanor saw me leering at it while sipping bubbly, leaned into me and said, "New money always collects the avant-garde." Then, while rolling her eyes, she added, "And the avant-garde is nearly always poop." The way she annunciated poop was a thing of beauty.

She tugged on my arm and pulled me over to a small group engaged in noisy debate.

A pallid man of short stature, and with graying mane saw us coming and opened his arms. "Ellie!" He squealed as Eleanor leaned into his embrace. When she pulled away, the man stepped back and gave me the twice over.

"And, who is this?" He asked with genuine glee.

"Chief Town, this is my dear friend Leonard Finch." I stuck out my hand and applied my best smile.

"Leonard, this is the Chief. Don't ask how he got that name, just accept it and move on."

Though Leonard was slight, his handshake was firm. "I love a man with a secret," he said.

Eleanor introduced me around, and I made small talk for a while, then took a stroll and made it a point to tune into the conversations around me, in the hopes of hearing something useful. At one point I picked up on a conversation between two middle-aged women in silk gowns, who were sipping champagne and swearing like the housewives of New Jersey.

One, a heavily botoxed brunette, leaned her fit frame against a massive stone vase, while the other, a bottle blonde with a puffy face and too much lip liner, stood beside her, arms folded. My back was turned to them, but I could see them clearly in a mixed media piece that I was pretending to admire. The "art" consisted of shards of mirrored glass and an array of woman's hygiene products, which had been spray painted in neon colors. Endicott had probably paid six figures for it. Of course, he'd probably sell it for a fat profit someday too. The thought of it made me shake my head, and as I was doing so, I overheard this: "And that Mayor. What a mess he is. My husband says he's stoned all the time. I mean, all the Goddamn time," said the fit one.

"Have you seen the way he looks when he leans over the lectern, like a dog eyeing a steak," replied the puffy one. "I swear to Gaia, someday he is going to leap from the stage, rip the throat out of a reporter and drink its blood. I hear he's always making his driver stop for snacks on the way to and from meetings."

"Yeah, because he's high as a kite." They both laughed a little too loudly.

I moved closer to the artwork and eyed it, before turning to the two of them. "Wow," I said. "Have you seen this? It's so powerful; really speaks to the struggle of women against the patriarchy. I especially love the artist's inclusion of sanitary napkins."

They were aghast. "You aren't serious." Puffy moved in closer and stared. "Gross! I think they're used!" People in a nearby group turned towards the commotion. Botox face now moved in and eyed it, then reared back, clasped a hand to her mouth and gagged.

Having successfully shared my appreciation for art, I made my way back to Eleanor and company. I was just in time to catch the heiress to a breakfast sausage fortune venting, "Christ, if I hear one more story about her little boy, Elon." Heads nodded, mouths murmured, and I excused myself again, as I'd finally found my bartender.

It was a more intimate scene in the sitting room next door, in which about a dozen of New York's most pampered engaged in conversation on their way to and from the temporary bar that had been set up along the back wall, behind which stood the Rooster. The little guy wore a white jacket sans Indian Head crest. I moseyed over.

"Making your special mojitos tonight, Rooster?"

His eyes widened, but he turned away before I could read him anymore.

"No sir, not tonight. I don't have all of my ingredients here," he told the wall. "I have champagne, wine, and IPA. Oh, and some of Mr. Endicott's preferred scotches."

"Oh," I said. Suddenly feeling a jump my step. "I'll have scotch neat, whatever you think is best. These brands are out of my league."

He had to turn around to pour. "Excellent, sir. Mr. Endicott drinks only the best."

"Rooster, you and I need to talk."

"We do, sir? What about?"

"About taking special care of me on Monday night."

"I don't ..."

"Don't bullshit me. You talk too much. I know what you said about taking special care of me. Now you're gonna tell me what you meant when you said it." He took a step back and bumped into the cart behind him, rattling the bottles. He just about jumped out of his skin at the sound.

Just then, a distinguished looking older gentleman and his niece appeared next to me. He wore velvet shoes in scarlet with his black tux. The shoes matched her dress, which was nearly showing cleavage, but not only in front, which was more than an eyeful, on her lower back as well. She was dripping in diamonds and pinching a silver cigarette holder between the index and middle fingers of her right hand.

I hated to intrude on their evening, but I needed to maintain the moment I had created with Rooster, so I leaned into the man and whispered: "Could you possibly give the barkeep and I a private moment? He said something." I paused for effect, "Something most vulgar about myself and my date." I pointed across the room to Eleanor. She was engaged in conversation. However, Leonard noticed and waved to me. I waved back, then looked the man in the eye and said, "You know some people." I turned to face Rooster and glared, "Just can't accept that love is love, regardless of one's gender."

The man raised an eyebrow. "Ah, understood," he said. Then he turned to Rooster and said, "Shame on you son. What is it with your kind anyway?"

"Come on darling," he pulled on his arm candy. "I hear the help is more open-minded over there."

I smiled at Rooster and said triumphantly: "I can do this all night."

He threw up his hands. "No, màs." He moved closer and spoke softly, "I didn't do anything to your drink. That's what you think?"

"Yes, and no shit. I figured that out when I was fine after drinking it. Listen to me carefully and answer my question." I leaned in and spoke slowly. "What did you mean when you said you took *special care* of me?"

"I didn't mean doing anything to your drink." I felt my face turning red.

"See those two over there." I pointed to two young socialites, I'd seen on Page Six more times than I care to admit. "I'm going to inform them that you said you diddled both of them last month, and neither was a particularly good lay." I stepped towards them, and Rooster broke.

"No!" He grabbed my forearm and leaned in close. "I didn't do anything, I overhear Richard saying this. I told some members about it. That's all, I swear to God."

"Richard said this? Who the hell is Richard?" I demanded.

"Richard." He repeated it and looked at me.

"Who is Richard?" I asked again. Rooster shook his head like I was the problem. He stepped from behind the bar. I felt my right hand instinctively move toward my holster, but he breezed past me. He led me over to a large street-facing window, where he pointed down to a man standing in the glow of a streetlamp.

Richard was the smart-ass security guard with a wand fetish.

14

I took out my phone, zoomed in and snapped a photo of Richard for my Bad Guys of the Upper East Side collection.

"What's Richard's last name?"

"I don't know," replied the Rooster. "He's just Richard to us."

"When Richard said this, who was he talking too?"

"I don't know that either," he said, as he poured glasses of red wine for two men at the bar. Traffic had picked up as the later arrivals made their big entrance and began filling the empty spaces. He leaned across the bar, looked to each side, and whispered conspiratorially: "It was in the men's locker room, I was in the toilet, I heard him and another man talking, and I know Richard's voice, but the other man, I don't know him."

"When was this?"

"Tuesday, after I come to work. About 3 p.m., I start at three and work to close. I was about to start."

"You work until the bar closes?"

"Si, I mean yes."

"Did you work the Saturday before last?"

"Yes, every weekend until Columbus Day, then they change the hours. I have to find part-time work in winter."

"Do you know James MacArthur?"

"Yes," he replied emphatically. "Everybody knows Mr. Mac."

I pressed on. "Did you see him on the dock before he left that Saturday night?"

He thought about it and nodded, but then pointed to a waitress standing behind me impatiently waiting for an order, so I simmered while he made a half-dozen Kir Royales. When he was finished, he came back over and said, "Thank you. Okay, I hear them first."

I must have looked confused because he added, "On Saturday night. I hear them on the dock. They shout, loud, angry."

I leaned in closer. "Who was yelling at who?"

"The Commodore, I mean Mr. Sterling, and Mr. French, and Mr. Mac. They all were."

"What were they yelling about?"

He looked over my shoulder, as a waiter approached, and whispered, "I don't know. Mr. French and Mr. Mac were yelling at one another. Then the Commodore shouted, but to calm it down."

"Who else was there?"

"Mrs. Saunders and another woman. I don't know her though."

"What'd she look like?"

"I didn't see. I only hear her voice. She crying." He shrugged his shoulders. "Bad luck."

I chewed on this while the Rooster poured bubbly.

He topped off my scotch, and I decided to move on, after warning him that I might be back with more questions. Rooster's relief at seeing me go was palpable.

I decided to speak to Richard now before I had time to overthink and complicate it. I'd go downstairs and confront him, but just as I reentered the great room, a cheer went up, and the crowd began to applaud. I wondered if I'd been mistaken for someone else, but I was looking at everyone's back. The crowd's rapt attention was directed at the far end of the room, where a small stage had been erected in front of the French doors. On it, stood Gibson French and Whitman Endicott. Lights were dimmed on the edges of the room, so only their space was illuminated. I decided to stay for the show.

Eleanor had told me to expect a speech from our host tonight, and it looked like Gibson French was just the right lackey to introduce him.

"Thank you, thank you, everyone!" French shouted over the not fully quieted crowd. He raised his voice and went on.

"This is the twelfth year Whitman has hosted this wonderful event, and before he speaks on behalf of the foundation that he so generously established, and which I proudly and humbly support, I want to say a few words about him, and the giving spirit that fills this amazing man!"

The crowd applauded rapturously, and I wondered how much of the response was genuine and how much was political. How many of these people were indebted to Endicott or wanted his money or influence for something. Rich people problems.

I moved along the wall to get a better look. I got close enough to read French's face but could see nothing that stood out about him, except for how perfect he looked.

Mr. GQ, Gibson French was tall and athletic, with intense blue eyes, a square dimpled chin, slicked back Wall Street hair, and a perfect smile. His voice was a deep baritone with more than a sprinkling of gravitas.

I surveyed the room. Many of the women were entranced. His looks and charm were lethal. I even caught a couple of the wait staff staring into French's baby blues. It occurred to me that the ladies in the room outnumbered the men by a decent margin. Maybe the office was a boys' club, but charity galas were the realm of the fairer sex.

French went on for several minutes about how Endicott had worked tirelessly to establish the foundation and the foundation's many accomplishments, which were not inconsequential. Whatever one thought about the man, Endicott had done important work for those in need.

French exchanged a knowing smile with the host as he finally brought the epic ass-kissing to a climax. At one point, I thought I might have to pull my gun and demand that he relinquish the microphone, but he finally handed it over to the man of the evening. The crowd didn't wait for Endicott to speak before giving him a long, rousing ovation.

Feeling the need to fit in, I applauded along with them, and as I was doing so, I felt a delicate squeeze on my left shoulder. Tinsley Saunders had materialized on my right flank and wrapped a slender arm around me. She leaned in close and purred in my ear, "Hello coach."

I felt my heart beat faster and had to force myself to wait before replying, so as not to give away my glee at seeing her again.

"Hi there." It was all I could say without stuttering.

"Strange seeing you here, Earl. Are you giving Whit a private lesson after the affair?" She had a peculiar way of speaking, it was a drawl, but not southern – she was a Yankee blue blood through and through. It was a seductive kind of a thing.

"No," I said recovering my sanity. "The old man's got a sore elbow. I'm here for the booze," I said, holding up my glass which was getting dangerously low.

"Awe, and I thought you were here to see me." She tilted her head and smiled up at me. She was tall, probably a full six feet in heels, and every inch was catnip.

"That's a benefit that I just became aware of. Now that I am, I consider the scotch to be a weak second to you, Miss Saunders."

"I don't want to hear that name come out of your mouth again, Earl. You call me Tinsley. But why are you really here?"

She had loaned her place to Beth MacArthur for our meeting, she knew why I was here. "Well, Tinsley," I said her name slow and deliberate. "Since so many of James MacArthur's friends and associates are here this evening, I thought I should be too. Maybe he'll turn up, and I can go home."

"Maybe," she replied. "Have you seen him?" She looked around the room.

A roar of laughter erupted from the crowd, and I followed Tinsley's gaze back to Whit, who was telling a story about bringing a rock star to meet sick kids in the hospital. Apparently, the rock star whipped out his phone and started showing pics of topless groupies to a 10-year old leukemia patient, or something like that.

"How did you get in here? This is," she paused considering her words, "quite exclusive."

"Do you know Eleanor Harriman?"

"I'm familiar with Eleanor."

"She's my doubles partner."

She laughed and swept wavy brown hair from a bare shoulder. Her fingernails were painted a rich cobalt blue to match her dress, which sparkled and boasted a deeply plunging neckline.

"You're too spry to play the senior circuit, detective. You should try a match with someone more youthful." She was sipping a clear cocktail with a wedge of lime waiting for the next volley.

The crowd suddenly went quiet. No one could speak, even whisper, without being overheard. I looked past Tinsley as she turned her head. The audience was rapt by the performance before them. Whitman Endicott had gotten down on one knee and was staring up into the eyes of the naked angels painted above on his ceiling. He held the microphone in one hand, his other hand outstretched like he was summoning strength from the little cherubs and the heavens surrounding them. He spoke in a whisper as if possessed by a spirit, holding long pauses between each word.

"I couldn't go into the room. I could not step through that door." He lowered his gaze and looked at the faces around him making eye contact with everyone in the first couple of rows. "I could not watch one more child die from this disease without doing something about it. I've spent time in too many hospitals. I've seen too many sick children." He paused and sniffed as though being overcome with emotion. He was selling, and he was damn good at it.

"This is why I want, no, that's not it!" He spun on his heel and reviewed the crowd again, occasionally smiling at a familiar face and giving away the game. Then he stopped and got back to the business at hand. "This is why they, the survivors and those fighting for their lives in a hospital or hospice right now, and the spirits of those who have passed at the hands of this vicious killer! They all want, no, they need, each and every one of you, to take something home tonight."

I looked around to see what people would be taking home, but unless they were planning to bring home Whit's "art" collection, I didn't see what was up for auction.

Having secured at least a nomination for an Oscar, Endicott pulled himself together and said, "Now, I also have a special announcement to make."

He eyed the frizzy-haired drummer in the jazz group, who responded with a lengthy drumroll. When it was over, Endicott puffed out his chest and gazed at the assemblage of wealth and privilege before him. For a man in his early sixties, Endicott was in great shape. He was only about 5'5", 5'7" in heels and lifts, but he was muscular and looked like he lived a disciplined lifestyle. He had a ring of gray hair that started above each ear and met in the back while avoiding the peak. His teeth were bright white and perfect. My ex-wife called this a Greenwich smile. Her antiquities business took off when she networked her way into the hedge fund community. Apparently, the first thing these guys do when they make a few million bucks is buy a set of gleaming white caps. Incidentally, most at that time drove Hummers too, and this made me wonder if a prominent Greenwich dentist also owned a dealership and offered a two-for-one special. Anyway, they're a swell bunch. At least Roxy thought so, she left me for one. Endicott spoke.

"Many of you know that I have been involved in some major negotiations over the past month. Some of you have been a great help in this effort." He looked at Gibson French, who stood straight and proud, like a dog receiving praise from his master. 'Heel boy, heel. That's a good boy.'

Endicott continued on. "I am pleased to announce that the merger between Wayne Trust and JKB SA was signed and sealed just hours ago." A groundswell of applause went up, along with a few whoops and whistles. "Thank you, thank you all!" He soaked up the adulation.

"You can read about the details in the Journal tomorrow. I would just like to say that I've been very fortunate in my life, and I am a man who gives back. Therefore I pledge to match whatever is raised tonight up to one million dollars!" Another roar swelled and rippled through the crowd, and he waited for things to quiet down again.

"So, everyone, bid early and bid often! Enjoy the music and the champagne!" He held a glass high above his head. "Let's raise some money for a great cause! Make me a million dollars less rich. I dare you!" Endicott downed his bubbly and handed the mic to a young woman. He was then swallowed up by the crowd to the left of the stage. It was awfully good to be Whitman Endicott.

I had been enraptured by the performance of a great salesman and finally turned back to face Tinsley, but she was long gone.

✳ ✳ ✳

I hoped Eleanor was planning on buying for the two of us in the charity auction; otherwise, it'd be difficult explaining my expenses to Joanna.

Back to the mission, I thought as I headed towards a windowed alcove at the front, where I thought I'd have a good view of the security detail on the street below. I peered down into the shadows and found the little guy with his clipboard, but I couldn't spot Richard and his wand. I turned back to scan the great room. If he'd moved inside, his height and gleaming dome would make him easy to spot.

As I was scoping the crowd, Larry Ferncroft stepped in front of me with a goofy look on his face. He punched my right biceps and said, "I can't believe it! You really made it in, you don't mess around, Earl. I'm impressed!" Buddies for life, me and Larry.

"I'm a man of my word, Larry." Then I poked him in the chest and added, "Hey, you clean up good." I figured I'd say it to him before he said it to me.

"You too," he replied.

He cocked his head towards a diminutive man with an awful wig standing by the stairs, one arm on the railing. "See that guy? That guy is number three behind Lloyd at Goldman Sachs. Made over thirty million last year. You know what he told me a few minutes ago?"

"I do not," I said eagerly.

"He is making a six-million-dollar alteration to his estate in South Hampton."

"Wow," I said, wildly underwhelmed.

"No, that's not it. The thing is, he doesn't want to make the alteration. He hates the idea of it, says it will ruin the flow of the house and detract from the view of the water." I squinted my confusion, and he went on.

"He's doing it because of his rival at Morgan." I don't know if he was referring to Stanley, J.P. or Tracy, I didn't ask, "who just added a

10,000 square foot guest wing and family entertainment complex to his place down the street."

"I don't get it," I said.

"Exactly! So, this guy over there is spending six million to add 12,000 square feet to his place, and destroying the flow and view, just to maintain his status as the owner of the largest home on the street."

"Wow, imagine how much he'd have to spend to make changes he actually wanted."

Larry spotted a passing waiter and latched onto two glasses of champagne, one of which he offered to me.

"Thanks, but I'm sticking with scotch tonight."

So, he tilted his head back and downed one of them in a single gulp, then set the glass down on a pedestal next to another God-awful contemporary art piece consisting of a mélange of early twentieth-century cooking utensils and contemporary sex toys. He then began to sip from the other glass like a perfect gentleman. You know, he was starting to grow on me. And, I hoped that the cleaning staff would mistake the glass he'd set down for part of the composition. I imagined seeing the piece in an auction catalog with champagne flute included and chuckled. Then, Larry broke back into my conscience.

"Hey, McNierney is looking for you."

"Who?"

"He's security at Indian Head."

"Richard McNierney? Bald guy, about yay big?" I held my hand above the top of my head.

"Yeah, that's him."

"What do you mean he's looking for me?"

"When we got here, Caroline overheard his partner, the guy taking names, say 'here comes Town's drinking buddy.' And she said he meant me. He's at the club most nights, must have seen us in the bar."

"Are you sure about this?"

"Yeah," he said. Then Larry turned and waved to a gorgeous 40ish woman in a little black dress. She had a thin waist and lean legs, which were adorned with stiletto heels. She wore a double strand of sterling silver beads around her throat, had shoulder length jet black hair and blood red lipstick.

Larry introduced me to his wife, Caroline, and she held out her small white-gloved hand, which I shook while staring into a marvelous set of intense blue eyes. I wondered how this dork had managed to marry such a beauty, and the only answer I could come up with was that he had a lot more money than I realized or was hung like an NBA power forward. Both scenarios pissed me off.

Larry asked, "Caroline, would you mind telling Earl what you over-heard on our way in here?"

She proceeded to recite the exact story Larry had told me. Then she excused the two of them and pulled Larry away, saying he abso-lutely had to speak with so and so. I sent a text to Ed asking him to look into McNierney, then spotted Eleanor and went to join her and a small clique standing over by melting Matthau and Hervé. I scanned the room for Richard as I went, but still no sign of him. Just then, someone stepped back on stage to announce the winners of a silent auction to have Jean-Georges Vongerichten come to their home and cook dinner. Apparently, the auction items consisted largely of net-working opportunities for rich people to get together and stumble upon ways to make even more money.

"This is one of the night's most sought-after items. Jean-Georges and his staff will cook for you and up to seven additional guests. He will come to your home, provided it's not more than five blocks from the Athenee." A small chuckle went up from the crowd, and the speaker actually said, "Just a little Upper East Side humor. And, the winner of dinner by, and with, Jean-Georges is ..." The drummer started a roll.

A woman behind me said, "Please let it be me."

The man with the microphone revealed the winner, as a cheer went up from across the room, but it was hard to discern the name over the crowd noise. An egg-shaped older woman was jumping up and down, shaking the floorboards and making a racket. I heard the voice from behind me say, "Christ, it's a fix. The bitch from Chappaqua got it. Just look at that pantsuit. Poor Jean-Georges."

15

I'd been keeping an eye on Gibson French. I saw that he was moving through the mob unaccompanied and cut him off by the stage.

"Mr. French. I'm Earl Town," I said, holding out my hand.

"Gibson French," he replied with a firm handshake and a thousand-watt smile.

"I'm investigating the disappearance of James MacArthur." Oops, someone flipped off the smile switch.

"Ah," he said, recognition sweeping across his chiseled face. "You're the man from Indian Head?"

"I am, and I have the lump to prove it," I said, rubbing the back of my head. If he knew anything about the attack, he didn't show it.

"Look, I think you're mischaracterizing James's absence, but let's talk about this someplace more private."

He held up his right hand, and a man with an earpiece appeared. Endicott had stationed security around the room. He whispered something in the man's ear, then walked over to the wall no more than 10 feet from us, pushed open a hidden door, and disappeared.

"That's impressive," I said. "You'll have to introduce me to the man who installs your secret passages."

He motioned for me to follow him through the same doorway, so I did.

"I could use a good trapdoor man too, if you happen to know one," I said, as we made our way down a long hallway. There were dozens of framed photographs along the passage. It was a display of Endicott's power and influence. There he is in a tux, arm around Madeline Albright, and there he is on a golf cart, arm around Jeff Bezos. Hey, is that him and Mick Jagger on a helipad?

So, this is the inner sanctum, I thought, as we reached the end of the hallway, which stopped at a pair of intricately carved doors, one of which had a golden knob in the shape of an eagle clutching a ball in its talons. French palmed the eagle's head and twisted, and the door swung open.

I followed him into Endicott's office, or maybe it was a library, or is this what they call a study? Conservatory? No, lair, that's more like it.

And, it was movie-villain perfect. It was big, maybe forty by forty. Two of the walls were covered in walnut paneling and floor to ceiling bookshelves, while the other two had walnut wainscoting beneath rich silk panels into which were woven scenes from feudal Japan. There were intricate depictions of warriors, streams, birds, cherry blossoms and temples. The ceiling was a good eighteen feet high and coffered into sixteen sections.

The delicate silk that lined the walls served as a backdrop for paintings in gilded frames. English landscapes, horses and hounds hung on one wall, contrasted by an assortment of mid-century abstracts – Miro, Kandinsky, Davis, on the other. A monumental stone fireplace sat in the center of the far wall. Along the front wall was a long dark table with stacks of old yellowing, manuscripts.

I heard the door shut and realized French had snuck out. It was just Endicott and me. Cue the eerie music.

Endicott approached with hand extended. "Whitman Endicott," he announced. The little dandy stood up straight as he could and raised up off his heels a bit, and still had to look up at me as I took his hand.

He pointed to the furthest away of two old Art Deco club chairs seated in front of the smoldering fireplace. I suddenly felt like I was Columbo, and I swore to myself that I would never do insurance work again.

I sank back into the rich, dark leather. "French, Deco, 1920s?" I reluctantly came to learn quite a bit about twentieth-century furniture from my ex. I can tell an Eames from a Le Corbusier, and I know the difference between Art Deco and Art Nouveau. Though I can't afford any of it, at least not the real stuff, but I do appreciate the lines.

My question (or was it the person asking it?) amused him. He chuckled as he answered. "1920s, yes, Art Deco, yes, but American actually. Those chairs were owned by Jesse Livermore, the great bear of Wall Street. He had them custom made shortly after making his third fortune. He made four fortunes, you know?" No, I didn't know, not that I wanted him to know this, so I nodded and looked bored.

He opened the doors of an ornate Chinese rosewood cabinet and took out two glasses and a sparkling crystal decanter filled with an amber liquid.

These guys and their scotch, I thought to myself. "Is that Dalmore?"

Endicott reeled back like he was choking, "God no!" he roared. He waved a rocks glass at me and asked, "Have you been drinking with the Commodore?"

"Yeah, I've seen where you park your battleship. It's a hell of a view from up there."

"Yes, Indian Head is wonderful this time of year."

I went for the old knock 'em off balance routine. "By the way, do you know who cracked me on the back of the head and left me floating in the Sound the other night?"

He didn't sway. "No, I've no idea. I'm sorry about that." He walked from the bar to the chair opposite me, handing me a glass as he passed. He paused to inhale the scent wafting from his tumbler before speaking again. "You know, my father had a saying about trespassing on another man's property."

"Really?" I looked up at him, as I swirled the liquid gold around in the thick crystal. "What was it?"

"He said, don't ever trespass on another man's property, it's a good way to get killed."

He leaned back and smiled like a kid at a carnival. His caps had been shaped and installed by a damn fine doctor, and they glowed in the soft light of the fire.

"That's some oddly specific fatherly advice."

"Yes, he was a practical man. You should hear the one about sleeping with other people's wives."

"Speaking of that. Where's Mac?"

He squinted at me as though I wasn't making sense. "*Damned* if I know. I wish I did, I could've used him these last few weeks, but you know what they say, Mac is Mac."

"Mac is dead," I said. I thought it would surprise him, but he was rock solid. He sniffed the air, then gave a look of disappointment.

"I heard what you told the FBI. I don't know what game it is you think you're playing Mr. Town. Do you have something against me?" I gave him a cold stare and a sigh.

He went on offense. "Joanna Hill has been a loyal employee, but I'm afraid we may have to let her go if this rumor mongering keeps up."

"She's concerned about her boss. Who, whether you want to admit it or not, has been murdered. You're going to fire her for worrying about his safety?"

"You don't know her very well," he said, with smug certainty. "She's concerned about more than his safety."

"What does that mean?" I demanded.

"Why haven't you told her your story about finding Mac's body?" Jesus, this guy had good intel.

"So, you're keeping close tabs on her," I volleyed back. "Why is that? Why have you been avoiding me? Mr. Endicott, these are these actions of a man who has something to hide."

He laughed in my face. It was a belly laugh, and he clutched his stomach and threw his head back while I waited for him to stop.

"Avoiding you? I was in the middle of a negotiation that will dramatically alter the lives of thousands of Wayne Trust employees. Do you not get it? I needed Mac here. His division is responsible for nearly one-fifth of Wayne Trust revenue, and he's nowhere to be found. His absence hasn't been beneficial to Wayne Trust or me." He sipped his scotch and gazed at me, his disappointment apparent. "I haven't taken time to meet with you because I was negotiating the sale of an international corporation without a vital member of my leadership team. Mac put the deal in jeopardy, but I got it done. If you really think Mac is in trouble, or dead, which I refuse to believe, I'd start looking at people who wanted to scuttle this deal. It was in their interest that Mac disappeared, not mine or my employees."

"And, who might that be?" I asked.

"You're the detective. I didn't get to this station in life," he paused and looked around the cavernous room for emphasis, "by doing other people's jobs."

"Mac sent you an email?"

"Yeah, the Sunday before last." He motioned me to drink up, and I took a long sip. It was fine scotch, though I didn't notice much of a difference from the Dalmore. But, I am a mere peasant.

"As I recall, Mr. Endicott, he said he was taking a break and not to worry. That's all! As you said, he's an important leader. There's a big deal brewing. You're his boss, and that was all he said? That makes no sense."

"Yeah, I can't explain it. Other than to say that Mac has behaved similarly in the past."

"Who's Rebecca?"

"What's that? Rebecca?"

"Mac named his boat after her. You're his good friend, so who is she?"

"I don't know. He never told me. Just Mac being Mac again. Look, Mr. Town, why don't you stop playing hero and go back to living in exile in South Boston. You are in exile, aren't you? From the place where you grew up, and your ex-wife, Roxanne?"

I set my scotch down on the table between us, leaned back into the big, enveloping leather chair, took in a deep breath and smirked at him. "You've misread me. You think I'll go away with my tail between my legs. You should have done more research, Mr. Endicott. I respond to humiliation with anger, rage even, not retreat. Keep throwing fuel on my fire, and you're liable to get burned."

"Be that as it may. The facts are the facts. You're trampling through here like a bull with an erection looking for a cow to poke. Now that the deal is done, Mac will likely turn up in short order. I'm sure of it. And, then you'll realize what an ass you've made of yourself, while in a rage, as you so eloquently put it."

"Stop lying, you and I both know he's dead."

He began to rise. It was a signal that we were done. So, I hit him with a right hook. "Why did the Commodore call you with an urgent message while you were negotiating last Sunday afternoon?"

He shot me a glare but didn't answer. The door opened, and a great hulking man with a bulge under his jacket motioned me to get up and follow him out. Endicott said, "Please enjoy the scotch, and have as much as you want Mr. Town. Enjoy the good life for the brief time you have access to it. If Eleanor weren't a dear friend, I'd have you escorted from the premises."

"Why did you send Gibson French to Indian Head after you received the call?" He tilted his head as though he couldn't wrap his mind around my knowing this. The big man clamped a large vice-like mitt down on my shoulder and propelled me toward the door. I looked back over my shoulder at Endicott and said, "I'm not done with you."

I left him stunned as the giant led me back down the hall.

"Hey, where'd French go?" I asked. If the ogre could talk, he didn't show it. He opened the secret door, which looked like a door from that side, and shoved me back into the great room. I turned quickly and wedged my left shoulder in the gap so he couldn't close it, and I stared up at him. "You know Richard McNierney?" He smiled but didn't say a word, and pushed the door against my shoulder, which hurt. "You tell Richard, he and I need to talk. Tell him to come and find me." I extracted myself and was soon staring at the wall.

I turned around and stood there rubbing my shoulder, sipping finely-aged scotch and simmering over Endicott's dismissal of me. I felt like calling it a night, but I had more work to do, and it was open bar.

A few minutes later, I was cutting across the floor towards the bar for another very much needed dose of liquid courage when Eleanor crossed into my path. "There you are," she said. "Chief, please don't think me rude, but Leonard is going to take me home." She seemed to be saying this for the benefit of anyone within earshot. Do these people not know he's gay? She leaned in close. "I know you've got work to do here, and this old gal's had enough champagne for one night."

I took her hands in mine and thanked her profusely. I told her that I hoped she never called me, but that I'd be ready if she did. She gave me a peck, and I shook hands with Leonard and thanked him for taking care of her.

As I was saying goodbye to Eleanor, Tinsley reappeared.

"Having a good time?"

"Hell yeah! This is the best one of these I've ever been too."

The auction and fundraising were over, and it was time to party. The band had been joined by a horn section and was really humming, and a dozen or so couples were tearing up the parquet, so I took Tinsley's hand, and we joined them. I scanned the room for Richard as we shimmied, but he was still out of sight.

I decided to enjoy myself for a while. The room, the crowd, the beautiful woman on my arm, it was all quite surreal, and I wanted to soak it in.

We took a break after a rousing version of "All of Me" and grabbed a couple of cocktails at the bar in the great room. She wanted a gin and tonic, so I ordered two. The scotch was burning a hole in my gut, which isn't used to the good stuff. We stood over by the mixed media piece. To my everlasting dismay, Larry's discarded champagne flute had been removed.

"My husband was here tonight."

"He was? So, he's not anymore?" I replied with a quick scan of the room.

"No."

"Gee, that's too bad."

"He says you're handsome."

I nearly choked on my gin.

"You pointed me out to him?"

"Yeah, I also pointed you out to several girlfriends tonight, and they said the same thing."

"What did they say?"

"They said you're handsome."

I smiled, and she laughed and gave my chest a light shove. "You're just eating this up."

The band took a break, and the MC came back to announce the evening's take. "Tonight, thanks to your generosity and the generosity of our host and his matching pledge, we have raised ..." The drummer had been making time with a member of the wait staff, and the MC glared at him as he jogged over to provide the drum-roll. At its conclusion, the MC announced, "Two million three hundred and seven thousand dollars to support the search for the cure to non-Hodgkin's lymphoma!"

A huge cheer went up, and Gibson French stepped on stage to raise a glass to Endicott, who was acting bashful at the back of the room. Then the MC took the mic back and announced that via his annual galas, Whit Endicott had raised more than ten million dollars. How can you not like a guy like that? Actually, having just met him, it wasn't all that hard for me.

After another toast, the band kicked back in, and Tinsley and I hit the tiles again. I should've gone back to looking for Richard. I was paid to find Mac or his killer, and I was dancing like a jackass instead. But, I'll admit, I wasn't thinking with a clear head or my big head.

At some point, the Ferncroft's cut in on Tinsley and me, and all of a sudden my hand was pressed onto Caroline's swaying hip, and she was staring up at me through a pair of big sinful azure eyes. She was something. She put her hand on my ass and pulled me into her. She smelled nice. Her breath was warm in my ear. I caught myself and realized that while Caroline was distracting me Larry was making time with Tinsley. I spun Caroline and found them. Larry had his arm around Tinsley's waist, and he was pulling her close the same way Caroline pulled me in. They looked a little too comfortable. I felt a finger on my chin. Caroline was pulling me back around to face her. "See something you like, Earl?"

"I do," I said, staring into her eyes. I lifted her hand and spun her again and enjoyed the band. The music, booze, and women were intoxicating.

Larry and I traded partners, and I danced a few more songs with Tinsley, before taking a break at the Taittinger Champagne bar that now occupied a corner of the ballroom. "What is this?" I said, waving an arm at it. "I was told Endicott only drank Bollinger."

"Corporate sponsorship," She said, bored. "Last year, Whit had Bulgari."

"Companies sponsor charity balls?"

"Whenever people of means get together, corporations fall all over themselves to promote their products to us. Taittinger donates a few cases of champagne, and in return, they raise their profile with people who have the resources to drink a lot of their product."

I'd have to talk to Dom Perignon about the next casino night at the Southie Kiwanis Club.

We took our glasses and headed out onto the massive brick terrace. There were two couples smoking and chatting at one end, while we had the rest of it to ourselves.

The air had cooled, and Tinsley's shoulders were bare, so I took off my jacket and draped it around her. As I was doing this, she wrapped her arms around my waist, pulled me in close, and laid one on me. It was electric, but I couldn't help but feel shame for engaging in this activity in the course of an investigation, and with a married woman, which, sad to say, was the lesser of the two shames.

I pulled my face away from hers while maintaining the embrace. "Didn't you tell me your husband was here earlier?"

"You're right," she grinned. "We need to go someplace more private."

Tinsley's eyes sparkled despite the dim light on the patio, and it was hard to resist, but I tried. "Is he cool with this sort of thing?" She answered with a three-letter look – DUH.

"What time is it?" she asked.

I pulled my French-cuffed sleeve back to check my watch. This was the first, and almost certainly will be, the last time I'll ever wear a French cuff. Phillipe had been thoughtful enough to include a pair of links. I wonder how he knew I'd need them. "It's a quarter to one."

She reached up and undid my bowtie. "It's after midnight, time to let your hair down. I love a man in a tux and an undone tie just hanging around his neck." She placed her right hand on my chest and slid it down to my navel, all while staring into my eyes. Then she said, "It turns me on."

"You didn't really answer my question." It took all the strength I had to push the issue.

"Fine, I'll answer you if that's what it takes to get you to take me home. He is cool with this." She waved her hands, and added, "With all of this. Our relationship is more advanced than most."

I'm not sure I agree with the notion that allowing private dicks, double entendre intended, to sleep with your wife is a sign of an advanced marriage, but who was I to argue.

* * *

Tinsley said her place was only a couple of blocks away, so we made a fast exit. For the sake of appearances, she went first and waited at the end of the street for me to catch up. Though Tinsley's affairs apparently aren't all that secret, leaving an event with a man who is not one's husband is simply not done in polite society, or so she assured me.

I don't recall the short walk to 62nd Street, but I know I was feeling terribly high. The flirting, especially Tinsley's aggressiveness, was intoxicating. Roxy and I had finalized the divorce nearly five years before, and I'd been with women in the interim, but Tinsley Saunders wasn't anything like those women. Well, apart from the anatomy. Tinsley was of a different class of woman. As much as I hate class structures, because my class is working and not leisure, I'm a realist. I'd never been with anyone like Tinsley, and probably never will again, and that's probably for the best.

She practically attacked me after we'd made it across the threshold of a large open apartment at the top of a four-story townhouse. Being a little intoxicated on scotch, champagne and gin led to a bit of fumbling, and a somewhat humbling spin around the living room, where we ended up in a heap on one end of a very modern sofa that looked like a handful of lollipops. This was followed by a more graceful romp in the bedroom loft above.

Round two and some of the softest sheets I've ever rested on did me in, and I quickly fell into a deep slumber with Tinsley's arms wrapped around me. Her body felt like a bit of heaven pressed against my back.

When I awoke, it seemed like I'd only been out for a few minutes, but the day's first rays of light were squeezing through the blinds. I wanted to wrap my arms around my sleep buddy and get back to dreamland, but the sound of an intercom cut through the good feelings. I wasn't sure if I should answer it. What if it's an armed and angry Mr. Saunders looking for his wife?

I gingerly shook Tinsley's shoulder. She murmured something unintelligible, but her intent was clear. She wasn't getting up for anything. I pulled on my pants and managed to find my t-shirt. As I walked down the stairs, someone began pounding on the door. They'd made it past security and were now standing in the hallway.

I hurried down shouting, "Okay, okay, I'm on my way." I didn't see Tinsley's lace panties, which lay at the bottom of the stairs and stepping on them, I nearly careened into a table on which sat a tall, ornate porcelain vase. After regaining my balance and racing to the door, I spent more time than I care to admit fooling with several locks and chains, before finally pulling it open, exasperated and out of breath.

To my immense surprise and theirs, Ron Sullivan and Amalia Garcia were standing behind a uniformed New York cop. The cop showed no emotion, but the mouths of the two agents were agape.

I groaned as I leaned against the door frame, "Oh Christ, not again."

16

An hour later I found myself waiting in an interrogation room of an Upper East Side precinct of the New York City Police Department. The room smelled of antiseptic and urine. The walls were painted pale gray and chipping, and there was a two-way mirror opposite me. To my right was the only way in or out. I sat there for nearly an hour stewing in my tux before Sullivan and Garcia finally made their entrance.

Sullivan sat across from me, while Garcia leaned back shoulders against the space next to the door. She pressed the sole of her left foot against the wall, folded her arms across her chest, and showed no emotion. Sullivan, on the other hand, was clearly incensed. He'd been subdued at the apartment. He simply told Garcia to put the cuffs on me, and she'd walked me down to an unmarked squad car. He came down a few minutes later, and they brought me here in silence. At one point I tried to speak, but he told me to shut the fuck up, so I did.

I could see the veins in his neck now, and his face was flushed. I had the feeling they'd done some checking on my recent movements while I was left to chill, and what they'd learned had set him off even more. He was Mount Vesuvius, and I was a Pompeii peasant.

"Somebody is working above his pay grade. What the fuck are you doing, Town? I believe we told you, not 48 hours ago, you are off this case!"

"Yeah, well my client said otherwise. Besides, spending time with a woman I met at Indian Head isn't exactly ..." Sullivan cut me off.

"We know you arranged to take Eleanor Harriman to the event last night. We know you questioned Whitman Endicott. We know you spent the night with Tinsley Saunders, at Elizabeth MacArthur's townhouse."

I blinked at the mention of Beth MacArthur and Sullivan took notice. "Yeah, that's pretty crazy, right? We pay a visit to Miss MacArthur, and who opens the door but you." He smiled at me. It wasn't a nice smile; it was 'you're fucked.' Then he added, "As Garcia's countryman once said, you got some splainin' to do."

"Racist," muttered Garcia.

"You're Cuban?" I asked her, trying to make a friend, but she ignored me.

"I still don't know why you showed up at the apartment this morning," I said looking from Sullivan to Garcia. "How about letting me in on the big secret?"

Sullivan leaned back and looked disgusted. He motioned to Garcia, who was still leaning against the wall, and she took a copy of the New York Post from under her arm and placed it in front of me. In a small box on the lower right corner of page three was the following headline: "Rich Financier Found Dead in L.I. Sound."

I looked up from the paper to Sullivan, "I told you he was dead."

"And, I told you, you are off this Goddamn case!"

I sighed but said nothing in my defense. There was no point.

"But you didn't listen, and now you turn up at the dead guy's ex-wife's apartment. Soon, we are going to have an approximate time of death, and you had better have an alibi, Town because you are starting to look good for this."

I laughed. "You think I'm good for murdering a guy who I didn't know existed until a week after he was killed? What are you smoking, Sullivan?"

"I didn't say he was murdered or when. We don't know what killed him yet, but if it was murder, you're sure as hell incriminating yourself."

I turned towards Garcia and shook my head, pleading with her to call off her partner before he embarrassed himself anymore.

"I told you two days ago that Mac looked like he'd been dead for a week. I already told you this. It's on the record. Stop jerking me around, and maybe I'll be nice and compare notes with you. I don't know where you two spent yesterday, but I've been piecing things together."

"Hey bud, you aren't listening to me," Sullivan began again. "I'm serious about the alibi. Seems to us that Beth MacArthur is about to inherit some serious money, maybe you think you can get some of that too. Maybe Miss Hill hired you to take him out, not to find him, and after learning how much money he had, you cooked up a second scheme. Not only would you earn a fee for his murder, but you'd shack up with his ex and get a taste of his fortune too."

I turned to Garcia and said, "Did he run this by you or is he just making shit up on the fly? Because this is one wild fairytale." I eyed

Sullivan again. "Why would Joanna Hill want her boss dead? She's probably out of a job now, and I doubt she's in the will."

"You're right, maybe you've been making time with Beth Mac-Arthur and her friend for months and hatched the plan with them. Miss Hill is just a cover."

"Yeah, this is the crowd I hang with," I said with revulsion.

"It's just a theory," he said, smirking.

"Fine, play it this way. See what I come through with."

All of a sudden, Garcia came on angry. "Enough! You are going to tell us what you know, or we're going to take your P.I. license. You think busting cheating spouses and investigating insurance fraud sucks? You're about to find out what bagging groceries at Trader Joe's is all about."

Garcia was leaning on the table only about a foot from me. She smelled nice. "So, I spill my guts, or you take away my livelihood. This is how you do business?"

"You know how this works," she said. "You can choose not to co-operate, but there will be swift and lasting consequences for doing so."

"As I told you last time, you need to give me something too. I'm not up for a chew and screw. If I cook the meal, you gotta clean the dishes."

"Just start talking," she said. Sullivan grinned from ear to ear, enjoying his partner's new menacing persona.

I spent the next hour telling the dull duo about the last two days. They made me go over everything several times, trying to catch me in a lie. I stuck to my story, which was the truth with a few omissions, like Harriet Goldstein. She didn't need to be pulled into this. After I finished the recap, I mentioned a new development that I thought might encourage them to share a little something with me.

"Here's another piece of information for you. Last Sunday afternoon, at about 4:00 p.m., Endicott and French were in an important meeting at Wayne Trust offices, when Nathaniel Sterling sent Endicott a couple of urgent messages. Shortly after receiving the second one, Endicott hired a car service to take French to Indian Head Yacht Club. He returned five hours later. At 6:03 p.m., Mac's final email was sent to my client and Whit Endicott.

"We know about the email. How do you know about the other stuff?" asked Sullivan.

"I plead the fifth." I wasn't about to drag Ed into this, but it turns out, they were already aware of him.

"Your nephew ...," Sullivan turned a couple of pages in his notebook, "Edward Chase, he works for you huh?"

I glared at him.

"You should tell him to be careful."

"What the hell does that mean?"

"What else did you discuss with Endicott?"

I let him change the subject. I was afraid of what else he might say about Ed. I said, "We discussed his motive or lack thereof. He says the deal will make him millions, and not having Mac involved made it more difficult to get it done. He says that whoever wanted the deal scuttled is the likely culprit, but he didn't give me any examples of who that might be. Maybe you know who wanted to kill this deal?"

They shared a look before Garcia answered. "There are two corporations we are looking at as having had a motive to kill the deal." She stopped talking, that was it. Silence reigned.

"Would you be so kind as to share the names of those companies with me?"

"No."

I looked at Sullivan in frustration. He ignored me.

"Did you tell Endicott about us? Specifically, about us working with someone inside Wayne Trust?"

"No, though the thought did cross my mind." I threw a question at them. "Are you sure your guys didn't find Mac in that fridge?"

Sullivan answered. "What does that mean?"

"I don't know, but I've seen Federal agents do some strange things in my day. Maybe you aren't leveling with me about the reason for the tail. Maybe you're working with Endicott, and you knocked me out and hid the body until the deal was done." Sullivan laughed at me and shook his head. I went on. "Mac could have threatened to kill the deal. It must strike you both like quite a coincidence that Mac's body turned up as soon as the merger was complete. How did Mac die anyway?"

"Are you kidding? We're not sharing that with you," piped Garcia.

Sullivan added his two cents while overtly gazing at his watch. "This is getting old, and it's still early. Start driving now, and you'll be eating dinner back in Boston."

I wasn't done asking questions. "What does your contact on the inside of Wayne Trust say about all this?"

Sullivan didn't like this question. He averted his eyes. Then I saw it. "Oh, Mac was your contact." Sullivan shook his head. He wasn't half the poker player Garcia was. "You thought maybe he'd gotten scared and dropped out of sight, but now the stakes have been raised. Jesus, he may have been killed because he was helping you! You were following Joanna last week because you were trying to find Mac."

"Times up!" Sullivan stood up and towered over me, face tomato-ing, but I wasn't done.

"The other day, you said I'd stumbled into something much bigger than I know. What was Mac helping you with? Who else were you following before Mac disappeared?

Garcia said, "If you think we're telling you that, you're out of your mind."

"Okay then, just tell me this. Would whatever it is have killed the deal? If so, then Endicott had motive to kill him and hide the body. The same goes for French."

"We're done," Sullivan said.

"No way. I'm just getting started. What about McNierney?" I had told them what I learned from Rooster.

Sullivan had been moving toward the door, but he stopped at the mention of the Indian Head security guy, Richard McNierney. He leaned forward, clutching the back of his chair. "What do you mean?"

"Are you going to interview him, because if not, I'm going to talk to him about the egg on the back of my head."

"I told you earlier, we will talk to him, and I meant it. You stay out of this, or I promise you, your license is finished."

Garcia said, "That's enough, for now, Mr. Town. You have a long drive ahead of you. I'll show you out."

"You guys are making a mistake," I said. "I'm not sure this is about Wayne Trust. Something stinks at Indian Head. Let me go back there and do my job."

Sullivan stared straight ahead and said nothing. I was dismissed.

As Garcia walked me out to the main lobby, I considered telling her about the shouting match on the dock, but to hell with them.

As I was about to exit onto Lexington Ave., she said: "Wait!" I stopped, eager for some good news. I should've kept on walking.

"If your story about what you found in the fridge on Monday gets out, we will come down on you so hard, you will not know what hit you." I spun, pushed through the door, and shielded my eyes from the intense mid-morning sun.

17

Joanna said, "I've been trying to get hold of you all morning. What happened to him?"

"I'm sorry," I replied. "I just left a police precinct, where I've been locked in a small room with two FBI agents for hours." When I got out to the street and turned on my phone, I found three voicemails from her.

"All the news reports say he was found in the water. Was this an accident?"

"I don't think so."

I gave her a full rundown of everything I knew and believed, starting with the whole truth of what had happened Monday night.

"Remember when we spoke on Tuesday, and you asked me if I was okay."

"Yes."

"Yeah, well, I didn't tell you everything." I walked her through the events on the boat, waking up with an egg on my head, and the FBI barging into my room. She gasped when I told her about finding Mac in the refrigerator and was upset that I hadn't told her sooner, but she calmed and showed real concern when I told her about being attacked, both on the boat, then by agents Dumb and Dumber. After that, she was more sympathetic and concerned about my head injury.

"I'm sorry I didn't tell you about the boat, but after the blow to the head and the FBI telling me they didn't find anything, I really didn't know what to think. I wish it hadn't gone this way."

"Me too, he was a wonderful man," she said choking back tears. "Who would do this?"

"Well, maybe the death was an accident. I wasn't able to examine him, and given the money involved in the merger, there's a chance whoever put Mac," I paused, "where they did. They may only have done so to delay the finding of the body until the deal was done. They might not be responsible for his death."

"But they nearly killed you!"

"But they didn't, and they easily could've."

I told Joanna about my conversations with Commodore Sterling and the CEO, Whitman Endicott, as well as the phone call between the two of them on the day Mac was killed, and the car service that subsequently took French out to Indian Head.

She was blown away at the prospect of conspiracy. "But doesn't it stand to reason that whoever hid Mac also killed him?"

"It seems logical, but they only had motive to hide the body. You yourself suggested that Mac's disappearance made the deal more difficult for Endicott. If Mac's body had been found, the deal might have fallen apart, so they conspired to hide him, but I can't find a motive for murder." Though there was the thing Beth MacArthur mentioned about her inheritance.

"What do you know about Mac's stock in Wayne Trust?"

"Uh. Not much. I know he was the second largest individual shareholder behind Whit Endicott. Why?"

"I heard a rumor that Endicott and French might try to get their hands on some of it, which would be a motive, if true. Do you think you can find out if there's a clause about his stock changing hands upon the event of death? Something like that?"

"Yes, I can try."

"Look, I need to tell you something else. Endicott didn't only shift the blame to whoever might want to break up the deal, he also mentioned you."

"What did he say?"

"He made it clear, he doesn't want me poking around anymore, and he threatened to fire you if I don't stop."

"How does he know that I hired you?"

"I believe he's in contact with the FBI. They've been working with people inside Wayne Trust. Mac may have been one of them. They followed you to my office the other day and have been keeping tabs on me ever since."

"Why was the FBI following me?"

"I've no idea. They told me I'm involved in something much bigger than I know. They're with the National Security Board."

"I don't understand!"

"What I'm saying is that this could have something to do with Mac's death. On Monday, they followed you, and then me, in a Wayne Trust car to hide their identity."

"They told you this?"

"We swapped some information. They're playing hardball and

threatened to yank my license if I don't drop the case. Any idea what they might be investigating?"

"No, I don't understand any of this. What should I do?"

"Well, reach out to your contacts and try to find out how he was killed. Until we know that, we don't know what we're investigating. Or, maybe you'll find out it was an accident, and case closed."

"Okay," she said. "I understand. I'll find out what I can." She sniffed.

"Look, about what Endicott said, I don't want you to lose your job."

"My job is over. I worked for Mac, not for Wayne Trust. There's nothing left for me there."

I mulled this over and replied, "Okay, I'm gonna find out who did this, but I don't think I can work for you anymore."

"Why not? I can pay you! I'm not a broke single woman, you know. Mac paid me, well. And I want to find out the truth too!"

"The FBI told me to forget this case on Tuesday, and now they're pissed I didn't and threatening my license if I don't drop it."

"You didn't tell me about Tuesday! I could've helped. Maybe I can tell them to leave you alone."

I chuckled.

"Okay. What are you going to do?"

"I'm going to pull on a few loose threads and see what unravels. I'll touch base when I can, but it'll be best if I'm not officially on the case anymore."

"Thank you. You're a good man, Earl."

Maybe I was, but I knew the smart thing to do was to go back to Boston and forget about these people. Working for free on a case that could cost me my license was beyond stupid, but I was in it, and lacking a strong will to stop something I'd started, even if it was self-destructive, at least that's what Roxy used to tell me was my big flaw, I didn't really have a choice.

❉ ❉ ❉

It was a short walk from the precinct back to Whit Endicott's mansion, and I reached his street before hanging up with Joanna. I looked around for any sign of Endicott's security detail, or more specifically Richard McNierney, but all was quiet. I decided to duck into the basement stairwell of a nearby building and make a call.

Long ago, I made a habit of taking note of phone numbers when on an investigation. It invariably came in handy later when I realized I had forgotten to ask a question about the scene, or I'd left something behind. Often, I'd collect the number in a witness or victim statement, but I also started writing down numbers printed on phone receivers, which are things phones used to have when they also had wires that physically connected them to the earth. Endicott was old-fashioned, and last night I took down two numbers from landlines in his townhouse. One was on a phone that sat in a small alcove just off the main entrance, and the other was in a corner of the room that Rooster had tended bar in. I figured the one in there would be my best hope to speak with a staff member with some authority.

A man with a distinct English accent answered. "Endicott residence."

I reverted to Cary Grant. "Er, ah, yes. I desperately need to speak to the security man who wanded myself and my date outside of Mr. Endicott's wonderful gala last evening. He was rather forceful with her, and me as well, frankly. He has large, intrusive hands. I haven't been touched by a man like that since my days in the Queen's Navy if you know what I mean."

The man on the other end cleared his throat but said nothing.

"Well, she's come to the conclusion that he may have, innocently I'm sure, dislodged a brooch from her bosom. She hasn't seen it, and she's not wearing it in any of the pictures on the society pages today. Thus, she believes, and I concur, that the gentleman may have liberated it with his wand device and picked it up, for safekeeping, of course. Is he available by chance? You know the one. He's tall and bald with dark, menacing eyes."

"Could you hold one moment, sir? I will check for you."

"Yes, I'll hold."

The Beatles came on the line. It was "Love Me Do," and I thought how cool is this? After I get a secret passage installed in my Southie apartment, I'd be sure to look into hold music. The debt collectors would be impressed.

He came back on the line. "I'm afraid it'll be one more moment, sir. I understand your gentleman is nearby. I've sent someone to inquire about the brooch."

"Great. I mean, Cheers!" I replied.

"Ah, yes, cheers," he said reluctantly.

I watched as one of the two front doors opened and a young woman strolled down the steps. She was smartly dressed, and I recalled seeing her instructing staff the prior night. She crossed the street, and I ducked as she walked right past my stairwell. I crept up the steps and followed her down to where 61st Street met Lexington Ave. She took a left and disappeared around the corner. I followed, but by the time I took the turn, she was gone.

Two doors down was a small diner. I carefully peeked around the menu in the window at the thin crowd inside. The woman was speaking with two men seated in a blue leatherette booth in a far corner. One of them was shaking his head, and the woman was apologizing for asking the question. It was McNierney and another young guy I recognized as also working security the prior night. He had been stationed near the top of the grand staircase. They were dressed casually like they were grabbing breakfast before heading back to Greenwich.

I walked past the diner and waited for the girl to leave. Then I kept my chin down, strolled in, and stealthily made my way to the counter where I found curious Carla.

"You go to a big to-do last night?" she said, chewing a wad of gum.

"Do I look like the type?"

She looked me over. "You are wearing a tuxedo."

I looked down. "Oh, you're right, I am." That drew a laugh. "Yeah, I'm part of the hired help. They wouldn't let me in otherwise." She made a motion with the coffee pot, I nodded vigorously, and she got to pouring. "Hey, those guys in the corner there. They been here long?"

"Yeah, they're almost done," she said. "They work with you?"

"Yes, but we're not on great terms." I leaned into the counter in a conspiratorial manner. "I need to speak with the big evil-looking one before he leaves, but I've got to make a quick phone call first. Could you make sure they're still here in ten minutes?" I pulled out a $20 and set it on the counter. "I promise that's all I need, well that and two eggs over medium and three pieces of bacon. I'll pay for that separately."

She picked up the $20 and stuffed it in her bra. "Ten minutes, that's it."

"That's it," I said.

I pulled out my phone and dialed Ed. He answered after one ring.

"What did you find out about Richard McNierney?" I said in a whisper.

"You owe me money."

"And I will pay you, very well too. Look, he's twenty feet away from me. What do you have?"

"Hold on." I heard him set the phone down and scramble, probably looking for his computer under a mess of food wrappers. "Alright," he began. "You need to be very careful with this guy."

"Go on."

"He's ex-Army, and the recipient of both the Purple Heart and Bronze Star. Apparently, he killed some enemy combatants in Iraq."

"Awe shit."

"I know," Ed said, "He'll kill you."

"It's not that, I don't want to mess with a vet who put his ass on the line for this country."

"Yeah, plus he'll kill you. You better be careful, Earl."

I sighed. "Every man has a weakness, I just have to find his and use it to my advantage."

The line was quiet for a few seconds, then Ed said, "Actually, I think I know what that is."

"Really, perhaps you'd like to share this with me, Ed?"

"It says in his bio, he was seriously wounded in Afghanistan. Injuries included a broken pelvis and a shattered right arm, all thanks to an IUD that went off under the Humvee he and five other soldiers were riding in." He was summarizing as he read. "He's one of only two survivors. Why is this guy working? He deserves a fat pension. He's a hero."

"Is he licensed to carry?"

"Yes, he is."

"That's not ideal."

"Don't mess with him, Earl. It's not cool, he's ..."

I ended the call, scoffed down the eggs and bacon Carla had just set in front of me and laid down another $20. Nothing's cheap on the Upper East Side. Then I made my way back to McNierney.

He looked up and grinned as I approached. He was confident, cocky even. He said something to his companion, and the guy got up and left the restaurant. Yup, he was cocky alright.

I slid into the booth across from him.

18

"I hear you've been keeping tabs on me."

He sipped his coffee, then dipped his last triangle of toast into a pool of egg yolk and bit off a chunk. He did both of these things with his left hand. As he did Carla showed up with his check. She saw the expression on my face and hurried back to the counter.

I said, "You have nothing to say for yourself?"

He leaned back into the worn blue booth. "Look old timer, I get that you think you're some hotshot detective, but you're way out of your league here. You best go on back home and forget about all this." He ran his eyes over my tux, which was perilously close to turning rank.

"You're the second person in two days to tell me I'm out of my league, but I haven't seen any evidence to prove it. So far, all I've seen is a bunch of wannabe aristocrats trying to cover up a murder and doing a piss poor job of it."

"Okay. Last time I will say this, then I'm going to kick your ass right here in this diner. I got friends in this town, so, it won't cause me any trouble. Go home old man, before it's too late."

"Don't threaten me, Richard, it's not going to end well for you." He was wearing a black windbreaker with the IHYC crest on the left breast and 'Security' on the shoulder. There was a distinctive bulge by his right armpit. His hands flexed as though he was preparing to strike. I shifted my hips and got ready to spring up from my seat.

He reached into the right side of his jacket and smiled as I watched him, knowing that I was looking for any move towards his gun. He took out his wallet instead and winked at me, then placed two twenties on the table and moved towards the edge of the booth. He said, "I'm going to leave. You can keep your mouth shut and leave on your own, or you can mouth off again and leave on a stretcher. It's your call. I don't care either way."

I replied, "You walk out of here, and your ass will be doing hard time. Man, are you blind or just too stupid to see you're being set up?"

He rose from his seat and fired a quick left jab straight at my nose. I stood too and easily dodged the punch. I latched onto his wrist as it thumped into the booth back and jerked it down hard against the edge of the table. His face and upper body followed his arm, and his yolk-covered plate and silverware were thrown in the air and made a racket as they scattered across the floor. The noise helped cover the loud cracking sound emanating from the ulna bone in his good arm as I snapped it in two.

"Ah damn, I'm sorry. I didn't mean to break it. But, come on, I warned you." I was standing over him, holding his arm and neck, and pressing him against the table. His head was turned to face me. He could only see me through one eye because the other side of his face was squished against the lumber. Making it worse, the one eye wasn't seeing so good, as it had been briefly submerged in egg yolk, which was now dripping from his brow. I squatted down and reached into his jacket, removing his 9mm. Then I stood and handed him a napkin.

He sat up and leaned back into the booth. Carla had begun to collect the plate shards and wanted to know if she needed to call the cops. He was tough and responded before I did.

"No ma'am, I slipped a little. Sorry about the mess."

He cleaned his face, gritted his teeth and rubbed his broken wing while staring through me. Finally, he said, "I'm going to gut you, slowly, so you can watch yourself die."

"You gave me no choice. Look, you're missing the big picture."

"What's that, dead man?" he said, left eye twitching a little, as the pain seeped out.

"You're being set up, and I can keep your ass out of jail." I stood and handed Carla the check and McNierney's money along with an additional twenty.

I hadn't meant to break his arm, but the last time I'd used this move it had ended the same way. When I was the chief in Princetown, the town drunk would threaten to kill me every couple of months. Then he'd do a short stint in the county jail, and be back out again, drinking and terrorizing the barflies at the local Legion Hall, as well as his poor, elderly parents. One summer shortly before things in town really hit the fan for me, his wheelchair-bound father and ailing mother lived out of a small camper in my backyard for a week. All because they feared their little boy was going to get loaded one night and kill them.

Anyway, Barry ran into some trouble during one stint in the joint and came out wearing a sling on his left arm. A few days later, he and I sat across from one another in the legion hall, as I tried to convince him to leave peacefully. He responded to my offer by throwing a roundhouse. After that, he wore slings on both arms for a while.

I looked across the table at McNierney and said, "You knocked me out Monday night, and you moved the body off the Rebecca while the Feds investigated. Don't try to tell me you didn't."

"I didn't knock you out, and I don't know anything about a body. Give me my gun."

The eye twitch was gone. He'd absorbed the pain. I think it made him stronger.

"So, you admit to moving my unconscious body?"

"I don't admit to shit, except for doing my job as club security. You were trespassing and drunk as a skunk, and you know it. You were sleeping like a baby when I put you back on your raft and sent you ashore. You're lucky I didn't send you out into the Sound instead."

He leaned in close enough for me to smell the coffee on his breath. "I'll play your game one time only. This is your shot. What am I being set up for?"

"You really don't know? Son, you are being framed for the murder of James MacArthur."

"That's what you meant? His body?"

"Yeah, James MacArthur's body. It was on the boat. I found it, then you knocked me out and brought me ashore."

"Where?" I looked at him like he had two heads. "Not where did I set you ashore. Where was his body?"

"It was stuffed in the refrigerator, like a side of beef."

His eyes widened.

"Yeah, kind of makes you an accessory, don't you think?"

Richard forgot about the wrist for a moment and slumped back into the cracked blue Naugahyde. "Awe fuck. I knew these rich pukes were gonna get me into trouble. I shoulda listened to my little brother. He runs security at Con Ed, wanted to get me in there, but I wanted to be where the money is."

I shook my head. Sympathetic.

"What am I supposed to do?" he asked.

"Who told you to attack me?" I replied.

"Answer my question first. What do you know about me being set up?"

"The Feds seem to think you're a prime suspect, and they didn't just stumble onto you. Someone, maybe Sterling, or French, or Endicott, pointed them in your direction."

I was lying. What can I say? Admitting that the only thing I had on him was what Rooster overheard, wouldn't have gotten me anywhere. I'm an ex-cop. Lying is in poor taste if it involves faking evidence, but if it'll get someone to incriminate themselves and provide evidence. That's another story altogether.

"Let me guess, Sterling sent you out to the Rebecca to investigate an intruder, and you knocked my ass out and brought me ashore. Is that it?"

He had a change of heart. "Nope, forget it. You can't talk your way out of this. My arm will be in a cast inside of three hours, and then I'm gonna find you and settle up."

"You think the Commodore and his friends are gonna take the fall for this? They have a lot of sway in this town, and even more in Greenwich. I'll bet you're charged with Mac's murder before ..." I looked at my watch; it was 10:53 a.m. "Twelve-thirty, one o'clock tops."

"All I did was move your drunk ass off Mac's boat, and safely to shore. None of this is my business. These people are animals, they eat their own."

"They also use guys like you and me as patsies. It's only when that no longer works that they start eating their own. Where were you Sunday before last? When Mac was killed."

"I was working at the club."

"That's a problem, not an alibi. Mac was likely murdered on his boat."

"According to who, and what is it you can do to keep me from taking the fall for it? Let's go back to that. What did they say exactly?"

He was off balance, so I fired another question at him. "How did the body get into the Sound?"

"I don't know. I never saw a body. Until I heard the news this morning, I thought the guy was banging a model under a palm tree somewhere. I haven't been to the club since Tuesday."

"When did you get to the city?"

"Yesterday."

"So, depending on how long he was in the water, you may have an alibi for that one."

He shrugged his shoulders. "Look, I gotta get this set." He glanced at his wrist.

"Have the Feds interviewed you?" He shook his head no.

"They will. Soon."

"Yeah, why would I believe you?"

"Who told you to tow me ashore?"

He sighed and stared like he was trying to make my head explode. I pushed a little harder. "I think I can help you if you let me."

"The Commodore told me there was an intruder on one of the

boats, and to come with him."

"How did he know I was on the boat?"

"I don't know. He told me to get in and row us to the Rebecca, so I did."

"Does he usually use a rowboat?" I asked.

"No, but he said he thought it might be some kids from the club looking for a place to screw, and he wanted to sneak up and scare the shit out of them. So, they wouldn't do it again."

I nodded. "Then what?"

"We get there, and he tells me to stay back. He's going to take the lead."

"That seem odd to you? You know, you being you and him being a soft, middle-aged rich guy? Cause that seems messed up to me."

"Yeah, I figured it might be his kid."

"So, then what?"

"We glided up, no lights, he climbed aboard. Things are quiet for a while, and I'm wondering what's going on. Then he comes back and tells me he caught an intruder instead of kids and to come and help him."

"Wait a minute, you didn't see anything?"

"I was too low in the water to see what was happening below deck."

"Oh yeah."

"So, I go on board and find you laid out on the floor in the galley, bleeding from a head wound. I start to dial the police, and he tells me to stop. Says you were drinking in the bar earlier and it'll be better to just get you out of there. Otherwise, you'd probably sue, and he'd catch hell from the members. It made sense to me. We put you on your raft, and I towed you back to the shoreline beyond club waters."

"You didn't look around the galley at all?"

"No, I did as I was told. I was barely on the boat."

"Then what?"

"I left you on the shore and went back to collect the Commodore."

"He didn't come with you when you dropped me off?"

"No, he said he wanted to assess the boat. You know, see if you damaged anything."

"Did you go on board then?"

"No, he was waiting for me. I pull up, he jumps in, we leave."

"You've been around these people for a while, know anyone who would want to bash MacArthur's head in?"

He leaned back, winced slightly at the pain in his arm, and thought about it for a while. "Probably an angry husband. That guy dipped his wick in everything, and he wasn't subtle about it either."

"Who was he screwing?"

"Your date, last night."

"He was fucking Eleanor Harriman?" I was genuinely shocked.

"Jesus! No, the one you left with."

I peered at him. "Yeah, I saw you," he said.

Was I surprised to hear Tinsley was one of Mac's girls? No. Did it bother me? It removed some of the shine off the night.

"Was he screwing someone named Rebecca?"

"Not that I'm aware of."

"Are there any club members named Rebecca?"

He shook his head. "Give me my gun."

I took the Sig Sauer P228 from my pocket, removed the magazine and extracted the bullets, which I placed back into my pocket. I returned the empty clip to the gun and set it between us.

He acknowledged my cautiousness and reinforced it when he said, "Clean mag, you're smarter than you look. We'll meet again, Town."

I left in a hurry, looking over my shoulder as I went.

19

I finally made it back to the hotel at twenty minutes before noon. I shed my clothes as soon as I shut the door and climbed into a hot shower. The urge to collapse face down on the bed and sleep was strong, but I packed up my things and prepared to leave.

As I was stepping into the hallway, bag in hand, my phone buzzed. It was Ed. I answered, planning to say I'd call him back after I'd checked out, but he was hot out of the gate, so I went back and perched on the end of the bed.

"I was about to go out just now, and guess what? There's a black sedan with black-wall tires parked on the street in front of my freaking house, and it's got a government plate. What the hell is going on, Earl?"

"It's my sister's house, Ed. You live in her basement."

"You're not paying me nearly enough for the cops to get up in my shit, Earl! I'm gonna need a big ass raise. No, screw that! I'm not working for you anymore man. This is not cool!" I heard rattling in the background like he was knocking things over. He raised his voice as he spoke until he was yelling at me and breathing heavily into the phone.

"Calm down," I said trying to mask the rush of concern that had washed over me.

"Stop telling me to be calm and tell me what is going on."

"Well, Ed. I think you should get some lunch down at Joe's."

"Ah," he paused. "Dammit, all." He disconnected.

Ed and my sister, mostly my sister Emily, took care of a couple of spinsters who lived a few blocks from them. The women were in their eighties, and my big sister dropped in a couple of days a week to clean up after them and make sure they were eating. They had a phone in their basement that sat on a small table beneath an antique porcelain-and-tin sign from a diner that used to be in downtown Worcester called Joe's Place.

The phone was paid for by a son of one of the two who lived in Los

Angeles. They hardly used it, but he insisted they keep a landline for emergencies. They insisted it was placed in the basement, so telemarketers wouldn't be a bother. Eddie and I had never used this phone before, but Eddie told me about using it to talk to a friend of his who was a serious hacker and who thought the Feds were recording his calls. He saved the number into my contacts under 'Joe's Place.'

He called me back about ten minutes later.

"Okay, Earl, what have you gotten me into?"

"Nothing I can't fix, Ed."

"Oh, well that solves everything. Thanks for putting my mind at ease. I'll hang up now."

"Laying it on thick, Ed."

"Stop deflecting and start explaining, Earl."

"This thing has obviously blown up."

I spent the next ten minutes catching him up. I finished with Mac's corpse showing up and my morning with Sully and Garcia. Then I added, "The Feds told me you should be careful."

"Me! What does the FBI know about me? Jesus Christ, Earl!" He dropped the phone, then picked it up. "I should be careful! Oh my God, what does that mean?"

"It means everything is fine, Ed, trust me. Just be cool about things, and this will all blow over."

"You think the Feds are tapping my line! Why didn't you tell me sooner?"

"Calm down," I said. I'd learned from experience that the key to getting Eddie to chill is to mention money. "They might be tapping your line, but probably not, Ed. This is about me. They're just threatening you to get at me. It's all bullshit. Look, I could really use your help on something else. You know just ordinary Google search type stuff. And I'll pay you $100 an hour."

"You think money can solve this, Earl? Don't just tell me this is gonna blow over. I don't want to be your scapegoat, Earl. Don't leave me hanging out to dry here."

"You're no one's scapegoat, Ed," I assured him.

"Tell me you're walking away from this case before it gets worse. Tell me you don't need my help anymore, Earl, because you are getting out and taking the heat off of me."

"Ed, I can't do that yet," I heard the slap of his hand against his forehead. "But, listen to me. I just need a little time to tie up a loose end, and then I'm out. And, more importantly, you're out. I swear to it."

He sighed, "You better make this right."

"I will, nephew. When have I ever let you down?"

He began to recite a litany of times I had, so I disconnected. I was just about to leave my room for a second time when my phone rang again. This time, it was Maria Moore.

"Who did this to him, Earl? He didn't deserve to go out like this." Her voice was halting, she was crying.

"Maybe nobody, Maria. They don't know what happened to him yet. Unless they told you something different?"

"They told me nothing," she said angrily. "But once a journalist, always a journalist."

"Yes?"

"So, I called in a favor from an old friend who's high up in the Connecticut State Police, and he told me a few things."

"Great work, Maria."

"Thank you," she paused, and I realized she needed to steady herself before telling me what she knew. "His skull was fractured. He was struck in the back of the head."

That fit with what I'd seen in the fridge.

"The speculation is that the killer came up behind him and he never saw it coming."

"Do they know where he was killed?"

"Yes, they're pretty sure it was on his yacht. They used an ultraviolet light inside, and the galley lit up. My friend said a lot of blood had been spilled in there recently. They're testing samples now."

"If so, he probably knew the killer. It'd be hard to sneak up on him on the yacht," I interjected.

"They didn't suggest familiarity, but that's what I inferred too."

"How about a time of death?"

"At least a week, but probably something closer to ten days."

That fit my timeline perfectly. He was killed Sunday morning. The body was found Sunday afternoon, then stashed and the scene cleaned Sunday evening, around the same time the email was sent. But who killed him? I still had no idea, though I felt the pieces beginning to come together.

Both of us were quiet for a bit as we mulled all this over, then she bore through the silence. "You gotta find whoever did this, Chief. Mac didn't deserve this."

"Do you have any friends in the FBI?"

"No, but I know a few people that do. Why do you ask?"

"I've spoken with a couple of special agents this week. Twice actually, both times against my will, and they're threatening to take away my license if I don't get off the case."

"Why would they do that?"

"There seems to be a larger investigation at play, and they're afraid I'll interfere."

"I want you on this case. Whoever did this is not going to get away with it. Let me make a call and see if I can straighten things out."

"No! Please, don't do that," I said panicking. "Look, I'm not planning to stop my work here, and your speaking with them will only make my job harder." I caught my breath. "Thank you though. One more question. I understand he had an argument with Gibson French on the Indian Head docks late Saturday night. There were three other people there, including Nate Sterling and Tinsley Saunders. The other person is a woman. I'd like to know who she is. This group may have been the last people to see him alive. Other than the killer."

"You mean one of them could be the killer?"

"I am not saying that, but it would be helpful to know who the other party was."

"Okay, I don't know that crowd as well as I used to, but I'll try to find out. Tell me something though. Who do you think did this?"

She was helping me, I didn't want to lie to her, she'd see right through it. "The method used was violent, personal. A lover, an ex-lover, the husband of a lover, that's my guess." I considered telling her about my theory that Endicott, French, and Sterling were involved in hiding the body, but I didn't see it doing me any good. As much as I liked Maria, she was an ex-wife and a suspect. For what it was worth, Maria was on the same wavelength.

"Although I'm in that group, I agree with you. And, I made my bones on the Charles Stuart case."

"Yeah, I'm sure I watched your reporting on it. Hey, one more question for you. Mac's boat is the Rebecca. Do you know her?"

"No," she paused. "Rebecca? Really?"

20

I didn't have many moves left. Sterling, a.k.a. the Commodore, was the one loose thread I could pull, so it was back to Greenwich for me. I caught a curveball when the elevator doors peeled back to reveal the hotel lobby.

"Joanna! What are you doing here?"

She sprung from a settee. "Sorry, I forgot to mention that I was in New York. There was a meeting regarding one of Mac's projects yesterday, and I was asked to help fill in the blanks. I was planning to take the Acela back to Boston, then I got to thinking after we spoke, and, well, going back to the office isn't going to help us find out what happened to Mac, and I thought if you won't let me pay you, maybe I could at least help you."

This was unexpected and unwelcome. Civilians are trouble. I sat down in a stylish egg-shaped chair to the right of the bench on which she had been perched and motioned for her to sit as well.

"This is serious work, Joanna. I was nearly killed the other night. I don't think it's safe for you."

"Look," she touched my arm. "I know these people. I can help you tiptoe through all the bullshit they sling, and I can handle myself."

"You have a license to carry?"

"No."

I shook my head.

"Come on, Earl. I brought you into this, and now you won't even let me pay you. Plus, I can't work right now with everything that's going on. And I can't sit around mourning the loss of Mac, wondering what you're doing, and waiting for you to call and tell me. Please, I can't bear that. You know, I can help you with these people. Let me." She gripped my forearm tight and looked into my eyes. I'm a natural born sucker for any woman who does this, and I'm convinced they all know it instinctively.

I exhaled forcefully. "Okay, well I'm running out of leads to follow, so you may not be able to help me for long, but there's something I need to look into back in Greenwich."

"Really? At Indian Head?" Her eyes widened.

"Yeah, sort of, Nate Sterling, the club's commodore. He wasn't truthful with me the other night. Plus, I'm pretty sure he gave me the lump on my head."

"You're kidding?"

I shook my head, and she asked to look at my injury. I turned, and she stood and gently used her fingertips to my part my hair.

"Ooh, you poor guy, that looks painful. Are you sure you don't want to see a doctor?"

As she stood, I noticed how great she looked, even in a gray pant-suit. The pants fit snug at the ankles and accentuated her long legs, as did the heels. Her thick red curls rolled down over her shoulders and caught the sun in the southwest-facing lobby. It made her look like an angel.

"Yes, I'm fine now. Thanks though."

"What are you going to do when you see him?"

"Try to hold back my anger and get some answers, I guess. Look, you can join me if you want. But, if things get physical again, you gotta go. I can't keep my butt safe if I'm watching out for yours."

"Sounds fair," she said.

Twenty minutes later the two of us exited the Midtown tunnel headed north on the expressway.

"So, how did you end up working for Mac all those years? Fourteen, if I remember correctly."

"Uh huh, fourteen years and now I don't know what I'm going to do."

I glanced at her. "You don't even look like someone who's been an adult for fourteen years. Did you meet him right out of college?"

She took a pair of shades out of her designer purse, pulled down her visor, put them on, and examined herself in the mirror. Hers was a beautiful view. "I was still in college actually. I did an internship at Wayne Trust the summer before my senior year. I didn't know what I wanted to do with my life. It took a while, but I eventually found that I enjoyed working with Mac."

"What kinds of things did you do then?"

"What didn't I do. I started with a group of interns picked by Wayne Trust. I remember my first day. How nervous I was, how I felt in my suit. How competitive it was. Some of the other interns were brutal. I just wanted to learn the ropes, but a few of them thought they should be running the company already. Our job was to analyze companies for the investment banking division. I was assigned oil and gas ventures in Eastern Europe, made friends with a few Russians, including some oligarchs."

"It sounds like fun. I mean more fun than the Police Academy."

"Not really, they worked us like dogs, fourteen, sometimes sixteen hours a day. I burned out quickly and was going to leave, which would've meant forfeiting my credits and delaying graduation. But, a woman in H.R. told me Mac was looking for someone to help him with a project involving a U.S. company that was partly owned by a Russian oil venture. Mac was trying to take over their U.S. retirement plan, which, being huge, produced substantial revenue, especially back in those days when they charged a lot more to manage money. The U.S. division wanted to work with Mac and Wayne Trust, but Oleg, the head of the company in Moscow, had to sign off on it. One of my connections knew Ollie, and I helped Mac close the deal. Mac brought me on full-time after I graduated."

"Do you still help Mac with deals?"

"All the time, though I don't leverage my old contacts in Moscow much anymore. Doing business with Russia these days is a bit more difficult."

I nodded. "So, you've never worked for anyone other than Mac?"

"Yes, that's where I now find myself. I'm screwed."

"I doubt that," I said. "You're obviously highly skilled and well-connected. You'll land on your feet."

"I guess so. I think most people at Wayne think I'm just a glorified answering service, but Mac involved me in all his projects. I just don't know that I want to be in this business anymore. I don't work for Wayne Trust because of an attachment to this company. I liked working for Mac, and I liked helping him grow the business, but we could've been making widgets instead of administering retirement plans, and it wouldn't have mattered to me."

"You know, some of the people I've spoken with have painted a different picture of Mac than the one you've experienced. They've also suggested you and Mac were more than just co-workers."

"People have said things about Mac and me forever. They're jealous."

"So, there's no truth to it?"

"There was, early on, before he married Beth, and for a very brief period after, but not for years now. And, that's not why I have the job. Mac employed me because I did damn good work for him. He needed me as much, as I, hell, more than I needed him."

"I don't doubt that. Tell me, was Mac a kiss-and-tell kind of guy?"

"No, absolutely not."

"Really?"

"What did you hear?"

"It's been suggested that Mac was involved with a woman at the club and wasn't being particularly discreet about it."

"Oh." She gazed out the window at I-495.

"Oh? It sounds like you have some thoughts on this?"

"Well. Mac had two personalities. It's probably the main reason we didn't last as a couple. There were two Mac's: Work Mac and Play Mac."

"So, Work Mac is all buttoned up, and Play Mac is not?"

"Play Mac spent his time with a group of friends who are, to put it mildly, juvenile delinquents. They try to one-up one another in everything – cars, real estate, women, yachts. Everything is," she caught herself, "was, a contest to see whose was the fastest, biggest, most beautiful."

"And this group includes Mac's boss, Whitman Endicott, and Wayne Trust counsel, Gibson French, no?"

"French yes, Nate Sterling, yes. But, I'm not sure about Whit Endicott. He's a member at Indian Head, but I always got the impression that he stays above the fray. Mac and Gibson French grew up together. Sterling is a later addition to the boys' club. There are others too, most are club regulars. Some golf at Brookline, where Mac is also a member."

"What about women?"

"Oh, they're in the mix. There's a lot of shenanigans."

"Did Mac confide in you about who he was seeing as of late?"

"Absolutely not. We stopped dating because of this crowd. He knew I didn't want to hear about them and never brought them up. I ended my association with Play Mac a long time ago."

We were getting close to Greenwich, and I suggested we stop and grab a late lunch. She agreed.

Over a traditional turkey club, which is the only thing that should ever be called a turkey club, I asked her again about the mystery woman. "What about Rebecca? I gather she is..., ah, was, one of Mac's girls. Well, more than just one of his girls. I think he really cared about her."

"I told you, I don't know her."

"Yeah, but he named a million-dollar yacht after her, maybe you overheard something?"

"Well, I did get the sense he was getting more serious with someone he knew at Indian Head."

"So, she's a club member?" I threw open my arms and nearly knocked over her water, which I then proceeded to fumble with.

"I think so, I got the impression he had a special sailing buddy that he'd seen for a while. That doesn't mean he wasn't seeing other people though. He wasn't big on commitment."

My phone buzzed with the important news that some spam had arrived in my email. I would've been annoyed, but it jogged my memory about something I'd meant to mention.

"The email Mac sent to you and Endicott. It was almost certainly sent after Mac was killed."

"Yeah, I thought about that," she said while putting down a forkful of Cobb salad. "Whit's the likely culprit, though it can't be proven, which is even more reason to send it."

"Why can't it be proven?"

"He has access to the email accounts of all his direct reports. It's a legal thing for investment companies. He could've easily told French or Sterling how to log into Mac's phone, and they could've sent it from there."

"There you go. That pretty much seals it," I said.

"Seals what?"

"The two-crime scenario, three if you count me being jumped. I've solved two and three, but one remains a total mystery."

"What are you talking about?' Joanna pushed her plate away, leaned back and flicked a lock of hair over an athletic shoulder.

"One, someone kills Mac." I paused and looked at Joanna. "Sorry, I don't mean to be flip."

"It's alright, go on."

"I'm sorry to say, I'm feeling lost on one, but I'm good on two. In two, Endicott, French, and Sterling facilitate the hiding of the body until the merger is complete. The much less serious number – a minor third if you will – is when I wander in and find the body and Sterling jumps me and steals my phone to keep me from revealing what I found." I sat back and exhaled. "Plus, there's whatever the FBI was investigating, which may just be Mac's disappearance, or it may be bigger, as they suggested."

I sighed. "How is it that after three days of intensive work, I am no closer to finding the killer? I have nothing on number one, and it's damn depressing."

She gave me the full-on sympathy treatment with her big emerald eyes. "Hey, I didn't hire you to find a killer. I hired you to find Mac, and you did that within what, about sixteen hours? You've solved that crime already, you'll solve the other."

"Thanks for the pep talk. I need it. Hey, tell me, is it true that not having Mac made the deal more difficult?"

"Yeah. It was a real coup for Whitman that he held it together because the initial reaction to Mac's disappearance was chaotic."

I signaled for the check.

Joanna got a glint in her eyes, and she leaned in and said, "Hey, what if Mac was working with the FBI on something that would've incriminated Whit or Gibson in a crime, then they might have wanted to get Mac out of the way?"

"That's a solid point," I said, but it doesn't fit with Sterling's phone call to Endicott on Sunday afternoon and the need for French to rush to the yacht club. If French or Endicott had been involved in a plot to kill Mac, they would've been prepared in advance. Hell, they would've found a better place to hide the body. It makes far more sense that someone else killed him, then when the body was found, Sterling called Endicott to ask what to do, knowing that Endicott was involved in a huge deal to sell Wayne Trust. Endicott then sent French to Indian Head to oversee the clean-up so they could finish the deal."

Joanna nodded, and we were quiet after that. She was probably thinking what I was thinking, but neither of us wanted to say aloud. That's Mac's killer was someone who knew him intimately. As with Maria, Joanna was, technically, a suspect. However, I had no intention of asking if she had an alibi unless I found a damn good reason to. For now, her alibi was hiring me to find him.

We were walking out to the car when she asked: "So, are we going to Indian Head to confront Sterling?"

"No, we're going to 10 Shoreline Road in Belle Haven."

"Why are we going to Belle Haven?"

"That's where Commodore Sterling lives."

"Won't he be at the club?"

"Probably, but the Feds may be watching the club. If I go there, I could lose my license. Going to his home will bring him to us instead."

She considered this as I sped up and got back onto I-95. "But, won't he tell the FBI you visited him? So, you'll lose your license anyway."

I smiled. "That's where your wrong, kiddo. After I'm through with him, the Commodore won't dare rat me out to the Feds. If he does, I'll make sure he's charged with at least one felony.

❊ ❊ ❊

We drove the last few miles in silence just watching the landscape change from dense suburbs to rural lanes and then occasional ocean vistas.

"What's your story?" I asked.

She smiled again. "What do you mean? I told you my story."

"No, I mean where did you grow up? Where have you been? That story."

"You tell me yours first, and maybe, if I like it, I'll tell you mine."

"Okay," I said. "I started my life in a border town in northern Mass. I'm the youngest of three. The oldest is my brother Phil, followed by my sister Emily. Her son, Eddie, emailed me Sterling's address two hours ago. He helps me out."

"Interesting," she said, clearly not interested. I had nothing better to do, so I went on anyway.

"I had a good upbringing. My parents were reasonably happy. My old man was a bit of a dud, but my mother was vivacious, intelligent and hell-bent on spreading goodwill wherever she went. They're both gone now, but they lived happy lives."

"How did you become a cop?"

"My ex, Roxanne and I, well, we got pregnant, and I needed a job with good benefits. They were hiring, and I had a bachelor's degree, which gave me an advantage over most of the other applicants, and I'm a damn good shot."

"So, how many children?"

"Well, we had a miscarriage, and never gave it another go."

"Oh, I'm sorry."

"Thanks, it's probably for the best, given how things turned out between us."

We passed an old train station that was still in use but only as a restaurant next to the concrete monolith that passed for a new "modern" station. We drifted along a two-lane street lined with an assemblage of architecture from every period going back to the days of Hamilton. We passed over a small stream and then turned onto a wooded lane flanked by trees, old stone walls, and pastures. We drove on for several miles then made another turn, this time into a neighborhood that made Maria Moore's Andover street look like Cracktown by comparison. These houses were fifteen to twenty thousand feet apiece with towering columns and stone facades. They were mansions.

We were in Belle Haven, a peninsula on the southern edge of Greenwich, where the average home sells for north of five million.

Within Belle Haven is a gated community called the Association, that includes a few billionaires among its ranks, but Sterling lived outside of the Association. This was crucial because it would allow us to drop in uninvited.

We were getting close to the water's edge, and most of the mansions were backed by lush green lawns that stretched all the way to the Sound. Number 10 was a bulbous two-story chateau-style stone affair with a mansard roof and attached carriage house. The driveway split about 100 feet from the house with each side wrapping around an oval reflecting pool, I took the right fork, pulled up a few feet from the front steps and killed the engine.

"Okay, so now what?"

"We wait," I replied.

"What do you mean, we wait? Let's go knock on the door."

"There's no need. Someone will be out soon."

She looked at me like I had two heads, but as she did one-half of the big arched double doors swung open, and a slender man strode out in front of the car and approached my window. He had pale, wrinkled skin, thinning silver hair, and rigid posture.

"May I help you, sir?" He leaned and spat out the words in a rich English accent filled with a thick air of superiority.

"Yes, my name is Earl Town, and this is Joanna Hill. We're here to see Commodore Sterling."

"I'm afraid Mr. Sterling is not here, sir. He's gainfully employed, you see." A mean English butler. I wondered if everyone in Belle Haven had one. Must be great when Jehovah's Witnesses come knocking.

"Yeah, we figured that, but he's really going to want to talk to us. You need to call him and let him know I'm here to see him." I didn't want to bully this guy, he was just doing his job, but so was I. He looked not at all convinced and about ready to tell me to get lost, so I held out my phone and said, "Here, I just dialed the number for Indian Head," which I had done. "Just ask for the Commodore and let him know Earl Town is here. I'm telling you there will be hell to pay if you don't. Take my word for it."

He hesitated, but finally took the phone and pressed it to his ear. He turned away from me, covering the phone and his mouth as he spoke. I was disappointed in his dress, which was a gray cardigan and black pants with a shiny pair of black patent leather lace-ups. I considered inquiring about his lack of a coat and tails but thought better of it.

Despite his efforts at shielding the conversation from us, I could hear Sterling shouting at him. "Reginald? Why the hell are you calling from this number?" Reggie's response was muffled, then Sterling yelled: "Well, what the hell does he want?" I looked over at Joanna and smiled. She looked more than a little nervous.

"What is it you need to speak with Mr. Sterling about?" I looked up at old Reg, who had leaned down next to my window, and answered loud enough for Sterling to hear, "I just had a long conversation with Richard McNierney."

Before Reggie could speak, Sterling bellowed, "I'll be there in twenty-five minutes. Show them to the lanai!"

Reggie bent down and handed me the phone. "Mr. Sterling will be home shortly. Please come in."

21

We followed old Reg through an arched-stone doorway that could fit a marching band into a sunny and spacious room that ran the full width of the house. To our left were the sweeping curves of a grand staircase. To our right, a large study backed by a stone fireplace. Straight ahead was a bright sitting area with two stories of floor-to-ceiling windows. At their base sat a series of French doors leading onto a stone patio with space for two hundred.

Reggie opened a set of doors and invited us to step through. I walked out into a vista of the Long Island Sound that rivaled that of Indian Head. And, the amenities didn't stop at the doorstep. To our right was a long oval pool with spa and beyond that an outdoor kitchen that put my indoor one to shame. To our left, sat a tennis court, and straight ahead stretched about a hundred yards of rich green lawn that gradually sloped down to a private beach and dock that extended far out into the sound.

Using only his eyes, Reggie directed us to sit around a teak table. We faced the Sound, and the view momentarily took my breath away. It was just a slight upgrade over my office panorama of Smitty's Corner Tavern. Reggie asked if he could 'provide us with a refreshment.' I considered asking for a Dalmore but decided to follow Joanna's lead, as she had no qualms about asking for a cappuccino, which he quickly agreed to. In no time at all, he came back with a pair of them, in warm cups no less, and they were as good as I've had in any restaurant. One thing I've noticed about rich people, they don't skimp on their coffee. Or their bedding, I'd recently noticed that as well.

Reggie was about to leave us when I asked a question that had been nagging at me.

"Is there a Mrs. Sterling, and might she be at home?"

"Yes and no, sir, Mrs. Sterling works in the city."

He turned and left us before I could ask a follow-up.

I eyed Joanna. "So, there is a Mrs. Sterling. Have you ever met her or her husband?"

"In person, no, but I've talked to him on the phone, usually to deliver a message for Mac about a club commitment or a race they were involved in."

We enjoyed the view for a while until I heard a noise and turned to see Reggie emerging from the house. "Mr. Sterling is arriving." He was looking out at the sea, and I followed his gaze.

"That looks like a fifty-footer," said Joanna.

"Fifty-seven, actually," said Reggie. "Although, the commodore prefers to round it up to sixty."

The sleek cruiser pulled up to the end of the dock, and two young men in Indian Head polo shirts and tan shorts jumped out and tied the boat to its moorings.

Sterling appeared from the stern where he'd been steering the craft, climbed down to the long dock and began walking our way. I tried not to laugh, but couldn't contain it and said to Joanna, "I'll be damned, they do really dress like that." The Commodore was a stereotype of a, well, a Commodore. He wore a blue jacket with gold buttons over a white shirt and pants and boat shoes. And, to top it off, perched on his blonde surfer-boy locks was a white captain's cap with a gold insignia above the brim. He hadn't been quite so formally dressed when we'd last met.

He finally reached the lawn, and we stood up to greet him as he made his way up the slope. As he got closer, I realized this would be a brief meeting. He was seething, and I braced for impact.

He shifted his gaze from me to Joanna and barked, "What the hell are you doing here?" I started to reply, but she cut me off to snarl back.

"We're here to find out what happened to Mac, remember him?"

Her tone seemed to calm him a bit, and I instinctively started to sit back down, but he wasn't finished. "Don't sit," he ordered us. "You're leaving." He grabbed my right arm as if to lead me back to the house, but I didn't budge.

"Not the first time you grabbed me, eh Commodore? Of course, the last time I was unconscious."

"Hearsay!" He sneered. "You've got no evidence to support that. I want you off my property, and don't come back. If you do, I'll have you arrested." He stepped up into my space. He was about an inch shorter and about twenty pounds lighter, yet tried to physically intimidate me. I expect shits like him to use his wealth as a weapon and try to make me feel like a poverty-stricken loser. I used to get it all the time as a cop from guys in suits and ties. The attitude was a surefire way to get a ticket. But physical intimidation? I couldn't let him get away with that. I was about to lift him off his feet and shake him, but, before I could, Joanna jumped back into the fray.

"What are you hiding?" she asked while pointing an accusatory finger at him. I turned and looked at her as if to say 'hey, I'll ask the questions,' but she ignored me.

"Let's go. Now!" Sterling said as he took hold of my arm again and stepped toward the house. "You'll leave if you know what's good for you."

I grabbed his free arm and squeezed hard on his wrist. He let go of me, but I squeezed tighter and looked into his dark eyes. "Why did you do it? Why did you hide Mac's body? How much are French and Endicott paying you?"

He winced and said, "Let go of me!" I squeezed harder.

I thought the pain would break him, and he'd fess up, but instead, he screamed: "Reginald, call the police!"

"Where's my phone?" I asked him. "I know you took it, and I know why. Who helped you put Mac in that fridge? Did French help you?" Beads of sweat had formed on his temples and begun to run down the sides of his face, but, to his credit, he kept his mouth shut. "Your friend Endicott is not gonna save you from a murder rap," I said, finally releasing him.

He stumbled backward and rubbed his wrist, then turned to Joanna and whined: "You're done at Wayne Trust. I can assure you Whit Endicott will learn of this. You should be mourning your loss, but instead, you're trespassing with this ..." looking me up and down, "this backwoods ape."

That made me laugh, and hard from the gut, and I had to stop myself before replying. "Spare me the outrage, Sterling. This ape wasn't the one smashing heads the other night. You did that, and I can prove it. You're gonna do time for it too."

"Leave!" he demanded, as Reggie came rushing out of the house shouting, "They're on the way."

I turned to Joanna. "It's time to go."

I was going to give my regards to the Commodore, but Joanna beat me to it. "We're not afraid Nate, this isn't going to end well for you."

Sterling stood and watched as we trekked back to the house. Reggie opened the French doors through which we had come earlier and quickly led us back through the mansion and out to my car.

Joanna spoke first after climbing in.

"Asshole didn't give us anything."

I started the car and began rolling down the long driveway, small stones crunching under the tires. "I don't know," I said. "He didn't deny knocking me out, that's incriminating."

"Yeah, but we already knew that," she said.

"Uh huh," I nodded. "That didn't go as I'd hoped. I was certain he'd give me something when I dropped McNierney's name, but he's tougher than I thought."

Joanna looked at me with a sympathetic gaze. "You're not used to these people," she said.

"No, I'm not," I admitted.

"They don't back down easily. They don't know how. They've had money and privilege their whole lives. It has never occurred to them that one day they might be held to account."

I sighed.

She added, "Plus they have teams of lawyers at their disposal. Have you ever been sued?"

"Uh, once or twice," I said, trying to squelch the bad memories she had suddenly conjured.

She lifted her purse from the floor, extracted a cigarette and lighter, and rolled down the window. Despite being late September, the air was warm and humid. "That got me a little jacked up, and I could really use one, do you mind?"

"No, not at all."

We got onto the main road and were headed back towards Greenwich proper when I heard a wailing siren and saw two Greenwich police cars speeding towards us, lights flashing.

She smiled. "Guys like Sterling have a lot of people on the payroll, including cops."

I pulled over onto the shoulder, put the car in park and waited for the inevitable confrontation. It would be the worst kind too. One in which I could only lose. The lead cruiser pulled to a stop in front of us and to my amazement, two cops came out with guns drawn and pointed straight at me.

"Christ," I said to Joanna through gritted teeth. "These guys are maniacs. Follow my lead and slowly put your hands on the dash so they can see them. They look crazed." I slid my hands to ten and two on the wheel.

One of them was a good fifteen years older and was obviously in charge. He was mid-40's, tan, bald, tall and lean, and he was clearly into free weights and dietary supplements, as his shirt sleeves barely contained the bulging muscles beneath. He took up a shooter's stance about fifteen feet away, gun pointed at my chest. He had a gleaming

Greenwich smile, apparently thrilled at the prospect of terminating me, and I wanted to laugh at his chiclets, but the look on his face gave me serious cause for concern.

I could see the other cop in my rearview mirror. He had moved behind us and was pointing his weapon at the back of my head.

The big one said in a loud, gruff voice, "Keep your hands where we can see them." He smiled again, then added, "Do not move." I glanced at Joanna and saw that she was rather calm. Sure, why not? I was the one in their sights.

The one in front holstered his weapon, slid up to my door and aggressively yanked it open. He told me to unbuckle my seatbelt, and as soon as I did, he pulled me out of the car by my neck and shoulder, similar to what I had done to Craig the pimp a few years before.

But, instead of planting my face on the sidewalk, he stood me up and slammed me into my roof. I had a split second to turn my head, or he would've broken my nose. Then he snapped me back and sneered at me.

I decided it was time to say something, and led with, "I'm an ex-cop, I know how this goes," but that was all I got out before he spun me around and into 'the stance.' He pulled my hands behind my back and set me up with a nice pair of bracelets, then proceeded to give me a rough patting down. He announced. "I'm Chief Matthew Boone of the Greenwich Police Department, and you're under arrest for assault and battery."

Then he dragged my ass to his squad car. I was thrown into the back seat half angry for being treated this way and half happy about the money I was going to make suing this town. I looked over my shoulder and saw that Joanna was gently maneuvered into the back of the other unit, which was one of those newer model Dodges with the Hemi. Yup, it was nice being a cop in Richtown. Maybe after we settled my suit, I'd buy a Hemi too.

The ride took all of ten minutes. Boone didn't say a word to me throughout. This was appreciated because my head had begun throbbing when he slammed me against my roof. The safety complex was constructed of two four-story stone buildings, one for police and another for the fire department, connected by a glass atrium. The police side included a multi-story parking garage.

Boone walked me through the atrium to an entrance for the police department. We waited to be buzzed through, then cut down a short cinder-block hallway that reeked of cleaning solution and body odor, and into a booking area. The other cop, whose name tag read

Penner, entered the room sans Joanna, and the two of them sat me down across from a steel-frame desk and freed my right hand from the cuffs. For a second, I thought he was removing them altogether, but then the little shit named Penner attached my left wrist to a loop that was bolted to the wall next to me. At this point, I'd had enough, and said, "I spent a decade as police chief in a town of seven thousand. I'm not gonna try to escape."

Chief Boone looked over his shoulder at me. He was pouring a mug of coffee from a small pot on a counter that ran along a wall. Next to the coffee was a box of doughnuts, and next to that, sat a jar of creatine powder.

My outburst hadn't gotten a rise out of either of them, so I gave them some more lip.

"Drip coffee. I thought you'd have espresso, you know, in a little cup with your seal on it. This is Greenwich, right?"

Boone looked at me and sniffed, and I began to think it was going to cost me some money to get out this mess. I said, "I'd like my call now. I want to speak with my lawyer."

Two minutes and twenty-four seconds of silence passed by. I know because I counted 144 one-thousands, it gave me something to do. Boone was a making a show of ignoring me and wasting both our time. Finally, he spoke. "You'll get your call in a minute. In the meantime, you and I are gonna talk." He was leaning back in an old oak chair, squeezing a stress release ball that looked ready to explode. He went on.

"Former law enforcement or not. You assaulted an important member of this community."

I lifted my free hand and examined my nails.

He raised his voice. "You think you can come into my town and walk all over its citizens, and I'm going to sit back and let you get away with it?"

I looked down at my chest and pretended to remove some lint from my shirt. "My lawyer. I want to speak to my lawyer."

He laughed and said, "And you will, in good time." He sat up and leaned across the clean steel desk, close enough for me to smell the combination of drip coffee and supplements on his breath, and I thought I might gag. "We look after the members of this community." He was interrupted by a man's voice coming from the phone to his right. It wasn't the voice of Penner. It was older, deeper and scratchy: a longtime smoker. He said, "Chief, sorry for interrupting, but I need to speak with you right away. It pertains to your guests and cannot wait."

Boone sat there, mouth agape, staring at the phone. I thought for a second, he was going to pick it up and throw it against the wall. Then he trained his eyes on me and glared, and it was all I could do to keep from smiling at him, which probably would've pushed him over the edge. He lifted his massive frame from the sturdy oak chair and moved to the door that led back to the front of the station.

He paused, one hand on the knob, turned back to me and said, "Sit tight, *former-Chief*, you and I are just getting started."

The impenetrable door of steel and bulletproof glass slammed shut. There's was nothing for me to do but wait in silence.

22

About ten minutes after Boone left us, the same door burst open, and Joanna was escorted in by a female cop. Unlike me, she wasn't cuffed, and she and the young, fit, officer appeared to be getting along well. She winked at me as she was led to a desk on the other side of the room. Unlike yours truly, she wasn't shackled to the wall either.

As I sat and waited, I wondered what would make a cop like Boone decide to rough me up. Was he on the payroll of Sterling or Endicott and trying to intimidate me on their behalf, or was he just a jerk in a steroid-induced rage? I hoped for the sake of the case that it was the former, but suspected it was just the latter. On this day, hope won out.

After another five minutes passed, Chief Boone roared through the door like an angry bull released into a ring. The muscles and veins in his neck were pulsing, and I swear I felt heat radiating from his violet, enraged face.

"Town! Hill! You're free to go. Get the fuck out of my sight and get the fuck out of Greenwich! You don't want to cross my path again."

He stomped across the room and disappeared behind a steel door to my right. I wished it wasn't so thick so I could hear him losing his mind. Penner jumped up and walked straight over, keys in hand, and freed me from the wall.

"What's up, Penner? Your chief looks none too happy."

"You shut up," he said. Nice comeback.

"Why'd Sterling decline to press charges?" I rubbed my wrist as we walked towards the exit, where Joanna and her escort were waiting. She mouthed "What did you do?" I shrugged my response.

Penner opened the door and waited for us to go through. As we entered the atrium, he said, "If you know what's best for you, you'll do what Chief Boone says and leave town. And, you'll stay the hell away."

"Or what, Penner?" I was losing patience.

He didn't bother to explain and pulled the heavy door shut.

I turned to Joanna, who was staring transfixed on a striking woman who was waiting for us by the exit door. She was tall, thin, draped in Neiman Marcus and wearing dark glasses. She turned up again, I thought. What does Tinsley have to do with all this?

She took off the glasses and bounced on her toes as Joanna, and I crossed the atrium.

"Hi, Earl! Long time no see." She giggled and gave me a peck on the cheek, and I felt Joanna staring through me. I was beginning to regret my utter lack of willpower and inability to separate my work and sex lives.

"Tinsley. You sprang us?"

"Uh huh!"

She giggled again, and I started to introduce the two of them, but Tinsley cut me off. "Oh, Joanna and I have met. Long time ago, right Joanna?" Joanna nodded but didn't say anything.

Tinsley said to Joanna. "I'm so sorry to hear about Mac. You must be devastated. You poor thing." Joanna just looked at her. I tried to catch her stare to gauge where we were now, but she wouldn't look me in the eye. In the doghouse, that's where I was.

"What on earth are you doing here, Tinsley?" I finally managed to ask.

"Well, I was about to go for a sail, when I was recruited for a mission to collect the two of you. So, here I am." She smiled at me, then Joanna, who looked away.

"What mission? Who asked you?"

"I can't say, but if you follow me, all your questions will be answered. I hope you're hungry." She opened the door and held it for us, then led us to the street, where she turned right, which meant we were headed towards Old Greenwich. It was early evening, and the sun was low and beginning its slow slide into the horizon.

As we walked, I tried again to get Tinsley to reveal our benefactor, and where we were going but she wouldn't give it up. She asked what it was we'd done to end up in police custody, and when I mentioned arguing with Sterling, she suggested that my temper may be short because I got so little sleep last night. I winced and immediately changed the subject. The conversation was stilted the rest of the way, with Joanna offering only an occasional grunt or cough.

It took all of ten minutes to reach our destination, a small restaurant, with maybe fifteen tables, called San Sebastian. Rather than walk in through the front door like the hoi polloi, Tinsley stopped and looked into an alley to the right of the place. "This way," she said, as she pulled me in. Joanna followed, and we walked about fifty feet then took a left into a restaurant kitchen via the back door. Tinsley spoke Spanish to a man who was preparing food, before turning to me, saying: "Mission accomplished. You two are to have a seat there," she waved to a stainless-steel table in a corner near the door to the dining room. "Your date will be here soon. Do have the grilled squid, it's delicious."

Then she looked me in the eye. "Maybe I'll see you around, Coach."

I managed to eke out an embarrassed "Sure," as she spun and strolled out. She had a way with exits, and I felt Joanna watching me watching Tinsley. I couldn't take my eyes off her.

I pivoted back to Joanna to find her eyeballing a man standing just inside the doorway to the dining room. He had a cell phone to his ear, listening more than talking. He nodded to us and held up an index finger, then gazed down at the floor as if listening intently. Whit Endicott must be on the other end, I thought. Joanna and I were studying Gibson French.

He pointed to the stainless-steel table, signaling us to sit since neither one of us had followed Tinsley's instruction. This time we did, and within seconds two waitstaff appeared and placed a gleaming white tablecloth over the scratched steel. On top of this, they centered a small red and green striped vase containing a single white orchard, the three colors of the Basque flag. I knew this because my ex Roxy had made a few trips to Bilbao. She wanted me to go with her, but I couldn't get away, something that's probably not a problem for her hedge fund guy.

French tucked the phone into his sports coat and came over to us. I got up to make the first move.

"Mr. French, we meet again," I said, accepting his handshake.

"Detective Town," he replied looking me in the eye, then he turned to Joanna, "and Miss Hill," before showing her the best smile his money could buy.

He was Greenwich casual: brown loafers, probably Italian, perfectly tailored tan pants with a French cuff, and monogrammed blue oxford shirt under a silk jacket in navy blue with an almost imperceptible herringbone pattern. All of this was topped with a neatly folded pocket square, and gold Rolex Submariner with a blue face, which I happened to know retails for about twenty-five grand. How do I know this? Said hedge funder wore one when I ran into Roxy and him a few months back, and I looked it up while drowning my sorrows.

We sat down, and within seconds, plates, silverware, napkins, and a bottle of red wine were expertly placed around us. French asked if we were okay with Rioja, which he assured us was terrific. Joanna was okay with it, but I decided to be a pain-in-the-ass and mentioned how much I could use a scotch. That is if the place had something decent.

"Decent?" he said, overdoing the gracious host routine. "You're gonna love this." He raised his right hand, and a young waiter ran right over. French mumbled something in his ear, and he headed off to the bar.

I fought the urge to ask French what the hell he thought he was doing. After all, I appreciated the get-out-of-jail-free card, but he obviously wanted something in return. I decided to let him make the first move. Hell, I was too tired to ask questions anyway. He looked us over for a bit, leaned back in his chair, and announced that he was concerned for our well-being.

Oh, how about that? The guy just wants the best for us.

The waiter returned with a square glass, which he placed in front of me, and into which he dropped a perfectly square ice cube from a set of bamboo tongs. Then he slowly poured an ample dose of a viscous caramel liquid over the top. The waiter seemed to be taking precautions to ensure that I didn't see the label. Before he left, he recommended I give it a couple of minutes to breath, but I considered throwing it back in one gulp while staring into French's cold eyes. Then I decided to try and be an adult, for once.

"You gave me the slip last night. Your friend Nate Sterling has us arrested today, and now you, of all people, save us from Chief Boone's dungeon. What gives, Gibby?"

"Now there's a good question!" Joanna exclaimed. I turned and caught her eye. Our space in the corner of the elongated kitchen was lit by a large bowl-shaped fixture suspended about eighteen inches above our heads and lined in gold leaf. The golden light made Joanna's auburn locks sparkle, and I wondered if Mac had ever been in love with her.

The waiter brought the first course. In front of each one of us, he placed a large white porcelain spoon. In the center of said spoon sat a red bubble about the diameter of a quarter and the height of a thumbnail. French watched for our reaction. Mine was disappointment, given how hungry I was and how little food, if you could call it that, was put in front of me. He couldn't wait to tell us what it was, so I delayed his pleasure.

"Wow, this is, mmm," I said sipping the scotch, which was smooth, sweet, warming and wonderful. "You must tell me what it is."

"Ah," he said, glancing up from the spoons. "It's a Yamazaki Single Malt Whisky. Twelve years old from Suntory. I prefer Japanese whiskeys."

"Damn."

"Yes, damn," he said.

"You were saying ..." Again, Joanna was pressing the point. I glanced over at her and added: "What she said." We both stared at French and waited.

"Okay, but eat this first, it's the most delicious gazpacho you'll ever taste." He looked from Joanna to me and back. "Eat it, you won't be disappointed, and then I'll tell you why we are here, while they bring us a whole bunch of other delicious things to eat." He paused, then added, "I promise, you're going to love this."

Joanna put spoon to lip, tilted her head back and sucked the crimson blob between her plump pink lips. She did that thing when you bring up your hand like the food is going to fly out of your mouth but doesn't. Then she began to ooh and ah and make bedroom noises, and that I was all I needed. I sucked the shimmering mound through my lips and saw God. It was more than gazpacho. It was the essence of the freshest tomato, celery, and bell pepper, with the perfect amount of seasoning. It was a revelation.

I exhaled and shook my head. "Can I just get a bowl of this please?"

A young man whisked away our spoons and quickly returned with more dishes. There was chorizo sausage, grilled squid, Iberico ham, pork belly, and mussels. Who needs vegetables? On and on it went. As soon as a plate was emptied, it was replaced with another delicious tapas.

Finally, our host addressed the elephant. Wiping mussel broth from the edges of his mouth, he announced, "I want to hire you to find Mac's killer."

Joanna cut in before I could respond. "You can't. He's already working for me, and to find Mac's killer, something you could help us with for free."

He looked at me and smiled, "Do your investigations always involve your clients?"

"Technically, I'm not working for Joanna anymore, and at her insistence, I am allowing her to temporarily assist me." Joanna bristled at my use of the term temporary, but that's what it was.

I sipped my delicious Japanese whisky and continued. "I plan to find out what happened to Mac regardless of compensation. This is personal now. Someone nearly killed me the other night. Maybe, Sterling told you about that?"

I watched for a reaction but got none. I glanced at Joanna. She was also staring at French. He looked at her, then at me, and said, "Earl, about what happened the other night, could we discuss that alone?"

I turned to face Joanna and asked rather meekly if she might need a smoke. She sighed her disgust with me, then grabbed her handbag, stood up and headed for the back door.

When she was gone, I said, "I'm going to tell her whatever you tell me. She brought me into this, and she deserves to know."

French smiled uneasily. "I wish you wouldn't, but if you do, it'll be your word against mine, and mine carries a hell of a lot more weight around here."

"Alright," I said. "Let's get to it."

"Fine," he replied. "Turn off your phone and put it on the table where I can see it."

23

"Look," he began while swirling his wine. "Let's say that an overzealous employee of Indian Head did something he shouldn't have done. Something that I had no prior knowledge of and am not at all okay with."

I frowned. "This is no way to begin an apology, Gibby."

"Come on, I don't know who killed Mac. Whit Endicott and Nate Sterling don't know who killed Mac." He paused, leaned way in, and whispered: "His death came at a horrible time, and some people, without my prior knowledge, apparently delayed the finding of his body for a few days."

I pulled back, laughed and shook my head. "Seriously? You think I'm stupid enough to believe this, and yet you want to hire me? Come on." I shook my head. "I was gonna be nice, and not throw this in your face, but I know about the call Sterling made to Endicott last Sunday afternoon. Remember, the one when you and Endicott were in a meeting, and your buddy Nate Sterling called Whit Endicott and said something like: 'Hey, I just found Mac's corpse, what should I do?' And Endicott dispatched you via Lincoln Town Car to Indian Head, where you spent about four hours ..."

"Enough!" He pounded the table with his fist. For a second, I thought I might have pushed him too far but screw that, I thought to myself. We needed to move past the bullshit, and now we had.

The work of the kitchen staff had ceased with the outburst, and French turned and glared at a man in a white coat, who then barked at the staff in Spanish, and they reengaged in their labor.

French leaned back into the banquette. His face had returned to displaying a cool confidence, but he couldn't entirely hide his anxiety. He unconsciously picked up his butter knife and began to shift it back and forth, between his thumb and index finger, up and down, up and down, like a see-saw. I smirked at him and waited.

"You're a bigger problem than I had realized. Mr. Town." Now I was

Mister.

"Yeah, you know I've considered changing the tagline on my card to *professional pain in the ass.*"

"Okay," he said with a sigh while opening his hands wide, as in 'you can trust me now.' "You've got to understand. This merger is a huge deal. Mac's heirs are about thirty million dollars richer because he wasn't found until after the deal was struck. It would've only punished them further if he had been found sooner and the deal had fallen apart. And, they've lost so much already."

"And the cops lost access to all of the evidence at the crime scene. It's hard enough to catch and convict a murderer with evidence, but without it?" I shook my head again. "Tell me something, French. What did you do with all the blood, and more importantly, where's the murder weapon?"

"Jesus Christ. Keep your voice down," he said. He turned and gave the head chef another stern look while gesturing towards the alley. The chef stopped what he was doing and said something to the half dozen staff. Burners were turned off, utensils put down, and the whole group of them went to join Joanna out back. It was an impressive show of power.

When they were gone, he leaned across the table and said, "There was no weapon. Only a mess. Things were scrubbed and disposed of. I'm sorry it wasn't my call, and I wouldn't have done it this way."

"That's easy to say now," I said.

He acted hurt by my comment, and sputtered, "What does it matter anyway? I, we, want you to catch the killer. Mac was a dear and loyal friend. We will help you as much as we can, but not if you bring us into this."

"Okay," I said. "The last time you saw Mac. Last Saturday night on the docks at Indian Head. You, Sterling, and Mac were all there. Who else was with you?"

The seesaw sped up, the tip of the blade now grazing the table with each flick of the wrist. "The woman who brought you here."

"Yeah, I know Tinsley was there. There was another woman. Who is she?"

He sighed, defeated. "Why bring her into this?"

"Because your reticence suggests you're hiding something, and I can't work for you if you're hiding something from me." I had no intention of working for him.

French set the knife down and sat back, arms folded. I did the same and stared through him. Finally, he said, "Caroline."

"Ferncroft?"

"Yes."

"Why are you protecting her?"

"Why bring her into it. She didn't kill him."

"Why not? What makes you so sure?"

"She's not the type."

"And, most people would say you're not the type to mess with a murder scene, but you did."

He grimaced and said nothing in his defense.

I noticed Joanna was standing in the doorway. The girl who had grilled the delicious squid was looking over her shoulder. I caught Joanna's eye and shook my head slightly. She shook her head to signal the others and walked back into the alley.

I switched subjects. "What about Mrs. French? Does she frequent Indian Head?"

"There is no Mrs. French," he answered.

"What was the argument about?" I probed.

"Club business."

"Fine, let the Feds and cops handle this. I'm out." I stood, and he grabbed my wrist and pulled me back down. I was surprised at the firmness of his grip and the ease with which he reversed my momentum. It didn't make me fear him, but I had a little more respect for him. Kicking his ass, should I be fortunate enough to have the opportunity, would be more fun than I'd anticipated. He held onto my wrist and leaned in across the table.

"Fine, have it your way, Mr. Town. I'm done being nice to you. Here's what you can do for me," he said. "You can keep your Goddamn mouth shut. I'd also like you to find out who killed Mac because I doubt the police will. Certainly not the jackasses you met this afternoon. But, first and foremost, I know you spoke with our chief of Indian Head Security this morning, and I'd like you to forget that conversation and what you saw the other night. Because that has nothing to do with what happened to Mac. What occurred the other night was done to help his heirs. It is what he would've wanted done. I'm sorry you got hurt, but it was the right thing to do. My conscience is clear on this."

"Rumor has it there's a clause in Mac's contract that on the event of his death, a big chunk of his stock diverts to Whitman Endicott. Any truth to that, Mr. French?"

"You know I'm not going to break attorney-client privilege."

"His contract is a matter of public record. Is your client going to try and abscond with Beth MacArthur's inheritance? Because that would undercut your heretofore stated position of acting out of magnanimity."

I caught him good with that shot, but that wasn't my point. I wanted to soften him up for my next question.

"Who is Rebecca?" I asked as he considered ways to explain his prior contradiction.

Unfortunately, he was smarter than ninety-nine percent of the creeps I run across, and he caught himself just as he started to reply, and he stopped and paused for a bit, then said: "I'm done answering questions unless we have a deal. You can either make the right choice, or we can make things difficult for you. Would you like to spend the next few days in a Greenwich jail cell?"

Now I was the one pausing as I weighed my options and threw him a look that I hoped communicated how little I thought of him and his friends.

He kept on selling. "Look, either way, we are going to get what we want. We hold sway in this town. I can have the charges reinstated. Boone would love that. Try me. I make a call ..." He took his phone from his jacket, held it up, and continued, "and he comes back here just salivating at the thought of arresting you again. You want to go another round with him?"

It was clear to me that he wasn't bluffing, and I didn't relish spending the weekend with Boone and Penner. I didn't have a smart comeback, so I just stared at him, until he filled the silence again.

"And remember, we haven't killed anyone. You should keep that in mind. We secured a great deal of wealth for his heirs. We did what he would've wanted us to do. He was our friend."

I'd heard enough and cut him off. "You heard of the first 48 hours? You morons destroyed the crime scene and all of the evidence. It's going to be near impossible to identify, let alone convict his killer without any hard evidence," I growled.

"That's the second time you made that point. I didn't deny it the first time, but dwelling on it does us no good," he said. "Do you want to get paid to find the guy who did this?"

"I don't want your money," I said wishing I had no principles so I could pay my bills without doing insurance work.

Then he asked a far more intriguing question. "Do you want some real answers?"

"Are you saying that if I agree to work with you, you'll answer my questions?"

He poured himself some more wine and nodded.

I decided to test him and said, "My rate is $3,000 a day, three days up front."

"Your rate is a thousand a day. What do you take me for?" He'd done his homework.

"That's for people who haven't committed a string of felonies and are now asking me to ignore this very pertinent fact."

"I've committed no felonies. I assure you that."

I laughed. "You're a lawyer, corporate law or not, you know what's at stake."

There was a commotion in the alley. A couple of the waitstaff were arguing. French caught the attention of the head chef and signaled him to come back in. Joanna came in as well.

"I guess, I can't keep them out there all night, can I?" How thoughtful.

I said. "Look, if you and your friends give me enough help that I find the killer, with enough evidence to get a conviction, which you've made damn near impossible." I just couldn't let this point go. "I'll forget what I saw on the boat, and the lump on my head, but I'll never work for you."

He said. "I guess that'll have to do, but you should be aware, detective, that we take a man's word very seriously. You do not want to find out what will happen if we put our trust in you, and you betray us."

"Please spare me the threats and get to the part where you tell me what the argument on the dock was about." Joanna had sat down again and now leaned in, chin in hand, waiting for him to answer.

He leaned back and asked as though he was bored, "Why the argument?" He glanced at Joanna, to show her that he was allowing her to hear this. "Well, Mac had changed. At some point in the past year, the guy stopped caring about appearances. This kind of thinking does not fly at Indian Head. Mac's drinking and ..." He paused and eyed Joanna again, but this time it was to say, 'you asked for it,' "his whoring had gotten out of control after his marriage to Beth fell apart. In recent months, he was too conspicuous with his, ah, activities. We, Nate Sterling and I, advised him to tone it down, and he wasn't open to our advice."

"But Mac wasn't married. Why should you care what, or who, he was with?"

"Because, several of his, ah, partners are married, and in some cases, to other prominent members of Indian Head."

"Who?"

He took a deep breath. "You're going to have to find that out on your own. I'm not airing their dirty laundry."

"That's not helpful," said Joanna.

His attitude was pissing me off, so I decided to poke him. Plus, I was showing off for Joanna. "I understand you and Mac had long been in competition for Endicott's affections. Endicott just made another hundred million, maybe a hundred and forty, if he gets his hands on the dear widow's money. Getting rid of the competition and having Endicott and his pile of money all to one's self, smells like motive to these nostrils." I sniffed.

"Nonsense. Mac was my friend and that money means nothing to me. I have no spouse, and no heirs, aside from a couple of prize-winning French bulldogs, Mr. Town, and I have more money than I could ever spend."

It was a good retort, so I said, "Who do you think did it?"

"I have no idea. Besides, I'm not in the business of doing other people's jobs for them."

"Yeah, I heard that one before," I said. "From your pal Endicott."

"Look, what if I'm wrong? You're the detective, you figure it out."

"What about the husbands? Might one of them have found out and become enraged?"

"Maybe," he paused, "but this sort of thing isn't uncommon around here. We don't fly into a rage and kill one another, we get back by having our own affairs out of spite." He looked at Joanna again, and I think she blushed a little.

"How about men?" I asked.

"What do you mean?"

"Was Mac only into ladies?"

He smiled. "Despite my best efforts back in the day, yes, Mac loved only women."

"What happened after the argument?"

"Mac left in a huff. He went out to the Rebecca, presumably to sleep it off. We commiserated for a few minutes then went our separate ways. I went home. I assume the others did too, but you'd have to ask them."

"Was Mac alone when he went out to the boat?"

"Yes. Look, I've got a commitment this evening." He stood, signaled the chef that he was leaving, and then shouted, "Charge this all to me, with a healthy tip for your fine staff, Andre."

He turned back to face us. "Here's my card. You can reach me at this number anytime. We have a deal, now. You need to remember that."

"That sounds like a threat, Gibby."

"It is. Try the flan before you go, it's amazing." He began to walk toward the back door.

I said, "I want to speak with Endicott again."

He stopped and said, "I'll arrange something." Then he disappeared into the alley.

"What's this about a deal?" asked Joanna.

I turned and looked her in the eye. "He said he'd only answer my questions if I agreed not to pursue him and the others for hiding the body."

"Did you mean it?"

"Absolutely, not."

24

I awoke the next morning wondering what the hell I was doing back at the Extended Stay, before recalling the events of the prior day. I lay there and considered my next move, which would probably be to call French and pressure him to get me another audience with his holiness, Whitman Endicott.

My phone flashed, and I grabbed it off the nightstand and squinted at the screen. I had two voicemails.

The first was from Maria Moore at 7:45 am. "Mr. Town. I'm letting you down on that name you asked for. I haven't turned up anything yet, but I've got a few other people to talk to. Just wanted to let you know, I'm trying. Call me if I can be of help with anything in the meantime." I didn't need her help anymore. French told me the other woman was Caroline Ferncroft. I could call back and let her know, but I decided not to. Maybe she'd be able to confirm it was Caroline, or maybe she'd come back with a different name. Maybe French hadn't been on the level with me.

The second message was decidedly more satisfying. It was Tinsley Saunders. "Rise and shine, Earl. Call me when you get this. I woke up with an itch, and you're the man to scratch it." Like one of Pavlov's pups, I called her back immediately and arranged it. It now seemed safe to assume she was working on behalf of French and Endicott, so there was a risk in meeting her. But it was one of the few pursuable leads I had, and I liked the idea of scratching her itch, regardless of her motivations. Some jobs come with perks like paid vacation days and others, well ...

I quickly showered and dressed while humming "Good Day Sunshine," and so Joanna wouldn't intercept me, I slipped quietly out of my room and waited until I was well away from the hotel before sending her a text to tell her I would be tied up for the morning, perhaps to a bedpost. I also told her I'd left my keys at the front desk, so she could get about while I was gone. I walked a couple blocks up the road to a little park where I waited for Tinsley.

She pulled up in a cream-colored circa 1980's Mercedes 450SL. She had the top down, wore oversized cream sunglasses to match the car, red lipstick, and a smile. The wheels of the SL passed within inches of me, and she swung the passenger door open and said: "Hey there cowboy!"

A sleeveless lacey white dress showed off her tan legs from thigh to red patent leather heel. I slid into the passenger-side bucket wearing my best smile, she popped the clutch, and off we went.

"Where are you taking me?" I asked as she worked through the gears. She knew how to handle a stick. Women like her usually do.

"It's a surprise," she said. Her hair was back in a ponytail, but there was a little chunk that had gotten free and was blowing around her chin, and every so often she'd reach up and move it back, only to have it return. She moved with the same fluid motion each time.

"When did you stop dancing?" I asked, showing off.

We were slowing to turn, and she turned and eyed me. "What makes you think I was a dancer?"

"The way you move. Like the way, you brush the hair from your face. It's the same precise movement every time. You made a few moves the other night too."

"You," she punched me in the arm. I hadn't been slugged like that in a long time. It brought my mind back to a girl named Patty and the summer before the sixth grade.

She drove us downtown, near where we'd dined the prior evening, and again we went in through the back door or at least pulled up to it. She turned into an alley that brought us to a service road behind a strip of shops and restaurants. She stopped and tooted the horn.

"What is this place?" I asked. We were a few feet from a back entrance, but from back here there was nothing to indicate what it was.

"The Blue Bird," she answered as we watched an adolescent boy emerge from a door carrying an oversized wicker picnic basket. He smiled, Tinsley nodded, and he gently placed it in the back seat.

Tinsley handed him a few bills and said, "Give the extra to your mother, Jorge, and tell her I better see her tomorrow."

"Si," was all he had time to say before she threw it in gear and peeled out of there. A minute later we turned back on the main road and headed towards the Sound.

"Wow, I can't imagine someone in Southie doing that for me. Does his mother work for you?"

"Yes and no. Getting good help is not easy around here. These people want the world. I just need someone to clean my house and look after my kids, not another dependent."

"You have kids?"

"Yes, two. Does that surprise you?"

"Yeah. I don't want to see them get hurt."

"Hurt? You think I'm falling in love with you, Earl?"

"No, of course not."

"Do you think you're my only breakfast-buddy?"

"No, I don't think that either."

"Then let's enjoy the morning, big fella, and leave the worrying about things you can't control for another time." She turned on the radio. It was tuned to opera, an Italian tenor, which, in that car, and that town, with that girl, seemed perfect.

She turned onto the road that would take us to Indian Head Point, and I said: "I'm not sure the Commodore is going to want to see my face at the club. He did have me arrested for assault yesterday." I caught her eye, and added, "If that's where we're going?"

She threw her head back and laughed. No response, just laughter. I turned up the music, and we headed towards Indian Head, but then Tinsley hung a left-hand turn about a mile and a half before the point and drove us into a large marina called Bob's Yacht Yard. She parked the SL in a dirt lot near the water's edge.

"Grab the basket and follow me," she said as she climbed out.

We walked onto a long dock that connected us to four other docks, some of which had docks attached to them as well. Anywhere from 8 to 10 boats – sail, motor, cabin cruiser – were moored to either side of each one. There must have been at least eighty crafts in all. At the far end of the main dock was a small wooden shack. That's where Tinsley led us.

Inside was a young man of maybe 20. He wore jeans and sandals under a white t-shirt with B.Y.Y. across the front. Tinsley walked right up and waved two twenty-dollar bills between his eyes and the cell phone that was consuming all of his attention.

She said, "Good morning, Junior. I need a boat for a couple of hours."

Without looking up from the screen, he palmed the cash, pointed past Tinsley and said, "Dock seven, slip three." At that point, he finally gazed up at us and added, "My shift ends at noon. I need it back by then."

"And you shall have it," said Tinsley, and off we went to find our ride.

As we were looking for our ride, I said, "So, I guess this is where the local riff-raff park their yachts."

"You could say that," she said with a giggle.

"I'm surprised Indian Head management hasn't found a way to keep this stretch of the Sound exclusive to it membership."

"Oh, it's not for want of trying," she said.

A minute later we were on a small craft motoring towards the Rebecca and the other big yachts anchored around Indian Head Point.

"So, I take it this is a backdoor into Indian Head?" I said, not really asking.

She laughed, gripped my biceps, and whispered in my ear. "It comes in very handy."

"How many people know about it?" I asked.

"I don't know. Mac introduced me to it. I'm sure I'm not the only woman he's told about it." She laughed and steered the small aluminum craft towards Indian Head Point, which was a short ride from the cove that was home to Bob's Yacht Yard.

We glided towards a sailboat similar in design to the Rebecca, but smaller, maybe 50 feet in length. The name on the hull read Every Boy's Dream, which seemed quite fitting.

"We're here," said Tinsley as she expertly guided us up to the stern. And so, we were.

❊ ❊ ❊

"This is yours?" I asked as I followed her down inside the cabin. There was a small galley to my left, where I placed the basket on a table in a dining nook. Straight ahead was a short hallway, on one side of which was a door. From what I'd learned on Monday night, I assumed one of these would be a pantry and the other a small bath. Beyond the doors, each side had a set of bunk beds tucked in behind curtains and at the end of the hall was a master bedroom, which in this craft was just large enough for a queen-sized bed.

"Yes, it belonged to my father-in-law. We acquired it a few years back."

"Acquired it?"

"Yes, when the old man succumbed to cancer."

"I see. About your husband?" I inquired.

Tinsley wrapped her arms around me and pressed herself against my back. She breathed warmly in my ear and placed her hands on my hips, then, she slowly slid her fingers along my stomach and up to my chest. She pulled me tighter and brushed her hair against my neck. She smelled like a tropical island. I realized I'd craved the scent since our last encounter.

"There you go, worrying again," she said. "He flew to Los Angeles yesterday and won't be home for days, and I've got to get that boat back before noon, so we better get to eating."

She turned me around to face her, pressed her mouth up to my ear and whispered, "Shall we start with an appetizer?" As she said this, she took my wrists and moved my hands to her behind.

"Sure," I replied while giving each taut cheek a squeeze. "What have you got in mind?"

She backed me up against the table, then reached around me into the picnic basket. She bit her bottom lip, stared into my eyes and extracted an aluminum canister.

"Whipped cream," I said. "Okay. It's dairy, that's a good way to start the day." She giggled and dropped to her knees. Then she set down the cannister, unbuckled my pants, and liberated me from my briefs. She looked up at me and watched as I swelled in her grasp. She stared straight into my eyes, placed the cap of the whipped cream between her teeth, tore it off, and spit it onto the floor.

She said, "Have I told you how much it turns me on that you carry a gun?"

I looked down into her big brown eyes and said, "But that's not my Glock you're holding."

"Oh, you're right, it's not," she said as she squirted a line of sweet sticky cream from the base to the tip. "But, you know," she purred and licked a good bit of it off, "it sure looks locked and loaded."

❋ ❋ ❋

We feasted on the rest of the basket's contents after finally finishing with our appetizer. She'd bought us a terrific spread, no pun intended. Buttery croissants and fresh jam, perfectly scrambled eggs, bacon, a mix of fresh fruit and cheeses, and a pot of coffee which we warmed on the ship's stovetop.

"I'm beginning to smell like sour milk," I said sniffing the air. "Please tell me there's a shower on this boat."

"There is," she said with a twinkle in her eye, "It'll be tight, but it can hold both of us."

"I'm all about conserving water," I said.

As I was dressing après-shower, I decided it was time to get the other thing I came for.

"You are something else," I said as I wrapped my arms around her and looked at the two of us in the mirror. I nibbled on her ear a little and breathed in the scent in her hair. She squealed and pushed me away. We were behaving like a couple of love-struck teenagers, even though we both knew this was the end of the affair. And, that there was nothing real about it any of it, except the part that is primal and more about satisfying an urge than any emotional linkage. It actually felt good to pretend, even if just for a few fleeting moments, that I was in love again.

"Were you a volleyball player back in the day?"

She stopped and eyed me in the mirror. "That's an odd question, detective." She applied lipstick. "No, tennis and sailing are my sports. You should see me on the water. Oh, you already did."

"Yeah, you're pretty good on a boat," I said.

"Hey," she laughed and punched me in the arm.

"You didn't tell me that was Beth MacArthur's apartment the other night. You should've seen the looks on the faces of the cops when I opened the door." She didn't react, so I went on. "You two must be good friends. Have you known her long?"

She stood and asked me to zip her up. I did, and she turned around and pulled me against her. "So many questions. You're going to spoil my mood." She gave me pouty face.

"How long?"

She sighed, "About ten years, I guess. We met at the club. We sail together." She paused. "Well, we used to, not so much now that she spends more time in Boston."

"Boston?" I asked. "I thought she lived in Manhattan. Why is she in Boston?"

Tinsley moved past me into the galley. She avoided my stare and spoke with her back turned to me. "Working, I guess." She turned to me and smiled. "She works with all kinds of charities, you know. She's a busy girl, no time for fun anymore. That's not the life for me."

Itch scratched, Tinsley moved fast now, and we soon emerged from the cabin into another beautiful day. "Here, give me the basket and untie us," she said, stepping down into our borrowed boat.

I climbed aboard and released the mooring. We started off, her expertly steering the small outboard motor again. I sat down on the bench across from her and admired the mansions along the shore. "What was said on the dock the Saturday before last? You know what I mean. I need to hear the truth."

She laughed and said, "That's a lot of drama, Earl. It was nothing, just another argument like any other night. In case you haven't noticed, we're not always the nicest lot of people."

"Yeah, I noticed nobody seems to care much about the guy who was murdered a few hours later. If they did, maybe somebody would tell me the truth."

"You want the truth? I gave you the truth last night. I gave you Gibson French."

"What does that mean? Are you saying he killed Mac?"

I could read her disappointment in me, even through her sunglasses. "I thought this was settled." She said. "Aren't you working for him now?"

"How would you know anything about that? And, no, I'm not working for him. I don't want his money. He and his pals are going to jail if I can help it. I want to find Mac's killer. If you've got information that could help me ..."

"You know, Earl," she was leaning back guiding the boat as though it was just another day on the Sound, and she wasn't discussing the murder of her lover with a private detective. "No matter what you do, he's not coming back. I'd like to find his killer too, but you'd better be careful, things are more complicated around here than you think."

"Warnings!" I looked up at the sky. "That's all I get from these people." We were quickly approaching Bob's, and Tinsley was running out the clock on me.

"What do you mean things are complicated?"

She shook her head and sighed, disgusted with my inability to understand that the rules of elite society were more important than punishing those responsible for extinguishing the life of one of its members. "Sometimes the truth makes things worse, Earl. Leaving well enough alone is the better way forward."

Now I shook my head.

She lifted her arms and spread them wide, "Life is good here, Earl. Please don't fuck it up. Play nice and let us be."

We arrived as she made her appeal, and she pointed to the mooring. I grabbed hold and pulled us up to the dock. She killed the motor, picked up the picnic basket and jumped out. She waited until I climbed up and said, "I'm sorry, Earl, but this is where this, well, you know the rest. I've got some things I need to do now, and I'm not going to be able to drive you back. You can get a ride, right?"

I've been dumped before, but this was exceptional. I held up my phone. "Yeah, I'm good."

She smiled, then turned and walked to the SL. As she sauntered off, I took a shot and shouted, "Rebecca!" She didn't turn around. Within thirty seconds, she had ripped out of the lot and driven out of sight.

The kid she'd called Junior had come out of his shack and recorded our split on his phone. From over my shoulder, I heard him say, "Man, that's gotta sting. Now uploading to YouTube, title: Dump City."

25

I dialed Joanna, thinking she'd come and save me from the effects of being literally left in Tinsley's dust, but she didn't answer. I was a good five miles from the hotel. I considered calling a cab or an Uber, but of course, I'd never used Uber before. Who was I kidding? I had no idea how to use Uber. I texted Joanna and decided to hoof it until she called back, after convincing myself it wouldn't be long.

Before leaving, I quizzed Junior about the informal boat rental service and more importantly, if the service was running on the Saturday night before last. He said a guy named Miggy, as in Miguel, worked Friday through Sunday nights starting at 11:00 pm. I asked for a number, he said he didn't have one. Miggy was mysterious but reliable. If I wanted to talk to him, I'd have to return that night. I tried Joanna again with the same result and set out on foot.

After about twenty minutes of baking in the afternoon sun, I was looking for a shady place to sit and call a cab, when a familiar black Caprice rolled up.

Sullivan gripped the wheel. Garcia rode shotgun. Both wore aviator sunglasses and a look of disdain. The car stopped, and Garcia's window came down. She motioned with her head for me to get in back. Inside, both temperature and atmosphere were decidedly cool.

Garcia spoke first. "Out for a stroll, are we?"

"Yeah, it's a nice day, why not?"

"Odd though," she began, "that you're here in Greenwich when my partner and I made clear that you were off this case."

I used a handkerchief to wipe the dust from my brow, then my loafers and said nothing.

"Well, Mr. Town. I believe, and I sincerely hope for your sake that you agree, you owe us an explanation, as to just what it is you are doing in Greenwich, and only a few miles from Indian Head Point."

She hadn't looked at me yet. She stared straight ahead with an occasional glance at Sully, who had begun driving west, towards my hotel.

"Well," I began, but she cut me off.

"Before you explain, Mr. Town, I'd just like to recommend that you don't try to bullshit us, because ..., well, I'll just leave it at because."

"Have you guys really taken a close look at Gibson French? You know, if I were still on the case, I'd look into him."

"Stay on topic," warned Garcia. "Why are you in Greenwich?"

I looked out the window at the signs of wealth everywhere around us, and I told them the truth, which seemed the only chance I had to keep them from following through on their threats and yanking my license. I wasn't even being paid, yet I was risking my livelihood. In other words, I was behaving like a total jackass, and it was time to do what I had to, to keep my job.

"Old dogs like me don't get cases like this every day, I have to do a lot of insurance work to make ends meet. It's not good for the ego, and I drink too much as a result. I thought that if I could crack this one, maybe I'd get better cases and not have to work insurance fraud and cheating spouses anymore. That's why I'm here." I continued to stare out the window, not wanting to look either of them in the eye.

Neither of them said anything, which I took to be a good sign. I'd expected Sullivan to jump down my throat.

He crossed the city line and passed the Extended Stay, where, I noted, the Caprice was still parked. He hung a right at a set of lights, then another right a minute later. We were on an old country lane now. There was a field to our left and a small general store and classic white-steepled New England church to our right. Sullivan steered the car into an empty lot in front of the church and parked. The old building sat proud as a peacock, perched on a hillside, the sun's rays shimmering on its steeple. Above it was a flawless blue sky. Behind it stretched a hillside smothered in deep crimson and ochre leaves fluttering in the breeze atop a grove of oaks and maples. I'd grown accustomed to the city, but I missed the country. Fall in New England is magic.

Under a large maple on the back edge of the lot sat two picnic tables. Sullivan killed the engine, and they slid out. I waited until Garcia opened my door, as there were no handles in the back. They took a seat on the far side bench, and I sat facing them, as far from Sullivan's reach as I could get without looking too paranoid.

"Gee, this isn't out of the way or anything," I said. They didn't find me funny. "Fine," I said and waited for one of them to take the lead. This time it was Sullivan.

"I want to get something clear. You're a pain in the ass, and I'm on the verge of charging you with obstructing justice. For a retired cop, you show no respect for the FB-fucking-I. We're Federal agents, fuck-face, we've told you twice to get lost, and you've ignored our orders." He paused and glanced at Garcia. Her lips were pursed, and she appeared to be glaring at me, but I couldn't be sure. She was still wearing shades. He cleared his throat and went on.

"However, that being said." He gazed up at the little bits of cloud-less blue sky that poked through the leaf canopy and continued, "although you sure as shit don't deserve a break, you may have infor-mation that could help us in a serious matter, which means if you cooperate with us, you might stay out of jail today." I smiled. Things were suddenly looking up.

"And you want my help?" I asked.

"Some people in the agency believe that you can be of assistance to us in this investigation. I have my doubts."

I said, "So, you want me to lay my cards on the table, and you'll do what?" I looked from one to the other. "You'll not take my license? I ap-preciate the ride, but I'm not spilling my guts to you."

Garcia chimed in. "That's what you said on Tuesday and again yes-terday, right before you spilled your guts. However, we are willing to go Dutch today."

"Really?" I said, leery. "Then, I'll tell you what, you two buy the first round, and we'll see if that loosens my inhibitions." Garcia shook her head dismissively, so I added, "I'll tell you one thing, though, I'm not a cheap date."

Sullivan started to speak, and I cut him off. "Why were you two fol-lowing Joanna in a Wayne Trust car?"

Sullivan looked around, leaned in and said, "We were brought in to investigate the disappearance of James MacArthur. Our contacts are a senior executive of Wayne Trust and a partner in a law firm that rep-resents Wayne Trust in a range of matters. I cannot name names."

"Yeah, I got it, Endicott and French. Why did they *really* bring you in?"

"We believe they were getting heat from the firm they were in merger talks with. After several days without MacArthur taking part, they were forced to admit to the other side that he was missing." He picked at something on the table, collected his thoughts and went on. "Now, they couldn't tell the executives of, what is it, Garcia?" She took a small notebook from her inside pocket, opened it, and said, "JKB SA."

Sullivan thanked her and went on. "They couldn't tell JKB FU, or whatever, he was missing and not get the authorities involved. A firm the size of JKD, S ...whatever, has contacts within law enforcement. So, Endicott and French used some leverage they had within our organization to get someone assigned to it, and we drew the assignment. This way when JK ...the company checked, they knew Wayne Trust wasn't bullshitting. MacArthur was legitimately missing, and the FBI was on the case. They could've walked away from the deal, but why leave money on the table. They focused on the negotiation and left us to find him."

So, there was no bigger case? That was bullshit?

Sullivan smirked at me, Garcia looked bored.

"So, you were following Joanna in a Beamer, why?"

"It wasn't just her. There were others who are more familiar with fine automobiles being parked outside their million-dollar condos, than squad cars."

I recalled Tinsley's comment about Beth spending so much time in Boston and realized that she must also have been under observation. She may have been a drama queen, but she was right. She was being watched, and from the comfort of a fine German automobile.

Sullivan said. "Don't blame us for your wrong assumptions. You also came up with that theory about Mac bringing us into this. I didn't want to ruin your little fantasy with the truth. You can take the detective out of New Hampshire, but ... well, you know the rest."

Garcia cleared her throat, then spoke. "Your round, Town. What did French tell you over dinner last night? All of it."

"I don't think he or Endicott killed him. He said he wants two things from me: to forget what I know about them stashing Mac in the fridge, and to find his killer. They say they'll even help me with the second one, in return for my cooperation on the first one. Though, the more I think about it, the less sure I am they want me to succeed at the second one. I think they want all of it to go away and would pay me well to make that happen. I'm insisting on the second one. Your round again. Why were you watching Joanna, specifically?"

"Simple, she was his Girl Friday. If anyone would lead us to him, it would be her. Until the body turned up yesterday morning, we were under the impression he was still alive, and just hiding out to scuttle the merger."

"Why would he want to scuttle the merger?"

"It was a theory floated by Endicott, he said Mac thought they could get more if they waited for a second bidder."

"Does he have a motive for murder? I haven't found one."

"Sorry, your round," Sullivan said. He looked at Garcia, and she went next. "Tell us what you know about Tinsley Saunders. Leave out the carnal knowledge."

"That's the best part, but okay," I began. "Tinsley is rich, beautiful, cultured, and obviously using me. She is acting as a spy for Endicott and probably French, and possibly sowing disinformation. I met with her this morning to try and get some answers, but she's a woman of few words, aside from pillow talk, in which she's a real pro."

"You said sowing disinformation; what do you mean?"

"Well, she and Beth have both suggested that French is involved in Mac's murder. They seem to want me to pin this on him. Would either of you happen to know why they want French to take the rap?"

Sullivan smiled. "That is the right question. How about that Garcia? He got one right."

The left side of Garcia's mouth twitched, and I said, "I saw that Garcia." Turning back to Sullivan, I added, "Saying I asked the right question is nice, but I'm also gonna need you to answer it."

"Well, we found that upon his passing, MacArthur directed his estate be split among immediate family, including his mother and a couple of siblings. His father is dead. This will be done through a series of trusts that were established through some fancy-ass family money manager based in Boca Raton. Elizabeth MacArthur was bequeathed MacArthur's holdings in Wayne Trust, which, as you probably know, increased exponentially with the merger."

"Yeah, I got it so far," I announced. "You still haven't really answered my question."

"Fine," he sighed. "It's come to our attention that there are bylaws at Wayne Trust pertaining to the allocation of equity in the event of the death of a general partner. Of which there are two. Ah, were two. Now there's Endicott. MacArthur was the other. In the case of Mac's death, two-thirds of his stock automatically transfer to Endicott. They set it up this way so that one of two of them would always maintain control of the company. The transfer worked the other way too if Endicott passed first."

I whistled. "So that means Beth loses forty of her sixty-million-dollar inheritance to him. So, why are they pointing at French and not Endicott?"

"Your turn, Town. Has MacArthur or Saunders suggested a motive, or mentioned evidence they have on French?"

"No. Beth MacArthur told me Mac warned her that if something happened to him, French would likely be behind it. Apparently, he also told her to watch out for her inheritance, so make of that what you will." Garcia had taken out a notebook and begun scribbling from time to time, while Sully nodded and stroked his chin. "For her part, Tinsley suggested that French was the answer to all my questions, whatever that means."

"Have you spoken with Beth MacArthur?" I asked.

"No, we've tried, but she's evasive. We obviously need to soon."

"I'd say so."

Garcia cut in. "And, Miss Saunders? She must have done more than just cast aspersions on French."

"The last night anyone saw Mac alive, there was an argument on the dock at Indian Head, between Mac, French, and Sterling. Tinsley Saunders was also there, along with another woman that I've yet to I.D." I looked at each of them to see if they knew about the argument. They did not. I held off on telling them the other woman was Caroline because I wanted to talk to her first.

"When did you ascertain this, Town?" I'd held onto this information when they grilled me yesterday morning.

"In the last twenty-four." He gave me the stink eye but said nothing more on the subject. I quickly moved on. "Yesterday, Tinsley met Joanna and me at the Greenwich P.D. She walked us to a restaurant where French ..."

Sullivan interjected. "Wait a minute. Greenwich P.D. You want to fill us in on why you were there, Town?"

"I decided to speak with Commodore Sterling, and he wasn't interested in conversing, so he called the cops on us."

"You weren't spotted at the club yesterday. Where did you speak with Sterling?"

"At his mansion in Belle Haven."

"You went around us, and against our orders," said Sullivan, shaking his head. Garcia rolled her eyes.

"Sorry, some things can't be helped," I said, as though that'd make it okay. "So, French was our get out of jail free card, and had Tinsley wait for us and bring us to him at a restaurant a few blocks from the police station. That's when he asked me to work for him. Anyway, when I asked Tinsley to tell me the truth about the argument on the dock, and who the other woman was, she told me that she gave me the truth when she handed me off to Gibson French." I paused and threw my hands in the air. "I don't know what the hell that means, but when I pressed her on it... Well, I ended up walking home. Next round is yours. "Why French, instead of Endicott?"

Sullivan replied. "The belief is that she is building the case for a civil suit that will get her the forty-million back. French is both counsel for Wayne Trust and chief confidant to Endicott. If he takes the rap, Beth will say Endicott conspired with French to acquire Mac's stock on the eve of a merger that would triple its value. She'll have one hell of a case. There's not much of a criminal case against him, so far, but if that also comes together, a civil suit will soon follow, and would be a lay-up for the kind of lawyers Beth MacArthur can afford to hire."

"Yes, but you didn't answer my question. Why not just smear Endicott?"

"He has a terrific alibi for the time of the murder. As you said yourself, Tinsley Saunders was there the night of the argument. She likely figured French doesn't have an alibi as it's pretty well known he lives alone. She's also reportedly sleeping with Endicott."

Just then my phone rang, and I looked at the screen and then at the two Feds. "It's a Manhattan area code. I should take this."

They looked at one another, then Garcia said, "Go ahead."

"Mr. Town, this is Whit Endicott."

"Mr. Endicott." I looked from Garcia's eyes to Sullivan's, as they sat, ears perked.

"We need to talk."

"Well, I've got a few minutes now, shoot," I said.

"Not over the phone. Where are you? I'll send a car to get you."

"Oh, that's very generous, but I'd prefer that we meet someplace public. Last time I was alone with one of your guys, I got my head beaten in."

"Have you forgotten about breaking my man's arm yesterday?"

His voice was loud enough for Sullivan and Garcia to hear, and Sullivan raised his eyebrows. Garcia looked intrigued, maybe even a little turned on, or so I imagined. I shrugged it off like I had no idea what Endicott was talking about.

"Ah, well none the less, I think a meeting on neutral ground is best."

Endicott said, "I'll be in touch," and hung up.

"What'd he say?" asked Sullivan.

"He'll be in touch."

"He wants to buy you off," he said. "You were smart not to take French's money. They are gonna raise the stakes. This could've been the most profitable case you ever worked. That is if you hadn't been honest with us. Now, if you take the money and clam up, I'll nail you to the cross."

"Yeah, yeah. I got it. You're lucky I've been so open. You should be thanking me instead of handing out threats."

"Look." I held up my phone, which showed that Joanna had called while I was on the line with Endicott. "I need to get back to my client, or former client."

"You need to call us as soon as you speak with Endicott. We want to document that meeting."

We got back in the car and drove to a diner a few miles from the Extended Stay, where they dropped me off. Joanna arrived in the Caprice about ten minutes later.

26

J oanna slid over to the passenger seat so I could get behind the wheel. She looked a little yellow around the gills, and I thought she might have come down with something.

I started to put it in reverse when I heard a man's voice from the back seat.

"I have a Remington 870 pump pointed at the back of your head. You keep your hands on the wheel until I say you can move them. Otherwise, I take your head clean off. You got me?"

"Yes." I croaked. I glanced at Joanna, and now I realized what she had a case of – fear of imminent death.

"I'm sorry," she said, but he cut her off.

"You shut up, and do what I say, or you're both dead. Now reach into his jacket and remove his gun. Do it by the handle, if your finger touches the trigger, I'll blow both your heads off."

I said, "My hands are not going to move from the wheel, and she's not going to try anything. You just relax." A single teardrop formed in the corner of Joanna's left eye and ran down her cheek, as she fumbled about with my lapel. I held my breath, afraid to move at all while she reached for my weapon.

"Keep talking," he said. "See where that gets you."

Joanna shakily removed my Glock and handed it over the seat. I caught a glimpse in the rearview, and it was McNierney's associate from the gala the other night, the little guy with the clipboard. He didn't look like much to worry about on the street, but now that he was pointing a shotgun at the back of my head, he somehow seemed more formidable. Once he secured my Glock, he had Joanna take my phone and hand that over. Then he ordered me to drive north.

"Take a left out of here and drive until I tell you to turn. Keep your mouth shut, and maybe you'll make it out of this car alive." We drove for a good thirty minutes. Eventually, the houses began to thin out and be replaced by forest and meadow. At one point I heard a crack and watched as the little thug bent my new phone until it shattered, then threw it out of the window. I'd had the thing for just about twenty-four hours and wondered if destruction by kidnapper was covered under warranty.

As I drove, I considered how foolish I'd been not checking the back seat. Now, I'd put myself and my client, whom I had insisted on not paying me, in a terrible situation. She'd practically gone catatonic on the drive. Every so often, out of the corner of my eye, I'd catch a glint of reflected sunlight as tears ran down her face.

We'd left Greenwich several miles back when clipboard guy told me to slow down. "It's up here on the right. Go slow and look for a dirt road."

I did as I was told and soon we were driving on a rough dirt track through thick woods. We drove on the old trail for 1.4 miles, according to the odometer, before I caught sight of a large black object up ahead. As we got closer, I realized it was a Mercedes Sprinter Van, or as had I learned on a prior case, it was a high-tech office on wheels for today's rich business guys.

To my everlasting dismay, the very large gentlemen who had removed me from Endicott's office not even 48 hours before, emerged from behind the van and stood in the center of the dirt road with a hand up in the universal symbol for stop, which I did. Though I would've gladly run his big ass over if not for the 12-gauge pointed at my cerebellum.

Clipboard guy spoke from the backseat. "Turn off the engine, leave the keys, and get out. Then do what he tells you, or don't, it'll be fun watching him tear you apart."

He had to be pushing seven feet in height, and somewhere in the neighborhood of four hundred pounds, but he wasn't fat. He was a solid mass of muscle, a brute force and I wondered where Endicott had found him. An SEC college football program seemed likely.

I shut off the engine, left the keys and started to open my door, and Joanna did the same. "Not you," the man in the backseat said to Joanna. "The skirt stays here."

I told her, "Don't worry, it's gonna be okay." Then I told him, "Lay a hand on her, and it'll be the last thing you do."

He laughed and said, "I'll do what I want, you're in no position to make rules."

I gave Joanna's hand a squeeze and stepped out.

The giant had pale skin and brown hair cut to military length and symmetry, seated on top of a big pumpkin-shaped head, with small, dark, eyes. He wore a voluminous navy jacket over gray pants. He spoke few words, but when he did, his accent suggested Eastern European, probably Russian.

He approached as I slowly extracted myself from the Caprice keeping my hands where they could be seen at all times, so as to keep my head. The giant towered over me. He grabbed me by the throat and lifted me off the ground with only his left hand, then slammed me against the side of the van and proceeded with a very rough pat down.

When I said, "easy there, big fella," he responded by placing his right hand on the top of my head and squeezing until I thought my skull would crack. His grip stretched from just above my eyes to the nape of my neck, and I felt like a basketball about to be dunked. He said, "You be quiet, or I make you be quiet."

Upon not finding any weapons, he said, "Okay. Come around to back. Don't run, or I'll catch you and snap your neck." He said this with a big toothy smile.

I caught a reflection of the Caprice in the van's window. Joanna was still in front, looking scared while clipboard guy remained in back, gun barrel resting on the top of the seat. He was saying something, his mouth close to her left ear. Her face read disgust, as well as fear.

I carefully made my way to the back of the van and waited as the giant gripped the miniature-looking door handle in his huge paw and pulled it open. Whitman Endicott was sitting inside, legs crossed in a comfortable-looking leather captain's chair.

"Mr. Town. I'm so glad you could meet with me in the place of my choosing after all. Arranging a kidnapping on the fly took some doing, but where there's a will."

He waved to the giant and said, "Bring him with you and shut the door." The big man gave me a shove, and I tripped up into the van, followed closely by my big new buddy. I could stand up straight in the surprisingly spacious and well-appointed vehicle, but the giant had to hunch over.

The van was long, and there was a good five feet between Endicott and me. The seats for driver and passenger were just beyond him. There was no one else in the van. I wondered if Sterling and French knew he was doing this.

The giant pushed me down into a captain's chair across from Endicott and then handed something to his boss, which I soon realized was my holster and Glock. Endicott said, "Thank you, Boris."

"B-, Boris, is that really his name?" I asked, before realizing the danger of getting my head squished for speaking out of turn. I instinctively leaned away from the giant.

Endicott smiled at me. "Yes, do you find that strange?"

"No," I insisted. "Not at all." I leaned back in my seat, which was encased in soft, rich Italian leather, and featured an array of buttons and sliders on its side.

Endicott pulled my gun from its holster and held it in his small hands. He was playing the role of a casual male today, being dressed in a forest green windbreaker, blue jeans, and running shoes. He wore a pair of aviator sunglasses, perhaps because he couldn't look me in the eye. The glasses and the gun made him look sinister, despite the short legs, and general prep-school vibe he was giving off.

He looked me over, then got to the point. "You should've kept up your side of the deal you made with Gibson last night."

"I am keeping up my side."

"Shut the fuck up!" He placed his finger on the Glock's trigger and depressed it enough to disengage the safety, then pointed it at me. "You chose to literally spend the morning screwing around and mouthing off about how you are going to put us in jail." Tinsley had gone right to him after she left me. Thinking with my dick was actually going to be the end of me. Honestly, thinking back on that moment, I was kind of alright with it. There are worse things to die for than an encounter on a sailboat with a woman like Tinsley Saunders.

I tried to reason with him. "Well, yes but I didn't mean what I said." Endicott looked past me to Boris, and all at once everything went black. Boris had slammed the right slide of my head with one of his big open hands, and I blacked out for several seconds. If he had made a fist, he'd have killed me. I came to, tried to shake the cobwebs out, and get my vision back. I watched through blurry eyes as Whit Endicott laughed hysterically at my plight. When I had regained some semblance of consciousness, he warned me that the next time I spoke out of turn would be my last time. I turned and looked at Boris. He smiled at me again, and I realized he had caps too, and I had a vision of him behind the wheel of a Hummer, his enormous head sticking up out of the moonroof.

"As I was saying, Mr. Town. You chose sex over life. I had originally planned to make you one more offer. One you couldn't refuse, but I've realized that you just have too damn much integrity to ever take me up on it, so I'm afraid that your work here is done. It's a shame to have to eliminate Joanna as well. I always envied Mac for bedding her. I tried, you know, several times, and the bitch fought me off. Actually, today just may be my lucky day. Third time's the charm, eh?" He laughed again, and I wanted to kill him more than anything I'd ever wanted. Except for Roxy, that is.

I looked over at Boris. He was sitting to my right, in another captain's chair. It looked like a child's playset underneath him. There were four captain's chairs in the van – two on each side – with room for a table between them, but that was folded up against the wall, leaving the space open. Boris was just out of my reach, but his arms were so long, he only had to get halfway out of his seat to crush my face with a left hook.

I looked at Endicott and made my appeal. "You're wrong about me. I'll take the deal."

"The deal is off the table. You missed the final sale."

"You're going after her stock, aren't you? Otherwise, you would've gotten rid of the body. Without it, you couldn't trigger the stock transfer. You're going to take forty-million of Beth's inheritance. Which one of you killed him? French? Is he getting a share?"

This intrigued Endicott and bought me a little time. He leaned back and considered me for a while before surprising me with his response.

"You're not very good at this, are you? You really believe we killed him? I assure you, we did not. I loved the man. We all did, and I'm quite certain he would've been fine with me taking that money from his *ex*-wife. You're not entirely wrong, though. I did tell Nate to make sure Mac would be found. You know, once the deal was done."

He paused and felt the weight of my gun in his hands. "I've never killed anyone before, which makes this all the more fun. But I'm troubled by something." He smiled, more sweet than sinister.

He said, "I can't decide if I should shoot you with your own gun or have Boris crush the life out of you. On the one hand, shooting you with your own gun would be so cinematic. Like in a great spaghetti western. I do so love those movies. I once played a round at Pebble Beach with Clint, back when he was the mayor of Carmel." Yeah, me too, sort of.

"But I've had this piece of equipment here," he nodded towards Boris, "for some time now, and I've never had the opportunity to take it to its limit. It's like my friend Carlos. He bought a Bugatti Veyron a few years back. Paid $1.5 million, as I recall. The first thing he did was to take that car to a track and push it all the way. The SOB took that automobile to 233 miles per hour, because that was its limit, and it would have been a damn shame not to. You know what I mean?"

"I do!" I said with enthusiasm. Anything to try to win him over.

"He was killed in the Veyron a few months later. Terrible accident, they had to peel him off the asphalt," he added, somewhat absent-mindedly.

"That's too bad," I said. Then I pushed my luck and added, "Hell, you know, all you did was hide a body for a few days. Let's not make a big deal out of such a small thing. Let's just let bygones be bygones."

My prodding triggered something in him, and the creep in him came back to the fore. His face twisted, and he spit out his words with force. "Why, if it's such a small thing, didn't you just take the money and go away, Mr. Town? No!" He leaned towards me and shouted, as though psyching himself up. His face contorted more, and I began to see the same man I'd watched down on his knees pleading with the crowd on a small stage in his Manhattan ballroom two nights before. It hadn't been an act after all. The man was genuinely certifiable.

He said as though speaking to himself as much as to me. "You're lying to yourself, and you're lying to me. Even with *my* lawyers, there's a good chance I'll be locked up in a cage for some, and maybe all, of my final years on this earth. I likely only have a couple left, you know. You think I started my charity strictly out of altruism? No, Mr. Town, I have been in and out of cancer wards myself. All of my years of hard labor, and when I'm finally able to enjoy it, I get handed a death sentence. Now you and that club security man want to move up the end date, and for what? Because I wanted to complete the deal, as Mac himself would've wanted it! No, I'm sorry, but you brought this on yourself."

"But I've already talked to the FBI. I was with them not an hour ago. Killing me doesn't end this for you!"

"Without you and the security chief, there is no case. Sorry, Mr. Town, but time's up." He gave a subtle nod to Boris, and I knew I had only a split second to act.

In a single, well-practiced motion, I pulled the razor-sharp knife from my belt buckle and used the ball of my left foot to push off and turn my chair to face Boris, who'd begun to lunge at me. Using all the power I could muster from my tired, old calves, I launched out of the chair to meet him, and with both hands, I drove the six-inch steel blade between Boris' thyroid and cricoid cartilage and straight through his windpipe. Then, as fast I could, I twisted my body and dove behind my personal Goliath, using his gurgling, writhing mass as a shield.

I heard a series of explosions as Endicott blasted rounds meant for me into the giant's midsection. I had little hope of surviving the next volley, as the preppy killer only needed to move a foot or so to have a clear line on me. I was coming to grips with my fate when clipboard man bailed me out.

Having heard the shots, he tore open the van's side door, and I immediately plunged into the opening and onto the unprepared henchman. He hit the ground hard, and I rolled off him and out of Endicott's sightline. I stood and saw clipboard man moving towards the shotgun, which he'd dropped when I bowled him over. The gun was in the line of fire, and I had no choice but to dive for it. I managed to knock it away from the little man's grasp, but it eluded my fingers too. I heard three more booms as Endicott fired again and somehow managed to miss me, the bullets whistling between the trees. Unfortunately, he also missed the other guy.

But the gunshots caused the henchman to jump back, and I reached the shotgun first. Having given up hope of hitting me, Endicott tossed my Glock to the hired help in the hopes of saving him, but it was too late. We locked eyes as he reached out to catch it, and I fired a round of buckshot into his body with such force that it knocked him backward into the van. Now I had a defenseless Endicott in my sights, but the rich prick was fast and managed to shut the door before I fired the second round. I should've gone for the tires because Endicott got the van started and raced out of there before I could get to my Glock.

I ran over to the Caprice, ready to get behind the wheel and give chase, but our kidnapper had left an eight-inch Bowie knife protruding from the driver-side front tire.

I peered into the front seat and found Joanna curled up in a ball on the floor, awaiting her executioner.

27

"So, you never saw Endicott?" I asked Joanna, dumbfounded at my luck. Once again, I was the only witness. That is, assuming that both Boris and the clipboard guy were dead, which was somewhere north of a 99% certainty.

"I'm sorry. I heard the shots and took cover. Besides, he told me he'd kill me if I left the car."

"It's okay," I said. "I'm just frustrated. It's like Monday and finding Mac all over again. The van and the bodies are gone, and aside from the blood on my clothes and knife in my tire, there's no evidence that this thing actually happened." My ears were ringing from the gunshots, and I was pretty sure I was shouting at Joanna. I struggled to hear her responses.

"Well, I'll vouch for you. I know you're not lying."

"We better get moving," I said. "He may come back with reinforcements."

I popped the trunk, removed the jack and spare tire, and got down to work. We were back on the road inside of ten minutes.

"Where are we going?" asked Joanna, as we came to the end of the dirt lane.

"To clean up and check out of the hotel. Then I'd like to get you on a train out of this town. Do you have a place you can go for a few days until I get this wrapped up?"

"Yes, I can stay with a friend in Manhattan, but I don't like leaving you here. What went on in that van anyway?"

I decided to keep it close to the vest. I had just killed two men and made her a material witness. "I'd rather not get into the details. Let just say, Whit Endicott was inside the van and planned to kill both of us. Luck was with me and not him, and certainly not with his henchmen. Now I need to speak with a few people and think through how to best handle him going forward."

"Handle him? You just said he was going to murder us. Let's go to the cops."

"Yeah, but you said you didn't see or hear him, so it's his word against mine, and as you know, he has an army of lawyers, and I have a guy named Irving, who's probably handing out business cards at a hospital emergency room right now."

"I'm sorry. Of course, you're right. Oh my God. I wonder if he'll show up to the memorial tomorrow."

"Memorial?"

"Yes, tomorrow afternoon at Indian Head Yacht Club."

"Really, tell me more," I said, as I pressed the gas and headed for downtown Greenwich.

* * *

After leaving the hotel, I let Joanna buy me another phone from the same salesperson that had served me the prior day. Given that we'd just gone through the process a mere twenty-four hours before, it went quick, and I managed to see Joanna board a 3:35 pm train to Grand Central Station.

The first thing I did on the new device was to send Nephew Ed a text urging him to call me ASAP. Having failed to kill me, I now believed Endicott's best option would be to eliminate McNierney. That way, if I were to testify about the conspiracy between him, French and Sterling, my primary source would not be able to corroborate my story. I needed to warn him.

Ten minutes later "Joe's Place" popped up on my phone screen.

"Edward."

"Oh, great, it's Serious Earl today," he moaned. "What do you need?"

"I'll tell you in a minute. First I have good news."

"Yeah?" he replied, sounding doubtful.

"Yeah. Look, I spoke with the FBI for quite a while this morning, and I think you're in the clear."

"What makes you say that?"

"I could tell they were just squeezing me for information when they brought you up. I think it's just the two of them working this case. Is the car still outside your place?"

"No, it left sometime in the middle of the night."

"Have you noticed anyone watching you, either on the street or through that porn box you're always using?" I asked him.

"Well, no," he said, "but that doesn't mean it isn't happening. And, it's a computer. Porn happens to be just one of its many fine features. Fortnight is almost as good."

"You're a grown man, Ed, stop with the video games and get out there in the world," I said.

"I am out in the world, I just access it through a device. You have no idea of the size of the world I live in, Earl."

He was probably right.

"You know what," he added. "Just call my cell from here on out. I don't want to have to sneak in here again. Last time, Fabiola, that's the older one. She got up and went into the bathroom by the cellar door, and I had to wait a half hour after our call for her to go back to bed. I could hear her in there, disgusting. And, I couldn't get a decent cell or Wi-Fi connection in the basement. I was going out of my mind with boredom."

"You should've worked on your Groucho impersonation," I said.

"Who's Groucho?" he replied. Kids.

"You said you needed something, Earl. Or did you call to work on your comedy act?"

"Yeah, right. Look, I need to speak with Richard McNierney, it's life and death stuff here, Ed. Do you have a number for him?"

"Life and death, my Mom's right about you having a flair for the dramatic, Earl."

"She said what?" I felt my fingers tighten around the steering wheel.

He ignored me. "I printed something out the other day. Let me look, hold on." I heard the usual sounds of things being moved and looked under.

He came back a minute or so later. "No, I'm sorry I don't have a number for him. I may need to call in a friend, but I'll get you his cell number. Watch for a text. Life and death!" He giggled.

I thanked him and hung up.

I considered calling Sullivan next, but I didn't have time to give a statement on everything that had transpired. Not to mention, he was going to be pissed when I told him I'd put Joanna on a train instead of driving both of us to a meeting with him and Garcia. But I had a case to close and a suspect to speak to, and I was already behind schedule. Plus, I had terminated two men, and stuff like that isn't always best disclosed to the authorities unnecessarily. One minute they're on your side, the next they're charging you with double homicide. Sleeping dogs and all that.

A half-hour after seeing Joanna off, I found myself driving to the residence of Larry and Caroline Ferncroft. Ed didn't find any information on her professional background, but he discerned her involvement in a half-dozen charitable and civic organizations, which led me to believe she didn't have employment and might be at home during the day.

The Ferncrofts lived about five miles from Indian Head in another millionaire's row. This neighborhood was a far cry from Belle Haven, but amazing in its own right. Here, the homes were a mere 10,000 to 12,000 square feet. They were mostly New England cape style, but on steroids; three stories tall, additional wings, oversized picture windows, balconies, and even a few crow's nest style roof decks. They were set back, separated from the street by beautifully curated lawns, shrubs, and flower beds.

Larry and Caroline lived in a gray-shingled number with white trim and minimal ornamentation. It was a corner lot, far from the road and backed by a long stretch of lawn set against a thicket of red and white oaks. I knew the Ferncrofts were loaded from the company they kept, but I found it hard to contemplate Larry generating the income needed to buy or build this place on his own. He was too meek. No, this was a family-money situation. The type of home that a wealthy father would bequeath to his little girl and her timid husband.

I turned through a gate flanked by square stone columns into a circular driveway and pulled up to a portico on what I guess was considered the west wing.

As I raised my hand to knock, one of the ornate double doors swung open, and a dark, gray-haired woman stared up at me with a suspicious eye. She said nothing, so I smiled to break the ice. Her face remained frozen.

"Is Caroline Ferncroft at home? My name is Earl Town, and I need to speak with her."

She shook her head no and gave me skeptical, but at least she didn't shut the door on me.

"It's urgent ma'am," I tried again. "It's about her friend James MacArthur." I leaned down to get closer to her eyes, which weren't much higher than my navel. "You know the man who was killed?"

She ran her tongue over her teeth, squinted at me and considered this, then pointed at my chest and then at the ground on which I stood, and shut the door. While I waited, I surveyed as much of the property as I could from my vantage point. After the portico, the driveway continued back out to the street on the same road that I came in on, but it also forked to the right just beyond the house. I suspected this led to a garage and possibly a side exit out to the road that ran along the north side of the property.

The door opened, and the old woman stepped aside. I went through into a two-story entryway. Above my head was a crystal chandelier about the size of a kiddie pool. Below my feet was a marble mosaic that must have cost thousands. The walls were mostly bare, off-white and judging by the moldings around the entrances to the living room and library, a good 18 inches thick. The old woman stepped in front and led me past a library, powder room, and then a modern kitchen with two sinks and two islands, a sea of marble countertops and walnut cabinetry. The aesthetic was snug, country kitchen, but on the scale of Madison Square Garden.

Beyond the kitchen was a breakfast nook with comfortable seating for eight, and beyond this was a set of French doors. The old woman stopped when we reached them, opened the right one, and pointed to another set of French doors on a smaller house on the other side of an expansive in-ground swimming pool. It was through these doors that I saw the profile of Caroline Ferncroft.

"Caroline," I said, once I'd made the winding trip through plants and patio furniture and entered the pool house. "Thank you for seeing me."

She didn't turn to face me. She stared straight ahead and asked meekly, "Have you caught the killer, detective?"

I stepped into a light, airy room with maple beams crossing beneath a cathedral ceiling. Skylights let in more of the late afternoon sun, which was being absorbed by an array of plants and trees scattered about in clay pots. Caroline was slumped into the corner of a long white sofa, her pale, slender legs extended out from under a red silk robe adorned with cherry blossoms. In her right hand dangled a rocks glass filled with a clear liquid and ice. Beads of sweat dripped from the glass in the humid air forming a stain on the arm of the couch. On the coffee table in front of her sat a silver bucket, in which leaned a bottle of Grey Goose vodka.

I maneuvered around a potted palm and plunked down in an armchair a few feet away. "Are you okay?"

"What do you want, Mr. Town? I've got drinking to do."

Her speech was slow and deliberate. "Caroline, I'm trying to find out who did this, and you can help me." She stared through me. I leaned in, put my hand on her shoulder and gave it a gentle squeeze as I asked, "What was the argument about that night on the dock?"

She turned her head to face me, eyes fighting against the booze to allow her to focus. "You're the detective, why don't you?" She paused and forgot to finish her sentence.

It'd been a long day, and I'm afraid I lost my shit at that point. I leaned into her and shouted. "What is it with you people?"

Just then the old woman entered carrying a tray, on which sat a silver pot, a couple of china cups and a few small containers. She gave me a cold hard stare as she went around a rubber tree in a big terra-cotta pot and set the tray down on a large square coffee table in front of Caroline and me. She glared at me while waiting to see if the mistress needed anything else. Caroline failed to acknowledge her, and when I finally said, "thank you," she pivoted and made a quick exit. If only I'd known, I would've thanked her at the front door and let myself in.

Another patio and garden lay beyond a set of French doors to Caroline's right, and she turned her gaze to the vista as she spoke. "You were saying something about 'you people,' please go on, Mr. Town." She was unfazed. My little outburst was par for whatever course she was on. Maybe I needed to start drinking myself.

"What can I do to get through to you?" I mumbled. A few days with this crowd and I was losing it. I reached for the coffee. "Do you mind?"

She waved a pale hand to go on, so I did.

I needed to get some caffeine into her too. "How you do you take it?"

"Black as the deepest abyss."

I poured us each one. As I took my first sip, she turned her head and caught my stare. Her eyes were moist and red. She looked up through the skylight. "Have you ever met *the one*, Earl?"

"The one?" I chewed on this for a bit, then said, "Yeah, I think so." I was admitting this to myself as much as to Caroline. "She threw me out of her life five years ago, but the more time passes, the more I've come to believe she was the one."

She turned and leaned toward me. Her cocktail, which contained only a few drops of ice water now, fell from its perch on the arm of the couch and spilled on her leg. She paid it no mind and asked me a question. "She's still alive though?" I nodded. "So, you can still win her back?"

"No, she lives a very different life now. She's moved on without me." I decided I had to ask the big question before she blacked out: "How long have you been in love with James?"

"How long were you in love with her?"

"We met young, so about twenty years."

She sipped her coffee and said, "I've been in love with James since we were teenagers. Was James ever in love with me? That's the question."

"Caroline." I leaned in close and looked into her foggy, but beautiful blue eyes. "Tell me what happened that night. The last night anyone saw James alive."

She laughed and gave me a seductive look, similar to what she was putting out on the dance floor a couple of nights before. "You want to know the big secret?"

I practically jumped from my chair. "Yes! Yes, I do, Caroline. Please tell me the big secret."

"They were arguing about Rebecca."

I sat up so fast, I rattled the china on the coffee table.

"What about Rebecca? Tell me everything that was said. Tell me everything that happened that night."

"They said he needed to cease being so reckless with his reputation and that of the club."

"Sterling and French said this to Mac, er, James?"

"Yes, Nate and Gibby, they said his actions were going to kill the deal." She turned away and looked out through the French doors again.

"What actions?"

"Being so obvious about his affair with Rebecca."

"Why would that kill the deal?"

"Wouldn't you like to know?"

"Yes, I would. Please tell me."

"Fine, I will," she sighed. "Her husband owns lots of Wayne Trust stock in his hedge fund."

"Rebecca's husband?"

"Yes," she insisted.

"Isn't Larry a lawyer?"

She looked at me and began to sob. She covered her face with her hands and then threw herself into the corner of the couch.

"Oh, I'm so sorry, Caroline. If Rebecca's not you, then who?"

She sprang up, tears streaking down her cheeks. "That's what you really want, isn't it? The million-dollar question! Who else was James fucking?" She made a fist with her empty hand and punched at the air. "He told me, it was me. Said I reminded him of the character in the du Maurier novel. But that's not what they said that night on the dock." She held out her rocks glass and asked for more. The coffee I'd poured for her was getting cold on the table.

I took the glass from her and walked to a well-stocked sterling silver art deco bar cart that had to cost as much as my Caprice. She didn't need any more booze, but I decided to give her whatever she asked for if it kept her talking. I refreshed the ice, added a wedge of lime, sat back down and poured a shot of Grey Goose into it. "Take it slow," I said as I handed it to her.

She immediately pressed it to her lips and threw her head back.

"Jesus, take it easy Caroline. What did they say about Rebecca that made you believe it wasn't you?"

"Larry is in no position to kill a billion-dollar deal, but you know whose husband is?"

"No, I don't. Please tell me."

She looked at me and smiled. "You should know, detective, she's your girl too."

I sat back and considered this for a bit. "Tinsley?" I asked rather shyly.

Caroline nodded and sighed.

"What did she say when they were arguing?"

"She said they were right. Mac should stop showing off."

"What did she mean, showing off?" I asked.

"In the novel," she slurred, "Rebecca's husband is cuckolded, humiliated by his wife's infidelities. Tinsley's screwed half the men at IHYC, and I guess that included Mac. What he saw in that bitch, I don't know." Caroline held out her glass again.

"Drink some coffee, before you pass out. Don't you have kids? Are they here?"

"They're all grown up."

Then she lashed out. "It must hurt to hear about the real Tinsley. Did you think you were special, Earl?" I already had this realization, and upon deliberation, I determined that I didn't really care, but I didn't want to spoil her moment, so I let it go.

Then the enormity of the information finally hit me, and I said, more to myself than to her, "Tinsley is Rebecca."

"Good God!" she shouted, her voice dripping with disgust. "Aren't you supposed to be a detective?"

I sat back trying to digest it. "Are you certain of this?"

"Ask her where she was that night. She wasn't sleeping in her bed."

"I was told Mac left by himself."

"So, he did. That doesn't mean he didn't have company later."

"What did you do after the argument?"

"I came home and drank myself to sleep, just like I'm doing now. Now, if you will kindly leave me to it, detective." Her slurred words tailed off. I walked over and seized her shoulders. I shook her, but she was out. Just like that. She'd dropped her glass on the rug, leaned her head against the arm of the sofa, closed her eyes and passed out.

I took out my phone and called Ed, but he didn't answer, so I took the plunge and plugged Tinsley's name into Google all by myself. Dozens of hits came back. Near the bottom of the first page, was a link to an article in the New York Times Society page about Tinsley and her husband Carlton Saunders III, known to his friends and fellow super-rich guys, as Tripp Saunders.

Caroline stirred a bit, then lifted her feet up onto the sofa, stretched out, mumbled something unintelligible, and went to back to sleep. I took advantage of the quiet and poured myself a fresh cup of delicious coffee, then Googled Carlton Saunders III, and within ten minutes, I had information to support Caroline's story.

After beginning his career at Goldman Sachs, Tripp Saunders was made partner in a Greenwich-based asset management firm called Avalon Partners. I assume Tripp had earned his title on the day he was born to the founder of Avalon Partners, one Carlton Saunders II. A search on Wayne Trust, JKB SA and Avalon Partners, brought me to several articles about the corporate activism of Avalon Partners, which was known to poke and prod the owners of companies in which it held large positions to divest certain divisions if they didn't meet Avalon's high standards.

Apparently, Avalon owned a large chunk of JKB SA and had made some noise in the press about Wayne Trust back when the merger was first being discussed. According to a piece in the New York Times, Avalon applied ESG screens to its investments, which stands for economic, social, and governance; apparently, this is a way to quantify how a company treats its employees, customers, and the environment. Wayne Trust, and in particular, Mac's unit, had been sued several times, and also fined, for overcharging participants in the retirement plans it administered. Avalon didn't like this and said so publicly until somebody convinced them otherwise. Were they worried Tinsley's husband would bring this up again and kill the deal if he found out about Mac and his wife? It sure made a lot of sense.

This internet search stuff wasn't so hard after all. I'd just saved myself $50. Ed was going to regret missing my call.

I sipped my coffee as Caroline gave a little snort and shifted onto her side. The opportunity to do some old-school sleuthing had presented itself, so I decided to have a look around. I'd already scanned the room we were in, but another set of French doors yielded a view of a sizable game room behind us. I finished my coffee, poured myself a small neat scotch from a crystal decanter, and went on in.

Pool table – check, ping pong table – check, giant flat screen television – check. Trophy case – unusual. I walked over and looked at all the plaques and awards. Most were won by Caroline for what surely must have been some serious equestrian skills. Larry's awards were fewer in number, but he had a section all his own too, as did the kids. The man of the house had won his awards for tennis, which seemed odd considering how when I had joked about being a tennis coach, he didn't mention his being one too. The awards were mostly from Indian Head Tennis Club, where Larry was apparently both a five-time singles champion and a youth instructor. Scattered among the trophies were a half-dozen framed photos of Larry and kids that he coached, and in just about every one of them was a kid I recognized. I'd seen him earlier in the week. It was Maria Moore's goofy son. The one who told me to go around through the Japanese garden, and who wore a necklace with a shark tooth.

I looked around a while longer, but the pool house didn't hold any more secrets. I left Caroline snoring into a sofa cushion and walked swiftly back toward the house watching out for the old woman as I went. I made it back inside and was strolling along a hallway peeking in doors, looking for an office or study to explore, when she caught up to me. I turned a corner at the end of the hall and came face to face with the old thing. She was waiting for me, perched in what looked to be an antique Chippendale chair. Her feet barely reached the floor. She stood, held up and waggled her index finger, and led me back to the door through which I'd initially entered. I began to say that I'd been looking for a bathroom but gave up when she turned her back on me. Soon, I found myself standing by my car in the portico, as she shut the door in my face.

Rather than completing the semicircle back to the street on the way out, I hung the right after the portico that I'd seen earlier and found that it did lead to a north side entrance as well as a two-story garage with in-law apartment above, which is probably where the little troll lived. As I exited through a brick archway draped in ivy, I told myself that in my next life, I'd own a house with two entrances – one for me and one for the help.

I needed a place to stay, and I didn't like the idea of being too predictable and getting another visit like the ones myself and Joanna had at the Extended Stay. Clipboard guy had shown up at her doorstep and forced his way into her room, where he had her call me and arrange the pick-up.

Google maps led me to a place in the center of a town. An old Victorian B&B with 8 rooms on four floors. I got it for $169 a night, which made me not mind the mildew in the shower grout so much.

An older couple, Mel and Rosie, ran the place and they seemed like a good lot. On the way there, I dialed the number Ed had sent me while I was prying information out of Caroline. Richard McNierney answered on the second ring.

"Speak."

"It's Earl Town, I need you to listen to me for a minute."

"Nothing you say is going to change my mind, Town. My arm is healing fast, it won't be long before I come and find you."

"That's fine, and not why I called. Listen up." I told him the key points of my afternoon with Endicott and why I thought he might be the next target. When I was done, he said. "Okay. Thanks, I'll take care of it."

"But, how will I know?"

He hung up, and I hoped to never hear from him again.

28

I rested for a bit, showered, then headed back out at 8:30 pm. I chatted with Rosie at the front desk while I dropped off the room key. It was that kind of place. I asked her about the local constabulary, and specifically Chief Boone.

She said: "Oh, we aren't much for gossip around here." Then she proceeded to inform me that Boone was the son of a former police captain, who was a "pillar of the community." However, "his son never worked for a damn thing in his life and is a crook." I told her this fit well with my impression and mentioned how enraged he'd been when I was sprung from his jail the previous night. To say she enjoyed my story would be a severe understatement, though I wondered if she'd take extra care in counting the towels after I'd checked out, given that I was a jailbird.

I planned to grab a quick coffee and something to eat at the old diner down the street, then get to Bob's Yacht Yard early and have a look around before Miguel, the security guard, started his shift at eleven. However, within a quarter-mile of the hotel, it was clear I'd picked up a tail. Not being familiar with the area put me at a disadvantage and I drove in circles for a couple of miles before I recalled the dual entrances at the Ferncroft residence and thought that might do the trick.

I drove slow most of the ten minutes it took to get there, but when I got within a half mile or so, I caught a gap in oncoming traffic, swerved into the other lane and stepped on it. After passing an SUV, I killed my lights and turned onto one of two roads that led into the neighborhood. No longer seeing the tail in my mirror, I pulled in between the pillars that stood at the Ferncroft's west entrance and continued down the drive. But, instead of pulling up to the house, I cut across the beautifully manicured lawn, avoiding sprinklers and most, but not all of, what had been a perfectly arranged flower bed, and made my way to the north entrance. I watched in my rearview mirror, and within seconds, I saw the tail car pass by. I exited via the north gate, turned left, then right, and came up behind the tail at a safe distance and without lights.

This time, it was only a minute or so before I saw brake lights come on as the driver realized he was no longer following anyone. Realizing he might turn around, I stopped and backed the Caprice between two tall hedges and into a long and secluded driveway. I parked, jumped out, and quietly made my way back to the road along the shrubbery. As I reached the street, a new car approached. It was a Greenwich police black and white, with Chief Matthew Boone behind the wheel. He stopped and waited for the tail car to reverse course and approach, and I knew who my tail was long before I saw his face. The two pulled up alongside one another not twenty feet from where I stood in the shadows of a tall ivy-covered red brick wall. They rolled down their windows to talk, and I heard every word.

"I lost him, but I know he's in here somewhere," said Penner.

"Christ, can you do anything right?" Chief Boone complained.

"I'm sorry Chief, the son-of-a-bitch passed several cars in a double, then killed his lights. We'll take his license."

Boone shook his head in disgust. "There are only two ways in and out of El Barrio Rich," he said waving a paw around as he surveyed the statuesque Tudor to his left. "If I take Norman and you sit at the top of Hycliff, we'll pick him up when he tries to leave. Call O'Rourke and get him out of bed. Tell him to come here now. If this jerk doesn't come out on his own, we'll use O'Rourke to flush him out."

Penner cracked his knuckles and smiled, and I slunk back into the ivy a little more.

They each drove off in opposite directions. They were right of course, I couldn't drive out of there without rousing one of them, and I couldn't leave my car and sneak out either. I jogged back to the Caprice and popped the trunk. I removed my black jumpsuit, ski mask, and a black utility belt. I also removed a small, fully charged Bluetooth speaker, which I slid into one of many pockets.

Once dressed, I began to move stealthily down the street in the direction Penner had driven. I used the shadows created by the long ivy-draped wall for concealment. Around a bend three houses away, I found Penner sitting under a big elm tree at the end of Hycliff Road. He was adjacent to the neighborhood's northern access point. He had backed in and turned the lights off, but his car was hard to miss, as it was a late model canary yellow Ford Mustang. Of course, he drove a yellow Mustang, I thought. He probably cruised high schools in it.

There was a long hedge that ran next to the stretch of sidewalk between Penner and me and I got down on my hands and knees and crawled towards him in the foot and a half or so of shadows that ran along the base of it.

Eventually, I got down on my belly and squirmed along the damp grass until I reached the shadows behind him. His window was open, and he might've heard me, had he not been foolishly playing the radio loudly. It was one those top-40 Kiss stations, and I watched as the back of his head bobbed to the beat of some God-awful rap song in which a deep-voiced dude said something like "mama gonna take all a me" repeatedly over an old Van Halen riff.

I extracted a collapsible aluminum baton from my utility belt along with a couple of strong magnets. Using zip ties, I attached the magnets to the top of the Bluetooth speaker and placed the whole thing into a set of grips attached to the end of the baton. I got down on my belly again and crawled within a few feet of the back of Penner's car. I carefully maneuvered the baton and speaker under the back bumper and used the magnets to attach the speaker to the gas tank. Then I made my way back to the Caprice the same way I came, on the ground. As I passed him, I noticed that Penner had his nose buried in a cell phone, making it all way too easy. If he was on my police force. Well, he just wouldn't be on my force.

Back at the Caprice, I pulled off the jumpsuit and mask, got behind the wheel and connected my phone to the Bluetooth speaker, which I had set to maximum volume.

I couldn't see Penner from my vantage point, but hoped for the best, as I did my impersonation of a panicked Chief Boone. I screamed in the microphone, "Jesus Christ, shots fired!" I paused, then added a frantic sounding "Penner, man down!" I heard tires squealing, then saw a flash of yellow whiz by.

I put it in drive and had just started to compress the gas pedal when an SUV drove past me in the opposite direction from where Penner had just gone. I immediately recognized the expensive looking vehicle because I had seen it a few minutes earlier when it was parked at the Ferncroft residence.

The SUV was an Audi with stickers for both Indian Head Yacht Club and Westchester Country Club on the rear window. After leaving the neighborhood, it next turned onto the main road out of Greenwich and headed for I-95. This was good because I was convinced Boone was going to roll up behind me any minute and I doubted he'd venture onto the highway, which was patrolled by state police.

We passed by an old church, then a farm stand already hocking pumpkins for Halloween, and I considered why I was following the vehicle. I was convinced Larry was behind the wheel, and that it was wise to see what he was up to. Something had been off about him. I couldn't pin it down exactly, but he just kept turning up. First at the club, then outside of Beth's, and at Endicott's gala. Then there were the photos of him with Maria's son, and now he just happens to drive by at the perfect time. I had to wonder: is Larry leaving me clues or is God sending me a message?

❋ ❋ ❋

The SUV took the onramp for I-95 South, and I wished I'd gassed up earlier. After the forced trip to the woods and losing Penner's tail, I had less than a quarter tank, and a drive to Manhattan would be pushing my luck, but we were only on the highway for a short while before Larry took the exit for Port Chester, which is just over the state line in New York. We drove downtown and passed the Capital Theater, which I recalled was the last place Janis Joplin sang in public and across the street from a bar where she supposedly wrote Mercedes Benz a few days before she took that final, ill-conceived blast of heroin. About a half mile later, the Audi turned into an asphalt lot next to a brown-shingled restaurant called McFadden's. It was an old-school place with a coat of arms on the sign. I drove past it and circled back in time to see him walking inside.

I pulled into a strip mall across the street and got to work. I began by extracting a duffel bag from the deepest recesses of my trunk. From it, I removed a wig that both darkened and added six inches to my tresses, which I topped with a oily 'Pete's Trucking' ball cap. Next, I added a pair of tinted glasses and a scruffy beard that matched the wig. Then I removed my jacket and oxford shirt and threw on a t-shirt with a skull on it and topped that with a leather coat. I've found that people usually don't ask questions of guys in leather. I climbed into the back seat and clumsily changed into worn, dirty blue jeans and then completed the ensemble with a pair of weathered leather boots. From to stylish P.I. to greasy townie in under five minutes.

I tugged my cap down tight as I entered the bar and scanned the room as best I could through the dark, smudged lenses.

Larry and his date, the one and only Tinsley Saunders, were easy to spot sitting opposite one another in the last of four red leather booths that lined the wall to my right. Across from them was a dark mahogany bar with eight stools, only three of which were occupied.

I kept my head down and strolled to the far end of the room making a conscious effort to not walk like Earl Town. I planted myself on a stool no more than five feet from their booth and signaled the bartender.

The Red Sox and Yankees were playing game two of a four-game series with the East Division title, and more importantly, postseason home field advantage, on the line. The game was on two flat screens behind the bar. The look the barkeep gave me suggested he wasn't all that eager to serve me. Maybe the oily ball cap and skull shirt were a little much for this neighborhood. I made a mental note to consider fine-tuning my disguise bag a bit.

The Sox were ahead by a run in the bottom of the eighth inning, and the Fenway crowd was roaring. Seth, according to his name tag, was a thirtyish guy with a paunch and bald spot. He raised his eyebrows at me, and I pointed to the Sam Adams tap. He handed me a tall cold one, and we watched the game in silence for a few seconds before he moved to the clearly soused older women at the other end of the bar. With Seth occupied, I set up my gear.

From an inside pocket, I removed a small, but powerful microphone. I plugged one end of this into my phone and the other in my right ear. I adjusted the little tip on the earpiece so that it was directed at the booth behind me and listened into the conversation. The phone allowed me to pinpoint the sound I wanted to capture and adjust the volume above that of the television. I could also record it.

The talk was a serious one. Larry said, "Look, I'm sorry about what happened, but I'm not to blame. Let's just go back to what we had. Let me help you forget him."

"You think I loved him?" Tinsley replied.

"I think he loved you." He paused, then added, "I've known you too long to think you're capable of love. I told you. I don't care. I love you, and I don't want to change you."

"That's what they all say," she replied.

"Yeah, what's the P.I. say? You still playing around with him?" I held my breath.

"No comment."

"You looked awfully friendly at Whit's shindig. You didn't really take him home, did you? I mean a guy like that may not understand how these things are handled in polite society."

"Handled?" she asked, sounding bored.

"Yeah, what if he falls in love?"

Her response was muffled as, in a case of severely poor timing, I accidentally moved the earpiece while trying to scratch an itch on the edge of my wig. I fixed it as she said, "He does have his strong points though," which she capped with a naughty laugh. Larry didn't see the humor in it.

"You really did?" he said, not really asking.

"Are you jealous, Lawrence?"

"No. Well, yes, but I told you, I don't want to change you. I just want to be with you."

"New subject, I tire of that one." The condescension was strong, but it didn't faze old Larry.

"Okay," he said. "Who do you think killed him?" I nearly knocked my beer over in excitement. He went on. "You don't think Nate and Gib actually had something to do with it, do you?"

"Who else, if not them? They had motive." She lowered her voice, and I struggled to make out what she said, but I believe it was this: "Beth is going after them. Seems to think they'll make a deal." Larry said something unintelligible in response, then Tinsley added, "She'll get screwed out of some of it, but there will be enough left over to keep her living like a queen forever more."

"Good, better her than them," he replied.

"Mmm," she purred her agreement. "I'm running low here, fella," she added, and the next thing I knew Larry was shoulder to shoulder with me at the bar. He signaled for another round, then stood there, not a foot from me. I froze and stared up at the closest tv and wondered if she was looking at me. I wasn't so sure this had been a good plan anymore and was happy for the dim lighting.

He ordered a round then glanced over at me, just as Aaron Judge led off the top of the ninth with a game-tying solo home run over the Green Monster. A guy two stools down cheered loudly and high-fived Seth. The Fenway crowd went silent as Larry nudged my arm and said: "Alright, go Yankees!"

I kept my eyes on the tube, saying in the most redneck accent I could muster, "Yeah, the Judge, fuckin-A." Thankfully, my pal Seth soon returned with two clear drinks, and Larry left me to the game.

I don't know if it was the alcohol, but I saw a change in Larry's character when he returned to the table. It was a side of him I hadn't yet seen. He was aggressive. He started in as he slid back into the seat. "Caroline is leaving on Sunday for a visit with her mother in Boca, and I want to see you."

"I told you, I need some time to think things through. I'm not sure I can continue this right now, Larry."

He raised his voice enough that Seth and the now giddy Yankees fan two stools away stopped and looked at him when he replied, "You think you can throw me aside like some detective from Boston?" Yup, that stung a little.

"What happened to how we handle these things in polite society, Larry?" she said through what sounded like gritted teeth.

He paused and lowered his voice. "We haven't been together in over a month." There was a long silence before Larry spoke again, in a pleading tone. "I can't live like this, baby. I have to be with you."

"Don't call me that," Tinsley said defiantly.

He lowered his voice to a whisper, and I pushed the volume to the max, as he said, "You're all I want. Please give me another chance." Her reply threw me for a loop.

"I saw you at the club that morning, Larry. You weren't in the city. How do I know you didn't kill him?" Then she got up and walked out. Leaving Larry holding back tears.

So, Mac was screwing Larry's wife and the love of Larry's life, and they weren't even the same woman. Mac even named his boat after Larry's true love. That was motive for the kind of beating that had killed Mac. And now Tinsley said he was also at the scene. The pieces were finally falling into place. Now I was feeling giddy, even though the Yankees had just gone back-to-back to take the lead.

29

I made two calls as I drove back to Greenwich. The first was to Gibson French. He started to feed me a line of garbage about honoring my commitment to him, and I cut him off.

"You heard from your pal Whit since this afternoon?"

"That's none of your business."

"Oh really? You remember that big bodyguard of his? The Russian guy, Boris?"

"Yes, so?"

"He's dead, severed windpipe. Another of his henchmen is dead too. You know the little guy? He took a shotgun blast to the gut."

He gasped and stammered. "I don't know what you want."

"I want you to call your pal the Commodore now and tell him that I need to ask him a few questions first thing tomorrow morning. You tell him I want five minutes and a couple of answers, and I'm telling you, he had better answer my questions, or I am gonna bring a real motherfucker of a conspiracy rap down on both your heads. You got me, Gibby?"

"Yes."

"Good! Now do it."

I hung up and made call number two to Ron Sullivan. He wasn't pleased with my decision to call him a few minutes before midnight, but he got over it when I filled him in on what I'd overheard in Port Chester. I did this because I needed some help that only he could provide. There were several tolls between Manhattan and Greenwich, and I'd noticed an E-Z Pass device on Larry's windshield. If Tinsley was correct, the data from this device, along with camera footage from the tolls, would destroy his alibi.

Sully said he and Garcia had been busy chasing down dead-end leads on the investigation into potential competitors of Wayne Trust taking Mac out as a means of sabotaging the deal. There was real joy in his voice as I told him what I'd overheard. He said he'd get on it and would let me know when he had something.

* * *

The dash clock read 12:03 am as I entered the dusty lot in front of Bob's Yacht Yard.

I made my way down the long dock to the security booth. Inside was a skinny young man with acne, chin stubble, and long dark hair tied back in a ponytail. He had headphones on, and his eyes were closed. I rapped lightly on the door trim, and he jumped out of his seat. He spoke with an accent that was part Spanish and part New York.

"Jesus man. What the fuck! You scared the shit out of me."

"I'm sorry," I said. "Are you Miguel?"

"Maybe," he responded, giving me the once-over.

"I have a couple of questions for you." I reached into my pocket and retrieved my wallet, which I held up. "I value your time and knowledge, my friend."

"Yeah?" He sat back down. "I don't know if I can help you, man."

I handed him a twenty-dollar bill.

He took it eagerly and said, "I'll see what I can do."

Miguel recalled a woman 'renting' a small boat in the early hours of Sunday morning. He said: "I was a couple of hours into my shift when she showed up."

"How long was she out there?"

"Long time. Dawn was breaking when she returned it."

Starting with Tinsley, I showed him pictures I'd saved to my phone of her, Caroline, Beth, Joanna, and even Maria Moore. I was covering all the bases.

"That might be her. She had dark hair. Well, I think she did. I remember those lips too. Look at those things, big, full, beautiful. Not a lot of white women with lips that like." Yeah okay, I thought, I liked them too.

Then, I showed him the others. He said no to Beth, Joanna, and Maria, but things got complicated when I waved Caroline's photo in front of him. "Yo, whassup? That could be her too. She got the hair and lips. Yeah, I'm not sure now, man."

"Okay, forget about that. How did the woman act? She seemed stressed out?"

"Not really, she seemed sad, I guess. Didn't say much, looked kinda down. That's the day the papers say that rich guy was murdered over there. You think she did it?"

"I doubt it, Miguel, but it's possible."

"Holy shit. I don't want to be a witness, man. I'll lose my job if they find out about the rentals."

"Don't worry about it. I'm not a cop, and I not going to tell anyone what you told me."

He nodded and looked around nervously.

"You said the sun was coming up when she brought it back. It must have been close to seven?"

"Yup, that's right. I was getting nervous that she wouldn't make it back before my shift ended, but then I see the boat coming this way, sun coming up behind it. It was a beautiful morning, all red skies, and shit."

"Any cops ask you about this stuff?"

"Nope, nobody, especially cops. I wouldn't talk to them anyway."

"You see anything out of the ordinary that morning?" I asked.

"No man."

"Thanks, Miguel," I said, thinking about Larry watching Tinsley pass by on her way back to return the boat and becoming enraged enough to go out to Mac's boat and beat his brains in. I turned to go, and he stopped me.

"Actually, you know, right as I was ending my shift, a skiff went by here going real fast in that direction." He pointed away from Indian Head. "I remember wondering what the hurry was."

"Don't small craft pass by here all the time?"

"Not that early on a Sunday. No one fishes around here, and fishers are the only early-birds. And, not that fast, either. They were really moving."

"Anything you remember about the skiff or the person in it?"

He sniffed and held out his hand, into which I placed another twenty.

"Thanks, I need it, no more work soon."

"What do you mean?" I asked.

"Summer's over. They keep us on until Halloween, by then all the yachts are set for winter, and we gotta find something else to do until spring."

"Sorry to hear that. What are you gonna do?"

"Work for my sister. She moved to Denver last year and opened a weed store. I still can't believe it's legal."

"Sounds like a real career opportunity. About the skiff?" I said.

"I remember it was red and had some white numbers on the bow. Like I said it went by fast, but I think it was 81, 15."

"What was 81, 15?"

"Numbers painted on the side of the boat, man."

"You remember the numbers on the boat?"

"Yeah, I was an altar boy until I was twelve. My mom wouldn't let me out of it. I even told her Father Roberto was molesting me, but she didn't believe me."

"Holy shit, was he?"

"Nah, I just hated being around priests all the time. They were nice to me though, just boring as shit."

"I don't see the connection to the boat."

"Psalm 81:15, that's why I remembered it. 'Those who hate the Lord would cower to him, and their doom would last forever.' Father Joe liked to break that one out when we got out of line. You know, the idea of being doomed forever put the fear of God into us."

"I get it," I said.

"But the number on the boat had a dash instead of the dots. It was 81-15."

"Thank you, Miguel, this is very helpful."

"One more question for you." He gave me a look again, so I reluctantly put another twenty in his hand.

"Thank you for your generous contribution to my Denver fund."

Who worked this shift two nights ago, when they found the rich guy's body?"

"Wednesday is my boy Mikey's day. He goes to NYU film school, says he gonna me put in one of his films next year. I told him to make sure I have a sex scene with a hottie!" He laughed, and I snorted and played along.

"You got a last name and number for him."

"I don't know, man."

I took out another twenty, and he didn't move until I took out another. "Flying first class to Denver, are we?" I asked as I forked it over.

"Gotta get some luggage," he said with a smile.

"Right, you need Vuitton?"

He gave me a cell number for Michael Pacheco of White Plains, New York, and made me swear that I would not tell him where I got it. I called him on my way out of the parking lot. I had trouble hearing over the sound of my tires on the gravel.

"Where'd you get my number?"

"Miggy down at Bob's." Those who overcharge forfeit their anonymity: my money, my rules.

"What do you want?"

"Just wondering if you saw anything out of the ordinary two nights ago? You know when they pulled the body out of the Sound. It wasn't far from the club."

"What's it to you?"

"Well, I'm trying to solve a murder, so there's that. I'll also make it worth your while to tell me what you saw, but no bullshit. I'll find out if you bullshit me, and I know where you work."

"Yeah, how much you got?"

I rolled my eyes. It's much easier to do these negotiations in person. Having money waved under one's nose is an A+ motivator. "A hundred bucks," I said, wincing at the amount.

"A C-note, huh?"

"That's what I said."

"Ahh, ha, ha," he laughed into the phone. "I was just screwing with you. I didn't see anything weird. I was fighting with my girlfriend and barely saw the ..." I hung up pissed about wasting forty bucks.

30

I awoke Saturday morning to the sound of rain pounding on the roof of the Mainsail B&B. The forecast was for a dreary morning followed by a sunny if somewhat chilly afternoon. The Indian summer had finally run its course. Autumn was about to fully settle in, and I didn't mind it for a change. I was looking forward to the feeling one gets when ducking into a warm neighborhood pub on a chilly fall evening.

I checked the time on the bedside clock and knew I needed to move if I was going to catch my prey before it left for the office.

Twenty-three minutes later, I parked the Caprice in the portico of Nate Sterling's Belle Haven mansion. The butler opened one of the colossal doors and did a double-take upon seeing me smiling back at him.

"Reginald, my man, top of the morning to you. I need to see the Commodore." He raised his eyebrows, but was too cool to say anything sensible, like "are you out of your mind?" Instead, he asked me to wait while he "checked on Commodore Sterling's availability."

A minute later he returned and showed me into the towering two-story entryway. This time, instead of walking through to the back lawn, we turned right into an office of sorts and then into a hallway that led to a spacious contemporary kitchen with sleek lines, beyond which was a semi-circular informal dining area. Sitting at a disk-shaped slab of white marble poised on a steel pedestal was Nate Sterling, and a woman who I figured must be the Mrs. I introduced myself and she said her name was Barbara. The Commodore ignored me and kept his nose buried in the New York Times, but Babs smiled and invited me to sit down. She even asked if I would like some coffee. I said I would love some and Reginald trotted over with a cup.

From behind the business section, Sterling said, "Barbara, would you mind giving our guest and I a few minutes alone?"

"Fine, it's about time I got moving anyway. Brad is bringing Lindsey for dinner tonight, and there's lots to do. You do recall that we're having your son and his fiancée for dinner tonight?"

He put down the paper and scowled, "Yes, I am aware of our dinner this evening."

Mrs. Sterling pushed back her chair and stood. She was wearing a thick white terry cloth robe, and she had a nice figure to go with her dark complexion and hair. The missus was about the same age as Sterling, 50ish, and was in terrific shape, although I suspect a plastic surgeon might have had something to do with that. I recalled Joanna mentioning that Mac and Sterling liked to share women and wondered if she was another of Mac's conquests.

Sterling folded his paper, set it down beside him, and glared at me. I glared back and waited him out. He'd been up for some time. He was dressed for the office, his white trousers perfectly creased and blonde hair exquisitely quaffed. A real Jim Dandy.

"I tire of your antics. What is it you want?"

I tried to stay calm. "Four nights ago, you knocked me out cold. You're lucky I don't pull you across this table and break your jaw."

He folded his arms trying to play tough, then reflexively leaned back away from the table and my grasp.

"I denied this accusation yesterday, and nothing's changed. That is unless you brought some evidence?" He looked down his nose at me. "I didn't think so. Gibson called last night and said there's something you must ask me. Let's get it over with so you can leave my property for the final time."

"Larry Ferncroft," I said, studying his reaction. His face betrayed nothing.

He said, "Yes, what about him?"

"Monday night at the club, did you ask him to meet me and then bring me up to your office?"

"No, he sent me a message saying he was with you in the bar, but I never asked why. Did you know him already?"

"Did you discuss this case with him, or tell him about the FBI coming to the club on Tuesday?"

"What the hell does Ferncroft have to do with anything? He's a long-standing member of the club, his wife's family is a legacy. Larry is," he considered his words, "a nice fellow, but he's not a confidant of mine or involved in club leadership."

"I thought he was the club's rear commodore."

"Ferncroft?" He chuckled. "No, Freddy Samuelson is."

Sterling wore a condescending smirk. I knew it was for Ferncroft, but I also knew he thought even less of me than Larry. After all, Larry at least had a claim to this place through his wife. I was just a dumb hick interloper. I would be gone soon, disposed of like the men and women who clean up after him and his neighbors in Belle Haven.

"Were you aware that Whitman Endicott planned to kidnap and murder Joanna Hill and me yesterday?"

"What?"

His face read surprise. "Yeah, that's right. He tried to kill us. You better be careful. He's getting rid of people who know about your scheme to stash Mac. You got a license to carry?" I chuckled. "Of course not. Guys like you, never get your own hands dirty. You should strongly consider hiring private security. You got a nice life here, Sterling."

"I don't believe you."

"Okay, don't." I sipped my still too hot to drink coffee and stood to leave. "Look, I need to speak to some people who will be at the memorial today. Therefore, I need access to Indian Head for a couple of hours."

"No!"

"Yes. Let me tell you what I told your buddy French last night. I've spoken with two FBI special agents several times in the last couple of days, and your name has come up each time. They know about the phone calls you made to Endicott on the Sunday Mac was killed. They know about the trip French made to Indian Head so the two of you could oversee the cleanup and hiding of the body. You think it looks bad outside here this morning." I took my thumb and pointed to the rain coming down outside the picture window beside me. "The forecast for your ass staying out of jail looks much worse."

"It all sounds circumstantial to me, and my lawyers can handle circumstantial."

The truth wasn't getting me what I wanted, so I did what I had to. "Endicott told me you gave him the idea to kill Joanna and me."

"That's a Goddamn lie," he shouted.

"I have a witness."

He sighed and said, "That's bullshit. But, fine, I'll put you on the list. But know this, Town. I will be watching you closely. You step out of line, and I'll have you physically removed from the club."

"Know this, *pal*," I replied. "This time, I'll be watching you too."

I stood and turned to go and found Reggie waiting, and watching, from the hallway. He spun around and led the way back through the house. When we reached the front door, he smiled and opened it with a flourish, as I passed him, he whispered, "Thank you for a wonderful morning, Mr. Town."

"Take care of yourself, Reginald," I said and hopped into my chariot.

*   *   *

I got to the club at 10:30 am. The service was scheduled to start after the morning races were completed, which I was told would be about noon. I knew it was time to go home to Southie when the kid in the gate shack saw me coming and waved me on through, just like a regular member.

There was no one waiting on the porch to welcome me this time, and I wondered if Larry was around. I wasn't sure where to go. So, I turned right at the trophy case and made my way into the club's bar, and what do you know? My friend Rooster was already mixing cocktails. The rich like to drink at all hours. That's the one thing I admire about them.

"Rooster," I said. "Good morning."

"Buenos dias, Mr. Town."

"I thought your shift started at three."

"Usually yes, but special event today for Mr. Mac."

"I see. Do you have coffee back there?"

"Yes, but how about I make you a nice cappuccino?"

"I would do just about anything for a nice cappuccino. Thank you, Rooster, you're a life saver."

A few minutes later, cappuccino in hand, I sauntered out onto the patio. The rain had stopped on the ride over, and the clouds had given way to brilliant sunshine. However, the warm, humid air of the prior week was gone, not to be seen again until spring. It was crisp now, the kind of fall day where when you're in the sun, everything feels so optimistic, but step into the shade, and you're forced to face the reality of impending winter.

To my great fortune, sitting at a table not ten feet away from where I stood was Maria Moore and her son. They were joined by a man with far too dark of a tan for late September. Though, maybe the tan wasn't as dark as I'd first thought. Maybe the gleaming chiclets made him appear darker. She introduced him as her husband, Cliff, and he gave me a friendly shake. She then introduced her son, the tennis player. His name was Hunter, and he didn't look happy to be there.

I wanted to ask Cliff if he'd ever owned a Hummer, in a friendly way of course, but Maria sent him on an errand, thus leaving me alone with mother and son long enough to get what I needed.

"I visited with the Ferncrofts last evening, and I noticed Hunter in several photos. I guess Mr. Ferncroft is your tennis coach?" Hunter had his head buried in his phone, and only responded with a grunt in the affirmative after his mother poked him in the ribs.

I looked at Hunter, "Did you happen to speak with Mr. Ferncroft on Monday afternoon? You know, after I visited with your stepmother."

The little shit smirked at me, and said: "Why do you want to know?"

Before I could answer, Maria grabbed the phone from his hands. "Hey, gimme that back!" he said loud enough for the surrounding tables to hear. This made Maria cringe, but she didn't back down. She handed the phone to me instead and said, "I pay for it, and you have my permission to review the phone log."

"Thank you," I said, smirking back at the little puke.

Sure enough, I found a call to Larry at 12:04 p.m. on Monday, not long after I left Maria's place.

I held the phone in front of him and said, "I'll give this back if you're honest with me." I spoke slowly, "Did you tell Larry about my conversation with your mother?"

"What's it to you?" Maria poked him again, then told him to smarten up.

"Yeah! I told him you were interested in Mr. MacArthur. Okay?"

He reached for his phone, but I jerked it back.

"Why, Hunter? Why did you call him?"

"Fuck you," he said.

I laughed. Maria was horrified and threatened to take the phone away for good. This got him to answer, but not until he'd sulked for a good minute.

"Uh. Alright. No reason, I guess. I knew that James was a big shot at the club, and I wanted to see what Larry knew about things."

"You wanted to impress Larry?" He turned red.

"So, he didn't talk to you about Mr. MacArthur before you called him?"

"No. Why would he?"

"I guess he wouldn't, Hunter."

I handed the phone to Maria and thanked her, and as I was doing this, I noticed Tinsley Saunders emerge from the bar. I excused myself just as Cliff came back with a couple of tall cool drinks. I smiled at Maria, as she took one from Cliff. She said, "It's never too early for one of Rooster's concoctions." I had to agree.

Tinsley was standing along a stone wall, staring out at the Sound. I sidled up to her.

"Miss Saunders, might you be amenable to a quick conversation with a homesick fool?" I said, trying to turn on the charm.

"I think we finished talking yesterday, Earl," she said, with a look of disdain. Her seductive drawl was gone, her tone now caustic.

"I have more to say."

"It was just a fling, Earl. Why can't that suffice?"

I laughed. "You think I want to talk about *us*?" I shook my head and dropped my payload. "You can talk to me now, or I'm going to call my friends at the FBI and tell them about your being on the Rebecca around the time of the murder, which makes you one hell of a suspect. Then I'm going to discuss your starring role in setting up what was nearly a double homicide yesterday. That's right Tinsley, we both know you're up to your pretty little neck in this. It's your call." I held up my phone.

She decided she would like to speak with me after all.

We went back inside the bar and found a quiet table in a corner. As we settled in, I heard Larry Ferncroft's voice and turned to see him and Caroline coming in from the patio. They looked wind-blown, sun-charred and invigorated after sailing. He saw the two of us and waved. I waved back and asked how the sailing was, and he reported it choppy. You ain't seen nothing yet, pal.

Caroline gave me the evil eye and dragged him into the dining room.

I turned back to Tinsley and charged ahead. "Tell me about that night. The argument on the dock, your trip out to the Rebecca, when and where you saw Larry that morning. I know even more than I've told you, so don't lie to me."

"Maybe I should call my lawyers." She emphasized the plurality of the word. "You know I have a terrific civil attorney. She's particularly adept at proving defamation."

I took out my phone again and started to get up, but she grabbed my wrist. "Sit down."

She signaled Rooster, and he came right over. She said, "Bombay Sapphire, rocks." He looked at me, and I shook my head. When he left, my beautiful little canary began to sing.

"We argued on the dock, and Mac was upset with me because I agreed with Nate and Gib. He was far too indiscreet. My husband and I don't have a traditional marriage, but there was no need to rub his nose in it."

"But, does your husband know you're Rebecca?"

"No, not yet, but it's only a matter of time."

"When did Larry find out?"

"I'm not sure, but I think it was that night too. It was clear from Caroline's reaction on the dock that she'd finally figured it out. I don't know what James saw in her, but she wasn't much more to him than an occasional screw. Anyway, he headed for his yacht to sleep it off, and I went home to do the same, but I was gutted by the way everything had gone down and wanted to be with him. So, I changed course and went out to see him on his boat."

As she was saying this a wave of members made their way into the bar. They were fresh from the sea and full of shouts and taunts and all the things that people do when they've finished a battle and are ready to compare war stories.

Tinsley paused while they passed, and Rooster returned. When it had quieted down, I nudged her: "You were saying."

"He had calmed down by the time I made it to him, and we made up. You can use your imagination how, or your memory, if you prefer." She smiled, but I didn't reciprocate.

"And then you bashed his brains in and left?"

"No!" She'd said this so forcefully that several people around us took notice. She paused and waited for their eyes to turn away again, then leaned in and lowered her voice. "He was fine, giddy even, afterward, and said he wanted us to be together. He said the merger was going to be the end of a chapter in his life. He wanted to take the money and run. Just the two of us, cruising the world on our Rebecca." She smiled at the memory.

"That's nice that he was happy," I said. "Would you have gone with him?"

"In a way, I did love him, I guess. But no, of course not. My leaving was out of the question."

"So, you left to take the boat back to Bob's?"

"Yes, that's when I saw Larry. He was on his boat. It's a forty-footer with a dock mooring. He was deckside."

"Did he see you?"

"He had to see the boat pass by, but I don't think he knew it was me. How do you know about this?"

I ignored the question. "Do you think Larry killed Mac?"

She mulled this over for a while. "I didn't think so at first, but now I'm not sure. I've noticed a change in him recently. He's more assertive, angry even."

"I'd be too if someone was sleeping with my wife and my mistress," I interjected.

She nodded, but this didn't seem to faze her, as though it was nothing out of the ordinary.

"Did you notice any other small boats on the Sound that morning?"

"No, why?"

I switched gears to another topic I'd been wondering about. "Where did you hide the microphone?"

"Microphone? What am I, the CIA? I hid my phone in the centerpiece, and we listened in from the Starbucks around the corner. You know the one."

"So, it was your idea for me to meet Beth at your apartment?"

"No, that was Larry's. He asked me to suggest it to her. And given her paranoia about being followed, she agreed."

"Paranoia? So, you don't believe there are people following her?"

"I've known Beth a long time," she said. "She's always been a bit of drama queen."

"What was Larry's reason for the espionage?"

"He said Beth was hiding Mac from Whit and Gib, and that if he could find him, they would finally give him some respect around here, maybe even make him a club official."

"You believed him?"

"I thought Mac was still alive. I had no idea he was dead until two days ago. You'd already been taken away by the authorities when I found out. If you'd have seen my reaction, you'd know how much it upset me. Until the police showed up Thursday morning, I had no reason to suspect he'd been murdered."

"Okay, but you really believed Larry went to all that trouble over his status at the club," I smirked at her, and she shot me a critical eye.

"I thought you were a smart guy, Earl. Open your eyes and look around you. Status is everything around here."

"And once you had learned of the murder, then what did you think about Larry's motives?"

"I'm conflicted obviously. I don't think he's capable of it, but I can't explain his actions otherwise."

"Why did you tell Whit about what I said to you yesterday?"

"He called me as I was driving away. He'd seen us from his craft. He asked me if we'd talked about the case and I told him what you'd said. He didn't actually try to kill you, did he?"

I said, "You know, I think the only reason you called me yesterday was because Endicott put you up to it. I'll bet that's why you took me home the other night too. You two must be awfully tight. What else do you do for him?"

She smiled knowingly, and said, "So what if I did, Earl? You were fine with it. All of it. You got what you wanted and so did I, and you know it."

I told her to go to hell, then went down to the beach, where the memorial was taking shape.

31

A large crowd turned out to honor old Mac. There must have been eighty of us on the small private beach in front of Indian Head Yacht Club. The sandy stretch was about half the size of a football field, and each end was lined with one- and two-person sailboats, many of them used by the member's kids during summer sailing programs.

There was a stone wall separating us from the flagstone patio that connected the bar and restaurant, where a few dozen more of Mac's friends watched and mingled. Many had drink in hand, and I spotted bar staff making rounds and taking orders. Cocktails on the beach is my kind of memorial. Maybe I should quit being a P.I. and just get rich.

I stayed back on the patio for a bit while I exchanged text messages with special agent Ron Sullivan. He confirmed that they had digital and visual evidence of Larry driving from Manhattan to Greenwich early the morning Mac was killed. His alibi was a lie, and he was in the vicinity of the club when Mac was murdered. Circumstantial, yes, but also compelling.

I told the G-man about the red skiff with 81-15 on its bow. He said he'd look into it, and not to do anything else until I heard back from him. If only I'd listened.

The service began with Sterling moving to the water's edge and turning to face the crowd. The Commodore's comments were more perfunctory than they should've been. He said a few words about what a great friend James was, and how much he would be missed, but he shared no wistful anecdotes of the good times. I'd chalk it up to emotion in the wake of the passing of a dear friend, but he didn't show any sign of mourning either. He was going through the motions, and it dawned on me as I watched that Sterling knew the noose was being tightened around his well-moisturized neck. His weak words were the result of distraction. Whit Endicott was nowhere to be found. I wondered if he'd tried his act on McNierney yet, and just how the wounded vet would handle him if and when he did.

Gibson French slipped in just as the service began. I assumed it was because he didn't want to run into me. I tried to make eye contact with him several times, but he always averted his gaze. However, he did bare some of his soul to the mourners, telling humorous, even self-deprecating, tales about sailboat races, nights on the town, and business successes shared by him and Mac. He even teared up and had to pause as he spoke of a boarding-school adolescence made bearable only by his friend James. I almost felt a little sorry for him, even as I fantasized about Sully and Garcia slapping a set of cuffs on him.

Old Hirst Albrecht went next and spoke of how he taught Mac and French to sail when they were barely out of diapers, and how much they loved the sea, the Sound and Indian Head Point. It was a touching moment, nearly ruined when Hirst lost his balance mid-way through and began to stumble backward into the water as the crowd watched frozen in horror. Fortunately, Beth MacArthur put her volleyball-honed reflexes to work and leaped up to steady him. Then she stayed by his side to make sure he was safe, and to ensure her turn at the microphone would be next.

She spoke briefly of good times with Mac. The adventures they had, such as sailing down the eastern seaboard through the Panama Canal and across much of the Pacific. I could see why she took a chance on him. In addition to all of his money, of course. Neither Tinsley nor Caroline said any words and the event broke up after about thirty minutes of recollections and the occasional prayer. I felt bad that Joanna hadn't been able to be there and say a few words, but when your dead boss's boss is trying to murder you, it pays to keep a low profile.

I had been keeping an eye on Larry and watched as he and Caroline moved in different directions following the service. She headed for the bar while he walked down to the dock and onto a yacht. I gave it a few minutes, then made my way to him.

❊ ❊ ❊

"Last Call, I like that name, Larry," I said as I approached his craft. He was standing on deck adjusting the rigging around the mast. Though the boat might be considered diminutive compared to the Rebecca, the Last Call was no small deal. It was long, sleek and modern, with graceful lines and as much cabin space as a North-end studio apartment.

"Earl. It's, ah, nice to see you," said the voice that came out of Larry.

Larry's face told a very different story. It screamed abject fear.

"Can I come aboard?" I already had a foot on the deck and was boarding regardless of the answer.

"Of course," he said, setting down the lines he'd been sorting.

"This is beautiful, Larry," I said gazing up at thirty feet of mast. "Having a boat like this has got to make you feel a great sense of freedom. You can hop on this thing and sail just about anywhere in the world."

"It was a gift from my old man. He used to take me sailing as a kid." He gazed out across the Sound, and added, "One of his favorite sayings was *a man with a sturdy ship and an ocean, is his own man.*"

"That captures the sentiment beautifully," I said.

We faced one another on top of the cabin, which sat directly below deck. The deck we were on was only about eight feet wide with rounded edges and no railing. I considered my options should Larry make a move and felt at a distinct disadvantage being unfamiliar with the surface on which we stood.

"You planning on taking any trips, Larry?" Subtle, but not too subtle, I thought. Larry must have been in a hurry because he cut to the chase.

"I know you're not here for a social visit, Earl. Just get on with it."

"I came here to try and help you. You've told me several things that don't add up, and you need to turn yourself in. It's bad now, but it'll be worse if you don't get out ahead of it. The cops know what I know, and probably even more."

"Aw," he groaned, sounding more like a wounded animal than a man. Then he sat down in a heap right there by the mast. He wrapped his arms around his knees and pulled them up to his chin. "Jesus, Earl. You're right, I haven't been entirely truthful, but I didn't kill him. I just didn't."

I dropped down beside him with my legs hanging over the edge of the cabin roof and let him think things through. We stared out at the Sound and said nothing for a while.

Finally, I broke the ice. "I think you're a good man, Larry. I really do, and I think you'll do the right thing. You can't run from this. You have to make this right to remain your own man."

"No!" He stood up, and I followed, not wanting to leave myself open to attack. "I'm not..." He paused. "This isn't easy, I can't just." He paused and looked out at the water, then back at the club, where I noticed Caroline was watching us from the patio. She looked away when I spotted her. He said, "I need some time, Earl."

I considered this while surveying the dozens of sailboats dotting the Sound. The elite of Wall St., Madison Ave., and U.S. media and manufacturing, and their offspring were out there having a great day riding the waves and the wind, unaware of the drama being played out only a stone's throw away. I wasn't sure if he'd done it, or was covering for Tinsley or Caroline, but in that moment, when he said he hadn't done it, I believed him.

"Okay," I said. "It's two o'clock. I'll give you a few hours to get your head together. Alright?" He nodded. "I'll call you at five. If you're up to it, I'll arrange a meeting with some people I've come to trust. They'll give you a fair shake. I promise you they will." I wasn't a hundred percent on this, but Sullivan and Garcia seemed decent enough.

He looked into my eyes and thanked me. "You're the first person in a long time." He caught himself and paused. "Thank you."

I tried to find Caroline on my way out, but she had pulled a disappearing act.

* * *

My phone rang at 4:35 pm. I had gone back to the B&B and was making use of the free coffee in the lobby, which wasn't bad as lobby-coffee goes. The screen on my phone read: Sully 4 (G-Man). I know a lot of Sully's.

"Earl's Bait and Tackle."

"What did you say to him?" Sullivan's tone was deadly serious. This woke up the butterflies that live in my stomach, and I immediately began to feel uneasy.

"Who are you talking about?"

"Larry Ferncroft. I told you not to do anything until you heard back from me. What did you do?"

I put down the coffee and plunked into a well-worn wingback chair. "I told him there were some inconsistencies in his story and that he should turn himself in. I offered to introduce him to you."

"Goddammit! Where are you?"

"At the Mainsail B&B in Old Greenwich."

"Go stand out front. A car will be by to pick you up." He hung up.

I downed my coffee in one long burning gulp, then walked outside under a roiling cloud of doom.

In a little under six minutes, a black Ford Crown Victoria with black-wall tires pulled up in front, and I hopped into the passenger seat.

The driver was a young man with neatly trimmed auburn hair and aviator glasses.

"You Earl Town?"

"Unfortunately, yes. What's going on?"

He pulled away from the curb and reversed direction with a chirp of the rear tires. "I can't say."

"You don't know, or you're not allowed to tell me?"

"I can't say."

We drove in silence for a while, before I said something that had been bothering me since climbing in. "Ford Crown Vic, huh? You get a choice in the matter? Cause the Chevy Caprice is a better car."

* * *

It wasn't long before I recognized where we were headed, and my stomach crawled down into my lower intestine. We were approaching the Ferncroft residence, which was surrounded on two sides by police cars, emergency vehicles, and an ambulance. I saw a couple of press types lurking on the civilian side of yellow police tape as well. "What happened?" I asked again.

"Special agent Sullivan would like to tell you himself," said the young agent as he turned into the driveway. We made it about halfway to the house before we had to get out and walk around the cop cars to reach the front steps.

Garcia met me at the door, and blurted out, "I managed to calm him down a bit. Come on, I'll take you back there."

I followed her between the library and living room to the kitchen, out through a set of French doors along the pool to the pool house. I didn't have to enter the room to see evidence of the horrible act that had taken place there. The white sofa on which Caroline Ferncroft was laid out the day before had been spray coated in a coagulating mass of blood, flesh, bone, and brain matter.

Sullivan looked up, saw us coming and came quickly over to meet us. "Come here," he demanded, as he walked to a set of patio chairs and a table. "Sit down."

I did as I was told, though it was hard to peel my eyes away from the scene inside. I hate rubberneckers, but I was transfixed by the carnage.

"Who?" I asked, glancing at the splatter that covered half the sofa, most of the coffee table, and a good deal of wall. There was a body contorted in a corner section of the couch with a sheet placed over it.

Between the sofa and wall sat a large potted fern. Its leaves had also absorbed a good deal of spray, and every so often blood, or a bit of flesh, would drip from the leaves into the dirt below. Even more chilling was the splatter outline of the fern that was now staining the white wall behind it, little rivulets of blood streaking down and pooling on the porcelain tiles below.

"First things first. I want to know what was said, word for word."

I told him about my brief conversation aboard the Last Call, a name that now held new meaning. I also filled him in on what I'd learned from Sterling, Maria, and Tinsley. As I was doing this, I heard a woman cry out from a nearby room, and I knew that Caroline was okay. It was Larry who had done the redecorating.

Once I'd satisfied him, Sullivan glanced at Garcia and said, "Let him look, then get him out of my sight." He got up and walked toward the main house. He didn't look back.

She was standing by an open set of French doors and directed me to come over with a thrust of her head.

"Don't go in, you can see everything from here," she said. She stepped into the room and pulled back the sheet.

Larry's body was slumped over. What remained of his head was turned to the left, the shot coming from the right, and at very close range. I recalled Larry's forehand being on his right side in several of the photos in the trophy case.

A 38 special, lay inches from his right hand. I wanted to tell myself that it wasn't my fault that he'd terminated his life, but I couldn't.

"Is there a note?" I asked Garcia.

"Not yet, but we haven't checked the back pockets." She put her hand on my shoulder, and I turned my head to face her. "It's not your fault," she said. "He was facing life in prison. He took the easy way out."

"Not necessarily," I said. "He could have been protecting someone."

She was skeptical, and I knew in my heart that barring the finding of a secret recording or some other evidence left by Larry, the investigation would end here. It was neat and tidy. Well, not this scene, but Mac's murder. Everything pointed to Larry. The lies, the motive, the suicide. No district attorney would look beyond a mountain of evidence such as this, and especially not when the rich and powerful were involved. They had everything they needed to put this case to bed, and that's what they'd do.

Garcia walked me back out front and handed me over to the same kid who'd brought me. I asked to speak to Caroline. I needed to see her reaction, but Garcia simply shook her head and pointed to the car. Behind it, my driver was directing a hearse to move so we could back out of there.

32

I stayed in Greenwich one final night to provide an official statement regarding my conversation with Larry, before making a
break for Boston late Sunday morning. Not surprisingly, I got
caught up in work-crew-incited jams on both I-95 and the Mass Pike
and didn't make it back to my apartment in Southie until late that
evening. I watered my severely malnourished plants, for which I had
forgotten to make arrangements, while reviewing the rash of voicemails that had come in since the story of the jealous corporate lawyer who murdered the rich financier in a love triangle with his wife
began to hit the media.

Tinsley clearly had some solid P.R. professionals behind her, or
maybe 'fixers' is the better term for them. She managed to stay out of
the coverage, even though I was certain it wasn't jealousy over his *wife*
that provided Larry with a motive to kill. I'd made this clear to Sullivan and Garcia, but it didn't matter. The media had their story, and
that was that.

Someone had told a reporter for the New York Post about some of
my role in cracking the case, and I had a pretty good idea who too. I
wasn't sure if I should send Maria Moore a Christmas card or a cease-
and-desist notice for doing so. On that day, I had no desire to talk to
the press about the case, even though I knew it would be good for business. I told myself that maybe in a few days after I'd had a chance to
decompress, it would be okay. But, until then, the odds of me getting
annoyed with a reporter's inquiries and saying something that could
get me sued, arrested, or both, were north of ninety percent.

I took a long, steamy shower and found a fresh voicemail from a
friend when I'd dressed again. "Hey Chief, it's Hiney! I pick up a copy
of the New York freaking Post this morning and whose ugly mug is
staring back at me on page 3. You son of a bitch! I know you're probably
getting made-up on the set of the Today Show right about now, but as
soon as you get a chance, you call me and fill me in. You old-dog you.

Congratulations, what a case!"

While the murder story made the front pages of the paper, in the back was a separate story about charges being filed against a couple of Greenwich residents, whose names were being withheld, which is just another of the many ways it pays to be rich. The pair was charged with obstruction of justice, witness tampering, tampering with a corpse, and conspiracy to commit offenses. One had also been charged with assault and battery and kidnapping, and I thought of Sterling's smug face and took in a deep, satisfying breath of fresh air. The article quoted an unnamed source saying that a third person was also being sought in the investigation. So, Endicott was still on the run.

I put on a pair of comfortable sneakers and blue jeans and walked to Smitty's on the corner, where I washed down a plate of corned beef and cabbage with a pint of Guinness. Then I finally retreated to the bed I'd so missed and fell into a restless sleep, rich femme fatales and evil scotch-swilling sailors filling my dreams.

I was up early on Monday, and was back in my office at 8:30 am, calculating the expenses I'd run up and realizing how reckless I'd been. I'd worked for free since Thursday when my retainer with Jo-anna had expired. In that time, I spent more than a grand on hotels, meals, and Ed's services, not to mention filling the tank several times. Apparently, the gas they sell in New York and Connecticut contains a high quantity of gold.

My buzzer went off, and I recalled Joanna arriving at about the same time one week prior. I fixed myself in the mirror before walking to the front door, where I found her waiting.

I gave the universal sign for 'come on in.' She knew the way and walked past the stairs and into my office. She sat down across from my desk, just as she had before. Because I needed another one, I asked if she wanted a coffee. She didn't. I leaned back in my chair, pressed my fingertips together and waited.

"You did it, Earl. You found Mac, and you found his killer. I will be eternally grateful to you."

"Just doing my job, Joanna."

"You did it well, Earl, and I'll never forget it." She began to tear up a little, and I offered her a Kleenex. She took two, dabbed at her eyes, and went on.

"I'll never forget what I felt in those woods. The fear of everything coming to an end right then and there, and at the hands of that evil little man. The feeling of imminent death followed by the joy of see-ing your face after all of the gunfire. You saved my life, Earl. That's not just doing your job. I didn't hire you for that, but you did it."

I shook my head. "I also created the situation that put you in danger. You should never have been in those woods. That was due to mistakes I made."

"No!" She stood and came around the desk. She leaned in close. "You played all of this beautifully. You did what you had to, and you and I came out unscathed. Well, except for that bump on your head." She ran a gentle hand over my still mostly brown locks and smiled with great warmth. It was one of those motherly looks, and I knew my initial read of her was correct, and even saving her life hadn't changed it. We'd never be more than friends.

It annoyed me a little. My male pride doesn't like being bruised, and I was, perhaps a little too direct with my next comment. "I'm not convinced Larry killed him."

The look of motherly love dissolved into concern, and she sat back down. "What do you mean, Earl?"

"Caroline doesn't have an alibi. She'd had just found out that Rebecca was Tinsley, and not her, and Caroline apparently loved Mac." She frowned.

"Just hear me out. Caroline likely told Larry that Mac was sleeping with Tinsley and lured him back to Greenwich. Larry could've seen Caroline visit Mac's boat and then gone out there and found the murder scene. Knowledge of Caroline's guilt is the perfect motive for all of Larry's lies. Larry could have been protecting her. And, when I gave him an ultimatum, and he told Caroline the jig was up, perhaps in the hope that she would turn herself in. He got dead."

She sat back and considered it for a good while. It had felt good to unburden myself of this scenario, which was beginning to dominate my psyche. She was wise, and I had to admit that I had enjoyed bouncing ideas off of her during the case. Though, almost getting her killed, reinforced my belief that I was meant to be a lone wolf, in a business sense, not in life, not if I could help it.

She reached her verdict and gave it to me straight. "Everything you said may be true, but the more likely scenario remains the one that everybody but you, apparently, believes occurred. Larry had two reasons to kill Mac: his wife and mistress. He was there at the time of the murder. His alibi collapsed, and when presented with these facts, he killed himself. You've got to accept this and move on, Earl. Look I have something here to help you get past this."

Joanna picked her bag up from the floor, reached into it, and took out her checkbook. I waved her off, saying, "That's nice of you. I'll take reimbursement for the additional expenses I ran up in the three days

I worked for you, but you don't owe me any more than that. Heck, you dropped $400 on a new phone the other day."

"It's okay, Earl. I got some crazy news on Saturday. I want you to take this money."

"Yeah? What kind of news?"

"Mac never told me this, but he put me in his will."

"Really?"

"Yes, and I want you to have this." She removed a check and placed it on the desk in front of me. I nearly choked when I read the figure.

"No way. Joanna! This is out of the question."

"He left me the Rebecca."

I stopped protesting and peered at her.

"That's quite a boat, and quite new too," I said, recalling what Larry said it was worth.

"Yes, it is, and I'm going to sell it, so you take this money that you *more* than earned. Okay?"

I had taken a serious blow to the head and was nearly murdered. I knew the killing of two men was not something that could be locked away in its compartment forever. I would have to deal with it at some point, and it wouldn't be pretty. Even though they were intent on murdering Joanna and me, their violent deaths at my hands will probably always haunt me.

"Thank you," I said, folding the check and placing it inside my jacket. Instead of being thrilled, I found myself thinking about the forty million my work had probably saved Beth MacArthur and wishing she'd also share some of the wealth. P.I. problems.

"What are you going to do now?" I asked her.

She caressed her chin and looked past me through the window. "I don't know, maybe go to Vermont and raise some alpacas."

"That sounds like a damn fine plan, Joanna." I meant it.

Soon after we said our goodbyes, and then my nephew Ed appeared at my office door just as Joanna departed.

He parked himself in the warm chair, and said, "Holy shit, Earl! Her pictures don't do her justice." Then the meathead set a bag on my desk and extracted a donut along with a cloud of powdered sugar. I gave him a death stare, and he gently placed it back in the bag and blew the dust onto my previously clean floor.

"Sorry." He handed me a bill for the rest of his hours on the MacArthur case, and I did something I rarely do, which was to take my phone and transfer the remaining money I still owed him without picking the charges apart.

"What gives, Earl? That hit on the head still affecting you?"

I leaned back and interlocked my fingers behind my neck "You know, Ed, I think this business of mine might just be taking off. I may not have to take on crappy cases anymore."

Just then the phone rang. It was Provident Insurance Corporation, where I had a contact that fed me a steady stream of fraud work. I glared at the screen for a few seconds, struggling to ignore it. Then I said, "Ah shit, I better take this."

* * *

Sleep did not come to me that night, because I could not stop dwelling on how neatly the pieces had all fallen into place. How convenient it was that Larry wasn't around to claim his innocence. I wondered about the skiff that Miguel saw race by. Maybe it was a fisherman or someone out for an early morning spin. Maybe it was Caroline fleeing the scene after bashing Mac's head in.

At 7:15 am, I climbed out of bed, dressed, repacked my overnight bag, and began to drive back to Greenwich. I had to speak with Caroline Ferncroft. I had no choice in the matter.

My phone rang about an hour later, as I was getting onto I-84.

"Special agent Sullivan, to what do I owe the honor?"

"Yeah, uh, morning, Town. I have a question for you. Last night, a Mercedes Sprinter Van registered to Wayne Trust was found in an abandoned quarry about forty miles northwest of Greenwich. It had been torched, and there were a couple of bodies inside."

"Really?" I said, doing everything in my power to sound disinterested.

"Yeah, really. You want to tell me what this is about, Town? Or should I send someone to get you and bring you to me in cuffs?"

"Well, if you send Garcia, the cuffs thing might be okay. I'm kind of a lonely guy."

He didn't respond, and I suddenly found myself in a panic. "You're not on speaker with her right now, are you?"

"No, you're lucky. Now, stop wasting my time, and answer my question."

"Why do you think I have something to do with this?"

"Well, as I said, the van is registered to Wayne Trust. And, it was last used by Whitman Endicott, who has seemingly disappeared. And no, his is not one of the slabs of barbeque we found inside." He let this hang in the air for a moment. Then, when I started to speak, he cut me off with his closer: "Oh yeah, I also happened to notice that you were wearing one of those crazy mercenary-type knife belts when we spoke with you on Friday. You do have one of those, correct?"

I felt a cold sweat forming on my hairline. "Yes, I do have one."

"You *do*, as in *still do*?"

I had a choice to make, and I chose the right one. The one that my decade and a half as a cop taught me, which might surprise you. The rule is to never admit anything that could be considered a crime to an officer of the law. People think the police are on their side. They are not. I took a deep breath and replied matter-of-factly: "Yes, I'm wearing it right now. Why do you ask?"

"That's a good answer, Town."

"You know," I said, quickly changing the subject. "I wondered why Endicott wasn't at the memorial on Saturday."

"Funny you never mentioned that concern to me, detective."

"Well, I had a lot on my mind this weekend, *special agent*." I chewed on his title a bit to let him know I didn't appreciate the grilling after all I'd been through. According to the papers, I had been instrumental in helping them catch a murderer. He owed me some respect, not that I expected him to give it.

"You know, Sullivan, Larry's lies can all be explained if he was protecting his wife."

"His wife?" He exhaled deeply and gave me a not so measured response. "No, she don't look like the type."

"Really? What type does she look like?" I asked.

"The non-murderous type. But, fine, I'll play along. What's her motive on MacArthur?"

"She and Mac had been having an affair for some time, and she told me she'd been in love with him since they were kids. He'd told her he loved her too and made a lot of promises. Then he told her that he loved her so much he named his million-dollar boat after her."

"But I thought Tinsley Saunders was Rebecca."

"Tinsley is Rebecca," I said. "Rebecca is a character in ..."

"Yeah, I know about that," Sullivan interjected. "I mean, I know about the novel and the wife flaunting her affairs. Why would Caroline believe it was her?"

"I don't know. Maybe she didn't believe, but she thought Mac loved her, and then she found out that Tinsley was Rebecca and that Mac was more in love with her. Caroline was the other woman on the dock when MacArthur, French, and Sterling were arguing."

"No shit? So, what happened after the argument?"

"My theory is that Caroline left the club and went home like the rest of them. After a few sleepless hours, she decided to pay Mac a visit to mend things. As she approached his boat, most likely from the water, she saw Tinsley leaving it, and flew into a rage."

"Yeah? You know how to weave a tale, but where's the evidence?"

"Wait, there's one more thing to consider. Tinsley was also sleeping with Larry Ferncroft. And, Larry was in love with Tinsley."

"Jesus. What the fuck is it with these people? Are you serious?"

"Yes. I told you I was witness to a lover's quarrel between Larry and Tinsley on Friday night. Didn't seem like he wanted to leave his wife for Tinsley, but he was wild about her."

"Yeah, well pardon me if I forgot that, after all, I was busy cleaning up the mess you made. Okay, so why not kill Tinsley instead? After all, she's the real problem here, as far as Caroline would be concerned."

"Caroline placed tremendous trust in Mac. Like I said, she told me Mac was her true love. I think when she found out he had been lying to her and was in love with Tinsley, her rage was directed at the betrayer, instead of the rival. Though, now that you mention it, Tinsley would be wise to watch her back. You might want to mention that to her, as a service to a rather substantial taxpayer."

"Okay, but again I ask, where's your evidence?"

"I don't know, but I have to talk to Caroline. I need closure there. Have you found out anything about the gun that killed Larry?"

"No," he said. "Saturday night special, no serial numbers, no ballistics match. Where a guy like Ferncroft got a gun like this, I don't know."

"How about a suicide note?"

"Nope. She said he came home very upset. Mentioned talking to you and told her he had done something very bad and was going to have to pay for it. She left him alone in the pool house for a few minutes, while she went to find valium to calm him down. She heard the gunshot while in the main house."

"What about the skiff? You got anything?"

"No, state cops looked into it, came up empty. No more questions, until you answer mine. What's the motive for killing her husband?"

"I told you this when I gave you my statement."

"Tell me again."

"Larry knew the jig was up after we spoke on his yacht a couple of hours before he died. I saw Caroline watching us from the patio at Indian Head. He went home and either confronted her or she caught on. She feared he would spill the beans. Maybe he was blackmailing her. After all, he loved someone else, why not? Any way you slice it, he had to be silenced."

There was a lengthy silence, then Sullivan said: "Dammit."

I disconnected my phone before he could say another word.

33

I made good time and arrived back in Greenwich twenty minutes before noon. I squelched the hunger growing inside of me with an energy drink and two bags of snacks from a gas station, then drove to the Ferncroft estate. Services for Larry weren't scheduled until Thursday. The widow would likely be in mourning at the family home, and I hoped my presence wouldn't cause a scene. Especially if it resulted in another round with Chief Matthew Boone.

I maneuvered back between the stone columns past the open gate and into the circular driveway. As I pulled up to the portico, I noticed a set of familiar tire tracks running across a stretch of lawn and over a small flower bed. It didn't look so funny now, given the events that had befallen this family since I'd made those indentations.

I pressed the doorbell by the large double doors off of the portico and waited. The old woman answered, and I froze for a second wondering how to handle her.

I said. "Hello there. I'm very sorry for your loss ma'am, and I hate to intrude at such a difficult time, but it's imperative that I speak with Mrs. Ferncroft right away. Is she at home?"

She gave me a blank stare again. Then shut the door in my face as she had done the first time I'd visited. I'd waited last time, and she came back, so I decided to try my luck again. A short while later the door opened, and instead of the woman, a young man stood there. I introduced myself and made my appeal again.

He looked at me blankly and said: "It's Tuesday afternoon."

I said. "I'm new to town. What does that have to do with this?"

"Miss Ferncroft rides at her father's stables on Tuesdays and Fridays."

I recalled the equestrian trophies in the pool house. "Ah, where are these stables?"

Twenty minutes later I was back in Belle Haven, wondering how they could call it exclusive if a guy like me could breeze in here for the third time in less than a week.

I followed my GPS and soon turned off the main drag onto a well-maintained dirt drive that led to the Belle Haven Stables.

The road went on for about a half-mile and was mostly surrounded by a forest of oak and pine trees, before opening into a vast expanse of green meadow separated every so often by a horse corral or an old stone wall. On a hill at the end of the lane stood a large Victorian-style mansion alongside a couple of well-maintained barns and what looked to be a covered riding ring.

I planned to make my way up to the Victorian when I noticed an arrow-shaped sign just barely poking out of tall roadside weeds on my left. It read: Boat Ramp, and I felt my heart rate quicken. I turned into a narrow and bumpy dirt trail and made slow progress for a couple hundred yards until I reached the end. There, I found a small secluded beach and, as advertised, an asphalt boat ramp about thirty feet in length and about as wide as a pick-up truck. What really caught my eye, though, were the two red skiffs parked on the far edge of the beach. I put the car in park and got out.

The small metal boats were worn and scuffed on the inside and out, but had well maintained outboard motors. Scratched red paint covered the exterior except for a space on each bow, which read Belle Haven Stables in small white lettering. Above this, painted in large white letters was the abbreviation: B.H.S. I stepped back and stared at the letters, then stepped back more, and then some more, until I was about a hundred feet away, which is about how far Miguel had described the skiff being from the dock. At 100 feet, B.H.S. could easily be mistaken for 81-15. In fact, it looked more like 81-15 than B.H.S.

I thought of what Miguel said, and muttered aloud to the waves breaking on the shore: "Those who hate the Lord would cower to him, and their doom would last forever."

All at once I felt sick to my stomach. I dropped to my knees and vomited a mix of Red Bull and junk food into the surf. It wasn't the road breakfast that made me ill. It was the knowledge that Larry didn't commit suicide and my visiting him on his boat, while Caroline watched from the patio above, is what got him killed.

I stayed there on my knees for a few minutes telling myself it wasn't my fault, but I wasn't buying it. Finally, I told myself to put my feelings in a box and lock them away for the moment. It was time to focus on the task at hand. I snapped a photo of the skiffs and texted it to Sullivan and Garcia with the message 'Caroline Ferncroft's riding stables, on the Sound, just south of IHYC.'

I got back into the Caprice and drove up to the old Victorian with a fury building inside of me. I passed the turnoff to the parking lot and pulled up alongside the first of two massive barns. That's where I thought I stood the best shot of finding Caroline. The barn was lined on either side with horse stalls, only a couple of which contained the magnificent beasts. Most of them were outside munching grass in the brisk fall air. I heard a human rustling about in the third stall from the back to my right and tried to think of I what would say as I made my way to it. I decided to go with 'serious message guy.'

"Is Caroline Ferncroft about?"

"Who wants to know?" asked a young woman, no more than 25 years of age. She wore a torn flannel shirt, grubby denim jeans, and mucky work boots.

"I'm a friend of the family, and I have some urgent news about the, ah, events of Saturday, that I must relay to her right away. It's good news, you know, as good as can be in these circumstances." I thought throwing in the good news part would get her on my side. Who doesn't want to cheer up a grieving widow? This wench for one.

"Good news, huh. She didn't seem all that upset to me." Blonde ponytail swaying, the girl waved a pitchfork and threw some hay around the stall. I took two steps back.

"Really? Well, she's a strong woman."

"Uh huh, well she went out for a ride. The trails connect to her father's property. She usually goes over there to train."

"Father's property?"

"Yeah, he owns this place and the place next door." She pointed through the rear door to a field. Then she looked me up and down and asked, "You any good on a horse?"

"Yeah, actually I am. I grew up around horses. It's been a few years, but I rode quite a bit as a kid."

"That guy over there." She pointed to a tall white and brown appaloosa across from us. "His name is Shoes. He needs to be exercised, but I gotta get this placed cleaned up. You up for a ride?"

I looked down at my dress pants and loafers and said, "Uh, yeah, why not?"

About ten minutes later, I was in the saddle. Shoes was an older horse, so I was instructed to take him on a gentle walk. A trot was acceptable, but a gallop was out of the question, which was fine by me.

He was a good horse, though as with most horses, it took me several minutes of tugging on the reins to prove to him that I was the one in charge. Whether he liked it or not, he was not going to pull me to whatever patch of grass or leafy bush he wanted and have at it.

The trail started on the other side of a meadow behind the indoor riding stable and meandered through a dense wood, across a small stream and up and over two small hills that the stable hand called 'the twin sisters,' before opening into a large field where I was told I would find Caroline. My phone buzzed with a series of texts as I made my way out onto the well-worn trail. They were all from Sullivan, who was insisting that I wait for back up before engaging. I kept on the trail.

After about twenty minutes, I reached the peak of the second sister and halted. Spread out beneath me was a long flat pasture divided into five sections by ancient New England stone walls. There was a small barn in a far corner, and a section of the field was filled with a series of small fences, walls, and other obstacles. I recalled that many of the trophies in Caroline's home were of horse and rider in midflight. She wasn't just an equestrian, she was a jumper. I realized she had a significant advantage on horseback and reached for the handle of my Glock to give it a reassuring squeeze.

As Shoes and I trotted down into the pasture, a rider emerged from inside the barn and I knew it was Caroline. Unlike me, she was dressed in proper riding attire: black helmet and jacket over a white shirt, with tan pants and black boots. She and her tall gray steed trotted towards the first of a series of fences. When they were about a horse's length away, she pulled up out of the saddle as her mount recoiled on its hind legs. The horse's head and chest rose as Caroline leaned in, nearly resting her chin on its neck, her white silk scarf billowing in the wind as the stallion leaped into the air. Then Caroline rose up out of the saddle lessening the impact on the horse's front legs when the beast came back down to strike the earth, only to drop back into the saddle as the animal's rear legs made purchase and the horse perfectly hit its stride. The pair repeated this process through another dozen or so obstacles as I gradually made my way towards her, in awe of her skill, as well as that of her horse.

I took a position a short distance from the makeshift course and waited until she finished her run and trotted over to me.

"Detective Town, rather surprising to see you not only here, but on horseback too. Do you jump as well as ride?"

"Mrs. Ferncroft," I replied, noticing things between us had gotten formal all of a sudden. "No, absolutely not. I like my horses old and calm, like Shoes here. No galloping and definitely no jumping." I patted Shoes on the neck, and he responded with a happy whinny. I went on, "You're an amazing rider. I hear you grew up around these stables."

"I did. Is there something you need, detective? Victory and I," she patted her noble beast, "are just getting started, and I've got to get back home soon. There's much to do. Perhaps you've heard, I have a funeral to attend for my late husband."

"Yes, ah. I'm sorry for your loss. I'll get to the point." I sat up straight in the saddle trying to steady Shoes, who was pulling the reins trying to reach the grass in front of him. "You called your husband the night Mac was killed. You lured him back to Greenwich. Why?"

The impassive expression she'd been wearing turned angry. "Really, detective? My husband died in my arms just days ago, and here you are interrupting my grieving to what? Accuse me of something? Why don't you say what you really think?"

"I don't have enough information to think much of anything. That's why I'm asking for your help?"

"My help? I was told the case was closed. Larry killed Mac and himself. I don't know what you're doing here, Mr. Town, but you should leave."

I had no option but to bluff. "Okay. I'll be straight with you. I have an eyewitness who saw you leaving the murder scene in a Belle Haven Stables skiff. You can tell me what happened out there, or I can go talk to the Feds, and they'll sort it out. It's your call, Mrs. Ferncroft."

I saw Caroline's lip curl up in what can only be described as a sinister smile. There was a glimmer in her eye, and in an instant, I knew I had made a tremendous blunder in not dismounting before engaging her. If I hadn't been on horseback, she might have called my bluff and tried to talk her way out of it. But she saw an opportunity to eliminate her problem, and given she was on a winning streak, she went for the trifecta.

I shifted the reins to my left hand and reached for my gun with my right, but Caroline was too quick. Before I could raise the Glock, she pulled a leather riding crop from inside her jacket, and in one fluid motion she leaned down, brought her arm all the way back and put everything she had into whipping old Shoes hard across his backside. There was a resounding crack as leather met flesh and Shoes cried out, reared back and sprang into a full gallop with me fumbling with, then dropping, my gun. I slipped and slid all over the saddle, trying desperately to hold on to keep from being trampled under the massive beast's hooves. I lost one of the reins and fought to hold onto the saddle horn. When I lost my grip on that, I took a handful of mane and pulled as hard as I could while shouting "Whoa Shoes! Slow down Shoes, whoa!"

As I struggled to hold onto a horse that showed no signs of slowing, Caroline came charging up on my left flank. I turned and looked into her eyes, and I knew for certain that Larry hadn't killed anyone. The poor bastard was set up and taken out by this evil bitch, and now she was going to kill me in what would undoubtedly be ruled an accidental death. I wanted to lash out at her before she struck me, but I couldn't release my grip.

There was a joyful gleam in her eyes as she leaned into me with an outstretched hand. It connected with my left shoulder driving me back and causing me to finally release the old steed's mane. I tumbled ass over tea kettle, somehow managing to avoid the flying hooves, as I slammed down hard into the turf. Pain shot through my right side as I landed. The wind was knocked out of me, and I gasped for air. Shoes kept on going, and I found myself lying defenseless in the middle of a pasture with what sure felt like a broken right collarbone and a couple of cracked ribs.

Having galloped by, Caroline pulled back on the reins and expertly turned her ride. She trotted up to me slowly like a lion strolling up to a gazelle with only three good legs. She stopped a few feet away and gazed down at me with disappointment in her eyes. I hadn't presented much of a challenge, had I? Like everyone else, I had read her completely wrong, and this was going to be my final mistake. What a piss-poor way to go out, I thought to myself.

I sat up and felt both sides of my cleanly broken collarbone shift beneath my skin. The pain was excruciating and made worse by my aching ribs. I laid back and focused on it until I could take it as a whole and place it in a small lockbox in the back recesses of my brain. Then I sat back up to face my destiny. My neck strained as I looked past Victory's slimy snout and up into Caroline's cold, calculating eyes. Over her shoulder, I saw the sun breaking through an opening in the clouds. It would likely be the last time I'd see its rays, so I smiled for an instant. She took notice.

"You're taking this a lot better than my late husband. He begged me not to kill him. That was a tough one. Mac was a lot easier. I just waited until he turned his back and bashed his brains in. You know what they both told me right before they died, detective?"

"That you're a Goddamn psychopath," I said through gritted teeth.

"That they were sorry." She chuckled. "Well, for the record, I'm not sorry. I mean, it's a shame it had to go this way. I do wish you could've left well enough alone, but your kind never does. You know, Earl. There's more to life than the truth. In fact, the best things in life are the things we keep secret. If only you'd have respected that." There was that evil smile again.

"You win, Caroline, but tell me something first," I spat out. "Why did you kill Larry? He was a good man. He tried to protect you."

She considered this a moment as she petted the neck of her mount and chuckled. "I don't owe you an explanation, but I'll give you this because you got balls, which Larry never had. That man couldn't kill a spider, but I did love him once upon a time. That night when I called him, I needed someone to hold me. But instead of coming home to comfort me, that SOB went to Indian Head to confront Mac. Not because he loved me. Not to defend my honor! But because he wanted to defend Tinsley's honor! After trying to drink myself to sleep and failing, I decided to go out there myself to see if it was true that Tinsley really was Rebecca, and what did I find? That whore leaving Mac's yacht, and my husband watching from afar, and crying over her."

Caroline's voice elevated as she worked herself into a fresh rage. "I knew, after I'd taken care of Mac, that I was done with Larry too. My bloodlust for avenging these betrayals had not been sated. I just needed the right opportunity. Thank you for placing suspicion on him." I groaned as she confirmed my worst fears. "You gave me an opening to complete the sweep, as they say. Or maybe, I'm about to complete it now, right, detective?" I groaned again, this time from the pain in my shoulder, as she smiled down at me.

"Thanks for coming here today and making this so easy, detective. I had thought you'd go away and that'd be that. But I knew it would be in the back of my mind that you might put things together and turn up one day looking to blackmail me, just like my little Larry would've eventually, but now my worries are over!"

"You're welcome," I said and added, "you murderous fucking bitch."

"I hope that makes you feel better, Earl. It's the last feeling you'll ever have."

She clutched the horse's mane tight in her gloved hands and yanked hard. The great black beast leaped forward and dug his front hooves into the ground inches from my chest. Then it reared back, energy rippling from hoof, to leg, to chest and finally settling into his gargantuan hindquarters. He used the power coiled up in these massive springs to launch himself back at me. Caroline lay flat against his broad neck as he lurched up then back down, hooves aimed straight for my head.

I attempted a barrel-roll to avoid the impact of well over a thousand pounds of horse and rider, but I wasn't moving nearly fast enough. I had no more than a split-second of conscious life left when I heard a gunshot echo across the field and out to the distant tree line and back. Then it rattled around the old stone walls as a hoof struck the earth inches from the back of my head, and the ground rumbled as Caroline's horse tore off for the nearest of the twin sisters.

I lost focus, which brought back the pain, and I collapsed. As I fell back into the green meadow, I caught a glimpse of Caroline lying face-down a few feet away from me, blood oozing from a hole in the center of her back. I closed my eyes and tried to stash away the pain again, but this time it overwhelmed me. I heard a voice and opened my eyes to see the beautiful face of Amalia Garcia looking down at me. Then I passed out.

34

Three days later I was back home in Southie, a little worse for wear, but in good spirits. My injuries, though painful, and a pain in the ass, given how much they restricted my ability to move, were relatively minor. I was told by doctors that one of my ribs narrowly missed puncturing my right lung, I guess I should have felt lucky.

Unfortunately, my mind kept drifting to Larry Ferncroft and my role in his demise, which soured my outlook. I wasn't second-guessing myself, as I said before, I don't do that. It's a waste of time. But I was kicking myself in the ass for being so blind to the evil within Caroline. But I suppose he was married to her. So, no matter how much I kicked myself for not seeing through her act sooner, it was Larry who sealed his fate the day he put a ring on it.

I hadn't had a chance to go through all the mail that had piled up while I was working the case. As I was sorting through it, a piece that had just arrived that morning caught my eye, because the label was handwritten in perfect block lettering and there was no return address. Inside I found a small slip of paper with the following eight words written in the same block letters: "Direct exchange. Threat eliminated. You're lucky, we're even." It was clear to me that McNierney was the sender.

Goodbye, Whitman Endicott, I thought. I only wish I could've been there to watch you die for your sins. I turned on my air purifier, cracked the window behind me, and set paper and envelope on fire.

Amalia Garcia was due to come by to take my official statement on everything that had gone down at the stables. I'd given the Feds a statement at the hospital, but, as I was under the influence of pain-killers and sedatives, I would have to go through it all again with a clear head. I had enlisted my nephew Ed to help me clean up the place before she arrived. A little while later, I was asking him to put on a pot of coffee when Amalia let herself in and appeared at my doorstep. She was early and a sight for sore eyes.

"My hero," I said. "Please come in and have a seat. I'd shake your hand, but ..." I glanced down at my arm in its sling.

She came in and took up residence in the seat across from me. Ed followed with two cups and the pot of java and set them down on the edge of my desk. I introduced the two of them, and Amalia mentioned that she had seen some of Ed's work and found it interesting. Ed decided it was a good time to excuse himself.

"Now that was funny, special agent. I wish I had his expression on film."

"You know, we don't get enough opportunities to bust balls in this business. We gotta take the layups when they're available, Town." I held up my mug, and we toasted to busting balls.

"No Sullivan this morning?" I asked.

"He sends his regards and his thanks for calling him and putting it on speaker when you engaged with the late Mrs. Ferncroft. Not all of her comments came through clear, but enough did to make our job a lot easier."

I waved her off. "No, thank you, Garcia. I know that shooting someone to death, even a double murderer about to kill again, is not easy to do, and not exactly great for a career in law enforcement these days. Politics being what they are and all. Anyway, I appreciate all the garbage you have to deal with as a result. Thank you for saving my life."

"Actually, it hasn't been as bad as you might think," she said, grinning. She was dressed in her normal business attire, dark gray suit, white blouse, and sensible shoes, but she had done something with her hair that softened her look and made her smile even more radiant.

"Not only do we have her admission to the murders on tape, but we also found what appears to be the murder weapon at the stables. It's about two feet of lead pipe. It was hidden under a loose board in the back of the stall belonging to Victory, Caroline's horse. We're also pretty certain she got the gun from a stable hand, last name Slaughter, who has two prior convictions for illegal gun dealing. We expect him to crack under questioning or else three strikes. So, these developments have put a muzzle on the rather loud mouth of Caroline's rich daddy, who was a real pain in the ass at first."

"Wow, that's fantastic," I said, meaning it but without much feeling, as it just made me think again of Larry and how wrong I had been about him. She read my mind.

"You know, Town, we were all wrong about Larry Ferncroft. This isn't all on you. He shouldn't have tried to protect her, or blackmail her, whatever it was they had going on between them. And, there's a damn good chance she would've killed him without your visiting him on Saturday."

"Thanks for saying that," I said, considering all that had transpired.

The Ferncrofts had all the money they could ever need. They were surrounded by beauty and splendor and had staff to take care of their every need. But they still weren't happy, not even close.

What's it's all worth anyway? We're all flawed, we all want the same things: love, affection, respect. No matter how good we seem to have it, if we don't get those things from the people we love and respect, then none of it matters. Caroline thought she had that from her true love, Mac, and her former love, Larry, but found out in a couple of hours that she had neither, and it pushed her over the edge. Or maybe she was just a natural-born psycho. Yeah, that's probably what it was.

We each sat there for a bit, just sort of eyeballing one another, not sure what to say when she took out her phone and asked if she could record my statement, which I said was fine. I began to walk her through the events of Tuesday and continued for over an hour until I reached the point where she saved my butt, and I lost consciousness, which I assured her was a very manly thing to do.

I wasn't sure what else to say to Garcia. I was attracted to her, but the case had placed some serious baggage between us, and I thought this might be the last time I'd see her. Happily, she was a thoroughly modern woman and took the initiative.

"So, I'm gonna be in town until tomorrow. You think you can buy a girl dinner tonight, despite that broken wing?" She even added an incentive. "I'll cut your food for you."

"Heck yeah, I can! There's a great place on the corner. The steaks are good, and the martinis are even better."

"That'll work," Garcia said, returning my smile. "But only if you promise to tell me how it is you came to know Clint Eastwood."

"Sure, but it's a long story. We go way back."

A NOTE ABOUT THE AUTHOR

The son of a policeman, who has spent a quarter-century working
with the world's largest asset managers, C. James Brown has lived a
fish out of water story. His goal is to make writing fiction his final
career and for Earl Town to become a regular part of the reader's life.
Indian Summer is his first novel.

Please visit him at www.cjamesbrown.com, on Twitter @C_James_
Brown, and Facebook @CJamesBrownAuthor

If you enjoyed the story, please rate it, and perhaps even leave a review, on Amazon, Goodreads, etc. Thank you!

Made in the USA
Middletown, DE
05 April 2022

63664174R00146